Ever Alice

H.J. RAMSAY

Ever Alice

ISBN: 0-9969239-4-2
ISBN13: 978-0-9969239-4-1

For Nick, Gracie, Annie, and Bradley.
Thank you for making every day feel like I've been unintentionally invited to one of the Mad Hatter's tea parties.
Pass the butter, please.

A

PART 1
RABBIT HOLES

A

Chapter 1
Alice
Warneford Asylum, Oxford
September 15, 1888

Alice stared at the spoonful of red syrup. It may as well have had a note saying, "Drink me."

Nurse Hazel said, "Open wide."

Alice took the medicine into her mouth and let it pool under her tongue while she made a show of swallowing. The taste of nutmeg and something metallic, almost like blood, made her eyes water.

"That's a good girl," the nurse said. She wiped the spoon, capped the bottle, and left the room.

The lock clicked.

Alice waited until the nurse's steps faded into the symphony of shrieks and moans that always rang down the hallway, and then she spat the medicine in the sink before her thoughts could curdle like an overheated custard.

She wiped her mouth on her sleeve and reached under the bed, wiggling the loose floorboard. Her tattered notebook lay in a cavity between the joists. She dusted off the cover and flipped past her drawings and recollections until she came to a fresh page.

Her hand itched to fill it, but she waited with her eyes closed. At last, he came to her, as he always did. She drew the White Rabbit, a timepiece in his paws, the chain dangling from his waistcoat pocket.

Chapter 2
Rosamund
House of Hearts, Wonderland
Lilly of the Valley 11, Year of the Queen

A light drizzle misted the air while the drummers played "March-O Death-O."

Rosamund, the Queen of Hearts, tapped her fingers to the beat.

So very appropriate.

Of course, Rosamund wouldn't have expected anything else. All ways were her way, and whatever way she wanted, she generally got, even if only in the end.

Her perch on the tower balcony gave her the best view of Thomas as her guards led him to the block. Her lips melted downward when she saw the proud expression on Thomas's face.

The traitor.

Rosamund wanted Thomas to look afraid, pathetic even, but he appeared exalted, as if he were walking to his coronation, not his death. It would be better if he acted a little remorseful, but that was Thomas's problem—he never did what she wanted.

She bit her lip until she tasted blood. Tears sprang to her eyes, and Rosamund dabbed them ceremoniously with her handkerchief. She glowed with satisfaction as her people followed suit, shaking their heads and giving her their bravest faces.

They'll always love me.

Rosamund forced more tears to flow until she could taste them. She took a breath as the drummers rattled out a long, steady beat that reminded her of a purring cat.

She hated cats, but that didn't concern her at the moment.

The traitor stopped before the block, and the drumming ceased. A dreadful calm lingered in the air. Slowly, he dropped to his knees and rested his chin on the chipped stump.

Thomas's eyes flashed towards her.

She expected to see anger in them, perhaps even hatred, but there was only pity.

The executioner raised the axe and the drummers started a low and steady roll.

Brrrrrrrrruuuuuuuuummmmm...buh DUM.

The axe sliced through the air, and his white head dropped into the basket in a baptism of blood. No one turned away. Not even as Thomas's legs twitched on the ground. They watched her, waiting for what she'd do next. She draped a black veil over her face.

"Lower the drapes," Rosamund said to a palace servant. "I am a widow today."

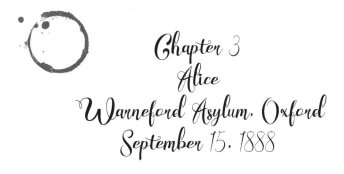

Chapter 3
Alice
Warneford Asylum, Oxford
September 15, 1888

Alice drew the last whisker on the White Rabbit. She sat back, admiring the likeness, and thumbed through her pictures of the Cheshire Cat, the Caterpillar, the Dodo, and the others.

All the creatures they said didn't exist.

"It was your imagination," her parents had told her. "You slipped in the river. You nearly drowned."

Alice gripped the leather edges of her journal.

She knew better. It was real. She had tried to tell them so, but her parents wouldn't listen. They refused to even acknowledge anything she had to say, telling each other over Alice's head that she'd grow out of it.

But years went by and she never did.

School was where she had the most problems. Headmistress Collins said Alice could not return until she "acted her age and stopped this childish nonsense." It was affecting the other students.

After that, her parents paraded Alice before every doctor in Oxford. She didn't mind too much at first. They listened to her talk about Wonderland in a way that her mother and father never would, and they asked pertinent questions about what had happened. When the doctors weren't asking questions, the nurses—the magpies, as Alice thought of them—watched her and scratched away in their books. Some of the nurses were pretty, and Alice believed it a shame that they wore such drab black dresses. If she were a nurse, she'd wear the brightest, most cheerful colors.

Her parents promised that Dr. Longfellow would be the last doctor. After he went through all the usual questions, she sat in his study, tapping her foot and gazing out the window, looking forward to finally having done with all these visits.

Dr. Longfellow adjusted his horn-rimmed glasses. "It's unmistakable," he said, addressing her mother and father. "She's mad."

Alice jerked backwards.

Mad?

She'd been called a lot of things. Inquisitive. Fanciful, perhaps. But mad? No, the doctor must have meant something else.

Her father sat forwards. "Are you certain, Dr. Longfellow?"

"Very." The doctor nodded. "It's rare for a child of…" He ruffled through his papers. "Of fourteen—"

"Fifteen," Alice corrected him. "Just turned."

"Yes, quite right," he said. "But as I was saying, it is rare for a child this age to exhibit these sorts of delusions. Perhaps it was the near drowning. She will have to stay here, of course."

"Here?" Alice gripped the chair. She heard her heart pounding in her chest and wondered if they could hear it too. "No, I won't. I couldn't possibly."

Alice expected her parents to be as dismayed as she was at Dr. Longfellow's request. Instead, they gawked at her as if she had arrived in a whiff of smoke—horrified and surprised.

"No, Mummy. No, Daddy. Please." Alice jumped from the chair and clung to their arms. "I'll be good. I won't talk about Wonderland anymore. I promise. I'll be good."

Her father patted her hand and said to Dr. Longfellow, "I don't think that will be necessary. I'm sure we can make other arrangements with Alice at home."

"Quite right." Her mother nodded. "Our daughter is fanciful, certainly, but leaving her here? Do you think that's really necessary?"

Dr. Longfellow pressed his hands together. "This is not a passing fancy. You've said so yourself that you thought she'd grow out of it, but she shows no sign of improvement. Alice needs proper care. She will receive it here in the asylum."

Alice searched her parent's faces, but they were as empty as drained tea cups. Her stomach knotted as if she'd swallowed a mouthful of bugs.

"For how long?" her father asked.

"Until she is cured. Treatment can't be rushed. It all depends on Alice."

Her father cleared his throat, and her mother dabbed her eyes with a handkerchief. They wouldn't look at her. It was as if she were invisible, as if they'd already agreed to let her disappear.

Her father glanced over at her mother and nodded.

Alice felt her insides crack. "No. No. Please. I'll be good. *Pleeeeaaasssse.*"

A blur of magpies surrounded her in their black gowns and white aprons. Their fingers bit into her flesh, holding her tight. The birds dragged her down a hallway with gaping doors, took her to a damp room, and shoved her into a crate.

"In you go," one of the nurses said as she pushed Alice's head down and slammed the top shut. The nurse leaned down and peered at Alice through the slats with eyes as dark as raisins. "The crib should calm you down a bit, deary."

The nurse walked away, following the others, and left Alice alone in the cold dark.

Alice screamed for her parents. After a while, she even screamed for the magpies. She said she'd be good and promised a thousand promises. Then she called for the White Rabbit—only more quietly. It was two days before the magpies finally let her out. By then, her voice was so hoarse that it hurt to ask for water.

After Alice was moved into her own room, Dr. Longfellow's treatments started: the bleeds, the baths, and the purging that left Alice weak and exhausted. At first, she tried to fight them, but fighting made it worse. If she closed her eyes, eventually, she'd go somewhere else, somewhere they couldn't touch her, and in that place, nothing could make her stop believing in Wonderland.

Alice tried to behave like a good girl. But no matter how polite she acted, Dr. Longfellow kept on and on with the medicines and the treatments. She grew silent. She stopped talking—at least to herself—and ate when instructed. Doing so pleased Dr. Longfellow and the magpies, and, at that point, that was all that mattered.

Dr. Longfellow came every morning. He flashed a light in her eyes and tapped her knees. He asked if she had seen any rabbits lately, and she shook her head, but she always saw the White Rabbit, waiting in his waistcoat, every time she closed her eyes.

Her parents came to visit—her mother mostly. She took Alice out of her room and sat her before the fire or out on the grounds if the weather was pleasant. Her mother acted as if Alice weren't at the asylum at all but on some holiday.

Alice should have felt something—pain, despair, anger at her parents for what they'd done, for betraying her like that, but the medicine didn't allow her to feel anything, so she stopped taking it. Then, when her mother visited, she felt the embers of hatred growing in her belly.

* * *

Alice sketched a rose and threw her pencil against the wall.

"I'm not mad!" she yelled. "I'm not."

Alice cupped her hands over her mouth as if she could push the words back down her throat. She hadn't meant to scream like that. Screaming caused bad things to happen.

Click.

She whirled her head towards the door. Its hinges yawned as it swung open.

Someone had heard. Despite all the other wailing in the asylum, she'd still been caught. It had to be Nurse Hazel. She had never liked Alice and must have been listening at the door. Alice shoved the journal under her mattress and sat as still as a candlestick while she waited for whatever was going to happen.

Several moments went by and nothing happened. Something wasn't right. The bedsprings squeaked as Alice got up. Part of her wanted to slam the door shut, but another part—the one that always seemed to get her in trouble—wanted it opened more. Maybe it was a test. Or a trap.

Alice stepped towards the door, expecting Nurse Hazel to come flying into the room at any moment. She wrapped her hand around the handle, its cold metal stinging her palm, and peeked outside.

Her eyes widened. She'd expected to see the gray stone of the asylum. Instead, she saw a familiar green-paneled hallway with portraits and paintings hung along the walls.

It was her home.

Had Dr. Longfellow given her a treatment and she hadn't remembered leaving? Or maybe it was a dream, and she was asleep in the asylum. Alice tried to find a reasonable explanation for why she was at home, but she decided it didn't matter.

Still in her hospital gown, Alice stepped into the hall. She turned to shut the door and gasped. It wasn't the room at the asylum but her old room. She hadn't realized how much she'd missed all her things. Her trinkets and books with plenty of pictures. Agnes, her dolly. Even the ruffled blanket on her bed. The more she looked around, the more she realized she really was at home—it wasn't a dream.

She closed her bedroom door and went down the hall. The farther she moved away from her room, the stronger the pull was to go back. It all felt wrong somehow. The same paintings remained on the wall: fields with multicolored flowers, watery ponds with lily pads, the occasional bowl of fruit, and the portraits of Queen Elizabeth and Mary, Queen of Scots. But while everything looked as she remembered, something about the way it was all too perfect made her feel as if she were inside a photograph.

Alice came to the top of the staircase. "Hullo?" she called. "Hullo? Is anyone here? Mummy? Daddy?"

There was no answer.

Alice swallowed, trying to cool the dry itch in her throat. "Hullo?"

She couldn't hear anything. Not the tick of a clock, not the shuffle of feet, nor the mumble of voices. Alice was alone; at least she thought so, but one couldn't be entirely sure of those things.

Her hands trembled as she crept down the stairs and into the parlor, where a fire burned in the fireplace. She stared at the backs of the two chairs with the patterned violets and lilies. Her mother had specially ordered them from France. She'd been awfully proud when they'd arrived and wouldn't let Alice sit on them until she was old enough and didn't drip her tea anymore. On the table between them was Alice's chess set, the pieces untouched, and a puff of steam swirled in the air from a tea cup. Was it her mother's or maybe her father's?

Alice leaned forwards until she could see past the wingbacks. Both the chairs were empty, except for a ball of yarn on one cushion and a folded newspaper on the other.

Curiouser and curiouser.

Alice brought her attention to the mirror on the mantel. Before she left for the asylum, she'd spend hours with her chin resting on the edge as she peered into the glass. Now she saw her face and recoiled.

It wasn't her—not really. Not like how she remembered. Alice touched her cheeks. She pulled back her hair. She puckered her lips. But it wasn't that—it was her eyes. Something was different, almost vacant, as if she were locked somewhere far, far behind them. She shook her head. It must be a trick of some sort. Mirrors did that sometimes. She was still Alice. She hadn't changed much. Taller, maybe.

The smell of cooking meat distracted her. She went to the kitchen and found a meat pie on the counter. Melted butter dribbled down its flaky crust as if it had been brushed on moments before. A fork lay beside it, and, despite herself, she tore into it, taking bite after bite, potatoes and gravy sliding down her chin. After she took the last bite, she looked around guiltily. The pie must have been meant for her parents. Where were they?

A dragonfly floated across the window. Outside, lemony sunlight pierced through the clouds, washing the flowers in light.

"Maybe Mummy and Daddy are having a picnic." The moment she said it out loud, she regretted piercing the house's silence. It seemed dangerous.

Alice hurried out the main door and off the veranda. Shielding her eyes from the sun, she went past the old sycamore tree with the swing and towards the bed of daisies. She grabbed a handful, pulling them from their stems much the same way little boys pried the legs off spiders, and held them to her nose.

Bees hummed from flower to flower. Alice followed their movements along a well-worn path, dropping daisy petals like breadcrumbs. Before long, she was standing before the river in the very spot she'd first seen the White Rabbit all those years ago. She glanced over her shoulder and saw the tree her sister, Katherine, had decided they'd sit under as they waited to be called to tea. It felt like ages ago. Dinah chased butterflies around the trunk all afternoon, a kitten huntress.

Alice hadn't seen much of Katherine since that afternoon. Her mother had told her Katherine had gone to the university—a place of learning. Alice imagined it as a place of books with no pictures, and she never understood why anyone would want to read any of those.

Katherine had visited her once at the asylum. She entered Alice's room with her lips curved upwards ever so slightly. "They say that you are not yourself," she said. "That you are unwell."

Alice had embraced her with delight, but her sister's arms remained lifeless.

"You'll tell them that I'm not mad, won't you?" Alice asked. "You saw him. I know you did."

"Who did I see, Alice?"

"The White Rabbit, silly." Alice shook Katherine. "He was right in front of us both. You can tell them I'm not mad, and I can go home."

Katherine grabbed Alice's hands, squeezing them hard. "I didn't see anything," she said. "There was nothing there. Stop all this nonsense, Alice. It's so maddening."

Alice didn't understand why her sister would treat her this way, as if she were nothing more than a trinket she didn't care for any more and had tossed aside.

Katherine didn't come to see Alice again after that. Perhaps it was just as well.

Alice stared at the river as the water churned and rolled as if it were a swarm of snakes. It used to be one of her favorite places, but not anymore. She threw the daisies and watched them disappear under the surface before turning to go back to the house. She didn't feel like being outside anymore and would rather sit next to the fire and wait for her parents—wherever they may be.

Alice stepped through the slick rocks and wiped her wet hands on the sides of her hospital gown. She hadn't gone far when a familiar voice said, "You're late."

Chapter 4
Rosamund
House of Hearts, Wonderland
Lilly of the Valley 11, Year of the Queen

Rosamund tossed the black veil aside for a red shawl as soon as she entered the solace of her personal chambers. She had never cared for black—red was her favorite color.

She sat down, triumphant, and hid the tear streaks with a sprinkling of powder. She had beheaded yet another traitor, and it gave her a thrill of satisfaction to watch their heads tumble.

Rosamund knew her advisors didn't believe Thomas was guilty—she had noticed every look, every whisper, and every raised eyebrow. None of these things ever got past her. She was the Queen and was well versed in watching for traitorous behavior.

Only when she received the cryptic notes—ciphers of a plot, she was sure—did her advisors take any notice. Notes left under her plate. Others left on her chair. The ones left under her mirror. Thomas told her they were his love notes. Well, at least he didn't deny writing them, even if they did contain some very nice things written about her.

She had proof beyond doubt, but her advisors still wanted more. Those useless toadies were blind to all the signs.

Rosamund remembered the time she nearly fell to her death on the loose carpet on the stairs. Thomas told her she was being silly because it was the very bottom step, but what if she had broken her neck?

He couldn't so easily explain away the servant who had choked on the chicken bone after testing her soup. Everyone knew chicken noodle had no chicken in it whatsoever. It was another assassination attempt.

Then came the final straw.

On a morning stroll, an arrow nearly plunged into her breast. It was a matter of luck that the arrow fell short and landed a hundred feet away, but enough was enough. Her advisors weren't going to appreciate the danger until one of these arrows had found its target.

Thomas tried to argue that there was an archery lesson nearby and she shouldn't have been in the area in the first place. He paraded witnesses in front of her to lie for him, saying he had told her all about it.

Rosamund couldn't recall such a warning, and she always said everything twice and wrote it down for good measure; therefore, she found him guilty and signed his death warrant. Thomas had been behind it all because he wanted the throne to himself. Well, she wouldn't let him have it. He would never have it.

She was the Queen.

Rosamund pulled a tiny locket from inside her gown. She clicked it open and gazed upon the stoic face of a young man with strawberry blond hair and Easter-egg-blue eyes.

Oh, Pedro.

"I wish you were here," she said to the picture. "You'd be so proud of me. I finally got rid of him and what a relief it is that he's dead. Hush, now. Don't fret, I felt completely different the day I had *you* beheaded. If you hadn't gone and ruined everything, you could have been here to share in the fun."

Rosamund brought the portrait to her lips and kissed it before slipping it inside the front of her dress. She wrapped her shawl tighter around her body and watched the rain cling to the windowpane in fat droplets, thinking of Pedro and how he always tried to get her to smile.

A noise at the door jolted her out of her reverie. She turned in time to see a letter sliding under the threshold. Rosamund marched towards the door and plucked it from the carpet. The wax seal was unmarked. She sniffed as she carried it to her desk and sniffed again as she flipped it from front to back to see if there were any markings. The paper was as blank as a seashell. She cracked the wax seal and slowly opened the letter.

Your time is nearly up.
Hickory, dickory, dock.
Ticktock, ticktock,
Ticktock.
P.S. It wasn't the King of Hearts.

Rosamund's eye twitched as she read and reread the letter before writing its contents down. When she was finished, she ripped the letter into shreds and threw it in the fire, staring at the tiny pieces as they curled into black wisps of smoke.

Not very appropriate, not very appropriate at all.

Even as she stood before the fire, an iciness crept into Rosamund's bones. This had never happened before. It was unbelievable, undeniable even, but there it was. She'd made a mistake. The traitor was still out there and that fact terrified her, but for killing Thomas, well, blunders happen. She'd challenge any one of those pompous pompotamuses to throw the first cherry drop if they'd never made one.

Hickory, dickory, dock...hickory, dickory, dock...ticktock, ticktock... The words rang in her ears, filling her with dread. She had to smoke out the real traitor like a blackbird hiding in a bluebird pie. She needed a plan, but her thoughts kept scattering like unruly school children.

Rosamund heard a tap at the door and nearly fell out of her chair. She lunged for the fireplace poker, her heart hammering in her chest. "Who...who's there? What do you want?"

Bess, the Duchess of Redwood Brae, opened the door juggling a tray in her meaty hands. Rosamund had first thought to execute her when that nutty duchess had the audacity to box her in the ears after she lost a game of I spy. Rosamund had said she'd spied something red, and, no, it wasn't her dress, her brooch, the painting of herself in a red gown, the ruby baboon on the end table, her teacup, the tea set, the roses in the carpet or in the curtains, or the tiny hearts on the wallpaper. It was a book she'd *read*—not "red"—and quite enjoyed. Bess said

Rosamund had cheated, to which she'd replied that the rules never said it had to be anything literal, and that was when the duchess went completely mad and struck her.

Just before Rosamund was about to take Bess's head, Thomas had suggested, "Wouldn't it be worse than dying if she had to do everything you told her to do for the rest of her life?"

It wasn't a bad idea for a traitor. From then on, the Duchess of Redwood Brae became her chief lady's maid, and it had worked out swimmingly ever since.

Bess looked at the poker in Rosamund's hands and tutted. "You shouldn't be tending to the fire yourself. I'll call for one of the servants."

"No, no," Rosamund said, putting it back. "That won't be necessary."

Bess smiled. "I thought you could use some tea. It is teatime by your declaration this morning."

"You dare to presume my thoughts?" Rosamund snarled.

Bess lowered her gaze. "Forgive me, Your Majesty. I should know never to think unless told to first."

"Precisely," she said, "and curtsy when you do. It's prettier that way."

Rosamund motioned for Bess to continue. The duchess busied herself with the tea and cut the butter. "One pat or two?" Bess asked.

"One. I'm watching my figure."

Bess placed the butter into the cup and poured the tea over, filling the air with the scent of rusted tin and soiled sock. "It's your favorite brew this week, Your Majesty."

Rosamund took the cup out of Bess's hands. "Yes, but I may change my mind within the hour. You must be prepared for these things."

Despite Bess's abilities as a lady's maid, Rosamund had never cared for the duchess's pinched cheeks and shifty eyes buried underneath her layers of hideous purple eye shadow. She always smelled like pepper, and it made Rosamund's nose tickle. Maybe Bess did that on purpose, to irritate her. Maybe Bess was the traitor. People who loved pepper had to be traitorous. It was such a disagreeable spice with a temper—everyone knew that.

Rosamund narrowed her eyes. "Were you at my door a moment ago?"

"Yes, Your Majesty, with the tea."

"Not that moment," Rosamund huffed. "The moment before."

"The moment before the moment?"

"Yes, that moment. You know the moment I'm talking about."

"If it's the moment before the moment and not the moment before, then no, I was not at the door a moment ago."

Rosamund's words dripped slowly like a leaky tap. "I hope we're talking about the same moment. Because you know it wouldn't be very appropriate to hover at the queen's door a moment ago."

Bess put two pats of butter in her own cup before she poured. "Very inappropriate, indeed."

"Indeed…"

Rosamund decided to have Bess beheaded—to be on the safe side. She'd have to remember to say it twice and write it down, since it was teatime and she didn't like to be interrupted with such things during tea.

"Do you suppose"—Bess lowered her voice—"All is well now that the traitor is gone?"

Rosamund peered at the etched lines in the duchess's face. "Just because you are in my employ that doesn't mean the safety of my throne is of any concern to you."

"Absolutely not," Bess said with an air of surprise and took a sip of her tea.

Yes, Rosamund thought, she'd have Bess beheaded as soon as she had a reason. Not that Rosamund needed a reason, but her uppity-tuppity advisors liked them.

Rosamund looked around. One of her lady's maids was missing. "Where is Sabrina?"

"That girl," Bess sighed, "is off crying her eyes out."

"Sabrina should know her place at court. Haven't you told her that she can't cry except at the queen's pleasure? As my lady's maid, she should know these things."

"I've told her so, Your Majesty, and she continues to blubber on. It's all over the fuss with that Count of Candlewick."

"That arrogant Reuben. The nerve of him trying to court one of my maids," Rosamund said, shaking her head.

"Quite right, Your Majesty."

Rosamund glanced at the duchess. "You should consider yourself lucky that you don't have to worry about that sort of thing. Isn't that right, Bess?"

Bess's eye twitched.

Rosamund heard a crescendo of voices outside her private chamber. The door flung open most unceremoniously. Stumbling across the threshold were her three advisors: Lord William de Fleur, Earl Charles LeMarque, and Sir Ralph de Longshoot.

Lord William de Fleur, previously known as the Hatter before Rosamund elevated him, stood before her with one hand in his breast pocket. "Pardon our intrusion, Your Majesty," he said with the usual spittle, "but this is a matter of most unimportance."

"Take off that ridiculous hat when you're in my presence," Rosamund snapped at him.

William did as he was told and ran his hand over his slicked-back hair, which caught the light like a prism. Clearly, he had been a little overzealous with the slug slime that morning.

Rosamund huffed, "Sometimes I'm ashamed to call you my cousin, honestly. Now what is all this fuss that you had to interrupt...to interrupt..." She grabbed the black veil and put it on. "To interrupt my mourning?"

"Only the most unimportant news," he said with his tongue sticking out of his mouth.

Earl Charles LeMarque, the featherbrained dodo, as Rosamund liked to refer to him, stood behind William with the tips of his wings in his breast pockets and a pipe in his mouth.

Ralph moved to Charles's side and opened, closed, and reopened his pocket watch. Before coming to her palace, Ralph had been in a touring magic show. She'd only discovered him because she happened to be paying attention when he was pulled from a top hat. It wasn't the trick that interested her (she'd seen it a thousand and two times), but Ralph's perfectly tailored waistcoat. A rabbit in a waistcoat? Who'd heard of such a thing? The longer she admired his taste in clothing, the more she realized she had to have him. Nobody would have anything like him, and she loved things nobody had. It was after he came to the palace that he started proving himself useful and he eventually went from magician's prop to queen's royal advisor—quite a leap.

However, she could do without his constant obsession with time.

Ralph opened his watch again, and Rosamund snapped at him, "Is there somewhere more unimportant you need to be?"

"No, Your Majesty," he said.

"Then PUT your watch away."

"Yes, Your Majesty," he said and dropped the watch in his pocket.

Rosamund picked up her gown and swept across the room before sitting. She neatly folded her hands in her lap. "Well, then, what is so unimportant?"

Charles took his pipe out of his mouth and said, "We have received word from Saint Holland's Fjord. The Queen of Spades has escaped."

She tore the black veil off her face as blood rushed to her cheeks. "How long ago?"

Ralph looked at the other two. "A month ago."

Rosamund felt as if she'd been kicked in the jaw. "A month?"

"The carrier snails got backed up in Stonewall Pass—an unexpected snow chain requirement. There's reason to believe she's coming here to seek refuge from the Spades."

"To seek refuge?" Rosamund gazed at her advisors. "What a bunch of rubbish. There's but one reason she'd come here."

Panic gripped Rosamund's heart and gave it a sharp tug. The Queen of Spades was coming for Rosamund's throne.

Her advisors stood there, watching her.

She slammed her fist on the arm of the chair. "Quit standing around like a pack of cards. Tell me what you're going to do about it."

“We are doing everything we can,” Charles said. “We’ve already alarmed the guard. Everyone is on low alert.”

Rosamund nodded. “Yes, low alert, everyone must be on low alert. It’s our number one priority.”

Hickory, dickory, dock.
Ticktock, ticktock,
Ticktock.

Chapter 5
Alice
The Riverbank, Oxford
September 15, 1888

Alice blinked—once, twice. But no matter how many times she did so, he was still there. He jumped down from a decayed log and shook his hind legs, flinging clumps of mud. He checked his watch and slipped it into his breast pocket.

Alice brought her hands to her cheeks in surprise. "It's you. It's really you—the White Rabbit."

"Is that what you call me?" He brought one paw to his coat. "Ah, that's right. I don't think we were ever properly introduced before. My name is Sir Ralph of Longshoot."

Alice smoothed down the front of her hospital gown. If she'd known she was about to see the White Rabbit again, she would have made herself more presentable. "How do you do, Sir Ralph of Longshoot?" She tried to curtsy, but her foot slipped on the wet ground.

He came close to Alice, peering at her. "You look different from how I remember."

"Yes, I suppose I do. I'm fifteen years old now."

"Are you the same Alice?"

"I believe so. It's hard to tell nowadays." Alice wanted to reach out and touch his cottony ears to make sure he wasn't a hallucination. "They told me," she whispered, "that you weren't real."

His whiskers twitched. "I assure you, madam, I exist no more and no less than I already do."

Alice clapped her hands, grabbed Ralph, and swung him around. "I knew it," she cried. "I tried to tell them, but they wouldn't listen, they wouldn't."

"PUT ME DOWN."

Alice lowered the rabbit to his feet. "Oh, I'm so very sorry. I didn't mean to offend you. I wanted so badly for you to be real, and you were real this whole time. My mother and father will be so happy to see you." She grabbed him by the paw and pulled him down the path. "You must come with me at once because, you see, you have to show them I'm not mad."

"I will do no such thing," Ralph said, and snatched his paw away.

Alice took a step back. "Why not?"

He checked his watch again. "Because, my dear, it is I who must take you somewhere and we haven't much time."

Alice bit her lip as she glanced towards the house. "Oh, I...I don't know if I'm allowed to go anywhere. You see, I've just returned home, and Mummy and Daddy would be worried if I left again."

"Stickfiddles," he said. "You are to go with me at once. Wonderland is at stake."

"At stake?" Alice breathed. "How do you mean?"

"The Queen of Hearts has gone mad. *Stark* raving mad."

"But wasn't she already mad?"

Ralph nodded. "It's become worse. Terribly, terribly worse. She has done the most unbelievable, unthinkable, unimaginable of all 'un' and 'able' sorts of things."

"What?"

"She beheaded the King of Hearts."

Alice took a step backwards. She remembered the King, an odd sort of fellow but pleasant in his own way. He had pardoned everyone the Queen ordered beheaded at the croquet game—everyone except the Cheshire Cat.

"The King? He's...dead?" Alice gulped.

"Deader than a lobster in a hot spring."

Without the King, there was no one to stop the Queen of Hearts. Alice had spent but a brief time with her, but discovered quickly that the Queen took immense pleasure in death and blood. "What will become of Wonderland?"

"I'm afraid," Ralph said, "that heads are rolling faster than ever. Who knows? I might be next. She'd have my head for sure if she knew I sneaked away to come here. Not easy to do when there are guards everywhere."

Alice furrowed her brow. "Sneaked away to be here with me, you mean?"

He waved his paw. "Here with you, there with her, there's no need to be so particular. I try not to be. The real question anyone should ask is not 'Where am I?' but rather 'When am I?' or, 'When am I not?' or the most pressing question of all, 'Am I late?'"

Alice shook her head. Her thoughts were muddling already. Maybe everyone was right, and the world of Wonderland was simply nonsense. "White Rabbit...err...Sir Ralph...I'm terribly sorry about the King, but what can I do? I'm not anybody important."

"Actually"—Ralph moved towards her—"you're most unimportant."

"Unimportant? I'm not sure that makes any sense."

"It does. *It does.* You must come back to Wonderland."

Go back to Wonderland? She had hoped to for so long, but now she wasn't sure. It wouldn't do to go rushing off when she'd so recently left the asylum. She missed her room. She missed her kitty, Dinah. What if she went and never came home? Or they put her back in the asylum and never let her out? Perhaps, this time, seeing the White Rabbit again would have to be enough.

Alice ran her hand along the tall grass. "Well, you see, it's not a very good time, and—"

"You have to help us, Alice," Ralph interrupted her. "If you don't come back, then we're doomed. The Queen will murder us all, one by one."

Alice's eyes lit with a sudden idea. "Maybe you can ask her to leave. I'm sure if you asked her politely—"

"How preposterous." Ralph laughed. "To ask her that, even in jest, is like asking her to say, 'Off with your head.' It's simply a question that is out of the question. No," he said. "She must be killed."

Alice gasped. "Killed?"

"Wonderland isn't safe. Heads line the bridge to Gardenia City. If things carry on as they are, then one day it'll be my head on one of the stakes."

"No," she whispered. "Don't think such a horrible thing. She wouldn't."

"Yes, she would." Ralph took Alice's hand. "But, you could stop her. You could kill her."

"*Me?* I couldn't possibly. I wouldn't want to kill anyone."

"That's why you're so unimportant. The Queen would never suspect you."

Alice shuddered at the memory of the Queen's gleeful face when she'd ordered Alice's execution. "But she hates me. She'd suspect me right off. She wanted to behead me the last time I went to Wonderland, and I doubt she has forgotten it."

"She never signed your death warrant," Ralph said. "She might have."

"Even if that's true," Alice said, "I wouldn't know the first thing about it. I've never killed anyone before."

"It's not so hard." Ralph leaned towards her. "I'm part of the Aboveground Organization—very hush-hush. You wouldn't be alone."

Alice frowned. "What you're asking—"

"It's such a simple thing, really."

"A simple thing to kill the Queen?" Alice looked around. "This isn't Wonderland, you know. Here, I'd be hanged for treason for merely talking about it. You can't kill a queen."

"But we have no other choice."

Alice wrung her hands in her hospital gown. "I'm sorry. I want to help, but I just can't. You have no idea what it's been like for me since I left Wonderland. It hasn't been altogether pleasant, I can assure you. Going back, especially to do what you ask, will make it worse. They say I'm not well, you know."

Ralph was quiet a moment. His ears drooped a little. "Don't you want to come back to Wonderland?"

Alice had dreamed about it for so many years. If only the White Rabbit had come sooner, before she'd gone to the asylum. "Oh, I do. Or I *did*, rather. Please try to understand."

"I see." Ralph shrank away from her, saddened, as if she'd broken his beloved pocket watch. "I have to go. The Queen will get suspicious if I'm gone too long. Goodbye, Alice."

He turned and jumped back over the log, disappearing on the other side.

"Wait," Alice cried, hurrying after him. "Don't go. I need to introduce you to my mother and father, so they can see I'm not mad. White Rabbit! Ralph!"

Alice stopped at the log. Ralph was nowhere in sight—almost as if he hadn't been there at all. Everything everyone had said about the White Rabbit came rushing back to her, but she shook those thoughts away. The White Rabbit was real—as real as the fern fronds tickling her legs.

A chill blanketed her shoulders as gray clouds filled the sky. They looked as if they could crack open like eggs and drench her within seconds. She sprinted home and threw open the door as it started to pour.

"Mummy? Daddy?" she called. "I'm back."

Darkness shrouded the rooms and shadows skulked around the corners. The remains of the meat pie were still on the counter and the teacups, now cool, hadn't moved from their places next to the chess set.

Alice jumped at the sound of a meow coming from the top of the staircase.

"Dinah?" she called, moving towards the sound. "Is that you?"

Sitting on the top step was her darling, striped cat.

"Oh, Dinah." Alice put her hand on her thumping heart. "You frightened me."

Alice ran up the stairs, eager to scoop up her cat in her arms. Just as she got close, Dinah bounded down the hallway, past the portraits and family pictures, and disappeared behind her bedroom door.

The door appeared ajar, even though Alice swore she had closed it. She inched down the hallway until she was standing before it, trembling. Dinah mewed on the other side with a high-pitched, impatient air. Alice slowly reached for the knob and pushed the door open wider. On the other side was her room, safe and familiar, and there was Dinah, right next to her bed, waiting for her. "There you are, Dinah."

Alice ran inside and picked up her kitty, holding her close.

"Oh, Dinah. I missed you so."

Alice rocked her back and forth, cooing and coddling, but she couldn't feel Dinah's soft fur in her fingers or her whiskers along her palm. She looked down.

In her hands were nothing but dirty rags.

"Dinah?" She shook her head. "Dinah? Where are you?"

Panic pushed up her throat. Her head jerked from left to right, taking in the lumpy mattress with the threadbare blanket, the water-slicked walls, the barred window… She wasn't at home. Not even close.

Alice scrambled to the door, but Nurse Hazel blocked her way and slammed it shut.

Chapter 6
Rosamund
House of Hearts, Wonderland
Lilly of the Valley 11, Year of the Queen

Rosamund shoved Bess out of the bedchamber; she couldn't think with that dreadful pepper smell. She sat at her desk and tapped her finger to her chin.

Think. Think. Think.

But the thoughts wouldn't come.

Rain splattered against the window, reminding her of a cat pawing at the door. Rosamund growled. *Bloody cats.* She hated all those shedding bags of uselessness, and there was one cat she hated above all others: the Cheshire Cat.

She had an outstanding death warrant with his name on it. If she could have beheaded him, she would have felt better, but knowing he was holed up somewhere, grinning his horrid grin under her nose, made her burn.

Rosamund jolted as the shutters blew open and banged against the wall. The curtains billowed towards her like ghostly fingers, causing the jitters to course through her body as if she'd drunk too much acorn syrup.

"Silly me," Rosamund said, swallowing the fear bubbling up her throat. "It's only the wind." She rearranged her crown, gathered her skirts, and forced herself towards the window, half expecting to see the pale face of the Queen of Spades lunging at her. Rosamund slammed the glass shut, and the curtains fluttered back in place.

She took a breath and leaned against the window. Her heart thudded away in her chest. She scolded herself for adding the pat of butter to her tea—too much butter always made her a bundle of nerves.

She heard a rustling from the corner of the room. "Your Majesty?"

Rosamund's knees nearly buckled as she whipped around.

Madame Diamond stood on the hidden stair wearing a hooded cloak. She curtsied when the Queen faced her.

"*Madame Diamond*," Rosamund sighed. "You scared the stockings off me. How many times have I told you not to sneak like that?"

Madame Diamond lowered her head. "I'm doing as Your Majesty asked—to keep our meetings a secret."

"But I didn't send for you."

"The spirits told me you would."

Rosamund nodded. "As usual, you are right, but you are not to frighten me so. Squawk like a chicken next time."

"As you wish," Madame Diamond said, motioning for Rosamund to follow her. "Come. Your cards are waiting. They have the answers you seek."

The fortune-teller removed her cloak, revealing a sparkling gown of white with a single red rose over her heart. She floated to the table in one elegant swoop, as if she had wheels instead of feet. Rosamund sniffed—no one should appear more graceful than the Queen.

Rosamund sat across from her and watched her shuffle the cards with deft, sweeping strokes.

Madame Diamond had entered Rosamund's court as a refugee from the House of Diamonds, which had not been allowing her to pursue her other interests. The fortune-teller had said that she'd come to the Queen because she knew her court was superior to all the other houses combined. Rosamund never asked about those *other* interests because it gave her a smug sense of satisfaction to hear that the House of Hearts had been her first choice. It was clearly better than all the others.

With a snap of Madame Diamond's fingers, the black cards spread across the table in a half arc. She grasped Rosamund's thumbs, closed her eyes, and spat on the floor. "They are ready," the fortune-teller murmured.

She flipped over the first card. It showed Rosamund at a tournament.

Madame Diamond said, "You will soon have something to celebrate."

"The death of the Queen of Spades?"

Madame Diamond studied the card. "It's hard to tell."

Rosamund snatched the card. It showed her looking especially stern: jaw set, eyes narrowed, nostrils flared. It was an expression she had spent many hours perfecting at the mirror. She peered closer and saw the tiniest, itsy-bitsy-est tilt in her eyebrow. "I say I look positively ecstatic, if you ask me."

"If you say so, Your Majesty."

Madame Diamond turned over the second card. It showed Rosamund signing a death warrant. "Someone will soon die," she said.

"The Queen of Spades?"

"It's still hard to tell, Your Majesty."

"Give it here," Rosamund demanded. "Clearly, I should be the one reading these."

Madame Diamond gave Rosamund the card. She squinted at the image, but the name on the death warrant was too blurry.

Gingersnaps.

Rosamund flicked it back to Madame Diamond. "Next."

The fortune-teller set the card by the others and revealed the third one. In it, Rosamund was raising a glass in the air. "You'll get the news you seek."

"*Yes.*" Rosamund rubbed her hands together. "The Queen of Spades is mine. I'm toasting to her execution. See all their faces? Everyone loves a good execution. I almost don't need to see the rest of the cards."

Madame Diamond arched her eyebrows.

Rosamund shrugged. "Let's see what they say anyway. I'm sure it will show me dancing or something like that."

When Madame Diamond revealed the fourth card, it showed a shadowy figure standing next to Rosamund, hiding something behind its back.

A cold sweat peppered Rosamund's forehead. "What does it mean?"

Madame Diamond didn't speak. For the first time, she seemed at a loss for words. Her lips pursed. "I don't know."

"WHAT does it mean?" Rosamund demanded.

"I...I don't know."

"Who is this?" Rosamund pointed to the figure in the picture. "Tell me at once, so I may have him beheaded."

"Or her," Madame Diamond said. "The figure is a shadow. It's impossible to tell."

"Rubbish!" Rosamund yelled. "I want to see the next card."

Madame Diamond's fingers trembled as she reached for another card.

Rosamund gripped the table. "Well, go on, you sack of flour. Get on with it," she ordered.

The fortune-teller turned it fast, but there was nothing there. The card was blank. She snapped over the next and the next, but the white nothingness glared back at them.

"It's a *plot.*" Rosamund swept the cards off the table. "The cards plot against me. I should have them incinerated."

"No, Your Majesty." Madame Diamond shook like a mound of jelly on toast. "The cards aren't plotting against you. It means the future...is uncertain. You are at a crossroads."

"Crossroads smossroads," Rosamund shrieked. "It's another plot. It's always another plot. Some fortune-teller you are."

"I'm sorry, Your Majesty. I've never seen this before..." Madame Diamond muttered to herself as if Rosamund wasn't in the room. "The future...it's disappeared."

"Well you better find the future and tell it to report to me at once," Rosamund ordered. "Or...or...it's off with your head."

Chapter 7
Alice
Warneford Asylum, Oxford
September 16, 1888

Alice's fingers twisted the sheets of her bed. She thought of the White Rabbit by the river. Her mind flip-flopped back and forth—*It was a dream…no, it was real*—until she felt thoroughly dizzy and confused, as if she'd fallen asleep under the hot sun.

The door opened and in came Nurse Hazel, dangling a set of keys from her fingers. "You have a visitor."

Alice's mother waited for her on the veranda in her usual spot, with tea set before her. Alice's stomach churned. If her mother wanted, Alice could leave the asylum this very instant, but her mother didn't want her to. She wanted Alice to rot here.

"Good day, Ma'am," Nurse Hazel said to her mother as she led Alice to one of the wicker chairs. "Always a pleasure to see you."

"Likewise," Alice's mother said.

Nurse Hazel nodded and turned on her heel, leaving Alice and her mother alone.

"Alice, love." Her mother beamed as she poured Alice a cup of tea. "I'm so very sorry, but I can't stay long. It's all because of the most wonderful news I have to tell you."

"Oh?" Alice held her breath. Was today the day she was finally going home? She'd take back every terrible thing she'd ever thought about her mother if she uttered those words.

"Katherine's engaged to be married," she squealed. "Isn't that glorious? Oh, some good news for once. Your father is simply thrilled."

Try as she might, she couldn't look happy at the news. Disappointment and sadness churned in her belly like a vat of butter. She wanted to cry. She wanted to sob, but she wouldn't. Not in front of her mother.

Her mother continued as if Alice wasn't even in the room. "Do you wonder if he's handsome?" her mother asked. "I bet he is. Katherine always had such good taste."

Alice bit the side of her cheek. She supposed she should try to be pleased for her sister, but Katherine was no better than her mother. Having a sister in the insane asylum didn't fit her perfect, little picture. Alice hoped her sister's fiancé had a giant mole on his cheek and a pig nose.

Her mother fiddled with the teapot, musing. "I'm sure he comes from a good family. It would be fitting, since they met at the university." She rambled on about Katherine's intended, until, finally, her mother realized that Alice was still there. She almost seemed surprised to see her. She took Alice's hand. "But that's not even the most exciting news," she said. "You'll be at the wedding as well."

Alice took a quick breath. "Will I?"

"Of course, silly girl." Her mother grinned. "Dr. Longfellow says you're practically cured. Honestly, I wondered what was taking so long. You've been here nearly eight months, and Dr. Longfellow came so highly regarded. I suppose that shouldn't matter. It's all in the past now."

Alice put her hand on her heart. The feel of it thumping away in her chest proved that she was real—that *this* was real—and not another dream. "Am I really going home? Truly?"

"Truly, my darling. I'm taking you home."

Home.

Alice wanted to jump into her mother's arms, but such acts could be taken in other ways—especially if Nurse Hazel was watching, and Alice suspected she was. Instead, she smiled, making sure it wasn't too big to draw notice.

"When I get home," Alice started, "I could...I could help with the wedding. Katherine would like that, wouldn't she?"

"Of course she would. She'd like that very much." Her mother glanced at the clock above the door. "Oh my, look at the time. Sorry again, but I must be off. Katherine is determined to have her wedding in a few short months, and there's so much to do."

Her mother stood.

Alice said, "I'll go get my things.

"Oh." Her mother's smile faded. "You see, my sweet, Dr. Longfellow said that you can't leave yet. He's making such a fuss over some final things. He really is so trying at times."

Alice stared down at the paint-chipped wood between her feet. "What about tomorrow?"

Her mother placed her hand on Alice's shoulder. "Don't fret, dear. Dr. Longfellow says it will be quite soon. I made him promise, after all. I told him, 'Now listen here, Dr. Longfellow. It wouldn't do to have Alice miss her own sister's wedding.' You'll see, Alice. I'll be back sooner than you know, and I'll have your room all ready when I do. Now give Mummy a kiss."

Alice didn't want to cry, but she couldn't help it. Tears welled in her eyes as she nodded, almost wishing her mother hadn't said anything about going home. That way, it wouldn't have to hurt so much that it wasn't happening today. Soon? What did that mean? She didn't want to press her mother out of fear that it would cause her to rethink the whole idea.

"Alice?"

Alice quickly wiped her eyes as she turned. Dr. Longfellow stood behind her. He snapped his pocket watch closed.

"Come along," he said. "It's time for your medicine."

Alice kissed her mother on the cheek before she followed Dr. Longfellow into the hallway. As they walked past the discolored walls and closed doors, she told herself that it wouldn't be much longer. She'd even take her medicine, just to be safe. Very soon, she'd be leaving for good, and she'd never have to think of this place again.

Nurse Hazel blocked the entrance to her room, holding something behind her back and grinning as if she'd swallowed a canary. "I think you need to see something, Doctor."

Only one thing would give Nurse Hazel that much satisfaction: the journal. Alice wanted to run back to her mother and scream for her to take her home today. It had to be today because, once Dr. Longfellow saw her journal, he'd never let Alice leave the asylum.

Every inch of Alice twitched to do just that, but her feet stayed rooted to the ground. She glanced from Nurse Hazel to Dr. Longfellow. He fumbled with his watch.

"I'm not sure if I have the time," he said. "Do you suppose it can wait?"

Nurse Hazel bristled. "I think not." She brought the journal out from behind her back and rustled the pages under Dr. Longfellow's nose. "Alice's treatment might not have been successful after all."

Alice tried to grab the journal out of her hands. "You had no right."

Nurse Hazel smirked. "I had every right, my dear. Every right."

"Please, Nurse Hazel," Dr. Longfellow said. "Let me see." He took the journal from Nurse Hazel's hands and perused it thoughtfully. "This is troubling. Troubling indeed."

Minutes later, Alice found herself in Dr. Longfellow's office in one of the overstuffed chairs that faced his wide, wooden desk. Next to the window that looked out to a garden filled with rhododendrons, a large framed painting of Queen Victoria sternly watched over the office.

Dr. Longfellow folded his hands. "This is a very precarious situation," he said. "You see, Alice, I told your parents that, in my medical opinion, you were well, but after this"—he gestured towards the journal splayed across his desk—"well, I am no longer certain."

Alice was determined not to cry in front of Dr. Longfellow. She already knew what he was going to say, and if she had to hear it, she thought she'd break inside. She stared at a paperweight on his desk, a golden hot air balloon. She concentrated on the lettering around the top that read "Merrie Olde England."

"That's the unfortunate news," he said, "but I have some good news too."

Alice lifted her gaze from the balloon.

Dr. Longfellow smiled. "I'm not a man that runs from a challenge. Oh, no. I see this as merely a temporary setback." He leaned forwards and put his hands on his desk.

"I have a colleague in Switzerland," he said, "who is making breakthroughs in diseases of the mind. It's all very exciting, and I've wanted to study his methods for quite some time now. What he has discovered is brilliant, but I won't bore you with the details because that's not what is important. What *is* important is that I think he can help you."

Dr. Longfellow waited for Alice to respond. She had but one question:

"If I see this doctor in Switzerland, can I go home?"

"Most assuredly, my dear Alice," he said, almost laughing. "You see, Dr. Gottlieb Burckhardt, my colleague, discovered that some mental defects could be fixed, not by medicine or treatment, but with a simple procedure. It's all a little unorthodox, but it is the future. Soon, every institution will be using his methods, and we will be one of the first. Isn't that wondrous?"

Alice didn't really understand, but she nodded anyway.

"Excellent." He clapped his hands. "I want to leave as soon as possible. I'll have Nurse Hazel make all the arrangements, and I'll write to your parents. I see no reason why we can't be on our way as soon as tomorrow. Does that sound all right with you, Alice?"

Nothing sounded more all right than going home.

Nothing.

Chapter 8
Rosamund
House of Hearts, Wonderland
Narcissus 21, Year of the Queen

Strange voices vexed Rosamund throughout the night.

"You killed me, Rosie," Thomas, the dead King of Hearts, moaned. "How could you do it?"

"Don't feel so bad," she heard Pedro's voice say, and nearly woke at the sound of it. "She beheaded me too."

"Yes, but you deserved it," Thomas retorted.

On and on it went while Rosamund tossed and turned. When Sabrina and Bess arrived in the morning, she needed an extra treatment of mayonnaise and sliced pickles for her puffy eyes.

"Didn't sleep well, Your Majesty?" Bess fussed. "I've insisted for ages that your mattress isn't lumpy enough, and now look."

"Stop with your hullabaloo for once." Rosamund groaned and shielded her eyes. "Where are my grounds? You know I can't function without my morning grounds."

Bess snapped her fingers at Sabrina, who was as sullen as ever. The young girl sighed, no doubt harboring secret hopes for that ridiculous Count of Candlewick, as she set the coffeepot before Rosamund. She wished Sabrina would get those silly thoughts out of her head. It didn't matter how many times that Count asked for Sabrina's hand in marriage, Rosamund would never allow it, and she couldn't wait for that fool to leave her court.

Rosamund dipped her hand into the pot and pulled out a handful of coffee grounds. She wadded it into a ball and shoved it under her bottom lip, fluttering her eyes as the juice seeped down her throat.

"Ah, that's better," she said with drool dribbling down her chin. "Now I can think properly."

After Madame Diamond's card reading last night, Rosamund was convinced that whoever the traitor was lurking in her House was in cahoots with the Queen of Spades. She also knew, as she knew everything else, that the plot against her had something to do with Madame Diamond's horrid shadow card, only she couldn't figure out the what or the how of it. She needed to do some sneaking.

After she was properly dressed, powdered and fluffed, and wearing her favorite pair of ruby high-heels, Rosamund went into the throne room. Intricate heart tapestries adorned the walls and rose-stained glass gave the marbled columns a pinkish tint. She climbed the steps to her throne. A sheen of sweat pebbled over her brow when she arrived at the top, but she was so high up that nobody could tell. She sat and beckoned to one of the guards to come closer. She yelled down at him, "I shall make a royal decree today, an exclusive for royal workers. Make sure everyone is gathered and be quick about it. You know I don't like delay."

"Yes, Your Majesty," he said with a click of his heels.

He shuffled down the stairs, telling everyone he encountered, "The Queen has a royal decree, royal workers only. Pass the word. The Queen has a decree."

The room filled with her palace staff, from the flower pickers to the pillow stuffers, from the pillow stuffers to the icing makers, from the icing makers to the tea stirrers, from the tea stirrers to the envelope lickers, and so on and so forth.

Rosamund rolled her eyes as Sir Pluckus, the rabble-rousing alligator, pushed through the crowd in his far too-tight union shirt. She hated rabble-rousers and how she'd ever agreed to a union was still a prickle in her paw. She chalked it up to her early days on the throne. She had been soft then, when Sir

Pluckus had made a case for servants' rights. Now that she'd had time to think about the whole idea, it was the most ridiculous thing she'd ever heard. Servants didn't have rights.

Sir Pluckus made his way to the front. "Pardon. Excuse. My apologies. Union steward coming through. Yes, pardon. Excuse."

"Pluckus." Rosamund clenched her teeth. "So glad you could make it."

"You know I never miss a royal decree, Your Majesty, and I do hope," he said, uncoiling a rolled parchment with his scaly hands, "it doesn't violate any of the bylaws and through-laws of the servants' contract."

"There's no need to be so disagreeable, Pluckus. You wouldn't want to lose your head, would you?"

"No, Your Majesty, but"—he pointed to a line in the contract—"it says here that you will refrain from beheading the Union Steward until the next triennium."

Rosamund's eyes narrowed. "And when's that?"

"The next triennium."

She pursed her lips.

Refraining could mean so many things.

The fiddlers played three sharp notes, silencing the hall, and all eyes settled on Rosamund—exactly where she liked them.

Rosamund brought her hands together. "I'm sure you are all wondering why you're here."

Her servants waited, and she allowed them to wait longer, enjoying all the attention.

Sir Pluckus whispered, "The royal decree, Your Majesty?"

"I'm getting to that," Rosamund snapped, and pushed a stray hair out of her eye. "I have decided on a royal decree that is good for this afternoon and this afternoon only."

Sir Pluckus scanned the contract, no doubt looking to see if that was legal.

Rosamund said, "I have decreed that everyone will have the afternoon off."

Smiles spread among the servants like a contagious disease. Rosamund couldn't have that. She didn't want them to think they were actually getting rewarded; besides, she also didn't want to catch it.

"Without pay," she added.

Some mouths dropped. Others gasped. She saw a few shaking their heads.

"What!" Sir Pluckus yelled. "You can't do that."

Rosamund tilted her head. "I can when there is a deficit. Look it up in your silly contract, Pluckus. We all must do our part. Think of the example you'll set with the workers outside the palace. They pay your wages, you know."

Rosamund never concerned herself with the royal coffers. All monies and the property of traitors, no-gooders, loiterers, gawkers, and general annoyers went straight to the Royal Bank.

"The union will fight this," Sir Pluckus shouted. "We'll make signs, we'll pass flyers, and we'll make a hullabaloo. Hullabaloos like you've never seen."

"Oh, don't crack your scales," Rosamund said. "It's one afternoon."

"This isn't over," he said, shaking his head. "Not by a short shot."

"Very well." Rosamund clapped her hands, ignoring the overgrown lizard. "Everyone can leave now. Go on. Shoo. Be gone." The servants continued to stare at her. "Last one here gets beheaded."

Mayhem broke out as everyone stampeded to the door. Bonnets, aprons, and knickers were discarded in the wake of the flight. Rosamund felt a little sorry for poor Mr. Hubert Snubert. The tortoise couldn't get out fast enough, but rules were rules, and the guards took him straight to the chopping block.

Rosamund wished it had been Pluckus instead, but not even the Queen of Hearts could always get her way. Such a pity.

Rosamund looked around the empty room.

She was alone.

Now she could finally implement her plan without a bunch of busybodies around.

Rosamund went back to her bedchamber and dressed all in green, a color she wholly despised because of its connection to the House of Clubs. If William hadn't thrown a ball with everyone dressed in the colors of the other houses, she wouldn't have had the green dress in the first place. Of course, that was when the houses were pleasant to one another and weren't plotting to take hers away. Or maybe they were. It was hard for Rosamund to remember precisely when it all started.

After Rosamund dressed; which took dreadfully long since she had to go about it by herself, she went to one of the rose arrangements in her room and plucked all the leaves from the stems. She carefully plastered them to her cheeks, forehead, and chin.

"There," Rosamund said when she finished. "Anyone who sees me will think I'm a fairly large and disproportionate Brussels sprout."

Rosamund left through the secret entrance that the chambermaids and the pillow fluffers used and crept along the corridor, keeping close to the wall. It wasn't long until she heard some whispering. She inched closer until she saw it was William, wearing his hat at a conspiratorial angle. He stood traitorously close to someone, probably whispering traitorous things.

Rosamund was about to confront William when she saw Lady Sabrina move away from him, blushing all the way to the tips of her fingers. Before she could question what that was all about, William headed her way.

Rosamund had to think fast.

She pressed against the red paneling and closed her eyes.

"How did a Brussels sprout get in here?" William huffed. "The servants get one day off and there are already Brussels sprouts? What's next? Asparagus? Green beans?" William stomped down the hall, grumbling under his breath.

Rosamund decided to move on but made a mental note to keep an eye on those two. She said it twice but had no way to write it down. She scolded herself for not bringing a notebook with her, but these were desperate times, and she hadn't had time to think it all through.

After lifting the manhole cover at the end of the hall, she took a few buggies, crossed a bridge, and walked a tightrope before she ran into another conspiracy at one of the palace's many three-way stops. Rosamund had no problem recognizing Bess's annoying voice.

She heard Bess say, "We need to talk."

We? Who could possibly be talking to Bess? But most unimportantly, who would possibly want to talk to Bess of their own accord?

"Now?" a familiar voice said. "I was getting ready to do a little preening. I've got a case of wing rash you wouldn't believe."

Rosamund crept closer until she saw Charles. She almost gasped but remembered she was undercover. What possible business could Charles have with Bess? She thought he despised the duchess.

"If it wasn't unimportant," Bess snapped, "I wouldn't be here in the second place."

"Very well. Come inside."

Rosamund knew they were planning to plot more plots, and she couldn't allow that. She whirled around to confront them, but they'd already disappeared behind a closed door. She raised her fist, getting ready to pound it open and demand to know what was so awfully unimportant when she heard—

"Why it's a Brussels sprout, but I have no time for Brussels sprouts."

Rosamund turned in time to see Ralph disappear down a hall with five and a half statues.

Where did he think he was bloody off to in such a hurry?

She followed the rabbit through secret stairs, secret passageways, secret ladders, and secret swing sets until he finally stopped before a row of secret doors of all kinds. Rosamund tried to remember ever seeing such a place. She'd have to ask her royal architect about getting a copy of the palace red-prints.

Ralph gazed over his shoulder. "I said I have no time for Brussels sprouts. No time. No time. NO TIME."

He circled around, pulling a key out from his pocket and heading to the smallest door. Rosamund took a step closer and wondered if the rabbit was a little daft.

How does he expect to get through that door? With a carrot and a corkscrew?

Ralph pulled out a vial from his waistcoat and took a small sip. "A little too tart," he said, smacking his lips together. In a twinkling, Ralph shrank to the size of a dormouse before her very eyes.

What in all that is roses...?

Rosamund had a vague recollection of seeing that type of magic before, but the memory was as soggy as her disguise. Even so, it didn't stop the warning bells from ringing, and, at that point, they were clanging around her brain. She had to stop Ralph.

Rosamund yelled, "Hold it right there, Rabbit!"

"I told you, Brussels sprout," he said, glaring at her with his beady eyes, "I'M LATE. You're being very rude. Now if you will excuse me, I have to go,"

He opened the door and slammed it shut behind him. Rosamund recoiled in disbelief, but it was quickly replaced with rage at the Rabbit's insolence. The nerve. Nobody walks away from Rosamund.

Nobody.

"OFF WITH HIS HEAD!" she shrieked. "OFF WITH HIS HEAD THIS INSTANT! Didn't anyone hear me?" Rosamund raised her voice even louder. "I SAID off with his head! Guards! GUARDS! Where the roses are you?"

When no one came, she remembered that she'd given everyone the afternoon off.

"Oh, bloody, bloody heads," she grumbled and glanced at the door that Ralph had gone through. "I suppose I'll have to do everything myself."

She crouched down, even though queens never crouch, and peered into the keyhole.

All she could see was white—white walls, white floors, and white jackets. Rosamund knew of but one place that had so much dreadful white: the House of Diamonds.

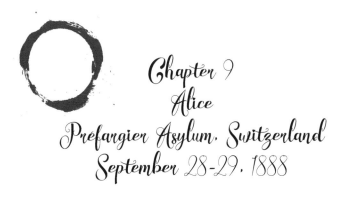

Chapter 9
Alice
Préfargier Asylum, Switzerland
September 28-29, 1888

It took five days to get to Switzerland—less time than Alice thought it would.

It was two days to the Channel and three days from the Channel to Préfargier. Dr. Longfellow decided it really should have taken three days, but Nurse Hazel said they would have had to rush and rushing was uncivilized.

Alice wished they could have left Nurse Hazel behind—far behind, maybe even somewhere in the middle of the English Channel. She had made such a fuss insisting that she come along that Dr. Longfellow had relented.

By the time the carriage came upon the asylum, the bloated, old nurse was the furthest thing from Alice's mind. Préfargier didn't look like an asylum—not really—but a palace of sorts with arched doorways, fountains, a labyrinth of hedges and trees, and a lake glistening in the distance with speckles of sunlight glimmering on the water.

They entered a courtyard, stopping before two double doors, where a line of servants waited. Baggage and boxes passed from hand to hand. The carriage had been thoroughly emptied before Alice took one step outside.

The servants disappeared with their belongings.

Nurse Hazel scowled. "What are we supposed to do? Wait out here all day?"

Dr. Longfellow laughed. "Come, come, Nurse Hazel. Cheer up. You wanted a tour. Here we are. It's amazing. Such efficiency, wouldn't you say?"

"A little too much." She sniffed. "I thought they'd take the bonnet right off my head."

A woman in a white dress descended the steps. She held a parasol in her gloved hand.

"Hullo there," she said, smiling. "Sorry to keep you waiting. Dr. Richard Longfellow, I presume?"

"You have presumed correctly, and might I say it's a great pleasure to be here." He stepped away from Alice as if wanting to put her on display and allow the woman in white a full inspection. "And this is my patient, Miss Alice."

The woman took Alice's hand. "I've been looking forward to meeting you."

The woman's eyes were warm, and Alice instantly took a liking to her. She was about to reply, to say something polite, maybe about the nice weather they were having in Switzerland, when Nurse Hazel huffed behind her.

Dr. Longfellow started. "Oh yes, how rude of me. This is Nurse Hazel."

The woman in white shook Nurse Hazel's hand. "It's always a pleasure to meet a fellow nurse. I'm Nurse Glass, the head nurse at Préfargier."

Nurse Hazel eyed her. "You don't seem like much of a nurse."

"Well," Nurse Glass said, still smiling, "we *are* a little different here at Préfargier."

She winked at Alice, and Alice bit her lip to stop the growing smile that was sure to irritate Nurse Hazel.

"Please, come along," Nurse Glass said, turning back towards the steps. "Dr. Burckhardt has been eager to see you all morning."

Nurse Glass took them down several long corridors with heavy draperies covering the windows, gilded mirrors clinging to the walls, and crystal chandeliers dangling from the ceiling.

"Magnificent," Dr. Longfellow whispered.

"Yes, isn't it lovely?" Nurse Glass asked. "Préfargier was designed by the French architect Francois Phillipon. Perhaps you've heard of him?"

"I can't say that I have, but from what I've seen, I'd wager he's a brilliant chap."

Nurse Glass lowered her voice. "Rumor has it that he was a little mad himself."

They stopped before a paneled door of edelweiss and lilies. If it weren't for the bronze handles, Alice wouldn't have known it was a doorway.

Nurse Glass motioned them inside. "After you."

Alice followed Dr. Longfellow and Nurse Hazel into a large study with expensive sofas and chairs. A man stood before a marbled fireplace with one hand on a pipe and the other in his jacket pocket. He had a white beard and a hooked nose.

"Dr. Burckhardt," Dr. Longfellow said, rushing forwards with his hand extended. "It's such a pleasure to meet you in person. I'm a huge admirer of your work."

Dr. Burckhardt's eyes rolled over Alice as if she were nothing more than one of the many ornaments in the room as he took Dr. Longfellow's hand. "The pleasure's all mine, Dr. Longfellow. And this must be the esteemed Nurse Hazel, head nurse of Warneford Asylum?"

"Indeed, sir," Nurse Hazel said, blushing.

"And you..." His eyes turned to Alice with even less interest than before. "I'm assuming you are the patient, Miss Alice."

Alice cringed under his gaze, wanting to make herself as small as possible. It was as if he saw her secrets without even looking for them. He finally released Alice from his spell and faced Dr. Longfellow, saying, "I'd like to explain my approach to Alice before we get started, if it's all right with you, Dr. Longfellow. But I'd understand if you needed a rest after your travels."

Dr. Longfellow said, "We came all this way to get Alice well. We can't delay. Go on, Dr. Burckhardt. Proceed."

Nurse Glass went to the door. "I'll bring some refreshments."

Dr. Burckhardt sat at his desk. Dr. Longfellow followed suit, taking one of the seats on the opposite side of the desk. Alice didn't know if she was supposed to sit or stand. She was used to being told, but then Nurse Hazel poked Alice in the back and directed her towards a chair directly across from the doctor.

Dr. Burckhardt folded his hands and stared at Alice. "As you may or may not know," he finally said, "doctors are different by nature."

"I completely agree," Dr. Longfellow said, bobbing his head.

"One kind," Dr. Burckhardt continued, "adheres to the old principle: first, do no harm. The other believes it is better to do something than do nothing. Luckily for Alice, I belong to the second category."

Alice jumped in her seat as the door opened and Nurse Glass rolled in a cart of tea and cucumber sandwiches, all arranged daintily with cream and biscuits. At the sight of the cart, Alice almost felt as if she were on holiday or at a tea party, but one glance at Dr. Burckhardt was enough to remind her that this was far from a jolly occasion.

After everyone had been given a cup of tea and a sandwich, except for Dr. Burckhardt, who waved his hand when Nurse Glass offered, he said, "Now, I am a man of science. I believe madness has a physical cause, like any other disease, and that's exactly what I'm going to treat. It'll be no different than having a tooth extracted or a broken arm mended—a small, trivial matter."

Alice felt a twinge of hope. Dr. Burckhardt seemed so confident, so assured that he could take the madness clean out of her.

"My dear Alice," he said, leaning forwards. "I'm going to have you out of here before you know it and you'll never be in an asylum ever again."

"Never?" Alice asked.

"Never," he said.

It was infectious, his belief, and the longer Alice sat there, nibbling her sandwich and drinking her tea, the more she believed it too. It would all be over soon, and she'd go home and attend her sister's wedding, and all her time at the asylum would be forgotten.

After all the cucumber sandwiches were eaten and the tea drunk, Dr. Burckhardt suggested that Nurse Glass take Alice to her room.

"We have a big day tomorrow," he said.

Alice followed Nurse Glass up a flight of stairs and down a bright hallway.

"I already had your things brought up," Nurse Glass said, stopping at one of the many doors and pulling a key from her pocket. "You should find the rooms here very comfortable." She opened the door and Alice peered in.

The room was nothing like the one at Warneford. It had furnishings, wallpaper, and a little window without bars.

Nurse Glass said, "Get yourself settled. There's a basin of water there in the corner if you'd like to wash up. Supper will be served in an hour, and then you'll have to promptly go to sleep. We want you to be well rested for tomorrow."

Alice stepped inside. She ran her hands over the soft duvet, walked over to the window, and pulled the gauzy curtains aside. She hadn't even realized Nurse Glass had left until the lock clicked in place.

Some things weren't so different.

A supper of bread and broiled beef came as Nurse Glass said it would. Alice ate next to the window, where she had a view of the garden with countless roses and gas lamps lighting the paths. It was easy for Alice's mind to wander, and she found herself thinking of the White Rabbit and the dream she'd had, because she was convinced now that it was a dream. There was no other explanation for how she could have explored her empty house, seen the White Rabbit, and then instantly been transported back to the asylum. She wondered if, after tomorrow, she'd ever dream of him again. Alice wanted to be well, but she couldn't help feeling sad at the thought of never seeing the rabbit again.

Nurse Hazel made sure Alice didn't dally at bedtime. She tugged Alice's hospital gown over her head, scowling. "I hope Dr. Burckhardt doesn't take long with you. The sooner we leave, the better."

"I rather like it here," Alice said.

"Of course, *you* would. You'd think they housed royalty here at Préfargier and not the mentally ill. It's not professional. If you ask me, I think they've all lost their heads. Now sleep."

Nurse Hazel locked the door behind her. Alice couldn't sleep no matter how many times she tried forcing herself. She'd never asked what sort of procedure it was, and she wondered all night how Dr. Burckhardt would take the madness out. Alice got more scared with each passing hour. What if it hurt? What if it was so painful that she couldn't go through with it and then she never left the asylum?

Alice didn't think she slept, but when Nurse Glass and Nurse Hazel came to her room, she opened her eyes to find it was already bright with daylight.

"Good morning, Alice," Nurse Glass said. "It's time to get ready."

Alice breakfasted on toast and tea as they pulled her hair back so tight that it gave her a bit of a headache. They dressed her in a hospital gown that was a little too short, but Nurse Glass promised that she'd have a blanket wrapped around her.

When they had finished, Nurse Glass took her down several flights of stairs, and through an assortment of hallways and corridors.

Alice slowed as she passed one of the rooms where she heard sobbing. A pretty girl, maybe a few years older than Alice, rocked back and forth, clutching a bandage around her head. Two nurses tried to soothe her, but she slapped their hands and screamed at them to stay away.

A chill passed through Alice, filling her to the core with fear. She couldn't move. She couldn't take another step. What had happened to that girl? Was it Dr. Burckhardt?

It'll be no different than getting a tooth extracted...

Alice started to shiver and shiver and shiver.

"Don't mind Sarah BreeAnn," Nurse Glass said, pushing Alice forwards. "She's a particularly difficult case. She's been having a hard time *adjusting*, but we have high hopes for her."

Nurse Glass opened a door at the end of the hall. It swung

on its hinges, ready to swallow Alice whole. "Here we are."

The room was nothing like the ones upstairs. It was cold and sterile, with white brick walls, deep sinks, and a table full of metal instruments. A bed had been bolted to the floor. As she got closer, she saw it couldn't be a bed because it was altogether too high up from the ground, and leather straps dangled from it.

Something was wrong. Very, very wrong.

Nurse Glass frowned. "What's the matter? Did Sarah Bree-Ann upset you?"

"N...no..." Alice stammered out. "It's that everything is happening so fast. I need time to think. Just for a second. Maybe I can go upstairs for a little while longer."

"None of this fussing," Nurse Hazel said, pushing Alice into the room. "I'm not going to wait around another month for you to decide it's a good time to get well."

Alice pushed against the nurses as they hoisted her onto the bed. "No, please, no!" Alice cried as they forced her down.

"It'll all be over soon," Nurse Glass whispered to her. "Very soon, my sweet. Do be a good girl."

Alice kicked at their hands as tears slid into the corners of her mouth, sending the taste of salt down her throat. She fought them, scratching and pinching and biting like an animal. All she could think about was getting away, but it didn't matter what she did. The nurses worked together, one holding Alice down while the other wrapped the straps around her hands and feet. They placed a rag over her mouth and nose that burned her lungs with a sickly sweet scent.

"That was more difficult than I thought it would be," Nurse Glass said. "We should fetch the doctors and tell them she's ready."

Nurse Hazel grinned at Alice. "Be back soon," she said before turning away.

They shut the door, leaving Alice alone. As soon as their footsteps faded down the hallway, she started tugging at the straps. She whimpered as the leather chafed against her flesh and burned it.

Something banged in the corner. Alice jerked towards the sound, but the light made it hard to see. She heard the faint sounds of a ticking clock and padded feet coming closer. It must be one of the doctors. Her heart was beating in her ears, and she closed her eyes, cringing. But then, she felt the strap around her left foot give way and then the strap around her right foot. Alice started kicking and fighting.

"You're having a proper wobbly, aren't you?" Alice recognized the White Rabbit's voice. He came to her side, releasing the restraints around her arms and then finally the one around her head.

"How'd you get here?" she asked him.

"That doesn't matter. You must come with me to Wonderland at once. We haven't any spare moments to find and many more to lose."

Alice dropped down from the bed, tears filling her eyes. "I want to go home. They said I could go home."

"Not here, no, no no." Ralph shook his head. "This is a terrible, terrible place."

Alice felt it too, deep down. The marbled floors of Préfargier were hiding something horrible—an asylum much worse than Warneford. She took a shaky breath.

Ralph cocked his head.

They heard footsteps, a lot of them.

"They're coming," he said. "We have to go."

Alice chewed her bottom lip and glanced towards the door.

Ralph took a step towards her. "Listen to me, Alice. This is your last chance... This is our last chance. If you stay, you'll be lost forever."

Sarah BreeAnn screamed somewhere down the hall. The sound shook Alice from the top of her head to the tips of her toes. Whatever had happened to Sarah BreeAnn, the same thing was going to happen to her. Dr. Burckhardt's cure wasn't a cure at all. It was a curse.

"Yes," Alice said, determined. "Let's leave now. Immediately."

Ralph nodded. "You've come to your mind and just in the nick of time."

Alice heard the jingle of keys outside the door. She turned towards the noise, shaking her head. "We're too late."

Ralph checked his watch. "Actually, we are right on time."

"On time?" Alice looked around. "How can we be on time? We're trapped. We'll never make it to Wonderland."

"All we have to do is go through the door."

"The door?" Alice pointed. "They're right outside it. They'll stop us."

"Not that one. *This* one."

Ralph pushed aside a cart and brushed a layer of dust off a tiny door with a silver knob. He pulled two bottles from inside his breast pocket and handed one to Alice. The tiny note attached to the cork read "Drink me."

Ralph held it up. "To our unbirthdays."

Alice swallowed the liquid. It tasted a little like roast beef, marmalade, and a twinge of peppermint. Her head felt light and woozy, and she thought she might throw up. Alice clutched her stomach and staggered. Her knees buckled underneath her, and the floor raced upwards as if to smack her in the face.

Faster and faster and faster.

Alice closed her eyes and put up her arms, expecting a painful crash, but then she felt an impatient tug on the back of her gown. Alice lowered her arms. Everything in the room towered above her. Giant feet moved inside. She could hear the thunderous voices of the doctors.

"Hurry," Ralph said. He took Alice's hand and pulled her through the door.

Chapter 10
Rosamund
House of Hearts, Wonderland
Narcissus 21, Year of the Queen

Rosamund threw her green garments to the side and ordered the servants back to their posts so that she might have a cool bath drawn. As she scrubbed her skin, her thoughts went around in rectangles, giving her a headache.

She hated the House of Diamonds as much as she hated the other houses. Rosamund couldn't help that they were all jealous of her; it was such a chore to be the best. The House of Clubs was too hot. The House of Spades was too much work. The House of Diamonds was too cold. But the House of Hearts… Well, it was perfect.

Which brought her to the crux of the matter. Why was Ralph sneaking away to the House of Diamonds? If it had anything to do with the untimely release of the Queen of Spades, then Ralph had a death warrant coming.

Rosamund threw a piece of soap at the gong to make it ring.

Bess rushed in. "All done, Your Majesty?"

"No, but I'm done enough."

Bess helped Rosamund out of the bath and into her robe. Rosamund eyed Bess as the duchess fussed about the room. Ralph's behavior certainly had Rosamund on edge, but she hadn't forgotten about the tryst between Bess and Charles.

Rosamund fiddled with her collar. "I nearly forgot with all the ruckus this afternoon that I was supposed to send a proclamation to Charles. I can't very well deliver it now." She turned to Bess.

The duchess said, "I could take it for you."

"How could you possibly?" Rosamund asked, whirling around. "You wouldn't know where his private chambers are. Why would you? I mean, what would you and the earl possibly have to talk about?"

Bess's face whitened.

How Rosamund hated that color.

"Y...you're quite right, Your Majesty. The earl and I... well... What would we have to say to each other unless he were interested in your doilies?"

Rosamund narrowed her eyes. "Interested in my doilies?"

Bess laughed nervously.

Rosamund sniffed and went into her bedchamber, where Sabrina was waiting by the armoire. She passed her with barely a sidelong glance on the way to her desk and wrote underneath Bess's name "To Do: Behead Charles," then covered it up with a napkin.

"Now then," Rosamund said, turning to Sabrina. "You may proceed."

Sabrina held up gown choices for the afternoon. Bess came in shortly after with the brushes and the nail files and combs. Rosamund pressed her fingers against her temples. All she really wanted was a cup of tea.

William threw open the door, startling Rosamund. Bess and Sabrina jumped to cover her with rejected gowns. Nobody could see the Queen without proper primping and fussing—not unless the next thing they wanted to see was the executioner's axe.

Underneath the satin and lace and silk, Rosamund shook with rage. "Are you mad?"

"My most insolent apologies," William said, "but I knew you'd want this information right away."

Rosamund growled, "Go on then. Out with it. And for the love of roses, take off that hat."

William removed his hat and held it behind him. "It's the Queen of Spades, Your Majesty," he said. "She's here, outside the palace, waiting under guard."

Rosamund smiled as she sank into the gowns like a cat finding a bird's nest. The Queen of Spades was her prisoner. "You have done well, Cousin," she said. "Better than well, even... You've done fine."

William glanced towards Sabrina. "I hope so, Your Majesty, and that it might be remembered when the time comes."

Rosamund raised her eyebrows. "That depends on *future* deeds. Now *get* out."

"Yes, of course," William said, taking a step backwards. "Shall I let your court know it is your pleasure to see the prisoner now, Your Majesty?"

"No, you shall not," Rosamund said smugly. "I am not properly attired. She will have to wait until I'm at my leisure."

Rosamund took her time to get dressed and then declared teatime. She chatted happily with Bess and Sabrina as she enjoyed her new favorite: fruit and oyster cordial. She finished her last biscuit and flicked a crumb onto the carpet. Sighing with contentment, she rose. "I suppose I should go and see the Queen of Spades. It would be the proper thing to do."

She wore her best crown, reserved for special occasions and fitted with rubies, garnets, and carnelian. She carried her scepter with the giant ruby heart, which had been passed down from one Queen of Hearts to the next for as long as time had been recorded.

Bess and Sabrina followed Rosamund into the Grand Hall towards her throne. Standing next to it were William and Charles. Most notably missing was Ralph. What conspiratorial activities was he up to?

Rosamund sniffed as she turned to allow Bess and Sabrina to fan her train. After she was certain she appeared positively regal, she sat and nodded to the guard.

And waited.

Rosamund drummed her nails on the rose engravings.

And then waited some more.

Finally, a troop of guards entered the hall, prodding along Constance, the Queen of Spades. Constance stopped before Rosamund, appearing weary and aged in her black gown and black cloak lined with ermine.

It was almost worth the wait.

Almost.

A hush settled on the room like a sprinkling of dust.

Rosamund extended her hand. "My dear sister. I find it somewhat satisfactory to see you again."

Constance kissed Rosamund's knuckle. "And I, you."

"Who should I thank for this visit? The King of Spades, perhaps?"

Constance paled at the mention of the King. "He is dead. I am here seeking refuge. I need your help, Sister."

"Refuge?" Rosamund asked, sitting back. "Whatever for? You're the Queen."

Constance pinched her lips. "If only the Spades knew how to treat a queen. It has been a trial. I was lucky to even escape. Now I'm a queen without a throne. They never would have treated me that way if my poor Edmund hadn't died, but, oh, bother," she said, shrugging. "I suppose we're both widows, aren't we?"

"*I* am a widow," Rosamund answered. "You've been charged with the murder of the King of Spades."

"Didn't you sign your husband's death warrant?"

"That is not the point," Rosamund snapped. "The Spades have levied some grim accusations against you."

Constance's mouth hung open. "None of it is true."

"I should send you back at once."

"You wouldn't dare."

"Wouldn't I? You dare presume what decision the Queen of Hearts would or wouldn't dare? How dare you?" Rosamund lowered her voice. "Don't think for one minute I don't know what you are trying to do."

Constance took a breath. "I'm not trying to do anything. I'm falling on the mercy of my dear sister. I'm appalled you'd think I mean any ill will."

"Rubbish," Rosamund said. "You can't fool me."

Constance looked over her shoulder and then leaned closer to Rosamund. "If you send me back, what's going to stop the Hearts from taking the throne away from you like the Spades did to me? We queens have to stick together. A precedent has to be set."

"My people would never do that to me."

Constance raised her eyebrows. "Are you so sure about that?"

Rosamund took a breath. "Is that a threat?"

"No... What in the world would make you think that?"

"Because I know you, that's why." Rosamund felt herself growing hot. "And I won't have you lingering about, trying to turn my people against me. Don't think I can't see right through you. I am and always will be the Queen of Hearts."

"Of course you are," Constance said. "There's never an end to your reign, my dear, only beginnings."

"I've had enough of this. Guards." Rosamund snapped her fingers. "Take her away and lock her in the tower."

Constance's chin quivered. "You wouldn't lock away your own sister like some common criminal."

"I will do as I please. A *queen* can do that."

The guards grabbed Constance by her arms. "You will take me as a prisoner? Your own sister?"

"You're not a prisoner, no, no, no." Rosamund wagged her finger. "Consider yourself my guest. And don't worry. It'll just be long enough for me to sign your death warrant."

"HICKORY, DICKORY, DOCK." Constance gazed about the room. "HICKORY, DICKORY, DOCK."

Rosamund froze. "What did you say?"

"Nothing." Constance shook her head.

"Those *words*..."

Constance was behind the plot. She'd probably orchestrated the whole thing. Constance had always been jealous of her. Rosamund was prettier, more talented, and, above all, a better ruler.

Rosamund ordered, "Get her out of my sight. Right now."

As guards dragged the Queen of Spades away, Rosamund exhaled, not realizing she had been holding her breath. She had been right. Someone from her court was in league with her sister—the same person who'd slid the note under her door.

Ralph, perhaps?

The pudding was thickening.

It was a bigger plot than Rosamund had imagined, maybe even the biggest, but she'd nip it in the rosebud. She always did.

William and Charles stared at her, and their silence coated the walls like red paint.

"Why are you standing there gawking?" Rosamund barked. "Issue the death warrant for the Queen of Spades."

Chapter 11
Alice
Lost Wood, Wonderland
Narcissus 21, Year of the Queen

Alice didn't know if she was in Wonderland. It was dark—frightfully dark. A spark ignited in the gloom, and she saw Ralph's shadowy face.

"This way," he said, holding a candle in his paw. "Follow me."

"Where are we?" Alice asked.

"The Lost Wood," he said. "You'd better stay close. If you get lost, you'll stay lost forever. Only those who know their way can make it out."

Alice gulped and looped her fingers into the top of Ralph's waistcoat.

The most unusual noises filled the air. A dog whined, a horse neighed, and she heard loud whooping noises—then a crunching sound. Large figures skulked from the yellow lights blinking on the trees like will-o'-the-wisps at twilight. They were giant, lumpy things and Alice had to swallow a scream every time she saw one from the corner of her eye.

Something grabbed Alice's shoulder and tugged, causing her to loosen her grip on Ralph. She glanced behind her. A wolf-ish creature with golden eyes tapped its talons against her skin. It cleared its throat. "I don't suppose you're going where I need to go? I must have become lost somewhere."

"I don't think so," Alice said and leaned closer to Ralph.

"Are you lost too?" it asked with a grin.

"N...no," she said with chattering teeth. "I am with the White Rabbit. He knows where he's going."

"Oh," the creature said and released its grip. "Pity."

Then it was gone.

Alice remembered a poem she read long ago in the Looking Glass Book:

"Twas brillig, and the slithy toves
Did gyre and gimble in the wabe;
All mimsy were the borogoves
And the mome raths outgrabe...."

Alice shivered. She knew what waited for those who lost their way in the Lost Wood.

"Jabberwockies," she said aloud.

"Yes." Ralph nodded. "This place is full of them. The Queen used to get rid of people here before she started beheading them. It was a favorite of hers. The Jabberwockies must miss being so well fed."

Something shrieked in the darkness, followed by the sounds of low, throaty growls and then deathly silence. Alice felt herself shaking and she held tighter to Ralph. She closed her eyes and chanted under her breath, "Please hurry, please hurry, please hurry."

Ralph suddenly stopped. She opened her eyes and peeked behind her. The jabberwockies lurked in the shadows nearby, watching them.

Ralph said, "Ah, I think this is it," and drummed his paw on the trunk of a tree.

Tap, tap, tappity-tap, tap-tappity.

Nothing happened. Ralph put his paw to his chin. "That's odd. I must have made a mistake."

Tap, tappity-tap, tap, tap-tappity.

The jabberwockies started coming closer. She could hear them growling.

"Hmm. How about this?"

Tappity-tap, tap, tap, tap-tappity.

Finally, a door in the tree opened and Ralph moved to the side. "Very good," he said. "Another minute out here and I believe we would have been lost. After you," he said and pushed her in.

Alice tumbled forwards into an abyss. She tried to scream, but her stomach pressed into her mouth, muffling her as she fell. She had gone from being nearly eaten by jabberwockies to falling to her death. If she had to choose which way she was going to die, she preferred this one. She squeezed her eyes shut, readying herself for impact.

The air shifted, and a breeze ruffled her gown and tickled her face. She'd felt this before. It was like the first time she'd come to Wonderland. She opened her eyes. Alice was floating down a torch-lit chasm. She passed so many curious things: mismatched socks, stacks of books rotating around each other, spoons and knives, a set of keys, and all sorts of jewelry. She reached out, but the objects bounced away.

Her feet touched solid ground without so much as a nudge.

"Move aside," Ralph shouted from over her head. "I can't very well control where I stop."

Alice jumped out of the way, and the rabbit landed beside her. "Was that another rabbit hole?"

"Of course," Ralph said. He straightened his waistcoat and checked his pocket watch. "Wonderland is full of them."

"Why do they have so many curious things inside?"

"It's where all the missing things go," Ralph said. "Everyone knows that."

"The missing things?"

Ralph started to walk away. "You know, from the nursery rhyme:

The rabbit holes are where's they go.
The things you misplaced, lost, or forgot,
Oh, but shouldn't have ought,
Never, oh n'er to be found again,
Deep down in the rabbit hole.

"It's a classic," he said.

Alice followed behind the rabbit. "I don't think I've ever heard that one before. How many lost things are in the rabbit holes?"

Ralph stopped before three passageways. "More than you can ever possibly count, times double, divided by half. This way."

They entered the tunnel on the left. Twinkle lights flickered along the walls like gems until Alice realized they weren't lights but glowing eyes. Creatures winked at them—some with one eye and others with three or four. As soon as they caught Alice staring, they'd blink out like snuffed lanterns.

"Such funny, little things," Alice mused. "Talk about feeling like being watched." She quickened her step, coming side by side with Ralph. "Where are we going?" she asked him.

"Headquarters," he said.

"Where do the other tunnels go?"

"One to a place of no significance, the other to Gardenia City, a place with plenty of significance."

"What's in Gardenia City?"

"The Queen of Hearts."

"Oh." Alice's stomach curled. What with the jabberwockies and rabbit holes, she had almost forgotten the reason Ralph wanted her to come to Wonderland in the first place. Her legs shook at the very thought of facing the Queen of Hearts, especially if they tried to make Alice kill her—murder her.

Murder.

Alice swallowed. Her throat itched as if she'd swallowed a tablespoon of salt. She wouldn't do it, of course. Alice could never hurt anyone, let alone kill them, but she couldn't go back to Préfargier either. What if the White Rabbit told her she'd have to go back if she didn't do what he asked? She didn't like to think of that.

Ralph turned to her. "Are you well?" he asked.

Alice nodded. "Yes, I believe so."

She followed Ralph through several twists, curves, abrupt rights, lefts, and rights again, and finally came to another door.

Ralph knocked.

Tap, tap, tappity-tap, tap-tappity.

Alice's heart raced. She wondered what she'd find on the other side. Villains of some sort, she was sure. Who else would plot the death of the Queen, even if it was the Queen of Hearts, but robbers, thieves, and crooks? People who were nothing like the White Rabbit. But then again, if she thought about it, she barely knew him. However, he did save her from the asylum, so that must mean he was good on the inside. At least, she hoped so.

A gruff voice barked, "Password."

Ralph cleared his throat. "*Hickory, dickory, dock.*"

The voice said, "You may enter."

"Come along," Ralph said and opened the door.

Alice followed the rabbit, but as soon as she stepped inside, someone slammed the door behind her and held a lantern up to her eyes.

"Were ye followed?" a voice demanded. "Have ye spoken to anyone? Did ye smell the scent of buttered croissant? Or perhaps jelly? Did the clock strike 7:37 on the way to the market?"

Alice shielded her face. "No, no, no, no, and I don't know."

Ralph shouted, "Leave her be, Bill, and for lobster mule stew, turn that blasted lantern off."

The light faded, but all Alice could see were bouncing black spots. She tried blinking them away, but no matter how many times she opened and shut her eyes, they stayed.

Bill, a green lizard with white splotches, said, "I'm tryin' to take precautions."

Alice felt a soft hand on her arm. "Sit here, deary," a woman's voice said as Alice was led to a chair. "I'll make you some tea in a jiff."

Alice rubbed her eyes until she could finally see the whole room. Papers lined the walls and a machine tapped out what she supposed was a code. Stuffed chairs, hard chairs, big chairs, and small chairs filled every space. She found herself sitting before a triangle-shaped table laden with jars, teapots, and cups—many, many cups.

"Here you go, deary." A furry hand placed a teacup before her. "It'll calm your knickers."

Alice took a sip and spat it out. "There's butter in it, and it tastes like a stinky, old sock."

A rat wearing a bonnet glared at her. "Well, my sty," she said. "I have never had any complaints about my tea, and I've served *queens*. And who are you...you... Well, what are you?"

"I'm a girl, I suppose," Alice said.

"Not any girl I've ever seen." The rat snorted as she sat across from Alice and put three pats of butter in her own cup. "Anyway, you better get used to it. That's how Her Majesty likes it."

"She doesn't seem like much of an assassin," a voice purred in Alice's ear, and she almost toppled her tea. She recognized that voice. She searched for the Cheshire Cat.

"Not to mention," the rat said to Ralph, drawing Alice's attention, "she doesn't act like one either."

Ralph's fur fluffed. "What would you know about it?"

"Wait, wait, wait 'ere." Bill waved the lantern over his head. "I knew I recognized her. Yer the girl that took the roof clean off Ralph's house. Blew up to a giant, you did. Took me a week to fix."

"Oh yes, I remember," Alice said, narrowing her eyes. "And I also remember you throwing rocks at me."

"Apologies 'bout that," Bill said, rubbing his hand over his scaly head, "but you did look like a serpent at the time, and you did kick me through the chimney in me knackers."

Alice heard the purring again in her ear. It said, "Yes, it was quite a sight."

She turned towards the noise, but nothing was there. She knew she'd heard the Cheshire Cat, but where was he? Why was he hiding? No doubt the Cheshire Cat was up to mischief like before. If it hadn't been for that silly cat, she wouldn't have been in all that trouble with the Queen in the first place. Alice was about to say something when Ralph turned to her.

"It seems like you already know Bill," he said, and pointed at the rat. "This is Lillian. And Chester...Chester, where are you?"

A wide grin materialized on Alice's lap, followed by a gray body with purple stripes, and finally a tail. "Hello, Alice. How splendid to see you again. I see you haven't changed—much."

Alice folded her arms. "I thought the Queen would have beheaded *you* by now."

"Oh, believe me, she's tried, but I'm much too clever for the likes of her."

"For now," Lillian said before turning towards Alice. "The Queen hates cats. Can't say I really blame her."

"Hmmm..." Chester flicked his tail. "And she's not too fond of rats either, from what I hear."

Lillian stirred her tea as if she were whisking cream.

"That's enough, you two." Ralph scowled at them and opened his watch. "Now, where were we? Oh yes, quite right. We still need to properly induct Alice into the Aboveground Organization."

"But we're underground," Alice noted.

"Of course we are," Lillian snapped. "No one would suspect us to be underground. That's the whole point."

Bill shook his head. "She has a lot to learn if she 'spects to kill the Queen."

Alice started to interject. "One minute please—"

"If she even has it in her." Lillian smirked.

"You see—" Alice began again.

"Oh, she has it in her," Chester said, disappearing until he was only a flashing pair of teeth. "You should have seen Alice before. She drove the Queen mad, absolutely mad. I think she'll be purrr-*fect* as long as the Queen doesn't behead her. It is such a lovely game the Queen likes to play."

Alice tapped the table. "And that's exactly why—"

"I agree with Chester," Ralph said. "She can do it. I know she can. She's the one who could—"

"BUT YOU SEE." Alice finally had their attention. "None of this really matters because I won't kill the Queen."

Chapter 12
Rosamund
The House of Hearts, Wonderland
Narcissus 21, Year of the Queen

Rosamund waited to receive the death warrant for the Queen of Spades. And waited. And waited. She could twirl her hair for only so long. Clearly, anything needing done in the House of Hearts she'd have to do herself.

She marched towards the Privy Council Chamber, a room her advisors had dubbed "the Cave," and poked her head in. She wasn't furious because William and Charles were playing billiards while servants served them drinks from the bar. Or because they had a nearly indecent puppet show playing in the background. The thing that really got her seeing red was that they weren't doing a single thing, not lifting a finger or feather, to get the Queen of Spade's death warrant in order.

Charles was in the middle of lighting his pipe, when she roared, "What's the meaning of this?"

William dropped his pool stick at the sound of her voice, which hit Charles's wing and caused him to burn himself.

"Why are you all dillydallying, filly-faddling while the Queen of Spades has her head on her shoulders? And where, for the love of all that's roses, is Ralph?"

William chewed on the brim of his hat. "That's who we're waiting for, Your Majesty."

"Since when did you need him to draw up a death warrant?"

"It isn't that," Charles said, blowing on his scorched feathers.

"Then what is it?"

William nudged Charles. "You tell her."

Rosamund picked up a billiard ball and gritted her teeth. "Someone had better tell me what is going on or, so help me, I'll knock you two into the next House."

"The issue is precisely this," Charles said, tucking his wings behind him. "You cannot execute the Queen of Spades."

"And whyever not?"

He picked up a piece of fancy parchment. "Because she had this in her possession." Even from where Rosamund stood, she could see the familiar golden seal of a cross and cup. The letter had come from Panoply City from Pope Cecil de Berg himself. "It's a Papal Bull stating that the Queen of Spades is the rightful heir of the House of Hearts, the true Queen, and if you execute her, he will set the Holy Wonderland Army on you and all your supporters until you are no longer queen of anything."

"The *true* Queen?" Rosamund crushed the billiard ball in her hand. Shards of plaster and wood escaped her clenched fist and fell to the ground.

"That's not all," Charles said as he grabbed a cherry cordial from the bar. "The Bull also commands every Proverbial to act on the disposal of the Queen of Hearts. If we want to get specific, it said kill you."

Rosamund placed her palm over her flaying heart. She felt hot and cold all at once, and her knees weakened. Every Proverbial. There were hundreds in Gardenia City. If the Bull was released, she'd never be safe, no matter how many executions she ordered. "Cecil wouldn't dare," she whispered. "I'm a Remonstration of the Holiest of all Holier Churches of Gardenia City..."

"I don't think that matters. If anything, it might make it worse."

She wrung her hands. Somehow, she was going to have to make this all go away. Perhaps she could appease Cecil and make him see that she was better than the Queen of Spades. She could send him a card. Or flowers. Maybe even ten batches of tarts. No… She bit her fist. None of those ideas seemed very good, but it was hard for her to think when one person kept bubbling to the forefront of her thoughts.

"This is all the fault of the Queen of Spades," Rosamund said. "I want her head, and I want it now. If I must fight off every Proverbial in Wonderland, it would make me feel better knowing she was dead. Besides, Cecil's all blubber, no bite. I'll have things smoothed over by the time he can rustle together an army."

William put a death warrant before her, held up his quill, and bowed. "As your most devoted advisor, I'll witness the warrant."

"Before you sign, Your Majesty," Charles said, lowering William's arm. "I think it's best that you know that our spies have spotted Cecil's troops in Clickity-Clack Fortress."

"Clickity-Clack? Are you certain?" Her gaze swept over their faces. "It was abandoned."

Charles said, "Not anymore."

Rosamund snatched the quill from William. A drop of red ink slid off the metal needle and soaked into the paper like a blood stain. "If that's how he wants to be, then so be it. We will declare war on him first. He'll see how strong the House of Hearts really is. He'll be defeated in a day."

She had nearly finished signing her name when Charles slid the inkwell away. "If we declare war on Cecil, the House of Clubs will join him, since he is the King of Clubs' second great uncle once removed from his mother's side. If the House of Clubs joins, then the House of Diamonds will too, and finally the House of Spades—vultures that they are—will follow suit. It would be like the Great War of Turnips all over again."

"The Spades will support us," Rosamund asserted. "Once I do their dirty work and behead their Queen."

"The Spades can't be trusted to come to our aid," Charles said. "They have always prided themselves on their duplicity."

Rosamund threw the pen down and ripped up the death warrant, tearing the pretty etching and loops into bits. "Everyone happy now?" she cried. "All this to stop me from killing the Queen of Spades? She's nobody special. She's not even really a queen anymore. It's all a bunch of hogwash. What about me? What about what I want? Does anyone care about that?"

"We do, Your Majesty," Charles and William said in unison.

"Stickfiddles. Everyone is against me. Even you two."

"Not true, Your Majesty," William said. "We've only ever cared about what you cared about. I don't think we have any other cares in the world other than that."

Rosamund slumped into a chair. "Then what am I supposed to do?" She kicked an ottoman and sent it flying across the room. It crashed into the puppet show, sending the half-dressed marionettes spinning. "I want her head."

"And you will," Charles said, "but we need more time."

"Time? *More time?* You sound like Ralph. Where is that rabbit, hmmm?"

Charles relit his pipe. "He said he was on the Queen's business."

"My business? Ha. Likely he meant the Queen of Spades' business, that vermin."

Charles said, "I see no reason to suspect him of treachery, Your Majesty. Ralph has always been a loyal subject."

William nodded in agreement.

"Funny," Rosamund grumbled. "I seem to have met plenty who have claimed the same but managed to end up on the block. Why should I even be surprised anymore. Here the Queen of Spades sits in the tower, getting ready to take my throne once some Proverbial makes good on Cecil's Bull, and here I am surrounded by fools. Worthless, the whole lot of you."

"Not so worthless," Charles said and glanced at William. "While we can't do anything about the Queen of Spades just yet, we do have a plan to handle any wayward Proverbials."

"Oh?" Rosamund asked. "And what is that?"

William held up a copy of the *House of Hearts Statutes and Administrative Rules*. "We took it upon ourselves to deploy the Aces. We can do that according to Article 327, Section-8. The Aces will take care of any Proverbial who steps even the slightest pinky toe out of line."

"The Aces?" Rosamund raised her eyebrows. Although she'd never admit to it aloud, the Aces did as they pleased, and Rosamund let them. The Aces were barely more than assassins and she didn't want to find herself at the receiving end of a sharpened cinnamon stick if she didn't.

"General Blunderbuss sent word this afternoon that the Aces have mobilized. No Proverbial will stand a chance against them."

"I suppose that does make me feel safer," she said, fiddling with the edge of her sleeve. "But I'm sure this means I'll have to cancel my summer tour. I couldn't possibly leave the palace with the Proverbials on the loose. Aces or not."

Rosamund loathed the idea of canceling the tour. She looked forward to it each year because it was the one time she was able to freely leave the palace. She loved traveling the countryside and seeing all the places near and far of her queendom. It also didn't hurt that at each stop there was a lavish party in her honor with hunting parties, feasts, and balls. The tour was the best part of being the Queen of Hearts, but being on the road risked being exposed to all sorts of villainy.

"Oh, I don't think there's any need to cancel," Charles said. "We can't let Cecil think he has the Queen of Hearts afraid to show her face."

"But would it be safe?" Rosamund asked.

"With the Aces traveling at your side, I can't see why not."

Rosamund thought about it for a moment and then slapped her hand on the table. "You're absolutely right. I refuse to care a whit or whistle about what Cecil says or does. I'm going on my tour."

Charles bowed his head. "Wise decision, Your Majesty."

"As you should know, all my decisions are." Rosamund got up and went to the door. "I'm still expecting that you make this problem with Cecil disappear. Don't forget that if I die, then who is going to give you your jewels, your manors, and your comfy lifestyles? Only I can. I'm the Queen. I've always been the Queen and I always *will* be the Queen."

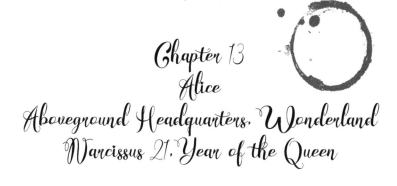

Chapter 13
Alice
Aboveground Headquarters, Wonderland
Narcissus 21, Year of the Queen

Alice's refusal to kill the Queen created quite an uproar. Bill scurried into the corner, Lillian gnawed on her bonnet, and Chester blinked in and out of visibility while they argued about what should be done. So far, no one had mentioned sending Alice back. She tried to take another drink of the stinky tea, but it made her stomach churn. Thoughts of flowers and lemon tarts helped keep it down.

Ralph addressed the group. "If Alice won't kill the Queen, we'll have to go with plan Z, which means one of us will do it. With the Papal Bull on one side and the Queen of Spades on the other, she won't see it coming."

Alice paled. "Are you going to kill her now? This very second?"

Chester turned to her with a wide grin. "Oh, it won't be that easy. Do you think we can tango right in and kill the Queen? If you do, you're as mad as she is."

"Don't call me that," Alice snapped. "Don't you ever call me that."

The room became quiet. Alice's face flushed, and she stared at the rim of her teacup. Why did she have to snap like that? It was a word. Only a word.

Lillian whispered, "Maybe she *is* mad."

"I'm not." Alice's eyes flashed. "I just don't like that word."

"What, *mad*?" Lillian said with a grin.

Bill wiped his nose with a hanky from his back pocket. "You best get used to it 'round here."

"Enough of this ... *madness*," Chester said, smirking at Alice. "We need to set our plan in place."

"Right-o," Bill said, and smoothed out across the table a large piece of parchment with dots, ridges, and squiggly lines. At the very top, in curling letters, it read:

A Cartographic Map
and Illustrative Illustration
of the Major Features of Wonderland,
its Environs, Population Density, and Notable Shrubbery

It showed the House of Diamonds in the north, bordered by mountains and scribbled with snowflakes. In the south, the House of Clubs was surrounded with water and little drawings of ships. To the east was the House of Spades, nestled in a valley with etchings of carts and horses and protected by high, jagged cliffs. In the west, "Panoply City" was written above a cathedral with high turrets, flags, and crosses. Right smack in the middle was the House of Hearts, hidden among a maze of rivers and flowers.

"To answer your question, Alice," Ralph said, picking up a long carrot to use as a pointer, "we won't kill the Queen right now because I have a better idea." He ran the carrot along a series of red dots that went over hills, rivers, woods, and villages. "This is the route the Queen takes on her country tour, and here"—he tapped on a house—"is one of her favorite stops. This is where she'll be the most vulnerable."

Alice asked, "Whose house is that?"

"Mine. It's Longshoot Castle," Ralph said as he leaned down to inspect the drawing. "I know every secret tunnel, hidden room, and trick painting. It's the perfect place."

Alice was surprised. "What about your cottage with the little garden and the thatched roof?"

Ralph scoffed. "Cottage? Someone of my stature?" He shook his head in disgust before resuming. "Now listen, the only problem with Longshoot is I can't just go home and wait for the Queen. She'd suspect. No, we need someone on the inside. Someone who can get close to her."

One by one, they all turned to Alice.

"Who?" Alice asked. "You're not suggesting I do it?"

"All you need to do is get her to trust you," Ralph said. "Since everything with the Queen changes on a whim, *her* whim, we must know what she's doing at a moment's notice. That's all. You won't have to kill her. Merely watch her."

"You want me to be a spy?" Alice asked.

"Precisely," Ralph said. "Only you must not give her a reason to suspect. If she does..."

Bill ran his finger across his neck. "Then it's off with your head."

Alice cringed and set her tea down. "I think it's a very good plan, I do, but the Queen didn't care too much for me the last time. How can I get her to trust me when I doubt she'd let me within a hundred yards of her? I suppose I could ask her if she'd like to play another game of croquet, except the last one didn't go so well."

Lillian wrinkled her nose. "Can't you figure anything out on your own, you fool? A croquet game? Really? Isn't it obvious? You'll have to become one of her lady's maids."

"*Me?*" Alice asked, hardly believing what she heard.

She imagined what it would be like as a lady's maid. She was a little curious about it, even if it was for the Queen of Hearts. It sounded like going to a party—dancing parties, tea parties, and supper parties. She liked parties, and after the time she'd had in the asylum, she wouldn't mind some amusement.

"Why do you think she'd want me?" Alice asked.

"You're not a rat, so that helps," Lillian blurted.

Ralph sighed. "Not that again."

Lillian crossed her arms. "It wasn't *your* hopes and dreams crushed."

"There is a post available," Ralph said to Alice, "and you're no better or worse than any other girl—"

"And you're not a rat," Lillian interrupted him.

Ralph rolled his eyes and continued. "As I was saying, you are no better or worse than the other girls she's had. Plus, I will recommend you, and, well, she trusts me. She'll listen to me."

"That's rich," Lillian grumbled.

"You think so?" Alice asked Ralph. "You think she'd let me on as a lady's maid? I thought only well-to-do ladies were maids to the Queen. I'm surprised there's a post open."

Ralph tapped his paws together. "It was unexpectedly vacated."

"Unexpectedly vacated?" Alice asked with a slight squeak in her voice.

"You'll have to tell her," Chester said, resting his head on his paws.

Bill shook his head at Ralph. "Don't."

"Tell her," Lillian said. "She should know."

Ralph took a breath. "The last girl was beheaded."

Alice gasped. "What?"

"Don't get worked up," Ralph said. "The girl had been caught stealing royal jewels. At least in that case, the Queen had cause."

Maybe being a lady's maid wouldn't be all parties after all. The Queen was too dangerous. She had wanted to behead Alice before. What would change now? Nothing. Absolutely nothing. She hadn't escaped to Wonderland so she could die on a chopping block.

Alice wrung her hands. "It seems so many lose their heads around the Queen of Hearts. What if I do something wrong, and I don't mean to? What if… I don't know if I can do this."

"Of course she can't," Lillian said, quite smug. "You should have known this wouldn't work. She's completely useless."

"Be quiet, Lillian," Bill snapped. "Leave her be."

Ralph rested his paw on Alice's shoulder. "You won't be alone," he said. "You'll have us. Besides, you've already come to Wonderland. There's no turning back now."

Alice wound her gown between her fingers. "If I do this, will you take me home?"

Ralph became very serious. "Once the Queen is gone, you'll have everything you've ever wanted. I promise you."

Alice took a breath. "Alright. I'll do it."

Ralph smiled. "You're doing a great service for Wonderland. Truly."

"Now that *that's* finally settled," Chester said, bouncing into the air and onto some invisible ledge. "She must be sworn to secrecy."

Bill nodded.

"Quite right." Ralph cleared his throat. "Please stand, Alice."

She did as she was told.

"Now lift one foot," he said. "Touch your finger to your nose, pat your head, and try not to sneeze."

Alice wobbled back and forth, ready to tumble at any second.

Ralph held up his paw. "You solemnly swear that you will keep the identity of the Aboveground's members secret? Do you swear to carry out your mission under pain of death and to honor the true Queen of Gardenia City...the Queen of Spades?"

Alice swallowed. "I do."

"Well, then," Ralph said and smoothed down his waistcoat. "It's time to take you to the Queen of Hearts."

Chapter 14
Rosamund
Palace Green, Wonderland
Narcissus 21, Year of the Queen

Rosamund crossed her legs and tapped her arm. She couldn't kill the Queen of Spades, but that didn't rule out a royal mishap—maybe a drop of poison in Constance's shoe, a needle in her soup, or a gumgum turtle in her bed. Rosamund couldn't be blamed for an accident, a small trick of fate. Take her own parents, for instance. Nobody thought anything sinister had occurred when their carriage plunged into Thistle Pointe Ravine—nobody at all.

These things happen all the time.

She stared out her window and sighed. In the distance, rooftops glinted in gold and maroon. Boats of all sizes made their way along the gentle waters of the Annaleigh. Gardens stretched before her with the blush of late spring. She felt trapped behind the palace walls with Cecil's Bull hanging over her head and his troops in Clickity-Clack Fortress. She needed to get outside and bathe in the adoration of her people. It always made her feel better. She was their Rose. It was the name they gave her as she climbed the steps to the throne, red hair flowing behind her back.

Rosamund called out, "Bess? Bess, where are you? I want to go out."

Bess hurried to Rosamund's side. Sabrina trailed behind, glum as usual.

Rosamund dressed in her velvet riding habit. Bess powdered her wig while Sabrina rubbed rouge into her cheeks. She wore ruby necklaces and had at least five rings on each finger.

There was a tap on her door. William poked his head in. "Hoo hoo. Hullo there."

"What do you want?" Rosamund sighed. "More unimportant news for me?"

He bowed so low he could have kissed the tops of his feet. "I wanted to stop in, so I could tell Your Majesty how striking your stockings are."

Rosamund snorted. "I suppose you can stay then."

She always had an appreciation for those who appreciated her excellent taste.

William followed her around the room, rattling off her virtues—vanity, greed, and envy, to name a few. There wasn't one she didn't possess. It was nice to be reminded from time to time, especially by one of her advisors, but William's drivel started to grate on her nerves.

"All right," she said, whirling around, "Put a lollipop in it."

William was staring at Sabrina like a squirrel that had found its first acorn. Sabrina caught Rosamund watching and quickly averted her gaze, blushing to the tips of her ears.

The very idea.

"William," Rosamund snapped. "What do you think you're doing?"

"N...nothing, Your Majesty. I'm here to admire your garters and your greatness."

"Is that so? I have half a mind to think that you were here to admire something else."

Sabrina couldn't possibly find William to her liking. He was much older than her, and didn't have much in the looks department. It was a pity William wasn't more attractive, but that didn't mean she could have him scavenging through her lady's maids for a wife either.

He shook his head. "Certainly not, Your Majesty."

"Mmhmmm." She turned away from William. "Sabrina. Fetch my ruby brooch. I have a fancy for it today."

She curtsied. "Yes, Your Highness."

"And *you*, William, make yourself useful and tell the stable boy to get my horse ready."

"Yes, Your Majesty." He put his hat on and skipped backwards towards the door.

When she knew he was gone, Rosamund stood before the mirror. She pushed down the flaps of her riding coat and strapped on her hat. She picked up her gloves from the table and glanced around for her lady's maid. "Sabrina? Can you please tell me what is taking so bloody long?"

"I'm so sorry, Your Majesty," she said, her hands wringing her gown, "but I can't seem to find the jewel. I searched all over."

"What do you mean you can't find it? I saw it last week."

Sabrina's lip trembled. "I looked, Your Majesty. I've looked everywhere, several times."

Rosamund left Sabrina. She marched over to her jewelry box and threw back the trunk-sized lid. She scanned the rows of rubies, garnets, agate, carnelian, and jasper and slowly made her way to the spot her brooch should have been. Instead, there was a blank spot of velvet.

She roared, "Sabrina! Bess!"

Her ladies surrounded her.

Rosamund clenched her fists. "Where's my brooch?"

Bess stammered, "Maybe...maybe it was misplaced."

"Brandimuck." Rosamund whirled on her. "I never misplace anything. Do I have to remind you two what happened to the last girl I caught stealing my jewels? Hmmm?"

Bess's lips quivered, and Sabrina stared at her feet, whimpering.

"It appears I do," Rosamund said. "Unless my brooch is found and put back in its rightful place, then it's off with your heads. You hear me? Off."

"Yes, Your Majesty," they said together, nearly in a whisper.

Rosamund put her hand to her ear. "I'm sorry...what was that?"

"YES, Your Majesty."

"Very good." Rosamund slapped her gloves against her palm. "Well, come along, my dears. We mustn't keep my public waiting."

They followed her out to the courtyard. The stable boy led over her horse, Scarlet, with rosebuds woven in her mane and tail. Scarlet was born white, but Rosamund had insisted they dye her red. No one else in all of Wonderland had a red horse, and that was how she preferred it.

The stable boy clumsily held her foot as she mounted Scarlet. She kicked him away as soon as she got on the saddle and guided her little procession over the drawbridge with the Aces trailing behind. Heart-shaped masks concealed their faces and fiery cloaks hid all sorts of weapons—nunchucks, throwing stars, poisoned darts, and banana peels (the deadliest of the bunch).

Rosamund focused on the road. Her people lined the streets, waving the royal banner, and as soon as she passed the palace gate, she heard shouting: "The Queen is here! The Queen is here!"

Mothers with babes in their arms leaned out of windows, bakers stepped away from their ovens, goose girls let their geese run amok, butchers wiped their hands on their aprons, and milkmaids dropped their pails. Rosamund waved as they clamored to get a glimpse of her. Papal Bull or no, nothing could change their love for her. All that nasty business with the Queen of Spades and Cecil felt far away, almost as if it had never happened.

"How about we give them a little show?" Rosamund said to Scarlet.

With one arm lifted high, she urged Scarlet up to a gallop and waved as if she were running off to slay jabberwockies. The voices of her cheering people faded in the background as she veered into a meadow with a layer of mist clinging to its shoots.

Rosamund slowed Scarlet as they neared Rose Wood—named after her, of course. As she was about to turn and go back, a hooded figure stepped out of the Silkwood Trees and into her path. She yanked on the reins.

Rosamund growled, "Out of my way, you idiot."

The figure did not move. Whoever it was stood there, defying her, poisoning her good mood.

The figure lifted his arm and pointed a musket at Rosamund. "God save the real Queen," he shouted. "God save the Queen of Spades!"

Rosamund barely had time to swallow, think, gasp, or scream before she saw a puff of smoke as the musket fired. A sharp pain burned into her shoulder like melted wax. Scarlet reared, dumping Rosamund onto the mushy ground, headfirst, leaving her with her breeches in the air and her petticoat in her face. The cool morning breeze blew across her bottom.

Bess's meaty hands gripped her arm, and Rosamund spat out a clump of grass as the duchess righted her.

Rosamund moaned, clutching her sleeve. "My arm, my arm."

Bess ripped a strip of cloth from her skirt and wrapped it tight around Rosamund's brow.

"How does that feel?" she asked.

"Better," Rosamund whimpered. "But I can't feel my arm. I fear I'm gravely injured."

"There, there." Bess fussed, while Sabrina sobbed like an otter with a splinter in its paw.

Rosamund wobbled as Bess and Sabrina hoisted her up. "Take me to the palace at once," she said. "I need the Royal Physician. I only hope we make it in time."

Captain Juker of the Aces kneeled before her. His hair had been clipped so short, she could barely make out the color of crimson. "We found the weapon," he said. "It was a cap gun."

"A cap gun?" Rosamund scoffed. "Is that all? Then why does my shoulder feel like it's on fire, and there's blood pooling down my arm as we speak?"

Captain Juker pulled a little piece of smoldering paper from her sleeve. "See, all gone. And that's not blood. It's a grass stain."

Rosamund's cheeks turned a dark cherry. "That imbecile could have got me in the eye. Would that have made it serious enough for you?"

Captain Juker coughed nervously and backed away.

"Where's the *assailant?*" she asked with emphasis. "I want him beheaded at once."

"I'm sorry, Your Majesty," Captain Juker said, shaking his head, "but he got away."

"He got away? What kind of Captain are you?"

"We'll find him. You have my word."

Rosamund leaned against Bess. "Oh, oh, my arm. It's making me so lightheaded."

They carried Rosamund back to the palace and the court physician put her arm in a sling after applying a hefty dose of jam to lessen the pain. Rosamund didn't know what hurt her most, her arm or the words—those dreadful words.

God save the true Queen. The Queen of Spades.

For the rest of the day, Rosamund kept to the palace and made sure guards surrounded her everywhere she went. It appeared Cecil de Burg had made good on his threat of the Papal Bull and pamphlets bearing his mark floated in every square. If that pompous walrus had been in Gardenia, she'd have shown him what to do with his Bull.

Rosamund sat at her writing desk and issued proclamation after proclamation.

Proverbials cannot see the Queen.

Proverbials cannot leave their homes when the Queen is out of the palace.

Proverbials cannot engage in any trade with the Queen's household.

Proverbials cannot practice their silly Billy religion.

She scowled at the last line and ended the decree with the statement: "Any breech of these rules is punishable by death. Those wishing to convert to Remonstration of the Holiest of all Holier Churches of Gardenia City will not have to follow the above rules—because Remonstrations are better."

Rosamund studied her list of proclamations. The new laws were for her queendom's own good, and she wanted them issued to the Assemblage of Hearts without further delay. She called for a carrier pigeon, who sent them along via snail.

Satisfied, she allowed Bess to lead her to bed and fluff up her pillows.

"I'm having some radish soup sent up, your favorite, Your Majesty," Bess said.

"Yes," Rosamund said, settling in. "Quite right."

"Try to rest now."

When Bess left, Rosamund remained sitting there, thinking and stewing in her thoughts. She wasn't going to let the Queen of Spades or Cecil or the Proverbials get away with this. She'd see all their heads roll before they ever took her throne. Even if it meant bathing Wonderland in blood.

Chapter 15
Alice
Gardenia City, Wonderland
Narcissus 21, Year of the Queen

Alice and Ralph followed the tunnel back to the crossroads and veered left for Gardenia City.

They reached a staircase made from the winding roots of an old tree and climbed each gnarled step until they arrived at a door. Ralph lifted the latch, and it swung open, blasting Alice with bright sunshine from above. She shielded her eyes as Ralph took her by the hand and helped her climb out.

They stood in a meadow with perfectly trimmed grass and clusters of wildflowers bursting with fuchsia and magenta. A pebbled road curved in the distance around rolling hills like a yellow ribbon.

Alice stared at the greenery, which seemed to glow in the bright light. "Where are we?"

"We're outside the city walls in Rose Wood," Ralph said. "Not much farther now."

Alice no longer felt curious. Now that they were close, her fear of facing the Queen of Hearts was stronger than her desire to go home. A knot grew in the pit of her stomach.

"How do you know the Queen will even see me?"

"Because I'll insist upon it. Besides, she loves her subjects, new or otherwise."

"I'm not a subject," Alice said.

"If you're in her land, then you're her subject."

Alice peered down at her hospital gown. Stains covered the front of it, and her bare feet were black from dirt. "I can't go before the Queen like this."

Ralph surveyed her. "You're perfectly adequate."

"Perfectly adequate?" Alice balked. "I look wretched."

"Do you want her to recognize you straight away and have you taken to the chopping block without so much as a word? The more wretched you appear, the better. Why don't you fuss up your hair a bit?"

Alice fidgeted with her locks, tangling them as much as she could as they walked past little houses with thatched roofs alongside the road. Badgers dug in their gardens, horses pulled their own plows, and kangaroos swung on their porches while their joeys hopped about.

Curiouser and curiouser.

"Everything is so peculiar," Alice said. "Nothing like at home."

Ralph suddenly stopped and turned towards her. "Why do you always talk of home?"

She shrugged. "Isn't that what everyone does when they're away?"

"Don't you like Wonderland?"

"Of course I do. But my sister, you see, she's getting married, and my mother and father, they—"

"They put you in that terrible place."

"Yes, but..." Alice started. "It's not their fault, because... because..." Alice didn't quite know how to finish. It *was* their fault she was in the asylum. She wasn't hurting anyone with her talk of Wonderland. They simply got sick of it and didn't want Alice to embarrass them.

Tears gathered at the corners of her eyes.

"Well?" Ralph asked. "Why do you want to go back there?"

Alice bowed her head. "It's where I'm supposed to be."

"You're supposed to be wherever you belong."

If Alice had to think about it, then she wasn't sure where that was. It seemed as if she'd always had a foot in both worlds, but now those worlds were drifting apart, forcing her to choose.

Ralph had walked a good distance in front of Alice. She ran to catch up. "You won't tell the Queen, will you? About the asylum?"

"I won't, I promise," he said. "Cross my heart and hope to die, stick a thousand peanuts in my eye."

Alice laughed.

"What's so humorous?" Ralph asked.

"I think the saying is 'stick a needle in my eye,' not peanuts."

"That doesn't make any sense." Ralph shook his head. "One needle wouldn't do anything at all. Now, a thousand peanuts—that would really hurt."

As they got closer to the city, more creatures and people were on the road. Alice jostled past pigs wearing petticoats and twirling umbrellas, zebras pushing buggies, and panthers reading the newspaper with *Gardenia Times* plastered across the front. Every so often, Alice would stop to stare at humans conversing with animals as if it was the most normal thing in the world to do.

A baker with a tray of golden crumpets passed, and Alice's fingers itched to snatch one until she saw sardines atop them. Whyever would the baker ruin a good crumpet with a sardine? Even so, Alice's stomach rumbled so loudly at the sight of them that a few chipmunks stopped and stared at her. She nodded and moved on quickly, clamping her stomach as if that could keep it quiet.

No one took any notice of Alice as they traveled through the bustling city. Her eyes darted from side to side, and she soaked in the tea shops, the shoe shops, and the Looking Glass bookshops. It was so lively and musical that she wondered how she had missed it on her first visit. After all, she had played croquet with the Queen—she must have been close the entire time.

"There's no time for gawking," Ralph scolded her. "This way."

They came to a red-and-white bridge surrounded by looming stone walls. The palace lay beyond. She could see the balconies and turrets, twisting towards the sun, with red flags waving above them. It was beautiful, almost like something out of a dream, and Alice couldn't believe she hadn't wanted to come, but then she covered her mouth and gasped.

Withered heads lined the road to the bridge: the head of a turtle blackened by the sun, a bear with a bloated tongue, a lion with tufts of hair drifting like dandelion seeds in the breeze, and a girl—blond like Alice—with crows pecking at her eyes.

Alice cried, "Oh, it's so awful."

"What?" Ralph asked, and followed Alice's gaze. "Oh, *that*. You get used to it after a while. After a week, they take them down. The Queen likes them fresh."

Alice felt as if the heads watched her as they walked along the cobbled bridge. Nobody else seemed bothered by the heads as they scuttled about their business, almost as if the dead things weren't even there.

They passed through a wrought-iron gate where two guards played draughts. They had the Three of Hearts embroidered on their tunics. They nodded at Ralph and continued with their game. They barely glanced at Alice.

Alice followed Ralph down the manicured drive towards the palace door. She stopped when she saw a hedged archway: the entrance to the labyrinthine rose garden. All those years ago, somewhere through all the shrubbery and rosebushes, Alice had come across the guards painting the roses red, and she'd met the Queen and King.

Alice caught her breath. Her time away hadn't softened the memory of the Queen of Hearts. Here she was, at the palace, under orders from the Aboveground Organization, about to go into the Queen's service—the very queen who had ordered her execution. Of all the things that were truly mad, this was it.

They came to another set of guards, this time with the Four of Hearts stamped on their tunics. The palace doors opened, revealing a hall ablaze in red. From the tapestries on the walls to the carpet, to the stained-glass windows to the entryways, everything was saturated in the color of blood.

They'd barely taken another step when another group of guards stopped them, and one demanded, "State your business."

"You know my business," Ralph said. "I'm the Queen's advisor. What's going on here?"

"Are you a Proverbial?"

"What?" Ralph asked. "Me, a Proverbial? I'm going to be a proverbial mad rabbit if you don't let us pass."

"Sorry," the guard said. "Queen's new rules."

Alice stood behind Ralph as he answered a series of questions. Finally, the guards moved to the side.

"Follow me," he said to Alice.

He took her upstairs, downstairs, up a ladder and down a slide, down a ladder and up a slide, and finally stopped before a door as tall as the palace itself. Two young chambermaids waited at the door, wearing matching red petticoats and aprons. They were identical in every way, from their wavy hair to the smatterings of freckles across their noses.

Ralph asked them, "Is the Queen in her chambers?"

"Yes," they replied with a curtsy.

"Tell her she has a guest waiting."

"Yes, my lord."

The girls curtsied once more and disappeared behind the door like two little mice going into the mouth of a cat.

Chapter 16
Rosamund
House of Hearts, Wonderland
Narcissus 21, Year of the Queen

Rosamund couldn't sleep. She got up and ambled around, stopping to play with her toy guillotine or rearranging her collection of ruby figurines. She went to the window and fiddled with the tassels on her curtains. As she did, she glanced outside and saw Ralph entering the gate. It was about time that rabbit showed his furry little face. It seemed awfully convenient that he'd happen to be absent just when there was an assassination attempt on her life. Some nerve. He had a lot of explaining to do.

Ralph had a girl at his side. Was this his so-called Queen's business? She was a knobby-kneed creature and dressed in what looked like a sheet. The girl's head darted from side to side as if she expected something to jump out and bite her. Perhaps she'd encountered one too many nests of flickwick beetles in her time.

Pressing her nose to the glass, Rosamund squinted to get a better look. There was something familiar about the girl, something she couldn't quite put her finger on. Maybe she had seen her on one of her summer tours. Or maybe out on one of her rides. Regardless of where or how, all she knew was that the girl had better not be a Proverbial, especially some charity case Proverbial, coming to dirty up her palace.

Proverbials.

She gritted her teeth and moved away from the window. She had half a mind to write to the King of Clubs and demand that his second great-uncle once removed from his mother's side eradicate the Bull at once, for the love of all that was royal.

And the other half of her mind would write it too.

Rosamund sat at her desk and pulled out a sheet of paper. She wanted to sound pleasant, but it didn't come very naturally. "Dear King of Clubs..." That didn't sound right. "Dearest King of Clubs..." No, too chummy. "To Whom It May Concern..." Too impersonal.

A pile of crumpled paper tickled her stockinged feet. Her tongue poked out of her mouth. "To the King of—"

A knock came at the door, sending the pen into a scrawled squiggle.

Rosamund growled, "What?"

Mary Lou and Mary Anne, her chambermaids, poked their heads into her room. "Ralph is asking for an audience with Your Majesty."

Rosamund dropped her quill.

"Is he now?"

She had no doubt it had something to do with his mystery girl, and she hated mysteries of all kinds; they made her head hurt.

"Very well," Rosamund said. "Bess? Sabrina? Get me into position."

Rosamund sat in her Official Receiving Chair, and her lady's maids pushed her—and the chair—so that she faced the door.

And then Rosamund slowly.

So very slowly.

Put her hands on the armrest.

"Show them in," she said. And waited.

PART 2
THE QUEEN'S COURT

Chapter 17
Alice
House of Hearts, Wonderland
Narcissus 21, Year of the Queen

Alice couldn't take her eyes off the Queen of Hearts.

She wore a gown of cherry, trimmed in red ermine. A ruby crown sparkled atop a tangled mass of scarlet curls. She stared down her powdered nose at Alice, raised her eyebrows, and sniffed.

Ralph nudged Alice. He had been bowing while she'd been standing there, unable to move. She fumbled for the sides of the flimsy gown Nurse Glass made her wear and curtsied as best she could but nearly tumbled in the attempt. When she looked up, the Queen's eyes narrowed. Alice smiled, but it didn't help.

The Queen fixed her stony gaze on Ralph. It was a wonder the White Rabbit didn't collapse under the weight of it. "And where have *you* been?" the Queen asked him.

"I'm so please to answer such a pointed question," Ralph said and stepped forwards. "You see, I realized that things have been difficult lately so I wanted to bring you someone I believe you're going to find quite amusing. Think of it as an unbirthday present."

The Queen motioned to Alice. "This wretched thing?"

"Yes, Your Majesty." Ralph pressed his paws together. "And if you'd allow me to say that ..."

The Queen held up her hand, silencing Ralph. She turned to Alice and demanded, "Are you a Proverbial?"

"Proverbial?" Alice asked.

"Don't make me repeat myself."

Ralph muttered, "Say *no*."

"No," Alice said. "I'm not a Proverbial."

The Queen sniffed again. "Then who are you?"

"I'm...I'm Alice."

"Alice?" the Queen said, surprised, and tapped her finger on her chin. "Now, why does that name sound familiar?"

Alice glanced over at Ralph, but he made no indication that he planned on doing any explaining. "Well, Your Majesty,"Alice started. "I—"

"Don't speak until spoken to," the Queen interrupted her.

Alice's eyes widened. "Oh, I'm so sorry. I didn't mean to upset you. I was simply going to say—"

"Did you not hear me?" the Queen snarled. "Be silent."

Ralph elbowed Alice and shushed her.

"Now, where was I?" The Queen continued to drum her chin. "Alice, Alice, Alice... Where have I heard that name before? Bess? Do you know where I've heard that name?"

Alice recognized the duchess immediately. She had the same dour expression on her face as before, except it was more pronounced now by the red shade of her gown. Bess leaned towards the Queen and said, "Perhaps in a book?"

"No." The Queen pursed her lips. "Doesn't sound right."

"Maybe at a Caucus Race?"

The Queen slapped her hand down. "I know, I know. I met an Alice playing a game of croquet."

Alice felt her stomach drop to her knees. She turned to Ralph. His nose was bouncing to the beat of her racing heart.

Everyone cheered for the Queen of Hearts and marveled at how good she was at working out riddles and all sorts of sums and subtractions of that kind. The Queen soaked in the adulation until her eyes fell on Alice, and her smiled melted back into the folds of her powder. "You don't look like the same Alice that I remember, but an Alice is an Alice and I believe I ordered your execution. It's about time you showed up. I hate tardiness. Guards, seize her."

The Queen turned to the duchess and began talking to her about the weather, as if ordering Alice's execution were nothing at all.

The guards squeezed her arms with gloved hands until tears came to her eyes. She knew she shouldn't have come. She told Ralph this would happen, but he didn't believe her, and now she was going to die. The guards started pulling her away.

Ralph smoothed down his jacket. "Your Majesty, if I may?"

"Yes?" the Queen asked.

"Alice has only just come back to Wonderland. Besides, I brought her here for you. Maybe we could wait awhile to execute her? She so loved Gardenia City and told me how lovely it was the whole way here."

The Queen held up a finger and the guards stopped. "Did she, now?"

"Oh yes, that and more," he said. "Why, Alice was telling me how the Queen of Hearts was a great Queen—nay, the greatest Queen in all of Wonderland. Didn't you, Alice?"

Alice nodded. "Oh yes. I did."

"My, my," the Queen giggled like a school girl with a new ribbon. "I suppose if that's how she feels, I *could* put her execution on hold, since she's obviously been gifted with superb taste. Come closer," she said to Alice. "I want to gawk at you."

Alice inched towards the Queen. The scent of roses grew stronger and stronger with each step.

"Don't stand so straight," the Queen said. "You must slouch. Everyone slouches in my presence. You certainly don't have much for manners, I see."

Alice slumped her shoulders.

"That's better. Now—" The Queen pinched her lips. "That hem. It's far too short—almost indecent. And that hair..." She clucked her tongue.

Ralph slid up to the Queen. "Perhaps if she were one of your lady's maids, you could have her properly attired."

The duchess gaped.

Another girl appeared at the Queen's side, almost as if she came from the very folds of the curtains. She was a little older than Alice, pretty, with brown hair and gentle eyes. She smiled at Alice, and Alice felt a twang of familiarity. Had she met her the last time she'd come to Wonderland? "Oh please, Your Majesty," the girl said. "Let her stay."

The Queen pointed at Alice. "*Her?* One of my lady's maids?"

"Your Majesty," the duchess said, leaning towards the Queen's ear. "She can't possibly be from a family worthy of your court. You must ask what house she is from first."

"Quite right." The Queen nodded and turned to Alice. "Are you from the Diamonds, the Spades, or"—she nearly spat out the words—"from the Clubs? I know you're certainly not from the House of Hearts."

Alice swallowed. "I am not from any house, Your Majesty."

Ralph said, "*That's* because Alice told me that the only house for her is the House of Hearts, the greatest house of them all. She was telling me all the way here that her dream, her reason for living—nay, for breathing—she couldn't stop carrying on so, and, between you and me, it was quite embarrassing—was to be one of your lady's maids. Isn't that right, Alice?"

"Oh, yes," Alice said. "It's all I've wanted."

"Hmmm..." The Queen sat back in her chair. "You know, normally, I would require that my ladies are from one of the houses—particularly my house—but considering I do have a vacant position, I might be willing to make an exception. It's the least I can do. I wouldn't want to break the girl's heart. What sort of queen would I be?"

Ralph bowed. "Your Majesty is most gracious."

Alice attempted another curtsy.

The duchess shot Alice a scathing look, but the other girl grinned approvingly at her.

"Now then." The Queen made a mooing noise, and the twin chambermaids appeared at Alice's side. "Mary Anne. Mary Lou," the Queen said with a wave of her hand. "Take Alice to the seamstress. She needs to be properly fitted and dressed. Something red would be nice. And burn that hideous gown. Whoever made that one should be beheaded. Put it on my to-do list, Bess."

The Hatter stormed into the room, keeping one hand on his hat. He faced Alice with his bushy eyebrows wiggling up and down. "I object," he said with a spray of spittle on her cheek.

The duchess hunched over and sighed, making the room strangely smell of pepper.

"Mad Hatter," Alice whispered. "Is it really you?"

He glowered at Alice. "What did you say?"

"You're the Mad Hatter," Alice said. "Don't you remember me? We had tea and—"

His cheeks burned red. "Nobody calls me *Mad Hatter*. Are you cracked, girl?"

Alice shrank away from him.

The Queen growled. "How many times do I have to tell you to TAKE OFF THAT RIDICULOUS HAT when you're in my presence?" She held up her finger. "One more time, William. One more time and I swear you'll lose the hat and the head it sits on. Understood?"

"Yes, Your Majesty," he said as he removed his hat. Alice couldn't remember ever seeing him without it. His hair was curlier than she imagined.

"Now, what is your objection?" she asked. "Objecting to the Queen's authority is dangerously close to treason, you know."

The Hatter shoved his finger under Alice's nose. "You can't allow her to be a lady's maid."

"Listening at the door again?" the Queen asked smugly.

"Not I," he said, placing a hand on his chest. "A little bee told me."

"A little bee?" The Queen raised her eyebrows.

"Yes, a little bee, and it said you cannot allow her to join Your Majesty's court."

The Queen sniffed. "Whyever should I not?"

"She could be a spy, a schemer... She could be a plotter."

"No," Alice said, shaking her head. "Not me. I would never." She glanced at Ralph, but he didn't flick a whisker.

"I know, dear," the Queen said, and scowled at the Hatter. "Alice is not from any of the other houses, so how could she be a spy? The poor girl's reason for living is to be a Heart. That's loyalty of the weakest kind."

The Hatter eyed Alice. "That's what she says..."

The Queen sighed. "Do you have any *other* objections?"

"Well...well..." He ran his fingers along the brim of his hat. "She offended the Dormouse," he blurted.

The Queen turned to Alice. "Is that true? Did you offend the Dormouse?"

Oh dear.

Alice had nearly forgotten about the little Dormouse at the tea party that day with the Mad Hatter and the March Hare. The creature had recounted the strangest story about three sisters and treacle. She remembered having so many questions and the Dormouse getting more upset with each interruption.

"What happened is ..." Alice twisted the hem of her hospital gown. "The March Hare had asked me to tell a story, but the Dormouse did instead and it was such an unusual tale that I couldn't help myself but be curious, you see. Perhaps if I had told the story, I could have recalled one about my dear cat, Dinah—"

"Your cat!" the Queen screeched. "Only the most offensive sorts would keep a cat as company. Such nasty, vile things."

"I told you, Your Majesty," the Hatter said. "Most offensive."

"Agreed." The Queen took a breath. "You'll certainly have to work on your manners, Alice, while you're under my employ. That is, if you want to stay under my employ."

Alice nodded.

The Queen clapped her hands. "There. That's all settled. Bess, bring me some pre-tea. All this talk about cats has upset my sensitive nerves."

Before Alice could thank the Queen, Mary Lou and Mary Anne took her by the arms. One of them whispered in her ear, "Never turn your back on Her Majesty. Skip backwards."

Alice paused, waiting for Ralph. He would come with her, surely. "White Rabbit..."

He faced the Queen and made no indication of going.

"What are you all waiting for?" the Queen barked. "Out."

"Come," Mary Lou and Mary Anne said in unison. "You don't want it to be off with your head do you?"

Alice took one last look at Ralph and realized she was on her own.

Chapter 18
Rosamund
House of Hearts, Wonderland
Narcissus 21, Year of the Queen

Rosamund was happy with her decision to let the girl stay. Bess was always a fussy-wussy, and Sabrina was such a bore. Alice might liven things up a bit.

Perhaps Ralph was right and the girl was just the thing she needed right now.

Rosamund picked up her quill to start a new letter to the King of Clubs, but changed her mind. She wasn't going to grovel to that puffed-up toad. No Queen of Hearts had ever begged, and she wouldn't either.

Outside, she heard a sudden ruckus of clanking pots and stamping feet. Rosamund covered her ears and peered out the window, but couldn't see anything past the palace gates.

"Bess," Rosamund called over her shoulder.

"Yes, Your Majesty?"

"Find out what that hubbub is about. I can't concentrate with all the noise. Tell the guards to make it go away."

"Of course," she said, and rushed out.

Rosamund sat back at her desk and decided to plan her itinerary for her tour. She considered the different manors, castles, and palaces where she might stop. Naturally, she'd visit all the homes of her advisors, that way she could see how rich she was making them. She might even pass by Bess's home in Redwood Brae, although she suspected it far too unfit for a queen and it probably smelled of nothing but pepper.

The door opened, and she heard the familiar sound of Bess's footsteps hurrying towards her.

Rosamund asked, "Did you tell the guards?"

"I did, Your Majesty, but they can't."

Rosamund glared at Bess. "And whyever not?"

The duchess wrung her hands. "It's your people, Your Majesty. They're protesting."

Rosamund gasped. "Protesting? Not possible. Not feasible."

"I think it's the Proverbials."

"Proverbials." Rosamund chewed on the word. "Of course, it would be them. Tell the guards to throw any and all Proverbials in the tower if they choose to continue this brouhaha. Those ungrateful wretches."

"Most ungrateful," Bess agreed, and she skipped backwards, disappearing behind the door.

Rosamund went back to her desk, but the shouting grew louder and louder. She stood up, pacing around her bedchamber. She didn't understand. Why were they still protesting? She was the queen; they were supposed to obey. They'd always obeyed.

It grew dark outside, and the racket gradually subsided. She left her bedchamber and stamped to the Cave, where she knew she'd find her advisors more than likely twiddling their thumbs.

Rosamund burst into the room. She was taken aback for a moment when she caught William, Charles, and Ralph poring over papers and books as if they were working for once. It must be dark days indeed.

"Are they silenced?" Rosamund asked.

William nodded. "Every hoot-whoer has been thrown into the dungeon."

"How many?" she asked, sitting at the oblong table underneath a portrait of a scantily clad Marilyn Montague—a local tart that called herself an actress.

Charles said, "Two hundred and fifty-two and a half."

"Two hundred and fifty-two and a half?" Rosamund breathed.

"There were more," he said through a puff of smoke, "but they fled when guards arrived."

"More? How can that be?"

Ralph closed the book he'd been reading and checked his watch. "It was on account of the new laws," he said.

"Why should they be so upset?" Rosamund snapped. "Don't they know it's for their own good?"

"We told them," Ralph said, "but I don't think they care."

"Don't...don't CARE?"

William unraveled a banner with the symbol of the House of Spades emblazoned in black paint. "They were waving this."

Rosamund snatched it out of William's hand and threw it in the fire. "I won't believe it. They love me, Proverbial or not. They wouldn't do this to me if it wasn't for that Queen of Spades. I want everyone's heads who waved her banner. Those traitors. They're no people of mine. Give me two hundred and fifty-three and a half death warrants."

"It might not stop them," Charles said, pulling a pinch of mint from his inside jacket pocket and stuffing it in his pipe. "We've uncovered a new plot. It involves the Queen of Spades."

"I see you're finally catching up," Rosamund grumbled. "I already knew there was. And how, pray tell, did you find out about it?"

"I have my ways." Charles put his pipe in his beak and slowly stepped backwards towards the fire. He puffed and looked at Ralph and William before turning back to her. "What you might not know, is that I suspect this plot involves someone from your innermost square."

William laughed. "Come now, Charles. Innermost square? Sometimes I think all that smoking is going right to your head. I haven't heard of such a plot."

"Nor I," Ralph added.

Charles put his pipe back in his mouth. "My crickets are rarely wrong. They said innermost square."

"I knew someone was helping the Queen of Spades." Rosamund scowled at Ralph. If that rabbit thought she'd forgotten about him disappearing behind that tiny door or being conveniently absent when the Queen of Spades showed up, he had another *think* coming. "Charles, if you know who they are, I want them beheaded at once. The people need to see this traitor's head roll."

Ralph held up his paw. "You know what the people need? They need a diversion."

William bobbed up and down. "A diversion is a lovely idea."

"A diversion?" Rosamund repeated. "We need a beheading—that's a diversion. And...and the plot. I must think of the plot."

"Plot-schmot," William said, flicking his wrist. "Let's have a party. That's what the kingdom needs."

"Queendom," Rosamund corrected.

"Yes, a party," Ralph said, standing on his chair. "You can make them see how much better you are than the Queen of Spades."

Now *that* was an idea. All the plots would end once the people saw she was the best, far superior to the Queen of Spades. They wouldn't want to kill her then. She looked at William and Ralph. "Maybe we can have a festival or a parade, with me at the front, of course."

"What about a tournament?" Ralph asked, leaning closer. "We haven't had one of those for ages."

"A tournament," Rosamund squealed. "Oh yes, I've nearly forgotten about those. But—" She stopped suddenly. "We haven't any knights. They are all with—"

"The Prince of Hearts," Ralph finished for her. "You could recall him from his Wonderland Excursion."

"Third-rate, chap," William said, slapping Ralph on the shoulder. "That's a brilliant idea."

Rosamund ran her finger along the top of the heart table. "No, I don't think it's a good idea. He's always been such a spoiled boy—Thomas indulged him too much. Not to mention it practically took an order of execution to get him out of my dungeon and gone from the palace on his so-called *excursion*. Besides, the people love me, not him, and when he's around..."

"They will always love you best no matter what," Ralph said. "But it would still be good for the people to see you two together. They do enjoy the young prince."

Rosamund glared at him.

"Not to say you're not *young*," Ralph blurted, "because that would be ridiculous. You're the embodiment of perpetual youth."

Rosamund's lips curved into a smile. "That's better."

William stood on his chair, brandishing an umbrella as if it were a blade. "We can hold a tournament with jousting and sword fighting. Everyone likes a good sword fight. Of course, we'd tell them that it was our benevolent Queen who thought of it."

"I do love a good tournament ..." Rosamund said, tapping her fingers together.

"We could plan one right away," Ralph said. "All we need is your consent."

"Very well, let's do it." Rosamund nodded. "Let's have a tournament. And believe me, I will give the people a tournament like they've never seen. It will be terrific. The best, really. They will all agree."

"Well done, Your Majesty," Ralph said and then added, "the prince is only a day's ride from here at Cross Buns Crossing. We could hold the tournament the day after tomorrow if you'd like."

"The day after tomorrow?"

"But not the day before," Ralph said.

"The day after tomorrow but not the day before." Rosamund clapped her hands. "Oh, it's perfect, and then, straight afterwards, we can have a ball."

Ralph bowed. "As Your Majesty wishes."

Rosamund grinned as she studied Ralph. He did have splendid ideas at times. She supposed it was on account of his early career in show business. Now that she thought about it, he didn't seem to have it in him for conspiracies and plotting. Maybe he hadn't been off with the House of Diamonds after all. Maybe he had a real unbirthday surprise planned for her since Alice didn't really count as one.

Charles ruffled his feathers. "Since that is settled, Your Majesty, I really think that we should discuss the matter of that girl,

Alice. My crickets and I agree that it's most suspicious that—"

Rosamund held up her hand. "Really, Dodo," she said. "That's sinking your spoon in the wrong pudding entirely. Alice is a simple lady's maid."

"Against my objection," William grumbled. "She offended a dormouse. Who does that?"

"Quiet, both of you." Rosamund ordered. "I refuse to hear another word more. Ralph is right. I need to keep my people happy, not dally with who will or won't be my Lady's Maid. All that matters right now is that my people love me and if I must give them tournaments, parties, festivals, balls, and a polka-dotted beast, I will. All I need now from you three"—she looked at each of her advisors in turn—"is to bring my son home."

Chapter 19
Alice
House of Hearts, Wonderland
Narcissus 21, Year of the Queen

The chambermaids led Alice through a bewildering maze of hallways—some with stained glass that reached towards the sky and others with low, curved ceilings they had to crouch to walk through. Alice marveled at all the doors—ones that she thought large enough to admit a giant and others too small for even a gerbil to use.

Mary Lou said, "Here we are," as she opened a door to a room filled with bundles upon bundles of clothes. Or it could have been Mary Anne. Alice couldn't tell them apart. They grabbed a measuring tape and started wrapping it around Alice's head and fingers as they scribbled numbers on a chalkboard.

Alice asked, "Are you two the seamstresses as well?"

"In a matter of speaking," Mary Anne or Mary Lou said. "There hasn't been a seamstress for years. Not since the Queen beheaded her."

"Beheaded her?" Alice gulped. "Sounds as if that happens a lot around here."

"Oh," Mary Lou or Mary Anne mumbled through some pins in her mouth. "At least once a week, sometimes twice."

Alice shuddered. "Aren't you worried it'll happen to you?"

"Oh no, she'd never behead Mary Anne Tweedledee," the one with the pins said.

"Or Mary Lou Tweedledum," Mary Lou added with a nod. "Our papas died in service to the Queen during the Great War of Turnips. The Queen promised to always care for us."

"Oh, I see," Alice said. "You are both fortunate in a way. I mean, it's terrible to lose your fathers, but you're lucky that you don't have to worry about losing your heads."

"Not really," they both said, surprising her. "We feel most exuberantly unfortunate—the best sort of feeling in the entire world."

Mary Anne and Mary Lou continued to write down her measurements. As quickly as Alice would work out who was who, they'd move about and she'd lose track again. When they had finished, they left her where she stood and busied themselves with fabrics in every type of red: crimson, brick red, scarlet, brickibrack red, flimflam red, and a few boring shades of regular red.

Red. Red. Red.

"I think we should make something red first," Mary Lou said.

"Oh, yes, I like that," Mary Anne said. "Good choice."

They hurried to the sewing machines, and the sounds of stitching fabric soon filled the room. Hours passed, and she waited. And she waited. She peeked outside. The sun shone overhead. It felt as if it should be dark by now. Maybe days were different in Wonderland. She wondered if the doctors at the asylum were in a panic and if word had been sent to her parents that she'd disappeared. Would they even care? Or would they be relieved?

Alice glanced up when the door opened, hoping it was Ralph. Instead, the other lady's maid entered, the one who wanted her to stay.

She waltzed over to Alice in a fitted gown of strawberry-colored silk with her chestnut-brown hair tucked away in a perfect bun. She took Alice's hands. "I stole away as soon as I had the chance. My name is Sabrina, the Lady of Lake Town. Can we be friends?" she asked. "I bet we'll be the best of friends. I just know it."

Alice had never had a real friend before. She considered the White Rabbit a friend, but she didn't know if that counted, since they were co-conspirators. She thought her sister had been her friend once, but that ended after she went to the asylum. Or maybe it ended before that and Alice hadn't noticed.

Alice smiled. "I'd like that, thank you."

Sabrina squealed, and hugged Alice, hopping up and down. "Promise we'll be best friends forever and ever and ever."

Alice wasn't sure she was ready to promise that.

Sabrina stepped away from her and crinkled her nose.

"What is it?" Alice asked, gazing behind her.

Sabrina leaned over and sniffed Alice's shoulder. "You smell like you've been in a rabbit hole."

Alice took a step back. Sweat beaded on Alice's forehead as she searched for something to say. She didn't want to lie to her new friend, but she didn't really have a choice. "Why would I be in a rabbit hole? It wouldn't be very civilized I'd think."

Sabrina shook Alice's arm playfully. "Oh, don't be so serious. I was merely teasing. Who would go into a rabbit hole? They're so musty and filled with such odd things. I wouldn't be caught alive in one. Come on, let's get you into the bath."

Sabrina took her to a side chamber with a giant porcelain tub. She helped Alice take off the dirty gown and get in the tub. She instantly started shivering.

"The water's freezing," Alice said.

"Of course it is, silly. Why wouldn't it be? Go on. In you go."

Sabrina pushed Alice into the cold water until she was submerged up to her chin and refused to allow Alice up until every inch of her was scrubbed and glowing.

"Mary Lou and Mary Anne must have finished something for you by now," Sabrina said. "I'll be back in a snap."

Alice waited only a moment before Sabrina returned with a crimson gown draped over her arms. "See, told you," she said. "Isn't it just beautiful?"

The color reminded Alice of blood.

Sabrina pulled the gown over Alice's head and then helped her get her arms through the puffed sleeves. When she had finished, Sabrina led Alice towards a dressing table and sat her before it. "Now for that hair of yours," she said. After a few winces, some groans, and a lot of whining mostly on Sabrina's end, Sabrina managed to wrestle Alice's hair into an elaborate knot at the base of her neck.

Sabrina clapped her hands. "You look like a proper lady. I think the Queen will be very pleased."

Alice stared at herself in the reflection. It couldn't be real. The mirror must be playing tricks because she was almost beautiful. Elegant, even. Not the plain girl who had been tucked away in an asylum.

"Is that..." Alice took a breath. "Is that *me?*"

"Of course it is," Sabrina said. "You're silly. Now, all that's left is your jewels. Where are they?"

"I don't have any."

Sabrina's mouth gaped open. "No rings? No necklaces? Not even a brooch?"

Alice shook her head.

Sabrina shrugged. "You'll get some soon enough."

A loud chime reverberated through the room, rattling the glass and shaking the perfume bottles on the dressing table.

Sabrina grabbed Alice's hand and yanked her towards the door. "Oh, we don't want to be late. She'll be fuming like a bandersnatch for sure."

"But where are we going?" Alice asked.

"It's teatime. Whatever you do, make sure you put two pats of butter in your tea, no matter what she says."

Alice didn't want any butter in her tea, let alone an extra serving, and she wasn't sure she was even ready for tea with the Queen. It was too soon. She'd barely made it into the palace with her head still on her shoulders. She needed Ralph. Where was he?

They hurried down more hallways in an impossible maze of rooms. "How will we ever make it in time?" Alice gasped for air. The bodice of her dress was starting to pinch.

"Don't worry," Sabrina said. "I know all the shortcuts."

They entered a hallway filled with portraits of women holding heart-topped scepters and wearing ruby-crusted crowns.

Alice slowed. "Who are they?"

Sabrina continued to pull her along. "All the Queens of Hearts who have ever reigned, dating back to our very first queen, Rosalynn Heart."

Many of the queens had sour faces, others were happy, a few were sad, and some had the sternest expressions Alice had ever seen. They wore their red hair in different styles and dressed in different cuts of gowns, but they all appeared alike—almost as if they were the same person.

"Here's *our* Queen of Hearts," Sabrina said and pointed to a painting at the very end. "It was done right after her coronation."

Something jolted through Alice's body. There was something so familiar about the picture—so very familiar. She gazed into the Queen's young eyes, and they stared back at her, defiant and sad in a way. But there was something else, something hidden inside them, that sent goosebumps down her arms.

"This one is my favorite," Sabrina said, "because it has the Prince of Hearts in it. Isn't he a dream?"

"The prince?" Alice asked, tearing her eyes away from the young Queen of Hearts. "I didn't think there was one."

"Of course there is," Sabrina said, sighing. "What kind of kingdom, err, queendom, would it be without a handsome prince? It wouldn't do. Isn't he the most handsomest thing you've ever seen?"

Alice peered at the painting. A tall young man with red, curly hair stood with one hand on the queen's shoulder and the other behind his back. Alice's eyes followed the strong line of his jaw to his mouth, which had the slightest hint of a smile. Her stomach fluttered for no reason at all, and she wondered if she was getting ill. "Yes," Alice agreed. "He is striking."

"They say he is a mirror image of the late king—oh my..." Sabrina looked around quickly and yelled over her shoulder, "I mean, the traitor!"

Alice examined the portrait again.

"Uh-oh, not you too," Sabrina said, staring at Alice. "You fancy him."

"No, I do not. That's absurd."

Sabrina wagged her finger in Alice's face. "You can't hide it from me. I know that look." She skipped around Alice, singing, "Alice and the prince sitting by the sea. K-I-S-S-I-N-G—"

"STOP IT," Alice cried and yanked her by the arm. "Please."

Sabrina giggled. "You fancy him, admit it."

Alice crossed her arms. "I don't, so I won't. It would take a lot more than a painting to decide whether or not to fancy someone."

"I suppose it doesn't matter if you do or don't," Sabrina said. "Because he's in love with that nitwit Marilyn Montague. They're off together as we speak, traveling all over Wonderland. He hasn't been to Gardenia City for over a year."

"Marilyn Montague? Is she a lady's maid too?"

"Hardly," Sabrina huffed. "She's an actress and not a very good one either. I've been to her plays and I've seen slugs put on a better performance."

Alice studied the picture of the prince. "Is she really all that bad?"

"Worse," Sabrina said and wrapped her arm around Alice. "Besides, you're much prettier than she is."

Alice's cheeks burned like fiery coals at the compliment.

Another chime echoed through the hall.

Sabrina gasped. "We're already late. If we hurry, we might be on time."

She yanked Alice forwards, and they sprinted the rest of the way. The duchess was waiting by the door, tapping her foot, when they arrived.

Bess said, "You're tardy, both of you, and, Alice..." She pinched her lips until they turned an awful shade of white. "It's your first day as a lady's maid and you can't even be on time. Wait until the queen hears about this."

Alice's mouth fell open. "I...I...didn't mean—"

"It was my fault," Sabrina said. "I dallied too long."

Bess's eyes narrowed. "Really? This is your fault?"

Sabrina glanced over at Alice. "I insisted on showing Alice the Queen's portrait. I'm sure the Queen wouldn't be terribly upset when I tell her how beautiful Alice thought she was."

Bess stabbed her finger at Sabrina's nose. "Insolent girl. You know how the Queen likes flattery, and you would use it too, you impertinent—"

Sabrina shrugged. "It's not flattery when it's true."

Bess took a long breath and tugged at the lace around her wrist. "You may be able to fool the Queen and this nitwit"—she pointed at Alice—"but you can't fool me. I'll be watching you. I'll be watching *both* of you."

Bess tilted her nose in the air before she pranced into an adjoining room. "Your Highness," she sang. "Don't you worry. I found them. Wasn't that good of me?"

Sabrina rolled her eyes and stuck her thumb at Bess. "Don't worry about her. She's been cranky ever since her baby transformed into a pig. It must have been all that pepper. I'm certain of it. Come," Sabrina said, wrapping her arm around Alice. "We'll go in together."

Alice let Sabrina lead her, feeling comfort at having someone close to her. As they entered, the Queen was already sitting before a table with a teapot, biscuits, and tarts. Alice's stomach rumbled at the sight of it.

The Queen snapped, "Your stomach is not allowed to talk unless spoken to. Please advise it such."

Alice bowed her head. "Yes, Your Majesty."

The Queen sniffed. "Sit next to me, Alice."

Alice moved towards the Queen. The many folds of her gown made it impossible to see the table's edge and she bumped into it. The duchess tried to hide her chuckle by holding a napkin up to her mouth.

"It's nice to see you properly dressed," the Queen said without even looking at Alice. "You must make sure you spiffy it up in my presence."

"Very spiffy," Bess added.

"Like me," Sabrina said with a nod. "I'm always spiffy."

"Well spoken, Sabrina," the Queen said.

Bess leaned forwards to pour the tea, and the Queen slapped her hand away.

"Alice will do that, Bess."

"Your Majesty," the duchess protested. "I always pour the tea."

"Not today," the Queen said. "Go on, Alice."

Alice reached for the teapot. She took several short breaths to calm her flailing heart. She didn't know anything about proper tea etiquette. It was always her mother or Katherine who poured.

Alice sat at the edge of her seat and tilted the pot. The tea spurted out in short bursts, spilling over onto the saucer. The duchess smirked.

When the Queen's cup was nearly overflowing, Alice set the pot down with a loud clack. "Oh, I'm so sorry."

The Queen pursed her lips. "Please, do be careful with that pot. It's a family heirloom passed down from my mother, who got it from her mother, who got it from her mother, who I believe took it from the Queen of Clubs."

Alice opened and closed her mouth, trying to think of something to say.

"Don't just sit there, brainless girl." The Queen nodded towards the platter of butter. "Finish."

Alice fumbled for the butter dish. She edged one pat into the teacup, and it dropped like a pebble, splattering tea on the Queen's doily. Flustered, Alice put the dish down and placed her hands in her lap.

The Queen eyed Alice with a slight twitch in her lashes.

Sabrina brought her hand to the side of her mouth and whispered in Alice's direction, "Offer another pat."

"Oh." Alice snatched the butter again and smiled at the Queen. "Would you like one pat or two, Your Majesty?"

"Oh, just one," the Queen said and fanned herself. "I like to watch my girlish figure."

Alice poured tea for Sabrina and the duchess, and no matter how hard she tried not to, the tea dribbled onto the saucers every time.

Alice gave a nervous giggle. "I suppose I need more practice."

The Queen picked up her cup. "Bess never puts enough tea in my saucer. Between you and I, I've always liked a little extra."

The duchess' eyes widened. "Your Majesty, I would have gladly done so. If you had told me—"

"You should have *known*," the Queen said, taking a sip and setting her cup back into its pool of tea.

Alice poured her own cup—absent of any butter—while the duchess begged the Queen's forgiveness and groveled at her feet. Alice took a drink and the taste of oily fish rolled over her tongue. She tried to swallow but couldn't. The tea stayed put as if her throat refused to accept such a sickening drink. Alice held the liquid in her cheeks until she could work out what to do.

"Enough, Bess. Now, I have some news ..." the Queen's red lips curved upwards, reminding Alice of the Cheshire Cat. "Gardenia City will be holding a tournament the day after tomorrow but not the day before. Isn't it such a marvelous idea? I practically came up with it myself."

Sabrina clapped her hands. "Oh goody, goody."

"Your Majesty is most generous," Bess gushed. "Most generous indeed. How lucky we are to have you. Wouldn't you agree, Alice?"

Alice nodded. The tea dripped down her throat and her eyes watered. She was going to start gagging. She stared up at the ornate ceiling, forcing herself to stay calm, but every ounce of her wanted to out of instinct. She couldn't. Not in front of the Queen. Not at her first tea time.

The Queen said, "Preparations are to start straightaway if everything is to be ready tomorrow when the Prince of Hearts comes."

Alice couldn't hold the tea in any longer. She coughed, sending a fishy spray across the table.

"I know," the Queen said. "My sentiments exactly."

Chapter 20
Rosamund
House of Hearts, Wonderland
Narcissus 21, Year of the Queen

Rosamund busied herself by watching everyone else work. She oversaw the making of the banners, tapestries, flags, and napkins. She noticed Alice wasn't so good with the needle, but after the Queen's grumbling and threats of beheadings, she improved.

Rosamund was always good at motivating others. It was one of her many virtues.

After the assembly posted the tournament notices, Rosamund rode Scarlet into town and paraded before the people, minus the Proverbials, since they weren't allowed. Her other people, the good ones, cheered and threw roses at Scarlet's hooves.

Before returning to the palace, Rosamund made sure to ride past the tower. She glanced up and smiled at Constance's crestfallen face as she watched from one of the turrets. Rosamund waved at her and then stopped to allow some of her nauseating subjects to kiss the hem of her gown. When they had finished, Rosamund insisted they sang her praises as loud as they physically could and then a little more for good measure, so that Constance could take it all in.

Rosamund then spent the rest of the afternoon sitting in the Cave and ordering her advisors to write letters to Cecil de Burg. Rosamund insisted they explain that Thomas had been convicted of treason and rightfully executed for it.

Her advisors grumbled that they had already told him in a million different ways, times twenty and divided by sixteen.

"Then tell him again," she demanded, "and don't stop telling him until he lifts the Bull like the fat, little walrus should."

She left her advisors with pens in hand and went to the throne room, where she forced herself to listen to the complaints and pleas from her peasants. It was the most bothersome chore of all her queenly duties. Her eyes kept closing, but no matter how many times she wished they'd all be gone when she opened them, they still stood in lines that tumbled out the door.

She stole my squash and it was my favorite one.

His shoe rooted in my garden.

Her cow got loose and ruined my pies.

And so on and so forth.

Rosamund had a migraine by suppertime. Everyone who was anyone—or those who considered themselves remotely related to anyone—had crammed themselves at her table, rising and bouncing on one foot as she took her place at the head. As Rosamund sat, servants rushed in, bringing platters of potatoes doused with orange sauce, rhubarb pie and cheese, and ham with cherry drizzle, while minstrels played "Ring Around the Rosie."

A servant plopped a dollop of whipped cream into Rosamund's soup bowl. As she went to dip in her spoon, she threw it down. "Will someone please stop that rumpus"—she pointed at the musicians—"before I have an eye hemorrhage?"

Bess jumped out of her seat and hurried to the corner, ushering the confused troop of musicians out of the room. "I've sent them from the palace, Your Majesty," she said. "Just for you."

"Yes, Bess, very good."

William wove through the guests, including several who were uninvited, until he came to her side. He leaned over and shouted, "We received word from the prince."

"Oh?" Rosamund asked. "And what did that spoiled little brat say?"

She ground some mint over her potatoes as she waited for his answer. "Well?" she prompted him as she looked up. William was staring off down the table. She followed his gaze and realized it went straight to Sabrina.

Rosamund flicked William's nose. "The Queen is over here."

"I'm sorry," he said, blushing to the tips of his oily ears. "I thought I saw something."

"My lady's maid, that's what you thought you saw, you fool. Stop acting like an aggravating gnat and tell me what the prince said."

"Quite right." William cleared his throat. "He has answered your summons, naturally, and he's expected at court tomorrow."

"Is that all?"

"That's all."

"Then go." Rosamund waved her hand. "Get."

She watched William return to his seat and again his eyes roved back to Sabrina. Rosamund sniffed. What nerve he had to make gaga eyes. At his age! He looked absurd. She was sure that everyone must be laughing behind his back. If they weren't, she'd make sure they did.

After supper, Rosamund didn't feel much like dancing and retired to bed early. Once her lady's maids had undressed her, she slipped into bed with her night candle flickering at her bedside. She sank her head into her prickly pillow and listened to the wind blow against the curtains.

As she was about to go to sleep, she heard Thomas moan, "You killed me, Rosie. You killed me."

"Wha... what? Someone say something?" Rosamund opened her eyes. All she could see was the red canopy of her bed. She must have fallen asleep and not even realized it. She closed her eyes again.

Then as clear as the pop of a soap bubble, she heard: "Oh, not this again."

A jolt shot threw her. She'd recognized that voice anywhere. That was Pedro. Definitely Pedro.

Thomas said, "*Excuse* me if I'm not over being dead."

Rosamund pushed the pillows against her ears and squeezed her eyes shut, demanding a new dream because she didn't like this one. She hoped that next she'd dream about something more pleasant, like the beheading of the Queen of Spades.

"Maybe," Pedro added, "if you weren't such a whiny, little baby you would be."

"Baby?" Thomas huffed. "At least I'm not a Polly Prissy-Pants, who can't stop complaining about wiping his nose."

"Polly Prissy-Pants?" Pedro scoffed. "Look who's talking."

Rosamund couldn't take it anymore. She'd rather be awake than listen to this nonsense. She threw the pillows away and sat up.

Just above her were the floating heads of Thomas and Pedro. Their skin had grayed and dried blood ringed their stumps, but it was most certainly them. They stared at her with milky eyes as they hovered mid-air as if suspended by invisible strings.

Rosamund slunk back into her pillows. "You can't be here. You can't. You're...DEAD."

"We know," they chorused.

Rosamund pulled the covers up to her chin. "I must still be asleep and this is all a dream. Yes, that's it. I'm sleeping."

Pedro winked at her. "This isn't a dream, Rosebud."

"He's right," Thomas said, rolling forwards. "It isn't."

Rosamund ignored them. "I've heard about these types of dreams before, the really vivid ones," she said to herself. "Oh, I knew I shouldn't have had so many tarts at supper. I've been told it could cause nightmares, but this—"

A mischievous grin spread onto Pedro's face. He floated closer and closer, as if he had a propeller hidden somewhere on the back of his head. His blue eyes that sparkled in life were as dingy as pond water.

"If this was a dream," he said, "could I do this?"

Pedro came closer, and Rosamund buried her head in the pillow. She chanted: *Not real. Not real. Not real.* But then abruptly stopped when she felt icy lips kiss her cheek. She howled and flung Pedro away, knocking him into the canopy post and not feeling the least bit bad about it either. She grabbed the candle next to her bed and waved it back and forth.

Thomas asked, "What are you doing, Rosie?"

"Get back!" she yelled. "Both of you."

"We can't," Pedro said, scrunching his face. "We have no feet."

"Then go away," Rosamund shouted. "Go to the Undying Lands where you belong. You're dead. You shouldn't be here."

Thomas's face fell. "There are no Undying Lands for us."

"Of course there are," Rosamund snapped. "That's where everyone goes when they die."

"Then why aren't we there?" Pedro asked.

"Perhaps it's because you haven't been properly ordered." Rosamund stared at the two heads and, with as much queenly confidence as she could muster, said, "I hereby order you to report to the Undying Lands at once."

Pedro and Thomas continued to bob in their places.

"At once," Rosamund demanded. "This very instant."

Nothing happened.

Rosamund slumped in her bed.

"I told you, Rosie," Thomas said. "There is no such place."

"Looks like you're stuck with us, eh?" Pedro said.

"I am not," Rosamund said. "I am the Queen of Hearts and you've defied my orders. If you weren't already beheaded, I'd behead you. Maybe I'll order your eyes gouged or your tongues cut out."

Pedro sighed. "Come, Rosebud. We both know you won't."

"*Won't?*" Rosamund's cheeks blazed. "Guards!" she roared.

Pedro's and Thomas's heads huddled together. Rosamund was certain she saw fear in their eyes—much to her satisfaction.

She smiled. "Not so uppity now, are we?"

The door banged open, and Rosamund heard feet rushing forwards. She jumped out of the bed and waited with her arms crossed.

An Eight of Hearts and a Seven of Hearts bowed.

"Your Majesty, we are at your service."

She pointed to her bed. "Remove those intolerable heads from my bedchamber and see that their eyes are properly gouged and their tongues hacked out. Then put them in baskets and drop them in the river."

"As you wish."

They threw open the bed curtains. Thomas and Pedro bumped into each other like two mome raths that had been caught making a feast out of picnic leftovers. Their eyes darted back and forth, from the guards to Rosamund.

"Take them away," Rosamund said with a wave of her hand.

"Begging your pardon, Your Majesty," the Seven of Hearts said, "but there's nobody here."

"Stickfiddles," she said. "They're right in front of you. Surely you can identify the late King of Hearts. And here." She pulled out the locket from inside her nightgown. "I beheaded Pedro years ago, so you might not remember him, but here he is. This is what he looked like alive. Recognize him now?"

The Eight of Hearts leaned closer. "Maybe if Your Majesty pointed them out to us..."

"You idiot," she seethed. "Must I do everything myself? Right here—" She poked Thomas in the eye.

"Ouch," Thomas cried, blinking. "Careful, Rosie."

"There," Rosamund said. "You heard *that*, didn't you?"

The guards glanced at each other and shrugged.

The Eight of Hearts said, "Maybe we should ask for one of the Nine of Hearts."

Rosamund mimicked. "*Maybe we should ask for one of the Nine of Hearts*. Just take them away or...or...it's off with *your* heads."

The guards shook in their tunics. They fell at her feet and clasped her gown, pleading. "Spare us, Your Majesty. We can't take the heads away. We don't know where they are."

"Stop it, Rosebud," Pedro said. "They can't see us; you can't fault them for that."

"See? That's why I had *you* beheaded," Rosamund said. "You were always taking their side."

"What else was I supposed to do?" he asked. "I was a knight."

"Not a very good one, as I recall," Thomas said, eyeing Pedro, "but it's true, Rosie, you can't punish the guards."

She glared into Thomas's foggy eyes. He was as obstinate in death as he had been in life. She hated that he was so soft. *Hated it.* He was never fit to rule. Maybe she had beheaded him by accident, but it certainly wasn't a mistake.

The door slammed shut. The guards had fled the second she turned her back. Rosamund balled her fists. "Oh, those insolent, those intolerable… They can't run off on me. I'll have them beheaded at once."

"Calm down, Rosebud," Pedro said. "You'll overexcite yourself."

She grabbed her favorite red shawl with the rose sparkles and wrapped it around her shoulders. "I've had enough of this."

She stormed out of her bedchamber and into the drawing room. She flopped down before the fire and stewed. And stewed. And stewed—

Until she heard an annoying ticking sound.

Ticktock, ticktock, ticktock.

Rosamund gritted her teeth and stood, grabbing a poker from the fire, and walked around the room. She lifted table covers, searched under chairs, but she couldn't find where the sound was coming from.

Ticktock, ticktock, ticktock.

"That better not be one of you two," she snarled into her bedchamber, but neither Thomas nor Pedro answered.

She crept towards a closet. The sound got louder and louder. She pressed her ear against the door.

TICKTOCK, TICKTOCK, TICKTOCK.

Rosamund tightened her grasp on the poker, and flung the door open.

A clock sat in the middle of the floor with the words "Hickory, dickory, dock" smeared across its face in dripping, black paint.

It started to ring with a high-pitched screech, shaking on its legs.

Rosamund screamed.

Chapter 21
Alice
House of Hearts, Wonderland
Narcissus 21, Year of the Queen

Alice helped Bess and Sabrina ready the Queen for bed. They pulled on her nightgown, told her a bedtime story, and placed a cup of soured milk on her nightstand. As soon as they were done, they tiptoed out into the hallway, shutting the door behind them. Bess stormed off straight after without so much as a word or a parting glance.

Sabrina didn't appear to notice or care. "I'm glad that's finally over," she groaned. "Here, come with me." She wrapped her arm around Alice and led her away from the Queen's bedchamber, though to where Alice had no idea. They headed down the hall, following the palace mice as they scampered along the sconces, replacing the burnt out candles with new ones.

"I need to talk to you," Sabrina said, lowering her voice. "It's very unimportant."

"You mean important," Alice corrected her.

Sabrina shook her head. "Important? Why that's nothing at all. No, it's definitely unimportant."

"Then what is so…unimportant?"

Sabrina leaned close to Alice. "The Prince of Hearts will be here tomorrow. I overheard William tell the Queen at supper. He's coming for the tournament, surely, but what if he's really coming back to take a bride? That's what princes are supposed to do—be handsome and charming and find a girl to marry."

Sabrina sighed. "Oh, Alice, what if? He hardly ever looks in my direction, but wouldn't it be glorious if he did ask me?"

Alice felt an odd churning in her gut and couldn't place it at first. Then she realized it was jealousy. Alice knew she was being silly. The prince was only a portrait to her. She couldn't be jealous, not of Sabrina.

"If he does," Alice said, pushing the feeling away, "then you'll be the next Queen of Hearts."

"Yes, there would be that," Sabrina said, "but it wouldn't matter if the prince did choose me. The Queen would forbid it."

"Could she do that?"

"She's the Queen. She has a say in everything, and she already said she won't let me marry. All I ever wanted was to be a wife and mother, and the Queen won't let me."

Alice shook her head. "But why?"

Sabrina's eyes watered as she stared up to the ceiling. A tear slid down her cheek. "My mother was one of her lady's maids and married the Queen's lover in secret. The Queen never forgave her for it. She hates my mother and me too."

"Why would she hate you? You had nothing to do with it."

Sabrina shrugged. "That doesn't matter to the Queen. She beheaded my father, Pedro, she banished my mother to the House of Diamonds—she knew how much my mother hated the cold—and then forced me to join her court on my sixteenth birthday."

"You didn't want to be a lady's maid?"

"Of course I didn't," Sabrina cried. "All the ladies of Lake Town are married at sixteen. It's tradition. I was to marry the handsome Count of Candlewick, my Reuben. We were betrothed from infancy. He even came and beseeched the Queen, but she sent him away. Last I heard..." She stifled a sob. "The last I heard was that he married Lady Mayflower. That fat pig always wanted him. He picked a pig over me. A pig. Everyone in Lake Town must be laughing behind my back. Am I so disgusting?"

"You're not disgusting." Alice took Sabrina's hands. "Don't ever think that. Besides, they're not laughing behind your back.

Lady Mayflower can't be that bad. She's not really a pig."

"No." Sabrina sniffed. "She really is."

"Oh." Alice looked about her as if somehow the words she needed to say would appear in tiny puffs of smoke. "Well... well, it'll be all right. You'll marry someone else. Maybe even the prince."

Sabrina blew her nose on the sleeve of her gown. "You really think so?" she asked, batting her wet lashes.

"I do."

"Can you keep a secret?"

Alice nodded.

"You must promise to stick a thousand peanuts in your eye if you don't keep this hush, hush."

"I promise."

"Very well." Sabrina looked behind her.

Alice looked too. They were alone. Even the palace mice had disappeared.

Sabrina whispered. "I'm not interested in the prince. There's someone else I have my nose on, and I think he fancies me too."

"Oh?" Alice raised her eyebrows. "Who is it?"

"I can't tell you that." She grinned. "It would jinx the whole thing."

"That's silly."

"Maybe to you," Sabrina said, "but not to me."

"I swear I won't breathe a word about it if you tell me who it is," Alice said.

"Oh, I can't. I mustn't. If I do, it might all vanish into a wisp of candle smoke." She twirled her hands upwards to further her point. "Perhaps in time, I will, but for now, let me show you your room."

They stopped at a door.

Sabrina removed a key from her pocket. "This is us," she said.

The door opened to a sitting area with two pink couches, a book case, and a table with a chess set. Alice gazed at the delicate tapestries and porcelain trinkets of eggs and hearts and dancers lining the shelves. Hanging on the walls were paintings of creatures she'd never seen before: oxen with the legs and feathers of an ostrich, dogs with antler horns, and horses with fish tails. A fire glowed in the corner, casting an enchanting light over rose-colored walls. On the right and left sides of the room were two more doors.

"This one over here is yours," Sabrina said and took Alice to the door on the right.

Alice stood before it.

"Go on," Sabrina said with a smile. "Open it."

Alice turned the doorknob and went inside.

A red velvet canopy bed took up much of the space along with a nightstand, a mirror, and an armoire. On the bed was an embroidered duvet with matching pillows. She hugged one of the pillows to her chest. Even with the scratchiness and the prickles, she'd never been in a bedroom this nice. Not even when she had traveled to France with Mummy and Daddy.

Sabrina said, "The Queen takes all the best prickly pillows and scratchy blankets for herself, but we make do."

Alice turned from the bed and went over to the armoire, opening the doors. Dresses of all shades of red filled the hangers. "Are these mine?"

"Of course." Sabrina pulled out a bottom drawer. "And your nightgowns are in here."

Alice took the garment and cradled the silk in her hands.

"You better hurry off to bed at once," Sabrina said, kissing Alice's cheek. "We have a busy day tomorrow. The Queen will want everything perfect when the prince arrives. Good night, dear Alice. I'm so glad you're here. Until you arrived, I thought I'd die of loneliness."

Alice wanted to chide herself for being so resistant in coming. So far, everything had gone well. Busy, but well. She could certainly do without the food and tea, but other than that, she was almost living within a dream.

"Yes, good night," Alice said. "Sleep well."

Sabrina left Alice alone in her new room. Alice went over to the bed and flopped down on it, sinking into the scratchy blankets. She was tired—more than tired, really. Her first day in Wonderland felt like five back home. If it hadn't been that Mary Lou and Mary Anne had made her gown specially for her and she didn't want to ruin it, she could have easily fallen asleep with it on.

Standing up, Alice fumbled with the clasps and buttons and zips of her dress. She almost went to knock on Sabrina's door a few times, but then she finally managed to free herself of the heavy gown and get her nightgown on.

Alice was taking the pins out of her hair when she heard a scream. She stood up, heart pounding, and pressed her ear against the wall. She heard it again. It was coming from the Queen's rooms.

She found some slippers and a robe. She thought of getting Sabrina, but then she heard the scream again. Panic spread its fingers along her chest, wrapping her heart in a fist. She didn't have time for Sabrina. She darted towards the hallway and sprinted towards the Queen.

Although the Queen's rooms were next to Alice's, Her Majesty's bedchamber alone was nearly the size of a cottage. When she got to the door, gasping for breath, she was prepared to go bursting inside, but she found herself hesitating. What if she wasn't allowed to go in without Bess? If only Bess were here, the duchess would know what to do.

Alice cracked open the door. "Your Majesty?" she called. "Your Majesty, are you all right?"

She heard a whimper and followed the noise. She found the Queen in a crumpled heap before the closet.

Alice dropped to her side. "Are you hurt? Do you need me to get help?"

The Queen sucked on her thumb and pointed a jittery finger towards the closet. Alice looked and saw an unusual little clock shaped like a tomato.

"7:37 a.m...." Alice frowned. "But it couldn't possibly. Is that what's troubling you, Your Majesty? Do you want me to set the time?"

"Who cares about the time?" the Queen snapped. "Look what's written on it."

Hickory, dickory, dock.

Alice's breath caught in her throat. It was the password to the Aboveground Headquarters. The same phrase Ralph had used when they were in the Lost Wood, but what was it doing painted on the face of a clock?

"It's a bomb!" the Queen shrieked. "You must destroy it quickly."

A bomb? It didn't look like one, but then again this was Wonderland. Was this plan Z that Ralph had talked about at the Aboveground Headquarters? Alice glanced over at the Queen. Ralph had promised that once she was dead, Alice could go home. But for that to happen, she'd have to walk away and let the Queen get blown up. Even if Alice hadn't planted the bomb, she'd be the one who killed her by doing nothing, and Alice refused to do that. Despite it all, the Queen had welcomed Alice, had been kind to her in her own way, had given her gowns, and a home within her palace. Maybe the Queen wasn't so bad after all.

"What are you doing?" the Queen cried. "Get rid of it before it kills us both."

Alice set the clock on a nearby table and frantically searched for something—anything—to destroy it with. She picked up a letter opener, a vase, a seat cushion, but none of them seemed right. She'd never destroyed a bomb before. What did one use for such things?

The Queen held up a fireplace poker. "Must I do everything?"

Alice smiled gratefully as she took the poker from the Queen. She went to the clock and held it over her head.

"Go on," the Queen demanded. "It could go off at any second."

Alice slammed the poker down and then shielded herself as thousands of pieces flew every which way. As the final cog whirled to a stop with a final sputter, they heard footsteps racing down the hall.

"Hurry," the Queen said, getting to her feet. "We must hide it. I don't want anyone to know about this."

"Whyever not?"

"Don't question me," she snapped. "I have my reasons."

Alice helped the Queen gather coils, wheels, and cogs, none of which resembled anything close to a bomb, but Alice reckoned the Queen knew more about it than her. When they had finished, they tossed the pieces into the closet just as knocking rattled the door.

"Your Majesty," the Mad Hatter called from the other side. "Is everything all right?"

"Y...yes," the Queen stammered. "Everything is miraculous."

"May we come in?"

The Queen smoothed her hair and sat before the fire, acting as if nothing had happened. Alice took her position behind her, kicking a stray wheel under the table.

"Your Majesty?" The Hatter poked his head in the door, followed by the rest of her advisors: the Dodo, who Sabrina said nobody called Dodo to his face except for the Queen, and Ralph. Alice's eyes lit up at the sight of him. She hadn't seen the White Rabbit since she'd left with Mary Anne and Mary Lou. She had hoped to talk to him at supper, but his place setting had remained empty. Where had he been? Why had he disappeared on her?

The Queen snapped at her advisors, "What do you three want?"

The Hatter scanned the room. "The chambermaids said they heard a scream."

"Oh? Well..." The Queen shrugged and tightened her robe around her. "I slipped on my way to the chamber pot, but Alice helped me. Didn't you, Alice?"

Alice nodded. "Yes, Your Majesty."

All their eyes fell on Alice; she didn't really enjoy the attention. The Dodo's feathers ruffled, and the Hatter sneered. Even Ralph gave her an odd look. Maybe the clock was a bomb, and she'd interfered in the Aboveground's scheme. What would they do? Would they kick her out? Send her back to the asylum? Alice shivered. No, she couldn't go back there.

The Dodo shoved a pipe into his beak and waddled over to the fire. "Yes," he said, staring at Alice. "We're so glad that she seems to have such a good sense of timing. An unusually good sense, I'd say. I wonder what the crickets would think."

Alice stiffened under the Dodo's gaze. It was as if he already suspected her. How, Alice didn't know, but even Ralph gave the Dodo a sidelong glance.

"It's certainly a good thing too," the Queen said. "Now, go away. All of you."

The Dodo bowed his head. "Very well."

The Mad Hatter, White Rabbit, and the Dodo shuffled out of the room.

"You too, Alice," the Queen said. "I need to be alone."

Alice curtsied and skipped backwards, eager to catch up with Ralph. Only he was already down the hall and speaking to the Dodo and the Hatter. As Alice was about to shut the door, she heard a chicken squawk. She watched as a hooded figure appeared in the Queen's room in a flash of blinding white.

"Thank goodness you're here." She heard the Queen say. "I need your counsel."

Alice caught her breath, hardly believing that anyone wore any color other than red in the House of Hearts. Who was this person? The figure turned towards Alice and a pair of green eyes glimmered out from under the hood, watching her as she shut the door.

Chapter 22
Rosamund
House of Hearts, Wonderland
Oleander 31, Year of the Queen

Madame Diamond went around the room lighting candles and blowing up balloons. She twisted one of the balloons into the shape of a horse and gave it to Rosamund. "The spirits told me, as usual."

"Ah, lovely," Rosamund said, taking it from the madame's grasp. "Did the spirits tell you the trial I've been through tonight? First the heads...then the bomb... What's next?"

She wondered if it was reckless to not tell her advisors about the bomb, but something told her to keep it close to the crown. If the Dodo's crickets were right and the Queen of Spades was in league with someone from her inner square, then she had to be suspicious of everyone—especially them. It wouldn't be the first time she had to behead one or more of her advisors.

"Heads?" Madame Diamond asked.

"Oh, don't get me started on them," Rosamund groaned.

Madame Diamond pulled a crystal ball from inside her cloak. "Come, let's see what the spirits say."

Rosamund took her balloon horse and went over to the table. She sat opposite Madame Diamond with the crystal ball between them. Madame Diamond spat on her hands, rubbed them together, and wiggled her fingers.

"Spirits and goblins," Madame Diamond chanted, "spirits and goblins...SPIRITS AND GOBLINS...Come to the crystal."

A mist swept over the ball, and Rosamund leaned forwards. "Well?" she asked. "What do the spirits and goblins say?"

Madame Diamond's eyes narrowed. "The spirits and goblins are restless. They are trying to tell me something, but I can't quite make it out."

"Not this again." Rosamund squeezed the balloon until it popped. Her little horse was now a blob of rubber. "Make it out at once."

Madame Diamond held up the ball, twisting and turning. "They say...they say..."

"Yes?" Rosamund nodded her head. "What do they say?"

"The spirits of those you've beheaded are angry. They want revenge."

"Revenge for what?" Rosamund snapped. "They all deserved it."

"They...they... Oh dear..." Madame Diamond covered her mouth. "They're saying they want your head to join theirs."

"My head?" Rosamund crossed her arms. "They dare plot against me? Well, it's never going to happen. Tell them that. Go on."

Madame Diamond peered into the ball. Rosamund tutted under her breath. What absurd business was this? Spirits wanting revenge? They were lucky she'd beheaded them when she did and should be glad for it. In fact, they should be raining down praises, not plotting. What a bunch of ungrateful ghosts.

"They're saying they heard you, but they won't rest," Madame Diamond said, looking up. "They won't stop until they have their revenge."

"Revenge? Revenge for being traitors? That's rich. Well if they want my head, they'll have to fight me for it first."

Just like she'd fought everyone. Traitors, conspirators, double-crossers, and now ghosts. From the moment she'd taken her throne, she'd spent every day defending it from those who wanted it, but nobody wanted it more than her.

"You can't fight spirits, Your Majesty. Your guards can't help you. Your advisors certainly can't, and there's not a saint in the Remonstration Church who can help. There's no one."

She sighed. "What do you suggest I do?"

"Hide."

"Hide? How disgraceful. I'm the Queen. I can't *hide*."

"You have to," Madame Diamond said, taking Rosamund's hands. "The spirits come at night, and you can't beat them if you're asleep and unsuspecting. You can't stay awake all night and all day, can you?"

"No, I suppose not, but where am I supposed to go? I can't walk away from my palace and turtle away somewhere. There's the tournament to consider and the summer tour…"

"What if you hid in the palace?"

Rosamund paused. "Now that is a thought. The palace is so large, the largest in all of Wonderland. They couldn't possibly find me, and if I run out of rooms, I can always build more."

"Well done, Your Majesty," Madame Diamond said. "You must put it in motion at once. The spirits already know how to find you. They could be here any second."

Rosamund jumped from her chair, racing around the room. "Oh, now, where did I put that air horn? I must call my lady's maids. They need to pack my belongings."

"There's no time for that," Madame Diamond said. "You must leave now, this very instant. I will help you."

Rosamund and Madame Diamond gathered Rosamund's things. They dragged her wardrobe, jewelry box, prickly pillows, tea set, and favorite doilies down the hallway and into another room. When it was nearly dawn, she finally crept into bed.

Madame Diamond tucked her in. "Good night, Your Majesty. I'd keep the information about the spirits between you and I for now. If they're hunting for you, they listen to whispers. The fewer people who know, the better."

Rosamund nodded. "Do you think I've escaped them?"

"I think so—for tonight anyway."

Rosamund sighed as she settled in, even though the mattress wasn't lumpy enough. She would have to make sure all her secret bedchambers had a proper lumpy bed, more prickly pillows, and extra-scratchy blankets in case she got a chill.

Light seeped through the curtains. Rosamund turned on her side and felt herself slip into a peaceful slumber. Seconds later, she heard shouting and hammering feet.

"Find the Queen! Find the Queen!"

Rosamund pulled herself out of bed and opened the door. Guards ran in five different directions in groups of threes and sixes. Servants popped their heads in and out of entryways. She couldn't help but feel the tiniest bit pleased to see all this fuss over her, despite the clumps of thistle-sand in her eyes.

Bess ran down the hallway with her skirts flying behind her. "Your Majesty, Your Majesty, where are you? Is this a game? Oh, I wish you had told me we were playing."

She passed Rosamund without realizing it.

"Hullo, Bess."

Bess whirled around, her lips forming a perfect circle. "Your Majesty, we've been searching all over for you."

"I've been here," Rosamund said with a yawn.

"You didn't sleep in your own chamber?"

Rosamund had to think of an excuse. As Madame Diamond said, the fewer people who knew, the better. "Honestly, Bess. Can't the Queen of Hearts enjoy some of the other rooms in her own palace once in a while? It is *my* palace."

Bess clasped her hands before her. "Yes, I suppose so, but—"

"Good," Rosamund said. "Now call off this nonsense and let me get some sleep. I'll ask for you when I'm awake."

"But, Your Majesty." Bess's voice rose to an annoying pitch. "The prince will be here any minute. The people are expecting you to greet him."

Rosamund scratched her nails across the wood of the door. "That insufferable child is spoiled even when he's not here. Fine. Get Sabrina and Alice."

Bess curtsied and ran in the opposite direction.

Mary Anne entered the room with a cupful of morning grounds. She set them before Rosamund as quietly as a goose before a holiday feast.

"Where's Mary Lou?" Rosamund demanded as she squinted towards the door. "What's taking her so long? She brings my breakfast and you bring my grounds. I want them both. I'm not in the mood for any nonsense. I've had a horrible night."

Mary Anne paled. "I looked for Mary Lou all over. I don't know where she can be. I woke up this morning and she was gone—disappeared. I'm terribly worried, Your Majesty. It's not like her."

Rosamund set aside her grumpiness for the briefest of moments at the sight of Mary Anne's distress. "Listen, Mary Anne. You tell her to come and see me the instant you find her. Mary Lou's behavior is most inappropriate. She will get an earful from me, I assure you."

"Yes, Your Majesty."

"Now run along and fetch my breakfast."

Mary Anne curtsied and skipped away.

Rosamund placed a wad of the grounds in her lower lip and closed her eyes as slobbery coffee filled her mouth. She spat a brown glob onto the floor and wiped the string of spittle from her chin with the back of her hand.

Bess opened the door, ushering Sabrina and Alice into the room. "Hurry along, hurry along. We haven't much time. Not much time at all."

She glanced over at Alice. The girl had saved her life last night. Bess certainly wouldn't have known what to do. She probably would have fussed all over the room until the bomb blew them both to bits, and she doubted Sabrina would have even lifted a finger. Alice was all she had. She could trust Alice. It was a good thing she hadn't beheaded her.

Rosamund watched as Bess prodded Alice towards the wardrobe, yipping at her heels like a crocodile. She didn't approve of Bess treating her most loyal subject like a common servant.

"Stop being so bossy, Bess," Rosamund snapped. "Leave Alice be."

Bess's cheeks bloomed a blood orange. "I'm sorry, Your Majesty. It won't happen again."

"Very good. Carry on." Rosamund motioned for them to continue with the powdering and dressing while she picked up the *Gardenia Times*. From the corner of her eye, she caught Bess sneering at Alice before returning back to work. As the morning grew brighter, the light chased away last night's fears.

She felt silly for acting so foolishly.

Spirits and goblins.

How ridiculous.

Or was it?

A sudden shiver blew on the back of her neck. One couldn't be too sure about these things, and maybe it would be best to follow Madame Diamond's advice to be on the safe side. Especially since there was that matter of the bomb to consider. Dealing with ghosts was one thing, but bombs were something else entirely. If the usurpers could gain access to her bedchamber—her most private of all private places—then changing rooms every night might be a good idea.

Unless, whoever had planted the bomb, already had admittance to her sleeping quarters. Then, it wouldn't matter if she changed rooms every night because they'd always know where she was. Rosamund could think of only a handful who were allowed the privilege of daily access: her lady's maids, the chambermaids, the shoemaker, the seamstress (although she hadn't seen her for a while for some reason), the wig maker, the late-night snack cook, the toe-nail clipper, and her advisors.

Her advisors.

Her thoughts kept returning to Ralph. Did he have something to do with it after all? His last absence was because of Alice, but what about that other time when he was sneaking about the palace, doing who knows what, cavorting with who knows who. Deep down, she hoped Ralph was innocent. After all, she liked the rabbit and his waistcoat, but he had done things lately that had given her pause and her instincts had always been impeccable.

"What jewels would you like today?" Bess asked, stirring Rosamund to the present. "May I suggest your ruby drop necklace with the agate or perhaps the rubies intertwined with rose quartz?"

Rosamund pursed her lips together. "The ruby drop, I think. I don't want to overdo it."

Bess hurried to the Queen's everyday jewelry box, mounted on a pushcart. Rosamund's most precious stones were locked deep in a vault at a location known by the royal locksmith, whose name remained even a mystery to her.

"Your Majesty!" Bess shrieked. "It's not here. Your ruby necklace. It's gone."

"Impossible," Rosamund said and shoved Bess out of the way.

She peered into the box. Just like the brooch, the necklace had disappeared.

Rosamund faced her lady's maids, gritting her teeth. "Which one of you took it?" She circled and circled them. "Which one of you? Tell me at once."

Bess, Sabrina, and Alice huddled together like aardvarks with their noses rubbed in raspberry.

Rosamund let her gaze fall on Bess. "You went to the jewelry box, so you must have taken it."

Bess fell to her knees, gripping Rosamund's hem. "No, Your Majesty, I swear it. It couldn't have been me. It must have been"—she glanced around frantically—"it must have been... Alice."

"Alice?" The Queen paused. Saving her life or not, stealing wouldn't be tolerated. How could she keep order when maids plucked her very jewels from under her nose?

Alice gaped. "I would never, Your Majesty. I promise."

"Then she should stick a thousand peanuts in her eye," Bess said. "She was the closest to the jewelry box when we dressed you. She must have taken it."

"Speak up, Alice." Rosamund demanded. "Did you or did you not take my necklace?"

"N...no. I..."

"Your Majesty," Sabrina said, stepping forwards. "Alice couldn't have taken it. She wasn't here when your brooch went missing. Whoever took your brooch must have also taken your necklace."

Rosamund turned towards Sabrina. "Are you suggesting you're the thief? Only a guilty person would say such a thing, everyone knows that."

Sabrina twirled a lock of her hair. "No, Your Majesty. Why would I steal your jewels? I mean, I have more jewelry than I need."

Rosamund crossed her arms. "Are you saying my jewels aren't good enough for you?"

Sabrina paled. "Oh, no. That's not what I meant. I mean it's...well... Oh muffins, I don't know what I'm trying to say."

"You don't, but I do." Rosamund lifted a shaky finger and pointed it at Sabrina. "OFF WITH YOUR—"

A herald of trumpets blasted through her most favorite sentence in the world.

Rosamund took a breath and headed towards the window. "The prince is here. Alice, grab me the ruby and rose quartz. I'll deal with you later, Sabrina. And, Bess—"

"Yes, Your Majesty?" the duchess asked, getting to her feet.

"Make sure you write this down for me."

Bess grabbed a notepad and licked the bottom of the quill.

"To do: Behead Sabrina."

Chapter 23
Alice
House of Hearts, Wonderland
Oleander 31, Year of the Queen

Alice clutched Sabrina as soon as the Queen left the room.

"She can't behead you," Alice cried. "We must think of what to do."

Sabrina had defended her with the Queen. She couldn't let her friend die because of her. Alice trembled at the thought of Sabrina's pretty head on one of those spikes.

"You must run away," Alice said. "Go somewhere she'll never find you. Oh, that horrible duchess. If she hadn't blamed me, you wouldn't be in this mess."

Sabrina smiled. "Don't worry, Alice. You fret too much."

Alice grabbed Sabrina's hand. "The Queen is going to *behead* you. If there was ever a time to fret, I think this would be the very instant."

"She won't behead me, silly," Sabrina said, "not when I tell my little love toad. He'll fix everything—oh!" She covered her mouth. "I said too much. I shouldn't have. It's supposed to be a secret."

"No more secrets," Alice said. "Who are you going to tell? Who's going to fix this? Please, Sabrina! I don't want you beheaded."

"I'm going to tell you-know-who I *didn't* tell you about."

Alice stared at her, confused.

"You know," Sabrina said. "The one I think fancies me. He'll make the Queen change her mind. I know he will. Besides, with all the excitement, she'll probably forget anyhow. She orders so many beheadings she can't ever keep track of them all."

"Not with the duchess," Alice said. "She won't let her."

Sabrina hugged Alice. "I told you we'd be best friends forever. Don't worry. Now come. We wouldn't want to miss the procession, would we?"

Alice trailed after Sabrina, not feeling as calm as her new friend. What if this secret crush doesn't help? The Queen had such a temper and her temper overruled everything.

Sabrina hummed as they walked down a carpeted corridor. Alice was glad Sabrina knew where she was going. It was so easy to get lost in the palace with stairs that led to nowhere, doors that opened to blank walls, and balconies with trap floors.

It was enough to drive a person mad.

They found the Queen standing on the palace steps. To take their places, Sabrina and Alice had to maneuver around the guards surrounding her. Alice stood on her tippy-toes. The rose gardens and fountains stretched out before her, but not a single person was in sight.

Shouts and cheers erupted from outside the palace gates. The prince must be close. The applause grew louder and louder as the procession made its way through the city, and knights in red armor rode into the gardens, carrying banners and streamers through a maze of crimson shrubbery, bleeding rose bushes, and fiery flower beds.

Alice saw the prince and she felt that fluttering in her chest again, except this time her heart was beating so fast she was sure it would stop entirely. He rode a checkered horse with curly ribbons in its mane and waved to the crowd that had spilled in from the gates. Alice didn't pay any attention to the jugglers or the elephants or mimes. All she could see was the prince's smile—the same warm, inviting smile as in his portrait.

He stopped his horse before the steps. He jumped off as light as a bird and did a little jig, causing all the women around to swoon. Then he bounded towards the Queen, his red hair swaying in loose ringlets that ever so slightly hung over his ears. He came so close that Alice could smell the scent of lemon drops on his skin. He threw his crimson cloak over his shoulder. "Hullo, Mum," he said as he got down on a knee, bowing.

The Queen reached out her hand and patted him on the head. "It's good to have you home, Thomas," she said to him. "We have a feast prepared for your arrival."

He followed the Queen and passed Alice without a glance in her direction. She had hoped his eyes would fall on her, but she was no more to him than another piece of furniture to adorn the hall. A nobody. Alice watched him go and wished that funny little feeling in her stomach would stop.

"What did I tell you?" Sabrina said. "Isn't he handsome?"

Alice said, "I suppose."

Sabrina elbowed her. "Oh, don't be so glum. The prince must pay all his attention to the Queen, at least at first. He notices us all eventually, if you know what I mean," she said with a wink.

Alice and Sabrina followed the procession into the dining hall. There were so many knights wearing scarlet plumes in their helmets. Sabrina giggled and batted her eyelashes at every one of them.

The table was laden with roasted beasts, jellies, tarts, bread, and pitchers of chocolate milk and strawberry cordial. The prince took the place next to the Queen, causing everyone to shuffle a seat downward. To Alice's amazement, a platypus took her spot with a flick of his bill, and she found herself at the very end of the table, far away from everything.

Sabrina tried to smile, but to Alice, from such a distance, it appeared as if she had indigestion. The minstrels came into the hall and played "Lizzie Had a Little Axe" and "The Heads on the Block Go 'Round and 'Round" along with some other tunes, but Alice didn't pay much attention. She watched the prince, hardly noticing the mice that ran up and down the table, stealing bits of cheese and grapes and dipping their whiskers in unattended tea.

"Are you going to eat that?" a gruff voice asked, startling Alice.

A spotted hyena sniffed her plate with his black nose.

"No," Alice said and pushed it towards him. "I'm not very hungry."

He chewed her food and then the plate, munching it into slobbery bits. One landed on Alice's arm and she flicked it off. When the hyena had finished, he patted his stomach and burped. It smelled like honey and gravy.

Alice wanted to get up from her seat, but she had to wait for the Queen. Hours passed and then more hours passed. The sun began to set, but the supper went on and on. After the Queen had sampled every dish, tried every dessert, sipped some tea and some cordial, and nibbled on a few crackers, she finally rose and headed to her throne.

Sabrina hurried over to Alice. "Wasn't that seating arrangement dreadful? You were so far away. No matter," she said. "The dances are starting soon. They're always great fun."

"Dances?" Alice hesitated. "I don't know how to dance."

"Oh, it's simple, really. Just follow everyone else."

Tumblers rolled onto the ground or tripped as they waved ribbons. The music became faster and louder. Everyone was merry as they made their way onto the dance floor, and even the Queen bobbed her head from side to side as if she were genuinely enjoying herself—something Alice had yet to see.

The prince stood next to the Queen with one arm behind his back. Alice didn't know why she cared if the prince noticed her. She hardly knew him, and he certainly did not know her. It was silly, really.

Sabrina tugged on Alice's arm. "Let's dance."

Two long lines formed.

"I really can't," Alice said, trying to dig in her heels. "I don't know much about it, other than a few steps my mother showed me, but those were years ago, and I—"

"Stop fussing," Sabrina interrupted her, pushing Alice into one of the lines.

A pig in a top hat stared across from her and wiggled his snout. She glanced over at Sabrina with raised eyebrows. Sabrina mouthed back, *You'll be fine.*

She groaned.

When the minstrels played "This Old Manatee," each line bowed to the other and then shuffled forwards.

"Watch me," Sabrina whispered and kicked her legs out with each step. Alice tried the same, but she felt like a crippled frog.

Everyone clapped, twirled, bounced, grabbed the arm of their partner, and whirled around. The pig's hoof kept pinching her arm and then he bumped her hip so hard that Alice flew in the other direction.

Alice tried to slip away, but Sabrina forced her back in line. She got ready to dance with the awful pig again, but the prince was in the pig's place. Alice froze at the sight of his grin. The minstrels started the next stanza of the song, and Alice barely felt herself moveforwards. Her knees threatened to buckle underneath her when they clapped their hands together for the patty-cake and then linked arms, skipping around each other.

The prince asked, "Are you having a pleasant time?"

"Y...yes," Alice stammered.

"This is my favorite dance," he said, and they switched arms.

"Oh, is it?" Alice wanted to kick herself for not having something more interesting to say.

He watched her as if he knew he was making her nervous. "You're new to the House of Hearts, aren't you? I haven't seen you before."

"Yes," Alice said. "I am new."

He released her arm, so they could bounce on one foot in a circle and then skip back to place. Alice returned to the line, scolding herself for not having something cleverer to say.

She turned for the next verse of "This Old Manatee," hoping to redeem herself, but the pig had reclaimed his place, ready to take Alice on another turn on the floor.

The prince had moved down the line and stood before another girl, smiling. She didn't understand why he'd so abruptly left without so much as a polite good-bye. Had she said something wrong? Did her breath smell? Alice heard the prince laugh with his new dance partner. The sound reminded her of the bubbling of a fondue pot. When the minstrels started playing the next stanza, she hurried off the dance floor and sat behind three rhinoceroses who fanned their faces and complained about the heat.

Sabrina found her when the dance ended and the musicians began to play a new song.

"Why aren't you dancing?" she said, out of breath.

Alice bit her lip. "I wasn't really in the mood." It wasn't fully a lie. If the prince had danced with her, she could have danced all night. Instead, she watched him flit from partner to partner like a bee in a field of flowers.

"Stop being such a sourpuss," Sabrina chided her. "Besides"—she glanced at the Queen tapping her foot and clapping to the music—"she won't be ready to go to bed anytime soon. The hall hasn't been this full since the prince left."

"I think I'd like to lie down for a while."

Sabrina took Alice's hands. "Oh, don't leave. Stay."

"It's just...it's just I'm feeling faint. You'll explain to the Queen, won't you?"

"Of course I will." Sabrina pouted. "But just this once and you have to promise me that next time you won't leave early."

"I promise," Alice said.

Sabrina kissed Alice on the cheek. "Don't wait up for me. There are too many knights here to steal my attention, and it's making my little Love Toad so jealous. Maybe he'll stop acting so wishy-washy and finally commit."

Alice responded with a weak smile, and Sabrina twirled back into the throng of dancers.

The music started to fade as Alice left the ballroom. She wasn't sure which way to go. Each hallway looked much like the other. She found one she thought seemed familiar and quickly became lost. She hit her head on the ceiling after taking what she thought was a staircase to the next floor. Then she turned the corner of a passageway and almost fell to her death when it stopped abruptly at a cliff. When she thought she'd finally found her bedchamber, the door opened to a smaller door and then an even smaller one, until it opened to a portrait of the Queen.

At times, Alice swore the palace was shifting around her when she wasn't paying attention. Sometimes she heard strange noises, and other times she'd see a shadow from the corner of her eye. She almost wished she hadn't left the dance. She had been childish, and now she had an uneasy feeling that she might get lost in the palace forever.

Alice debated about going back the way she came, but with every new bend or twist, she kept hoping she'd find her bedchamber.

"Excuse me."

Alice jumped at the voice, but it was only Mary Anne. The chambermaid stood before her with black smudges under her eyes. Her freckles had all but faded, and her nose didn't seem quite as upturned.

Alice touched her shoulder. "Is everything alright?"

"Have you seen Mary Lou?" Mary Anne asked. "I can't find her. I've checked everywhere."

"I haven't," Alice said. "Do you want my help?"

"That's alright." Mary Anne gulped. "If you see her, you'll tell her I'm looking for her, won't you?"

"Yes, of course."

"Thank you, Alice."

Mary Anne continued down the hall, whispering Mary Lou's name at every doorway. Alice watched her for a moment before she entered another corridor and finally saw the door to her bedchamber.

She quickened her step. All she wanted was to be alone with her thoughts, which would likely be centered on the prince and why he made her feel so peculiar. She already had her slippers off when she opened the door, but stopped short when she saw three mysterious silhouettes huddled together in the center of the room.

Chapter 24
Rosamund
House of Hearts, Wonderland
Oleander 31, Year of the Queen

Rosamund's heart did a funny little beat when she saw her boy, Thomas XXIV, as if she had missed him or some such odd thing. She pinched her lips together, demanding they stop spreading, but she smiled anyway, much to her dissatisfaction.

Thomas XXIV wasn't hers. Not in the traditional sense. In the early years of her reign and her marriage, Thomas had wanted a child. Every time the stork descended on Gardenia City, she'd hoped it would come to her, but that insolent bird never did. Rosamund thought Thomas would eventually realize that they didn't need a child, but as time passed, she could see how badly it wounded him, and he began to turn away from her. Rosamund couldn't have that. In those days, she needed him.

Then one morning, she'd been walking along the Annaleigh River and she heard a mewing in the tall grasses. At first, she thought it was a cat and went to drown it at once, but when she parted the reeds, she saw a little baby, swaddled in a damp blanket inside a water-logged basket.

She scooped up the child and held it to her breast, trying to comfort the little mite, and that was when she had an idea: all Thomas wanted was a child, and she supposed any child would do nicely.

Rosamund took the baby to the palace, burned the old, crusty blanket, replaced it with a royal one, and announced from her bedchamber that the stork had finally come.

Thomas never questioned it. He had rushed in and lifted the child into his arms. She'd never seen him smile so broadly, and she knew, from then on, Thomas would never leave her side. He was hers for as long as she wanted him.

Taking the child as her own was one of Rosamund's better decisions, despite the fact that the prince grew up to be quite insufferable and more attached to Thomas than her—even though she had saved the little brat from the Annaleigh. But, she supposed, what did it matter now?

Rosamund thought of these things as she sat next to Thomas, finding that she was enjoying herself at supper, with no clue why, and even becoming giddy when the festivities commenced. Rosamund never liked too much racket, but she ordered the minstrels to keep playing lively tunes for her pleasure as she watched Thomas dance and enjoy himself.

After another song ended, Thomas came to Rosamund's side with sweat on his brow. She picked up her kazoo and before she could give it a good blow, servants were already running for a chair. They juggled a throne, not nearly as large as her own because that wouldn't be very appropriate, and set it down beside her.

Rosamund asked him, "So…how were the Low Lands?"

"Very lowly," Thomas replied. "There wasn't much to do and not much to see, but even after all that, I'm still glad to be back."

"Gardenia City has missed you it seems."

"And I missed Gardenia City," he said. "There's no place like it—not in all of Wonderland."

Rosamund sniffed. "It really is hard to judge the House of Hearts against the other houses, especially since we are superior in every way."

"Truly," he said and took a sip of his chocolate milk. "Although, I wish I had been here for…you know."

Rosamund stiffened. She had hoped he wouldn't bring up the whole "beheading his father" thing, but she supposed it was unavoidable.

"You heard about the King, your father..."

His cheeks reddened, and he nodded.

"You know the law," Rosamund said, slowly. "I couldn't do anything about it. He was—"

"A traitor." Thomas slammed his fist on the chair's arm. "My own father."

Rosamund didn't know what to say, and she usually had something to say. She had never seen Thomas so angry, yet the sight of the stern line of his jaw and the way he pinched his eyebrows together reminded her...reminded her...well, of her.

Thomas took a breath.

Rosamund said, "He didn't give me a choice. You understand, don't you?"

A little voice inside her whispered that it was all a lie. The King hadn't been a traitor. He was innocent. She ordered the voice to shush.

"I know," Thomas said. "I wish I could have been here."

"What's done is done and we mustn't dwell."

"You're right, Queen Mum," Thomas said, turning towards her. "Let's not talk any more of traitors."

Rosamund said, "Right. Let's not talk about the tournament, shall we? Naturally, you will win."

Thomas placed his hand on his chest. "I vow to take the tournament championship and honor the House of Hearts."

"Well, if anyone does beat you," Rosamund said with a sly grin, "it's off with their head."

Thomas winked. "You're too good to me, Queen Mum."

"Anything for my little boy."

"That reminds me." He swirled his chocolate milk. "There is something I wanted to talk to you about."

"Oh?" Rosamund arched her eyebrows. "What is it?"

"I am not really a *little* boy anymore. I came to understand something with all my traveling. I realized there comes a time in a man's life when he needs to think about unimportant things like...why is the sky blue, how do they get the doughnut hole in the doughnut, and perhaps... marriage."

"Marriage." Rosamund spat the word.

Marriage meant a Princess of Hearts who would be a future Queen of Hearts. Rosamund didn't want some half-wit entertaining the idea of warming her bottom on *her* throne. Not in her lifetime. Besides, even if Thomas were serious, he wasn't even close to being ready for marriage.

Rosamund laughed. "There's still plenty of time for that."

"Queen Mum, I'm nearly eighteen. Most of my knights are married and some are younger than me."

"Yes, but I didn't have to kick any of them out of my dungeon, now did I? What are you going to do? Bring your bride down there so she can watch you play your ridiculous board games with all your little friends? No, Thomas. You're not ready."

"But—"

Rosamund held up her finger. "Even if you were, which you're not, but if you were, there's a lot more to marriage than finding a pretty girl. You are the future King of Hearts, after all. There's custom to follow, pageantry, negotiations, and so on and so forth. I hope you haven't told some ridiculous maiden that you'd marry her."

"Of course not," Thomas said, blushing as he stared down at his glass. "I wouldn't do that, not without consulting you first."

"I certainly would hope not."

Thomas reached into his doublet and pulled out a letter. "Which is why I'd like to consult you."

Rosamund immediately noticed the green webby seal of the House of Clubs. She felt the familiar burn of anger inching up her throat at the sight of it. What sort of conspiracy was this? Why would Thomas have anything to do with that insufferable house, the most coldblooded of all the houses?

"Are you in cahoots with the Clubs?" she demanded of him. "You dare go behind my back?"

"Queen Mum, please," Thomas said, and glanced around, but nobody was watching; they knew better. "You received the same letter. This one is my copy."

Rosamund narrowed her eyes. "I've never received any such thing."

"Then read it." Thomas said, holding it out to her. "I believe you'll find it most unimportant."

"Most unimportant indeed." Rosamund snatched the letter from his hand.

To the Queen of Hearts of the House of Hearts in the Great City of Gardenia City (which is second best to ours):

Rosamund sniffed as she read further.

Greetings!

We hope this letter finds you most unwell. We hear you are having dreary weather. We are enjoying a streak of sunshine, custom of the House of Clubs and the Great City of Tropicana.

Oh bother. Enough about weather. Let's get to the point, shall we?

As you may have heard, our beautiful, magnificent, and brilliant daughter, Penelope, has come of age, and it has come to our attention that we should begin the negotiations of her marriage, although we would never really want to part with our sweet, little tadpole.

The House of Hearts wasn't our first choice, but our precious pecan seems to have her heart set on the Prince of Hearts, and she won't budge on the issue. Trust us, we've tried.

At any rate, we shall be sending Ambassador Marco Polo to begin the process of arranging the marriage of our daughter, Penelope, Princess of Clubs, to Thomas, the Prince of Hearts. We hope Marco Polo finds the House of Hearts as hospitable as home—although I know it won't be quite like home. There is no place better than here.

The King and Queen of Clubs signed the letter at the very bottom and in small scroll wrote *CC: Thomas, Prince of Hearts.*

Rosamund crumpled the letter and tossed it aside. "Those insolent, those ostentatious, those croaking toads. No one from the House of Clubs will ever taint the House of Hearts. Not now, not ever." She pointed an accusing finger at Thomas. "You'd better not have been behind this."

Thomas's eyes widened. "On my honor, I wasn't."

Rosamund glared at him. "If you weren't behind it, then why is the princess so taken with you, hmmm, if you haven't been to the House of Clubs?"

Thomas sucked in a breath. "She must have seen a portrait of me. There's so many circulating... She must have stuck her hands on one. I swear to you, Queen Mum, I didn't know anything about it."

"They are the cause of all this trouble," Rosamund shouted. "Them and that blubbering walrus Cecil de Berg and his ridiculous Papal Bull. *The nerve.* They never sent me this letter because they knew I'd never allow it. NEVER."

Thomas shook his head. "But you see, I don't want to marry the Princess of Clubs. I thought that this letter was the real reason you called me home—to make me marry her. But I don't want to. I'd rather marry someone of my choosing—"

"Stop talking about marriage, Thomas! This is a plot. You're plotting against me." Rosamund felt the blood rushing to her face. "You're as bad as *them*. You want my throne. That's what this is all about. You can get those thoughts right out of your head. It's not going to happen. Never, never, never."

Chapter 25
Alice
House of Hearts, Wonderland
Oleander 31, Year of the Queen

The figures moved towards her. Alice tried to scream, but it came out as a squeak.

A familiar voice said, "Alice, it's us. We'll show you."

She heard the strike of a match. A candle was lit and the light brought the faces of Bill, Lillian, and Ralph out of the gloom. She didn't know whether to be relieved or nervous. Were they here because of the whole matter of the bomb and saving the Queen? She'd acted directly against the Aboveground Organization, and now they must want to remove her from her position, whisk her out of Wonderland, and shove her back in the asylum for failing them.

Alice took a breath. "You frightened me. What are you doing here?"

Lillian raised her bushy eyebrows. "It's been reported that you are getting too chummy with the Queen. These two think you're getting soft. Of course, I already knew that would happen."

Alice stepped backwards, ready to run if she must. She'd been right. They were here to take her away, but she wouldn't go. She wouldn't let them. "What am I supposed to do? She already believes there are plotters. If she suspects me, she'll behead me with a snap of her fingers. I'm doing my best, truly I am, but"—she glanced at Ralph—"I've been on my own. It's all been so dreadful."

Tears pooled in Alice's eyes. She didn't want to cry, but she couldn't help it.

Bill sighed. "Come 'ere," he said, motioning her over. His skin had gone all but white with a few green spots on his body. "Take a seat. We'll get ye some tea."

Alice sat at one of the pink couches. Bill placed a cup in front of her and nodded to Lillian. The rat had a clothespin pinching her nose while she poured. When she had finished, Alice lifted the cup to her lips and tasted tart raspberries and a hint of honey. She took one sip after another, closing her eyes and savoring the taste of real tea—not Wonderland tea. It reminded her of home and it made her ache to be back.

"There ye go, that's it," Bill said. "Feel better?"

Alice wiped her eyes. "Yes, thank you. I didn't think I'd ever taste proper tea again."

Lillian gagged. "Proper tea? I find it utterly revolting. Luckily, I brought some other tea for those of us who are civilized."

She pulled another pot from inside her cloak and the room filled with the scent of rotten eggs and soggy boot.

"Where's Chester?" Alice asked. "Isn't he here as well?"

"He never comes to the palace," Ralph said, "refuses to step a single paw in here."

"Naturally," Lillian nodded. "He does have an outstanding death warrant, you know."

"Enough of him," Ralph said, checking his watch. "We must discuss other matters. The Queen is getting concerned."

"Concerned?" Alice asked, setting her cup down. "I don't understand. I've done everything she's told me. I suppose there was that issue with the tea and my stitching could be better—"

"Not *that* queen," Lillian interrupted. "The other queen. The Queen of Spades. Honestly, keep up."

Ralph said, "It has reached Her Majesty that you saved the Queen of Hearts last night."

Bill slapped his hand on his leg. "We could have been rid of that 'ole tyrant had that bomb got her."

"That plan was against my advisement," Ralph said. "We'd already decided we'd do the Queen in at Longshoot Castle, as you might recall, not put a bomb in her room."

"A moment's a moment," Bill said. "And it would have been a good one if it weren't for her doing."

Alice jumped, spilling tea all down the front of her gown. "I didn't know, Bill. Honestly, I didn't."

"And they shouldn't have expected you to," Ralph said, glancing at the others, "since it wasn't part of the plan."

"Not to mention," Alice added. "I already told you I wouldn't kill the Queen."

"You weren't supposed to save her either," Lillian snapped. She glanced at Ralph. "I told you this would never work. She's useless. Honestly, I don't know why you brought her here."

Alice's bottom lip trembled as tears bubbled over and trailed down her cheeks. Why were Lillian and Bill making this all her fault? They'd left her out of their planning, and now they were blaming her for it.

Ralph placed his paw on her shoulder. "It's not your fault, Alice."

"He's right," Bill said. "It's not, but we have to make sure nothing interferes again."

Alice sniffed back her tears. "What are you going to do?"

She held her breath as she waited. Did not interfering mean having Alice leave the House of Hearts and Wonderland altogether?

Ralph stared at her. "It's not what we're going to do. It's what *you're* going to do."

"Me?"

"You must convince the Queen that she needs a new chambermaid. Lillian, to be precise."

Lillian smirked as she flicked her tail.

Alice said, "But the Queen would never listen to me."

"She'll have to," Ralph said. "I can't recommend Lillian after just recommending you. She'll start to suspect."

Alice stared down at her teacup. "She already has Mary Lou and Mary Anne. They have an arrangement."

Ralph flicked his whiskers. "Arrangements can be rearranged."

Alice jerked backwards. Rearranged? Is that why Mary Lou had gone missing? She searched their faces for clues, but they acted as if nothing were amiss.

"Besides," Ralph continued, "the Queen already had Sabrina and Bess, and I convinced her to allow you as a lady's maid. You can do this, Alice."

"I can't," she said. "She'll be angry. She's always angry."

Ralph leaned towards her. "You don't understand. If you can't convince the Queen, we'll have to take you away from court."

The words Alice dreaded had finally come. The White Rabbit would send her back to the asylum. Back to the white room with the white table and the tools with jagged teeth. She felt it as deeply as she felt the fear inside Préfargier the day she left.

She shook in her chair and struggled to breathe. "Not that," she managed to say.

"Listen, Alice. It would be for your own protection," Ralph said. "The situation here is getting too precarious. We suspect someone knows about the Aboveground. If the Queen finds out… I don't even want to think about it. I'm trying to keep you safe. It's for your own head. I can't be with you all the time. You need Lillian."

Alice glanced over at her. She would have rather had anyone but Lillian, but if it was between that rat and the asylum, then she'd ask for a thousand Lillians by her side. She didn't care about anything else—except that she stayed. Someway, somehow, she was going to make sure she did.

Alice nodded. "I'll talk to the Queen."

Ralph smiled. "I knew you would come to your senses."

Alice wanted to feel the confidence that the White Rabbit had in her, but all she felt was a pressing weight against her chest, making it hard to breathe.

Ralph nodded to Bill. "We should go. We never know who's listening behind windows."

"Yer right."

Bill stood and doubled over. He fell into the table, knocking the teapot onto the floor. Alice rushed towards him.

"Are you sick, Bill?" she asked him. "Do you need to see a doctor?"

He grimaced as he pushed himself up. "There be no doctor that can help me. I've got the sickness. It's in my scales. One more good rain and I'll be dead. We're not made to be living in this wet weather all year long, but don't be worrying 'bout me." Bill patted her hand. "The Queen of Spades promised me lands in the south, just as soon as she's queen of Gardenia City. A month there and I'll be as good as green."

Alice helped Bill to the door. The lizard moaned under his breath with each step.

The heaviness in Alice's chest felt worse. Bill's life depended on her too. Her shoulders were too bony to carry that kind of responsibility.

Bill wheezed as he stepped into the hall. "Thank you, Alice, for your kindness."

She wanted to say something, maybe a word of encouragement or reassurance that he would be alright, but she couldn't. She didn't know it would be true.

Ralph came up beside her, taking her hand. "Sleep tight, my dear. Don't let the bed slugs bite. Tomorrow is a big day."

Alice tried to smile. She didn't know how she could possibly sleep. She was tired, impossibly tired, but her mind was a whirlwind that she couldn't control.

Ralph shut the door behind them, leaving Lillian to glare at Alice from above the rim of her cup. Alice went to her room and the rat followed her, settling herself on a settee. Alice didn't feel comfortable with Lillian so close. Instead of undressing, she crawled into her bed, thinking about the task that lay ahead of her.

It was all too much. What if she failed them? What if it would be better if she did leave? Perhaps Ralph could let her stay in his castle. He was sure to have a garden there. She could tend it until matters were settled.

Alice had no idea she'd fallen asleep until Lillian woke her the next morning.

She snapped her tail on the floor. "You don't want to be late, do you?"

Alice looked at the clock near her bed. Every hour read "Queen's Time." She rubbed her eyes. Her head felt as if someone had squeezed it all night long. She pushed herself off her bed and put on her slippers, her stomach twisting like a gnarled blackberry vine. She stumbled towards the water basin where she got washed and then started fumbling with her hair.

Lillian watched her, stirring her morning tea. "Your hair's a positive beetles' nest. Who taught you to tie knots? That featherbrain from Lake Town? I suppose I will have do it."

Lillian placed her paws on Alice's shoulders and pushed her before the dressing table. With a few quick snaps of her wrists, she coiled her hair into a beautiful knot—without a single hair out of place—and even a piece of red cloth woven in.

Alice turned her head from side to side. "It's wonderful."

Lillian half smiled. "My mother was a lady's maid, as was my mother's mother and her mother's mother before her. These are all things I was taught before I got my first claw."

"You should be one of the Queen's lady's maids."

Lillian gazed down at her paws and sighed. "I would have been if the Queen of Hearts hadn't declared rats too ugly for her court. It ruined everything for me, everything for my family. The Rats of Shallowfielding held a place of respect at court for as long as I could remember, and now we are destitute. My mother, who ate from golden plates, has spent the last half of her life begging for scraps."

"That's awful," Alice said. "I'm so sorry."

Lillian twitched her nose. "Yes, well, rats do not put off the Queen of Spades. She promised to restore the Shallowfieldings to our former grandeur."

First Bill's health. Now the fortunes of Lillian and her family. What else was there? Alice swallowed, feeling a glob of guilt settle into her stomach. For Bill and Lillian to get what they wanted, the Queen of Hearts would have to go. Except Alice had been happy in the Queen's court. Truly, for the first time in as long as she could remember, and she didn't know what to do: betray the Aboveground, betray the Queen of Hearts, or betray herself.

Lillian fussed with Alice's gown and hemmed a few of the buttonholes in a blink, snapping off the thread with her teeth. "Now." She stood back, eyeing Alice up and down. "I believe you are ready to convince the Queen she needs a rat in her household. Let's all cross our claws that she doesn't strip you of your own position for requesting it. You never know with her."

Alice took a breath and headed towards the door. No matter what, that was the one thing she wouldn't let happen, Aboveground or not. For the first time for a long time, Alice decided her happiness would come first.

Chapter 26
Rosamund
The Arena, Wonderland
Wisteria 41, Year of the Queen

Rosamund stayed in a different room that night, without any sign of Thomas and Pedro. She should have had no problem falling asleep, but she tossed and turned. She couldn't stop thinking about Thomas—the one with a whole body. She didn't know why their conversation over the House of Clubs bothered her or why she cared, but she felt guilty somehow. Perhaps she had been too harsh on him. He was a simpleton after all—like his father. Even if she had supported the outlandish idea, it wasn't as if he were ready for marriage. He didn't know the slightest thing about it.

At daybreak, Mary Anne brought the morning grounds. Rosamund stuffed as much as she could in her bottom lip and let it seep down her throat. She sat with her head back, wondering what she could do to make it up to Thomas, when Bess came in with a notepad. "Would you like to behead Sabrina today?" she asked her. "It's on your to-do list."

"I can't behead her today," Rosamund snapped. "We're having a tournament, you dimwit. My Thomas is participating."

Bess shrugged. "Just thought I'd ask."

The duchess snapped her fingers, and Alice shuffled into the room, holding two gowns. The girl appeared strained today. Not that she'd normally notice such a thing, but since the incident of the bomb, Rosamund felt a little soft towards the girl.

Bess pointed to the gowns as Alice held them up. "Would you like to wear this red or that red, Your Majesty?"

Rosamund spat out the grounds. "Hmmm...that burgundy looks too rich for daytime use, but the cherry is all too mundane. What do you think, Alice?"

The girl studied both dresses.

"It's not some royal proclamation," Rosamund said. "Out with it."

"I prefer the darker red, Your Majesty."

"I prefer the lighter," Bess quickly added.

Rosamund grabbed the darker shade and held it against her. "I think Alice is right. The burgundy is rich like me. Wouldn't you say so, Bess?"

"Yes, Your Majesty," Bess said, unable to hide her disappointment that she'd gone with Alice's suggestion.

"Hurry," Rosamund said. "Let's put it on. I don't want to dally today."

Rosamund put up her arms and all three of her lady's maids pulled the gown over her head. When they had finished and her hair was properly knotted and curled, Mary Anne opened the door, trembling as she carried the breakfast tray.

Bess said, "It's about time. The Queen is starving."

Rosamund hadn't thought much of breakfast until then. She was too excited about the tournament and having a chance to make amends with Thomas. She bit into her toast and spat it out. "The sardines are cold."

"Begging your pardon, Your Majesty," Mary Anne said. "I warmed them, but by the time I went back for your breakfast tray, they'd already gone cold."

"This will not do." Rosamund wiped her hands. "This will not do at all. The Queen cannot live on cold sardines. I might as well be a pauper. Where is that Mary Lou? I must have two chambermaids at all times."

"Your Majesty?" Alice stepped forwards, her eyes on the tips of Rosamund's slippers. "I...I might know someone who could help. Until Mary Lou comes back, that is."

Rosamund glanced over at Mary Anne. The chambermaid stared at Alice as if her nose had been tickled with a feather. "I can do it," Mary Anne said. "I will find a way to bring the grounds and your breakfast. Please, Your Majesty. Don't replace Mary Lou. She's bound to pop up. I…I know she will."

"Do you?" Rosamund asked, taking a sip of tea to get the taste of cold sardine out of her mouth. She didn't like the idea of another girl taking Mary Lou's place either, but she was a Queen and was meant to be served as such. "Alice, what kind of servant is this? What are her qualifications?"

Alice rubbed her hands. "She… she comes from a very long line of lady's—I mean, *servants*."

"Oh? What family?"

"The Rats of Shallowfielding."

"A rat?" Rosamund shrieked. "A rat in my household? I couldn't possibly consider it. There's nothing more repulsive and diseased. They carry hives, you know."

"I assure you, Your Majesty," Alice said, "Lillian is very clean."

Bess grabbed Alice's arm. "The Queen already told you her feelings on the creature. How dare you press her?"

Alice stared at Rosamund with a pleading expression on her face that she normally found delightfully repulsive. If it meant so much to the girl, she supposed she could abide a rat for a while. It was only for a chambermaid position, after all, and it was just until Mary Lou appeared from wherever she went off to. Besides, she felt as if she owed Alice. It was a terrible feeling, and she promptly wanted to be rid of it.

Rosamund glowered at Bess. "How many times have I told you not to think unless told to? I can make my own decisions."

"Of course, Your Majesty," Bess said, retreating. "How silly of me."

Rosamund held out her teacup. Sabrina promptly poured the tea, placed in a pat of butter, and offered a second. Rosamund declined, and stirred, clanking the spoon against the porcelain as she considered the proposal.

"Since I am in need of another servant," she said, "I will permit it. Alice, you may tell your rat that she is employed, but if I find one hair or dropping"—she shuddered—"then it's off with that beastie's head. Understood?"

Alice nodded. "Yes, Your Majesty. Thank you, Your Majesty."

Mary Anne rushed out of the room, without any ceremony, and slammed the door behind her.

"What sort of mayhem is this?" Rosamund asked, glaring at her lady's maids. "Has everyone forgotten that I'm still the QUEEN?" She slammed her cup down. "I've been too lax, that's what I've been. After the tournament, I shall have a day of beheadings. That will help you all remember. Now, I need my powder. And you all better take care that not a single wrinkle shows."

Rosamund read the Gardenia Times while they finished getting her dressed. When they had finished, Sabrina suggested they play a round of hide-and-seek. They weren't long into the game when she heard the blast of the tournament horn. She ran to the window, clapping her hands. "It's time. It's time."

She made sure all her lady's maids took their places behind her before she left her rooms and made her way outside. Rosamund kept her chin in the air as she progressed onto the palace green, walking calmly among her subjects, who shoved each other to find seats. Everyone had heart-shaped jewels pinned to their hats or scarves and a few wore shirts that said "The Queen of Hearts Rules."

An Ace of Hearts led Rosamund to her box with her House banners flapping in the wind. She sat on a plush throne under a scarlet canopy.

Thomas rode over, looking quite the knight in his maroon armor. Last night's argument dissolved from her thoughts at the sight of him appearing so magnificent. Thomas stopped his horse before her with a bundle of roses in his arms and bowed. "Queen Mum."

Rosamund stood and took the offering of roses. She gazed around, making sure all eyes watched her before she said, "Prince Thomas. May you bring honor to the House of Hearts as the tournament champion."

Applause shook the scaffolding underneath her.

"May the tournament begin!" she yelled.

Feet pounded on the wooden stands as Thomas and another knight took their places in the arena for the first event: the swordfish fight.

Squires ran with the weapons. Rosamund chewed her fingernails as the knights gripped the fish in their gloved hands. A Two of Hearts raised the red flag. All eyes watched the ripple of the canvas.

The flag dropped.

Thomas and the other knight dived at each other. The clanks and clinks of the swordfish rang in the air. They dodged, circled, leaped, and skipped, but the fighting went on and on. Fish scales sparkled in the sun as the two darted up and down, here and there, around and straight.

Rosamund shouted, "Go, Thomas, go!"

The prince circled his swordfish about with a flick of his wrist, and it clamped onto the nose of his opponent. Thomas yanked the other swordfish out of the knight's hands and pointed the fish at his rival's chest, smiling victoriously.

Rosamund jumped to her feet, puffing with pride as she clapped. Thomas bowed as roses flew towards him, a few hitting him in the face. He picked up a handful and held them over his head, smiling.

Thomas walked out of the arena to the sighs of the crowd. Just as Rosamund settled back into her throne, readying to watch another set of knights, she smelled the sickly sweet scent of William's hair pomade.

"Sorry to interrupt, Your Majesty," William said with a spray of spittle, "but you have an unimportant guest."

"Whoever it is can wait," she grumbled. "Can't you see that I'm enjoying myself? Tell them to come back later."

"It's the Ambassador of Clubs."

"The ambassador?" Rosamund asked, confused. "Here?"

"Yes, Your Majesty."

Rosamund had nearly forgotten about that ludicrous letter from the King and Queen of Clubs—especially the part about them sending an ambassador. If the Clubs had actually sent her the letter, she would have replied that the ambassador's presence wouldn't be necessary because she wouldn't agree to a marriage between her son and Penelope. Only now that he was here, there wasn't much she could do about it. "You might as well bring him to me," she snapped. "I can't very well have him writing to the Clubs, spreading nasty rumors about me."

William stood aside as an egg rolled in beside him.

"May I present the Ambassador Marco Polo, Your Majesty."

Marco Polo tried to bow, but his legs wobbled. Servants ran to catch him before he toppled over.

"Pardon me," Marco Polo said. "It's an honor to finally meet the Queen of Hearts. I must say, portraits of your beauty are unjust. You're the most ordinary, humdrum creature I've ever laid my egg on."

Rosamund batted her eyelashes. She wasn't overly found of eggs, as a rule. They were either too runny or cracked in the head, but this one seemed to have a good shell on him. "My, my," she said. "I had no idea there were such gentlemen in the House of Clubs. You may take a seat next to me, Ambassador Polo."

She tooted her kazoo, and a servant placed a chair alongside her. The emissary nestled in and dabbed a kerchief to his forehead, taking deep, raspy breaths.

"This is quite the tournament," he said. "Very well done."

Rosamund beamed. "The House of Hearts has always been known for throwing the best of everything."

"Your ability to run a queendom is a work of art. Its great history is the first subject all young Clubs study."

"Is that so?" she asked. "Well, I can't exactly say I blame them."

"As you know," Marco Polo said, rolling towards her, "the Clubs would very much like an allegiance with your house and feel that both houses could be divinely combined in marriage between your Thomas and their Penelope."

Rosamund bristled. "My Thomas," she said, "is far too young for marriage. Besides, I'm not too keen on an alliance, as you say, with those pretentious Clubs. They've caused me nothing but trouble."

Marco Polo didn't waver. "That may be so," he said, "but the House of Clubs is able to strike a bargain that you might find most desirable."

"Oh?" Rosamund raised her eyebrows. "The House of Hearts is never lacking. Why…I can't think of anything I might even be remotely interested in."

"I can think of one thing."

Rosamund turned towards him.

Marco Polo looked around and then lowered his voice. "It has come to our attention that you're having a problem with a certain Papal Bull."

Chapter 27
Alice
The Arena, Wonderland
Wisteria 41, Year of the Queen

Under the shade of the Queen's tent, Alice couldn't take her eyes off the prince as he brandished his swordfish. He could have wielded a celery stick and she would have felt the same. The prince was so strong, so sure, so confident. When he won, Alice jumped to her feet, applauding as loudly as she could over the roaring crowd.

The prince left the arena and all Alice wanted was for him to come back. She'd watch whatever he participated in: a hopscotch competition, a three-legged race, or knucklebones. It didn't matter. Somehow, his presence took away all the confusion and fear, allowing her to forget for a moment about the Aboveground and the two Queens. She didn't understand how one person could make her feel that way. She remembered she would sometimes eavesdrop on Katherine talking with her friends about men in a funny manner that always left Alice confused. Now she understood why certain gentlemen could leave her otherwise reserved sister in a puddle of fits, because that was how she felt when she saw the prince.

"Psst."

Alice jumped at the noise.

A deep voice said, "Hey…hey, you."

The prince beckoned her over from the corner of the tent.

Sabrina jabbed her in the side. "Go on, you goose. What are you waiting for?"

Alice wobbled as she stood and managed to make her way over to him. Her movements felt sluggish, as if she were wallowing in a pool of maple syrup.

The prince smiled at her and said, "I didn't get your name the other night."

"My name is Alice, Your Grace."

"Alice. What a lovely name."

The way he said it did make it seem so. She bit her lip and blushed.

He said, "I didn't mean to dash off like that, but if I didn't dance with Countess Nickerbottle, she would have had my head." He chuckled.

Alice didn't know whether to laugh or not. Did he want a reply, or should she stay quiet? Ever since she'd arrived at the palace, she barely knew where to put her hands anymore, and having the prince so close just made it worse. She could already feel herself perspiring beneath the heavy folds of fabric.

"I came back," he continued, "but you had already left the dance line." He placed his hand over his heart. "It wouldn't do for the Prince of Hearts to act so rudely to one of his mother's ladies. Will you grant me the opportunity of another dance tonight, to redeem myself?"

"Yes," Alice blurted a little too eagerly. "Yes, I would like that, Your Grace."

"It's settled then," he said. "I will see you after the tournament. And, please, call me Thomas."

Thomas.

He disappeared behind the flap of the tent.

Alice went back to her seat in a daze.

"Don't be as quiet as a cricket," Sabrina squealed. "Tell me what he said."

"He asked me to dance with him tonight."

Sabrina's mouth opened. "He fancies you."

Fancies me? Alice warmed at the idea, but as quickly as the thought settled in her mind, doubt came to saturate it. She wasn't anybody special. What could the prince possibly see in her? "No," she said, shaking her head. "He was being polite."

"Oh, no. He *fancies* you, fancies you. I know it."

"No, he doesn't. Stop it."

Sabrina peered into the crowd, searching. "Oh, he doesn't, does he?" she said, pointing. "He's over there, staring at you."

Alice pushed Sabrina's arm down. "Stop being so obvious. Where?"

"Over there."

Alice followed Sabrina's gaze. She found Thomas atop one of the horses, gripping onto a giant red licorice stick. He winked at Alice before pulling down his visor. She felt her heart jump into her throat.

A Four of Hearts walked into the middle of the arena floor holding a flag over his head. Another knight on horseback took his position across from the prince, also with a licorice stick. The Four of Hearts dropped the flag, and the knights rocketed forwards. Alice's stomach dropped down to her knees. She didn't want to watch, but she couldn't look away. She held her breath as the licorice sticks slammed into each other with a splintering smoosh.

Helmets rolled away from the debris and pieces of armor skidded into the dirt. A dust cloud formed around the prince, making it impossible for Alice to see if he were injured. Her heart pounded against her ribs as she peered into the haze, hoping for one glimpse of him. When the entire arena had gone quiet, the prince skipped out from the mess, waving his bent licorice stick over his head. The people cheered while his opponent crawled away from the rubble on hands and knees. Thomas headed towards Alice, stopping to pluck up a rose from the ground. He bowed low before her.

"My lady?" he asked. "Will you accept this rose as a token of my victory?"

Everyone stared at Alice. Whispers passed from behind raised hands while others watched with arched eyebrows. The worst of it was the Queen, who narrowed her eyes like a she-wolf guarding her young.

The Queen snapped, "Well, girl, don't make my son look like a fool. Take the rose."

Alice slowly stood and walked to the edge of the box. The crowd leaned on the edge of their seats, waiting for what she would say. She managed to croak out a "thank you" and felt her cheeks match her red dress.

Thomas placed the rose in Alice's palm and bowed once more before joining the rest of the knights. She inched her way backwards until she knocked into the seat, sitting with a thud. She stared at the rose in her hands. A glow spread through her chest, sweeping down her entire body and filling her with the flutter of butterfly wings. Maybe Sabrina was right. Maybe the prince really did like her. The idea made her feel both excited and sick at the same time. She'd never experienced anything like it before. Not with her mother and father, not with her sister—certainly not her sister—and not with the White Rabbit. This feeling, it was something special, and Alice cradled the rose in her hands as if it might shatter.

The tournament ended with Thomas as the champion. He presented the Queen with the prize—a sword embedded with rubies—but the rose meant more to Alice than a hundred jewels.

Servants carried an enormous banquet table already set with food and dishes into the arena. They stamped right over the fallen knights and kicked the broken swordfish out of the way.

Alice followed the Queen to the table, barely feeling her feet touch the ground. She headed to what should have been her place, but a giant egg had stolen her seat.

"Not again," Alice grumbled.

The egg rolled around, twisting his moustache as he did. "Something I can help you with?" he asked.

Alice stared at him, and she remembered a faint flicker from a distant time when she raced on a chessboard through the Looking Glass House. "Humpty Dumpty?"

"No, girl," the egg said. "I'm Marco Polo. Humpty Dumpy was my cousin. Did you know him? Tragic what happened, don't you think? They just couldn't put him back together again. Usually the king's horses and the king's men are so good at that sort of thing too. I always told him not to sit on ledges, but he wouldn't listen. Such a shame."

He rolled his back to Alice, and she was left standing there once again without a seat. She sulked off down the table, far away from the prince, but she still had her rose and that was at least something.

Someone shouted, "Lady Alice!"

Her head jerked up. She looked around the room and saw Thomas waving at her. "Over here."

Alice counted her steps as she walked over to Thomas, her stomach in knots.

"Please," he said, gesturing to a chair next to him. "Have a seat here. I saved it for you."

Alice glanced over at Sabrina. She was grinning and waggling her eyebrows at her.

"Cherry cordial?" Thomas asked, snapping his fingers, and a servant filled their goblets. "To the tournament," he said, making a toast.

"To the tournament," Alice replied, and sipped the thick liquid; it made the churning in her stomach worse.

Thomas wiped his mouth on a napkin. "Do they hold tournaments where you're from? Queen Mum told me that you aren't from Wonderland."

"Yes, I'm from England," Alice said, surprised that the Queen would speak about her. "I think there used to be tournaments, but not for a very long time—at least I don't think so."

"You weren't locked away in a tower, were you?"

Alice twisted the goblet in her fingers, feeling herself grow hot. "In a sense, I suppose."

"Then you are a princess?"

"No."

"But only princesses are locked in towers."

"Not always."

"Huh," Thomas mused as a servant set a plate of steaming lettuce covered in chocolate sauce before him. "So in the Land of Eng, they lock princesses *and* maidens in towers. It sounds like a fascinating place. Tell me more. What did this man Eng do to have a whole land named after him?"

"I don't think there was a man named Eng."

"No such man? He must have been a god, then."

"I'm not sure, but I don't think so."

"Pity you don't know anything about Eng. What about the land, then?"

"Let me see..." Alice took a breath. "It's a lot like here in a way. Gardenia City, I mean. It rains a lot, but there are roses and flowers and tea—the English love tea. But the rules are, well, a bit different, and animals don't talk where I'm from."

"That's a pity," he said. "I find animals interesting sorts. Maybe in the Land of Eng someone should ask them their opinion. Animals are always so full of ideas, thoughts, and whatnot. Maybe that's why they don't say anything—nobody has properly asked them."

"No, I don't believe anyone has. Though I did use to talk to my cat quite a bit."

Thomas popped a clove of garlic in his mouth. "So, what brings you to Wonderland?"

Alice swallowed. What would the prince think if he discovered she'd escaped a mental asylum and that, back at home, everyone thought she was mad?

"It was the White Rabbit," she said. "I mean, Ralph."

"Is that so?" he said. "That furry knight. He traveled to your land, then? The Land of Eng? How peculiar."

Alice fidgeted with her napkin and wondered if she'd said more than she should have. She thought about the first time she'd come to Wonderland, when she'd seen the White Rabbit down by the riverbank. That was a safe story to tell, and it wasn't as if she'd be lying. "I think he was lost, really," she said. "He kept muttering that he was late for something. I suppose if he mistakenly came to England that would have made him very, very late."

Thomas laughed. "I suppose it would."

Alice swallowed, hoping she had satisfied his curiosity about why she'd come. "Anyway, I followed him, and here I am."

"Yes. Here you are." Thomas grinned and squeezed her hand. "I enjoy your company. There's something different and yet so familiar about you, as if we've met before. We haven't, have we?"

"I don't think so." Alice's hand tingled from his touch.

"Would you walk with me in the gardens tomorrow afternoon?" he asked. "You can tell me more of the Land of Eng."

Alice glanced at the Queen.

Thomas leaned towards her and whispered, "Don't worry about Queen Mum. I'll steal you away if I must."

Alice lowered her gaze, feeling her cheeks burn like bright coals.

Just as she was about to tell him how much she'd enjoy a walk in the gardens, a voice boomed from the other side of the arena. "Can I have your attention please?"

A possum dressed in a dinner jacket stood on a stage. A spotlight flickered on.

The possum cleared his throat. "On behalf of the Leaping Antler and Musical Earwig Theater and Production Team, the LAME, I'd like to commend the Prince of Hearts on his display of bravery and skill today."

Thunderous applause rang out.

"But that's not all," the possum said with an air of seriousness. "This very day...believe it or not...is the Prince of Heart's unbirthday."

Everyone gasped and turned to Thomas. He held up his hand and nodded.

The possum continued, "The LAME has arranged a performance to commemorate this special day. Please give a cool welcome to the lovely, the talented, the beautiful...Marilyn Montague."

Alice's mouth dropped as a blond in short-cropped hair sashayed onto the stage in a sparkling gown with a plunging neckline. Thomas immediately slid away from Alice towards the edge of his seat, a grin smeared across his face.

Marilyn took the microphone with her red-painted nails and parted her red-painted lips. In a low, husky voice, she sang:

Hap-py un-birthday to youuuu,
Hap-py un-birthday to youuuu.
Hap-py un-birthday, Prince of Hearts,
Hap-pyyy un-birthdayyy to youuuu.

Whistling and catcalls shrilled behind Alice when the song ended. Marilyn's high heels clacked down the steps, her hips swinging from side to side, and, to Alice's horror, she sauntered straight towards Thomas.

Marilyn pouted her red lips. "You didn't save a seat for me, Tommy?"

"Of course I did, uh…uh…" He looked at the Queen on one side and then at Alice on the other. "Can you move, Alice?" he asked. "You don't mind, do you?"

Chapter 28
Rosamund
House of Hearts, Wonderland
Wisteria 41, Year of the Queen

Rosamund was not a fan of Marilyn Montague's little performance—whoever invited her needed beheading. She had never liked that little tart, and the way she threw herself at Thomas was disgraceful.

But she had to endure it, and endure it she would until she could finally get Marco Polo alone with her advisors. She wanted to know exactly what he knew about the Papal Bull and how he could help her—if he could at all. The egg was probably a shell full of good-for-nothing with a heart of rotten yolk. What could she really expect of a representative from the House of Clubs?

After the last fireworks exploded in the sky, Rosamund sneaked away during the ball and headed towards the Cave. She found the ambassador already in the closeted room with her advisors, laughing and smoking cigars with a fire burning in the grates. They were having themselves quite the little gala without her, and it hadn't escaped her attention that William was acting the plum-nosed host at the head of the table.

She slammed the door. Everyone jumped and cowered—all but William.

"Keeping my seat warm for me, are you, William?" Rosamund growled.

"Your Majesty," he said with a nervous laugh as he slunk off her chair. "We weren't expecting you so soon."

"Clearly."

As she took her chair, Rosamund arranged a smile on her face as if it were a series of puzzle pieces. She was going to find out what Marco Polo knew about the Bull if she had to crack him to do it. "Are you enjoying yourself, Ambassador?"

"Oh yes," he said with a puff on his cigar. "The tournament, the food, and that Marilyn Montague—most exquisite. The House of Hearts definitely lives up to its reputation."

"I'm sure you'll be certain to tell the House of Clubs that."

"I shall, most assuredly." He chuckled and clapped Charles on the back. "Especially that Marilyn Montague, eh?"

"Yes, her." Rosamund narrowed her eyes. "But I'm sure the House of Clubs has something to tell me as well. Isn't that why you've come?"

"Quite right." Marco Polo whistled. A sentry with the insignia of the Clubs coat of arms came forwards with a parchment. "Now for business."

"If we must." Rosamund feigned a yawn, trying to appear aloof, but her hands glistened with the subtlest sheen of sweat as she waited for the ambassador's next words.

Marco Polo unfurled the parchment. "I have here a declaration from the House of Clubs approving the union of their house to yours through the marriage of the Prince of Hearts and the Princess of Clubs."

"I am already aware of that," Rosamund said, "but on what *terms?*"

Marco put on a pair of spectacles. "Let's see, it says here that the House of Clubs will give their eldest daughter in marriage if the House of Hearts agrees to surrender the Milkyam Lands and all of their quarterlies."

"Milkyam," Rosamund blurted. "Impossible. It has been part of the House of Hearts for hundreds of years."

"Three hundred and one to be exact," Marco Polo said. "And..."—he scanned the pamphlet again—"they also want the Providence of Peatown."

"Absolutely not," Rosamund scoffed. "I have a holiday manor in Peatown. This is ridiculous. What's next? My *crown?*"

The egg said, "If you'd like to use it as part of the negotiations, I'm sure the Clubs would be open to it—"

"Rubbish. These are the worst sort of terms I've ever heard. Go home, Marco Polo. I'd rather wait for better prospects." Rosamund got up and stamped towards the door.

From behind her, Marco Polo said, "Your Majesty, I think you're forgetting that little matter with the Papal Bull."

Rosamund paused with her hand on the doorknob and slowly turned.

Marco Polo watched her with deviled eyes. He knew he had her like a cherry topping on an avocado sundae. Still, she wouldn't give him the satisfaction of knowing he had her cornered.

"Oh?" Rosamund glanced at her nails. "What about that silly Bull?"

Marco shrugged. "Seems a pity to have it, especially since it could easily be swept away as if it never happened."

Rosamund retook her seat. "Go on."

"Let's say," Marco Polo continued, "that the King of Clubs is willing to beseech his great uncle twice removed on his mother's side for you to be released from the Bull once you have agreed to the contract."

Rosamund sat back. Released from the Bull? Now *that* was something. No more hiding. No more assassination attempts from Proverbials. No more guards surrounding her wherever she went—it made it so difficult to see her people's admiring faces. But, more unimportant, there would be no more Queen of Spades. She could behead the wretch anytime she wanted, which would be immediately.

"All you have to do," Marco Polo said, pushing the document towards her, "is agree to the contract and it all goes away."

The egg held a quill out to her. Rosamund tapped it on the table as she stared at the parchment.

Milkyam and Peatown.

Those were her lands, and she harbored no plans of parting with them—Bull or not. The Clubs were fools to think she would. The House of Hearts stole those lands away from them fair and square. Where would it end? How many Papal Bulls would they levy against her before they took her queendom piece by piece?

Rosamund clenched her fists. "We may still be able to find a way to settle the matter of the Papal Bull on our own without having to bend to the demands of the Clubs. And if we do, then the King and Queen of Clubs can take that parchment and shove it where—"

Marco Polo held up his hand to interrupt her, which was a dangerous thing to do. "They had a feeling you might have those sentiments. I believe, before you make your decision, you should look at this."

He took out a letter from his waistcoat.

"I have here," Marco Polo said, "an unofficial letter addressed to the House of Clubs on the most unofficial kind of unofficial business from the Proverbial Holy of Holies of the Holiest Church of Wonderland, in Pope Cecil de Burg's hand, no less."

Rosamund gritted her teeth. "And what does Cecil have to say now?"

"Read it for yourself."

Marco Polo handed her the letter, and she flipped it open with a flick of her wrist.

My Beloved Second Nephew Once Removed,

I have received your correspondence and I'm deeply grieved. I have spent many an hour wiping away the tears from my tusks.

The Queen of Hearts is a false Queen of Wonderland. She doesn't belong here. She never has—her rule is a mockery to us all. I would no more remove the Papal Bull than tear the liver out of my side. The execution of the King of Hearts was a travesty, but I blame myself. We are all to blame for allowing a crown to rest on her head—swindled by her innocence, the mask of her great terror. Why didn't we stop her when we had the chance? No, the sooner that woman—for I will no longer refer to her as a Queen of any sort—is dead, the better. Once the Queen of Spades, the true queen, takes the throne, I know peace will once more reign in the House of Hearts, and in Wonderland, for that matter.

This brings me to your letter. You have asked me to reconsider the Papal Bull as the House of Clubs wishes to enter into marriage negotiations with the House of Hearts. As you filed the formal grievance, I will have to rescind the Bull if you request to do so. Without house support, it cannot hold in the Proverbial Cannons.

My hope is that you will reconsider for the reasons I've listed above. But if you don't, I will do as you ask, and God help us both.

Have a blessed day,
Cecil de Burg

Rosamund's body shook as if lava spewed through her veins. She read it not once, not twice, but six times.

False Queen.

Mockery.

Dead—the better.

Queen of Spades, the true queen.

Rosamund ripped up the letter and flung the pieces in the air. She pushed away from the table and paced the floor, digging her nails into her palms until beads of blood stained her manicure.

She was so angry she could have kissed a cat.

Finally, Rosamund whirled on Marco Polo. "One thing, *Ambassador*," she said as if the words were venom on her tongue. "If I agree to the terms of the contract and I'm released from the Papal Bull, where does that leave Cecil's adored Queen of Spades?"

"Why, in your care I believe, Your Majesty."

Rosamund grinned. "That's what I thought."

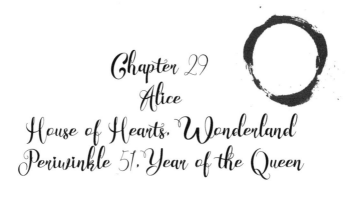

Chapter 29
Alice
House of Hearts, Wonderland
Periwinkle 51, Year of the Queen

The next day, Alice dawdled in the queen's room feeling as discarded as an old toy.

The prince hadn't asked her to dance last night, as he'd said he would, and she had stayed in the corner, watching him twirl Marilyn Montague across the floor. Sabrina tried to cheer her up by saying Marilyn probably didn't even know how to write her own name, but Alice doubted that would have mattered to the prince anyhow.

Alice supposed she shouldn't have expected anything more. She didn't even know why the prince had asked her to dance in the first place. Perhaps he was being polite. She was his mother's lady's maid and new to the House of Hearts. No doubt he was doing his duty by feigning interest when he didn't feel it a bit.

The sun shone in through the window. She could see the garden and the hedges of rose bushes. She sighed. It was a lovely day, but what she wanted was to lie in bed and nurse her hurt feelings.

"For you, *traitor*." Mary Anne shoved an envelope under Alice's nose. "Oops. I meant my *lady*."

She gazed up at Mary Anne, who glowered above her.

"Mary Anne," Alice said, breathing hard, "whatever do you mean by that? I'm not a traitor."

"You know you are." The chambermaid narrowed her eyes. "You think I'd forget that you had the Queen replace Mary Lou with that nasty rat? I despise you."

Mary Anne stormed off, leaving Alice gaping after her. She supposed she couldn't blame Mary Anne for feeling the way she did, but Alice didn't mean to hurt anyone, least of all Mary Anne; the Aboveground hadn't given her much of a choice, and now she had an enemy for her trouble—something she didn't need in the already treacherous House of Hearts.

Alice stepped away from Bess's recitation of "An Oyster, a Frog, and an Ocelot" and hid in a corner. She slowly peeled back the edges of the envelope. Inside was a note that read:

Meet me in the gardens.

—Thomas

Alice held the scrap of paper. She shouldn't go—not after he'd completely set her aside for Marilyn Montague without even a word. His behavior had been beyond insulting. She crumpled the note into a ball and was about to throw it in the fire when she stopped, feeling the twitch of butterflies in her stomach once again. Even after what had happened, the problem was she wanted to go. She flattened out the note and nicely folded it in halves. After all, what if he wanted to apologize? It would be bad manners to ignore his request. She should meet him, she decided. It would be the polite thing to do. Alice motioned to Sabrina.

Sabrina set her embroidery to the side and hurried over. "You look as if you've swallowed a stolen tart. What is it?"

Alice couldn't stop the smile that was spreading across her face. "The prince wants me to go to the garden."

Sabrina squealed.

"But the Queen..."

They looked over at the Queen, who studied a pamphlet with her tongue poking against her cheek.

Alice sighed. "She'll never let me go."

"Stickfiddles," Sabrina said. "She's been studying that thing all morning. I don't think she'd notice a troupe of jugglers if they came in. Come on." She grabbed Alice by the arm. "I have an idea."

They went towards the Queen. Alice began to doubt the closer they got. Even after the bomb and the Queen declaring that Alice had saved her life, she was still terrified of her and her unpredictable whims. "Your Majesty," Sabrina said barely above a whisper.

"Can't you see I'm busy, Sabrina?" the Queen snapped. "Whatever it is, ask Bess. I need to think."

"Pardon, Your Majesty, but Alice is feeling out of sorts. Something she ate, I believe."

Alice clutched her stomach for added measure, but her theatrics weren't necessary—the Queen didn't take her eyes off her document. "Tell her to go to her bedchamber," the Queen said. "Stop bothering me."

Sabrina nodded and steered Alice out of the room, away from Bess's watchful gaze. As soon as they got in the hallway, Alice gave Sabrina a quick hug.

"Thank you," Alice said before running down the hall. By now, she was getting used to the palace and knew where to go. She traveled down twisting staircases, jumped through a few hoops, and finally found the exit to the gardens. She spotted Thomas, leaning against a statue of himself.

"You came," Thomas said, and reached out towards her. "I didn't think you would after my behavior last night."

Alice grasped his hand with trembling fingers. Thomas pulled her close until she was nearly pressed against him. He smelled of gumdrops and moss, and she saw the hues of red in his eyelashes as he stared into her eyes.

"I hope," he said, "that you'll let me make it up to you."

Thomas bent his head and kissed the top of her hand. Alice held her breath while her heart thumped so hard against her chest that she could have sworn he could feel it too. With a smile, he released his grasp and moved to her side.

"Walk with me?" he asked.

He took Alice's hand and set it in the crook of his arm.

"Isn't it a disastrous day?" he commented as he led her into the garden.

Alice almost contradicted him but decided to give in to Wonderland's way of speaking and simply agreed with him.

He gave her a sidelong glance. "But it isn't nearly as disastrous as you."

Alice felt herself blush. She turned away, so he couldn't see the effect he was having on her. She didn't want him to think she was so inexperienced that she was unable to handle a compliment, even if it was a Wonderland compliment.

Thomas kept his hand wrapped around her fingers as he took her through arched vines and pathways lined with red daisies, mums, and tulips. He stopped to pluck a lily and placed it behind her ear. His hand brushed against her cheek, sending sparks up her spine.

"Here we are," he announced, and took her under a stone archway that opened into an alcove surrounded by rosebushes. Miniature winged horses and lavender dragons flitted around the blooms while the flowers appeared to reach towards the little creatures, welcoming them to come closer. Alice stood transfixed as Thomas headed towards a cherry blossom tree where there was a bench in the shape of a heart underneath it. "This is my secret place," he said, looking over his shoulder at her. "I used to hide here as a child when Mum was in one of her rages."

Thomas sat on the bench and stared at Alice. Everything was quiet inside the alcove, almost as if they were in their own world. She would have preferred to keep walking, because walking meant they were doing something, and she didn't know if she could be clever or witty or any of those things while she was sitting still. At least her sister never thought so. Katherine always brought a book whenever it was only them, preferring to read rather than talk to her.

"Are you going to stand there all day? Come," Thomas said, patting the bench. "Have a seat. I don't bite very hard. At least that's what I've been told."

Alice didn't know if he were being serious or not. How many ladies had he taken here? A couple? More than a couple? He seemed so at ease while Alice could barely keep her heart from wanting to jump outside her chest. She sat next to him and clasped her perspiring hands in her lap.

Thomas leaned towards her, and she noticed that he had the faintest freckle above his lip; the imperfection made him more beautiful. "The gardens are the one place where you can hide from all the formality of court," he said. "The flowers don't care if you're the Prince of Hearts—they've told me as much."

The roses were no longer open but tucked together into tight buds, as if they were closing their eyes. The horses and dragons had all but disappeared as well. Again, Alice wondered how many trysts Thomas had arranged in this very spot.

"Sometimes," he continued, placing his hand on top of Alice's, "I wish I weren't the Prince of Hearts. It doesn't even feel real, as if it's a role in a play that I didn't really want. Yet I'm compelled to play it and rail against it too. I mean, who else could be such a dashing Prince of Hearts? I don't know. I probably sound mad."

"No," Alice said, "I don't think you sound mad."

"I knew you wouldn't," Thomas said, turning towards her. "I think that's why I like talking to you. You're different from everyone else. You're not from Wonderland, and I like that you're not. It makes you special, and I like special things."

Alice lowered her eyes and smiled. Maybe Sabrina had been right after all and he really did like her and last night with Marilyn Montague had meant nothing to him. Could it really be true? The thought of it warmed her and filled her belly as if she'd swallowed an entire pot of tea with extra sugar.

"I'd like us to be friends," Thomas said. "Can we, Alice?"

Just like that, the feeling of warmth was gone and Alice felt her hope of being something more to Thomas dart away and disappear into the world of make-believe. Why had she been so silly? Of course he'd want nothing more than to be friends. Thomas would never have feelings for her. He was the Prince of Hearts and she was Alice, a lady's maid.

"Alice?" Thomas searched her face. "Did I say something wrong?"

"No," she said, shaking her head. "I'd like to be friends, too."

"Fantastic," he said and took her hand. His touch sent her heart racing and made it want to break at the same time. "Since we're friends, tell me more of the Land of Eng."

Alice kept her fingers intertwined with his, holding on as if it were the last thing she'd ever feel. The prince was like everything else in Wonderland—a dream that was always within reach but never in her grasp. She stared at the sky through the branches and leaves of the cherry blossom. It had been sunny earlier, but now it was a curious mix of purple, blue, and gray. She supposed it might rain soon. "What would you like to know?"

"What are the people like there?"

"They are always busy going somewhere or discussing some new thing. Then it can all change in a snap, and everything starts all over again. It's like running in a circle, trying to work out when to stop, but you never really do."

"It sounds like a place where one could disappear." Thomas sighed. "I wish I could disappear, but there's nowhere like that for me in Wonderland."

She didn't want to tell him that England was not such a place. If anything, things were more visible there, especially anything different. At least, that had been her experience.

Thomas gazed into her eyes in a way that made Alice feel unbearably hot. "Will you promise to take me there someday and show me all these wondrous places and people in the Land of Eng? Maybe we can even get the animals to talk again."

Alice didn't need her imagination to know how the prince would fare in her world. He would be like an orchid in a field of thistles, with no place to hide. He belonged in Wonderland, where it was safe to be different.

"Of course," Alice lied. "Whenever you'd like."

"I wish it could be now. I'd probably never come back, but you know, Mum wants me here. The Papal Bull has her on edge."

"You don't like being in Wonderland?"

"It's always one parade after another," he said. "And the parties, the balls, the tournaments, the tours. I want to simply *be* for a while."

Alice shook her head. "But you can do whatever you like, say whatever you like, and act however you like, and no one in

Wonderland will think...will think..."

"Think what?"

"Nothing," Alice said.

"No, tell me. We're friends, remember?"

Alice picked at a stitch on her gown. "All I was going to say was that, here, no one will think that there's something wrong with you."

"How can something be wrong with anyone?" he asked, getting up. "If I'm me, I can't really be anything I'm not."

"I wish everyone thought that way." And because he did, she couldn't help but like him even more and wish he wanted more than friendship.

"Why wouldn't they? You're a funny girl, Alice. Are you sure you're not a princess?"

She laughed. "I'm sure."

Alice was about to lean back and stare up at the sky and spend some time simply being, as the prince had said, when a scream shattered the stillness in the garden.

"What was that?" he asked, sitting up. "Do you think it was a lion?"

"I...I don't think so."

"Help!" a woman shrieked. "Help."

Thomas pulled Alice to her feet. They ran back through the garden maze, stopping at his statue.

A woman stood next to one of the palace walls, clawing her cheeks. A basket of laundry lay strewn about her feet. She saw Thomas and collapsed onto her knees, crying, "Your Grace, Your Grace," and pointing towards the hedge.

Alice followed the line of her arm to a slipper sticking out of the bushes. Thomas pushed Alice back. Two guards ran over, and Thomas took one of their swords and hacked at the shrubbery until they all saw a body lying unnaturally still.

Thomas had found Mary Lou—bloated, bruised, and very, very dead.

Chapter 30
Rosamund
House of Hearts, Wonderland
Periwinkle 51, Year of the Queen

No sooner had Rosamund returned back to the pamphlet than Bess had asked, "Would you like to behead Sabrina today?"

Rosamund gripped the sides of the contract. "For the love of roses, can't you see I'm working here?" she snapped. "One more interruption, and I swear, heads are going to roll."

"Yes, Your Majesty."

Rosamund sat back, rereading the Club's terms. Then she read them again and again, hoping for a mouse hole. "Leave it to the Clubs to have written it so solidly," she grumbled to herself. Nothing more than pirates, they were. Anyone with an ancestor by the name of Timmy the Barbarian had to have some unsavory blood.

No matter—there was always one little slip-up, one little misprint, and Rosamund would find it. She had started again from the beginning when Charles stormed into the room with Captain Juker of the Aces following close behind.

Rosamund's mouth opened. "Is ceremony completely at a loss around here?" she asked. "Bess? BESS!"

"Yes, Your Majesty?" Bess asked hurrying over. "Did you change your mind about Sabrina?"

"No, but I do want to set aside a full day of beheadings to get things back in order. I feel as if we're dangerously close to anarchy."

"Yes, Your Majesty."

Charles came forwards, fumbling with his pipe. "My apologies for the intrusion."

"You're not forgiven." Rosamund glanced around. "Where are Ralph and William? What's the matter?"

"I couldn't find them," Charles said, "and this news couldn't wait. The captain has informed me that a body has been found. We thought it most unimportant to come to you immediately."

"A body?" Rosamund asked. "Alive or dead?"

"Dead."

"That certainly makes a difference. Where was it?"

"Along the palace walls next to Your Majesty's garden."

"I see," Rosamund said. "That is certainly not appropriate. Well, find out who this body belongs to and return it at once."

"The body belongs to your chambermaid, Mary Lou."

"Mary Lou?" She put down the pamphlet.

A plate shattered behind the Queen. Mary Anne was as white as powdered sugar and tears bubbled in her eyes. Rosamund normally wouldn't abide such hullaballoo, but she did feel sorry for her little chambermaid. She remembered when Mary Anne and Mary Lou first came to her court. Little mites they had been. She'd made the no-beheading bargain with their fathers, the Tweedles, after forcing them on a suicide mission that changed the tide of the War of the Turnips. It seemed like a lifetime ago, but she'd never forget how that war had nearly toppled her after she first took the throne.

"This is most dreadful," Rosamund said. "But it doesn't excuse Mary Lou from being absent. Take her away and see to it that she gets a suitable burial after she is properly fined."

"As Your Majesty wishes," Charles said, "but there is a concern in the matter of how she died."

"Oh?"

Charles nodded to Captain Juker. The captain came forwards, clasping his hands behind his back. "My team has determined Mary Lou fell from Lady Alice's window. We found this stuck on a nail." He opened his hand and revealed a tiny piece of red cloth. "It matches the clothing Mary Lou was wearing."

Mary Anne came before the Queen. "Alice pushed her, Your Majesty. Mary Lou would never kill herself. Never."

"Calm yourself, Mary Anne," she said. "I'll get to the bottom of this. Bess, get her some cordial."

Rosamund watched Bess lead Mary Anne to the side cupboard before she addressed Charles and the captain. "What did Lady Alice have to say?" she asked.

The captain said, "We haven't spoken to her, Your Majesty."

"Whyever not? She was in her room. She left here no more than an hour ago, saying she wasn't well."

"I'm sorry, Your Majesty. But she wasn't there."

Rosamund sat back and looked up at the faces of Charles and Captain Juker. What sort of treachery was that girl up to?

"Well then," she said. "Find Alice and bring her to me. I'd like a full accounting from her. If she did push my chambermaid out the window, she will answer for it."

"There's something else," Captain Juker continued. "We searched her room—standard procedure—and we found this in the lady's possessions."

He brought out a velvet bag and dumped it onto Rosamund's lap. She turned the bag over and her missing brooch and missing necklace spilled out—not to mention a few rings, bracelets, and earrings she hadn't even known were gone.

"You...you found this?" Rosamund stammered. "All in *her* room?"

"As sure as I am a Heart," Captain Juker said.

Pushing a chambermaid was one thing, but stealing the Queen's jewels was an entirely different matter.

Sabrina stepped between Captain Juker and Charles. "But Your Majesty, it couldn't have been Alice. She wasn't even here when some of them went missing."

Rosamund glared at the girl. "You're the one who told me she was sick. Are you conspiring with her?"

"N...no, Your Majesty. That's what she said. Honest."

"How convenient."

Rosamund stared at the jewelry in her lap, feeling the rage growing within her. Alice's betrayal burned hotter than most.

She'd trusted Alice—taken her into her court, despite her better judgment. When the girl had saved her life, she thought Alice was one of the rare few that were truly loyal, but this girl was no better than any other plotter. She'd taken advantage of Rosamund's good nature and had been pinching her jewelry under her very chin the entire time. It made Alice worse than all the others, and she wasn't going to let the girl get away with it.

Rosamund clenched her fists. "Close the gates and search behind every pillow, under every cushion, on every shelf, and inside all the large pots. Find her and bring her to me at once."

Chapter 31
Alice
The Garden, Wonderland
Periwinkle 51, Year of the Queen

Thomas handed Alice a handkerchief. "Are you alright?" he asked. "Did you know her well?"

"Only a little," Alice said, taking the hanky from Thomas and dabbing her eyes. She couldn't tell him the real reason she was so upset. This was the work of the Aboveground, she just knew it. They had needed to make room for Lillian, and this was how they had done it. They had killed Mary Lou.

This was all her fault. If only she hadn't gone into the Queen's room that night. The bomb would have gone off and the mission would have been accomplished. The Queen would have been dead, everyone would have been happy, and Mary Lou would still be alive.

But she *had* interfered, and Mary Lou had paid the price for it.

"I should go," she said at last.

Thomas took her hands. "I understand. You have your duty to Queen Mum. We'll see each other soon, won't we?"

Alice nodded. She started to move away, but Thomas pulled her close. His hair felt like goose feathers against her cheek. She clung onto him, feeling his heart against her own. She could have stayed like that forever.

The stamping of boots into the garden broke them apart. "Lady Alice, you must come with us."

A troupe of Nines appeared and surrounded them. Thomas stepped before Alice, shielding her from the cards, but there were too many. They slipped around him and restrained Alice.

Alice struggled in their grasp. "What are you doing? Let me go."

Thomas ordered, "Release her at once."

"We are to take her to the Queen," one of the Nines said, "by direct order."

The Queen? Chills swept down her body. There was only one reason the Queen would send the guards: she'd found out about the Aboveground. It was over for Alice. For all of them.

"I am the prince," Thomas said, "and I say let her go."

"Begging your pardon, Your Grace," another card spoke up, "but the Queen signs the death warrants around here. We take orders from her alone."

"I'll fix this. I promise," Thomas said as the cards jerked Alice forwards.

She glanced over her shoulder. The prince appeared about as helpless as a kitten with an upturned bowl of milk. She doubted he'd ever utter another word to her again once the Queen told him she was a traitor. That hurt most of all.

The guards held Alice in such a tight grip that only the tips of her shoes brushed the ground as they dragged her towards the Queen's chambers. Once they arrived, the Nines dropped Alice at her feet as if she were a cumbersome piece of luggage. She glanced up at the Queen's severe face and trembled.

"Stand up," the Queen ordered.

Alice pulled herself up onto her shaky legs. She glanced over at Sabrina, but her friend ignored her completely. She must hate Alice now that she knew she was a traitor.

Bess, though, stared right at her with her lips screwed up in a smile.

The Queen asked, "Feeling better, Alice?"

Alice didn't know how to respond. It felt like a trap, and she supposed it was. The Queen knew she hadn't been sick. Alice lowered her eyes to the Queen's bejeweled slippers, unable to meet her gaze. The room grew hot, and the layers of her gown felt like a boa constrictor, squeezing and choking the life out of her. Alice's eyes watered with the threat of tears, but she forced herself to swallow them down.

"It appears," the Queen said, "that you've been well enough to steal my jewels and murder my chambermaid."

At first, Alice wasn't sure if she'd heard the Queen correctly. Jewels? Murder? Alice had no idea what she was talking about.

"Don't look so daft, girl," the Queen snapped. "Admit you stole my jewels and murdered my chambermaid."

Alice gaped. "But I didn't."

"You didn't, did you?" The Queen narrowed her eyes. "Then why were my missing jewels found in your room and Mary Lou's dead body underneath your window? Explain those two facts away, will you? I'd like to see you try."

Alice couldn't. She had nothing to do with Mary Lou's death or the Queen's jewels. Someone else had and, whoever it was, they were trying to get Alice blamed for it. Maybe Mary Lou's death wasn't the work of the Aboveground. She needed to talk to Ralph.

"No," Alice said, shaking her head. "It's not true. You can't possibly think that I—"

"I can think whatever I want to think," Rosamund interrupted. "I am the Queen."

Alice turned to Sabrina. "Tell her. You know I'd never do those things."

Sabrina remained silent. What was she doing? Alice stared at her, horror-stricken. Sabrina had insisted they share a bedchamber. Was she behind this? Did she tell the Queen that Alice had taken the jewels and killed Mary Lou? No, it couldn't be Sabrina. She had been so welcoming. So in need of a friend as much as Alice was. But maybe that was all part of her plan to lure Alice in. She didn't realize she was crying until she felt tears gliding along her jaw.

Bess leaned towards the Queen. "I bet Alice has been scheming the entire time, Your Majesty."

Alice suddenly couldn't breathe. She looked around. There was no one to help her, no one to come to her aid. This couldn't be happening—not again. Every ounce of her wanted to start screaming.

The Queen growled, "I'm going to do something I should have done the moment you walked in that door," and nodded to the guards.

The Nines grabbed Alice. She wiggled like a netted fish, trying to escape. She needed to get out—out of Wonderland entirely. She had done it once before. If she could just get loose, then she could make a run for the door and, somehow, make it back to her world. Only this time, the guards' hands clamped down on her arms, refusing to yield.

"Lady Alice," the Queen said. "You are to be executed second thing tomorrow morning. Until then, enjoy your night in the tower."

PART 3
QUEEN ME

Chapter 32
Alice
The Tower, Wonderland
Periwinkle 51, Year of the Queen

The Nines took Alice to the tower. Inside, the air was heavy and stale as if she were breathing a hundred years of despair. They climbed water-stained steps until they came to a room. Without a word, they shoved her over the threshold and locked the door behind her. Except for a chamber pot and a blanket, the small space was empty. Only one window brought any sort of light at all. Alice looked outside. Down below was the wooden block waiting to claim her head.

The air was chilly. She pricked up the blanket. It was threadbare with holes every few stitches. She wrapped it around her shoulders and rubbed her arms. Tears picked at her eyes. Tomorrow she would die. Why had she been so senseless? Had she not learned her lesson the last time she came to Wonderland?

Alice wanted her mother, wanted her more than anything she'd ever wanted in her life. If she could have one moment with her, she might be able to face death, but even if by some miracle her mother came to her side, she doubted anything could prepare her for the executioner. She buried her head in her arms and cried for everyone she was going to miss, most of all, the White Rabbit.

The door opened. Alice sprang to her feet.

"I didn't mean to startle you," a woman said. She stepped into the room and quickly closed the door behind her. She turned to Alice with a grave expression that matched her moth-worn gown of black velvet. Alice had never met this woman before, but she had a fairly good idea who she was.

Alice wiped her eyes. "You're the Queen of Spades."

The woman bowed her head and a wisp of black hair touched her pale cheek. "I am, but there's no need for formality in here. Please, call me Constance."

Alice glanced towards the door. "How did you get past the guards?"

"Them? They're easy," she said. She sat on the floor and adjusted her skirt around her. "They have Twos stationed at the doors. It's too bad they have Tens at the tower gate; otherwise, we could escape."

Alice wiped her eyes and stared at the queen, who smiled at her. "I've been hoping to meet you," Constance said. "Of course, I didn't expect it to be this way."

Alice moved her hand to her throat, brushing the skin the axe would sever, and swallowed. "I've been sentenced to death."

"It appears we have that in common. I'm expecting my death warrant any day." Her eyes moved about the room. "It's too bad we couldn't have a little spot of tea. Wouldn't that be nice?"

If it was to be her last, Alice would have accepted Wonderland tea and been grateful for it. There were a lot of "lasts" she'd miss—things that she hadn't known were going to be. She thought back to the last time she'd tasted a hot scone, heard a beautiful piece of music, held Dinah. All lasts.

Alice's eyes watered, but she blinked the tears back. If this was going to be her last conversation with anyone, she didn't want to cry all the way through it. "Your death warrant hasn't been signed. You might still live."

"At one point I thought so, but now..." Constance sighed. "My head will be taken as surely as yours." She gestured at the room. "This is a formality. What's the old saying? *The tower is the last stop before the block*, or something like that? I can't quite remember."

Alice thought of the block and the axe and the blood. She shuddered and brought her knees to her chest to stop shaking. It was getting dark outside. Shadows poured down the walls like water.

Constance motioned her over. "Why don't you come closer? It seems so formal to be far apart. In here, we're equals."

Alice moved towards the Queen of Spades. The Queen had a smattering of freckles on her nose and cheeks. Alice's sister had the same feature and hated it. She tried everything to get them to fade.

"See, that's better," Constance said.

Alice took a breath. "I want you to know that I'm sorry."

"Sorry?" Constance raised her eyebrows. "For what?"

"For ruining everything," she said, her bottom lip quivering. "I didn't mean to save the Queen that night with the bomb. I heard her scream and ran to help. I didn't even think about it."

"You can't blame yourself for that," she said. "You're not to blame. We all took a chance—I, for one, took a chance coming to Gardenia City. It seems it wasn't so fortunate, now was it? I thought I'd be received with love, or if not with love, then maybe with mutual regard. She is my sister after all."

Alice was taken back. "The Queen of Hearts is your sister?"

"Does that surprise you?"

Alice thought of her own sister, Katherine, and how she didn't do anything to help Alice when her parents sent her to the asylum. She hadn't uttered a single word in her defense. Alice thought sisters were supposed to look out for each other—another childish notion that wasn't true.

Constance picked at a hole in her black gown and then covered it with her palm. "Rosamund wasn't always this way. She was my baby sister. I watched her grow up. She was such a sweet child, always wanting to please and be accepted. She never felt as if she belonged, and it was heartbreaking to see her struggle." She sighed and glanced at Alice. "You know, you remind me of her as she was in the old days."

Alice tried to smile out of politeness, but she didn't particularly like the comparison. She wasn't anything like the Queen of Hearts, young or old. "Rosamund?" Alice said. "I don't think I ever heard her name. She was always *the Queen* or *Her Majesty.*"

"It's the name she chose for herself," Constance said. "Rosamund always hated her given name. It reminded her of a terrible time."

Alice shook her head. "But if you're the eldest, why didn't you become the Queen of Hearts?" she asked. "Where I'm from, the oldest is always the next king or queen."

"It would seem more natural, wouldn't it?" Constance smiled half-heartedly. "As soon as word reached us of our parent's untimely death, I was whisked away to my first prison in a blink—it was all planned, all arranged. Rosamund snatched my throne right from underneath me. There, I waited until the King of Spades freed me with his offer of marriage."

Alice stared up at Constance. "Why was she so awful?"

Constance shrugged. "It wasn't her. It was her advisors. They didn't want me as their queen. They thought Rosamund would be less likely to interfere with their plans. Rosamund was the Queen of Hearts, but in name alone. They ruled Wonderland."

Alice leaned towards her. "The White Rabbit... he did this to you?"

"Who?" Constance asked.

"Ralph."

"Oh, no, not him," Constance said. "When I was young, there were different advisors, similar though perhaps. Let me see, there was the Bishop of Newmark, the Sire of Pemberknee, and Colonel Mustard of Custard Cathedral. As old men do, they died and new advisors took their places, but those fossils certainly left a mess. They ran Gardenia City for the better part of twenty years with Rosamund as their puppet. They were the reason she went mad. I'm certain of it. They confused her, baited her, and made her believe everyone was out to steal her throne. It's their fault she is the way she is."

Constance became quiet and looked towards the window as if she were remembering something from the past. Suddenly, Constance inhaled. "Look at me rambling on so," she said. "Sometimes I forget the past, and when I talk, it reminds me."

The shadows had taken over the room and the temperature was dropping. Alice hunched over, shivering. She thought of her bed in the palace and the mountains of blankets. They were itchy but they were also warm and she would have gladly crawled underneath them.

As night pressed around them, it was harder to see Constance's face. Time was going fast—too fast. Tomorrow would come, and Alice would be no more. She twisted her hands in the blanket, feeling tears bubble in her eyes yet again. This time, she was unable to stop them from coming. "Oh dear," Alice said, looking out the window.

Constance used her gown to dry Alice's cheeks. "Don't cry," she said.

"How can you say that?" Alice asked. "I'm to die tomorrow. What else can I do but cry?"

Constance smiled. "I try very hard not to be sad. It wouldn't do to be pouty all the time, now would it?" She grasped Alice's hands. "I'd like to promise you something."

Alice sniffed. "Yes?"

"I promise, as the Queen of Spades, that you shouldn't despair. When you are executed tomorrow, you will go to the Undying Lands, where everything is green and warm. It's a place full of flowers and sunshine and happiness and freedom."

"But I don't want to go to the Undying Lands," Alice said. "I don't want to die. I'm not ready."

There was so much Alice still wanted to do. She wanted to finish growing up. Fall in love. Maybe have her own children someday. Write stories and draw pictures. Or simply live.

"Sometimes we don't have a choice," Constance said, and pulled Alice on her lap. Alice couldn't remember when she'd last been held, the last time she'd had someone to mother her. Alice wrapped her arms around the Queen of Spades and sobbed into her neck, which smelled faintly of black licorice and spice.

"There, there," Constance cooed, rocking Alice back and forth. "Everything will be all right. Don't cry, my little rose. Don't cry. Constance is here."

Chapter 33
Rosamund
House of Hearts, Wonderland
Periwinkle 51, Year of the Queen

At last, Charles and Captain Juker left the room, and Mary Anne followed behind them, wailing, "Mary Lou. Oh, Mary Lou."

Good riddance. The less racket the better. She had serious business to tackle.

Rosamund snapped her fingers at Bess. "Where were we?"

Bess cleared her throat and continued reading from the *Looking Glass Book of Wondrous Prose and Poetry* while Sabrina stared out the open window. Rosamund must have chosen a room near the kitchens because the marshmallow scent of fud-blood pudding wafted through the air, making her stomach rumble.

"Sabrina?" Rosamund called.

The girl wiped her eyes before turning. "Yes, Your Majesty?"

"Get me some tea."

Sabrina left and Rosamund grabbed the Clubs' contract and her spectacles. She'd settled back in her chair, ready to read again, when Ralph entered her chamber. She would have raged at another intrusion, but instead smiled when she saw him holding a familiar piece of paper.

"Ah," Rosamund said, "the death warrant."

He handed it to her, and read the flowing script: *Lady Alice of unknown origins is hereby sentenced to death by beheading.*

All it needed now was her signature. She dabbed the tip of her quill with her tongue.

"Your Majesty," Ralph said. "If I may?"

Rosamund raised an eyebrow. "What is it?"

Ralph's paw shook as he stuck it inside his vest, no doubt fumbling for his beloved pocket watch. "I don't think you should be so hasty with signing Alice's death warrant."

"Stickfiddles. I've executed hundreds, give or take a few thousand. Why should this one matter?"

"We don't know for sure if she was behind all this," Ralph said. "What if it was someone else? The Aces' search was rushed and careless. We haven't interrogated anyone. You love a good interrogation. Think of the fear you could inspire. Besides, it just doesn't make sense. Alice always held you in the highest regard. Why, she was telling me the other day—"

"Flattery won't help you this time," Rosamund interrupted him. "I have all the evidence I need."

Ralph lowered his voice. "You wouldn't want to execute an innocent subject, would you?"

She didn't like Ralph's tone. Like maybe he knew about the King of Hearts. He couldn't, of course. She'd kept everything secret. Why, he didn't even know about the bomb.

"Please say you'll reconsider," Ralph said. "At least until we have more evidence."

Rosamund squared her shoulders. "Is that all? *Reconsider?* If you were going to make a plea, I thought you'd come up with one better than that. I hope you're not getting soft on me," she said, pressing the quill against the parchment.

The signing of the warrants was the second-best part. The first was the execution.

Right as she was about apply her official autograph, Thomas barged into the room, knocking over a crystal cabbage sculpture in the process. It had been a gift from the House of Spades when they used to be friends.

"Stop!" he shouted.

"Not you too," Rosamund grumbled.

"Queen Mum," Thomas said, and bowed on one knee. "You must pardon Alice and release her from the tower."

"Yes," Ralph nodded. "I wholly agree. I was just telling Her Majesty—"

"Have you both gone mad?" Rosamund clenched her teeth. "The girl stole my jewels and pushed Mary Lou out of her window. Is that suddenly acceptable behavior? Should I dump my jewelry box on the palace green and overturn the sugar bowls in the streets? Is that what you two want?"

"Of course not," Thomas said.

"And you, Ralph?" Rosamund said, turning towards him. "Should I let you be pushed from a window? Because, believe me, I can make it happen."

Ralph's whiskers twitched about his face.

Thomas took a step forwards, holding his hands out in front of him. "Listen, Queen Mum. We're not saying the culprit shouldn't be punished, but Alice would never do those things. She is innocent."

"Really? Is that so?" Rosamund eyed Thomas and Ralph. What was this, a conspiracy? "If she's so innocent, then explain how my jewels made their way into her room? Perhaps a little monkey took them there? And what about the piece of Mary Lou's dress found in her window? I suppose that must have been a rhinoceros?"

Thomas shrugged. "It's possible."

"Possible shmossible."

"I'd believe that a monkey or a rhinoceros did it sooner than Alice," Thomas said. "Before you execute her, put her on trial. Let Alice prove her innocence."

"Why all this bother over a silly girl?" Rosamund asked. "You two act as if I'm executing somebody of unimportance."

Thomas jutted out his chin. "She's my friend."

"She's your *friend?*" Rosamund sniffed. "So, it's alright for your poor Queen Mum to have her jewelry stolen and her chambermaid pushed straight out of a window if it's your friend? Is that what you're saying?"

Thomas shook his head. "I didn't say that—"

"Yes, you did," Rosamund said, grabbing a rose-scented tissue and dabbing at her eyes. "You care about your *friend* and not me."

Thomas sighed. "You know I care about you above all, Queen Mum. It's just—"

"Good," Rosamund said, throwing the tissue over her shoulder. She picked up the quill and signed the death warrant before Thomas could say another word. "There. It's all settled." She stood and shoved it in Ralph's paw. "See to it that this goes straight to the executioner."

Ralph stared dumbly at the warrant.

"Go on now," Rosamund said. "Shoo."

Ralph skipped backwards towards the door with droopy ears. She wasn't sure, but she believed she saw a tear dampen his furry cheek. Ungrateful wretch. He should feel lucky that she wasn't blaming *him* for Alice. He had been the one to recommend her, and she'd ended up being a murdering thief.

When Ralph was gone, Thomas faced her with balled fists. "How could you?"

"How could I what?" Rosamund asked, returning his angry gaze. "You said that you cared about me most, and I care about my stolen jewels and my chambermaid. I thought you saw reason."

He nodded towards the contract. "I know what that's about. I know all about it and if you don't release Alice," he said, nostrils flaring, "then I won't marry the Princess of Clubs or any other princess—ever."

"Nonsense. You will do whatever I say," Rosamund said, plucking each word from her mouth as if they were fish bones. "You're being absurd, Thomas. Marriage was your idea in the first place."

"Not to the Princess of Clubs it wasn't."

Rosamund waved the pamphlet in the air. "It's nearly settled. You can't. I forbid it."

"You can't make me marry," Thomas said with a slick, little smile. "You know it and I know it. I'll ride out of Gardenia City and you'll never see me again."

Rosamund narrowed her eyes. "Don't threaten me, boy. If I want you to marry the Princess of Clubs, then you will marry her. I won't hear another word about it unless you want a royal spanking. I'm the Queen of Hearts and I make the rules, not you."

Thomas opened his mouth, but Rosamund held up her hand.

"Not another word," she said. "I'll have them do it in front of your precious Marilyn Montague. We'll see how smitten she is with you after that."

Thomas's cheeks turned a deep red. He glared at her. She'd never seen him look at her like that, and it stung a bit. As infuriated as he made her, he was still her little boy who loved her despite it all. Except for now. She saw no love in his eyes for her at all.

"This isn't over," he said, and kicked the crystal cabbage, shattering it against the wall.

Chapter 34
Alice
The Tower, Wonderland
Calla Lilly 61, Year of the Queen

Alice didn't sleep all night, not wanting to miss one last moment of her life. She lingered on every breath, every blink, and every heartbeat. Several times, she'd been convinced it was all a dream, like before, and she'd pinch her arm to make sure, but all she accomplished were several angry welts. This time, she wasn't going to wake up. She wouldn't find herself by the riverbank with her sister or before the fire in the parlor. This time, the Queen of Hearts would finally have her head.

She gradually came to accept her fate, if there was such a thing. Everyone had to die. Death was unavoidable, sort of like an acquaintance you couldn't fully ignore.

As much as she reassured herself that it would be alright, that it would be quick, the sun bathed the morning in reddish pink and she only felt more afraid.

Thump.

The sound came from outside. Alice sat up.

Thump. Thump. Thump.

Her legs shook as she walked over to the window. She clutched the curtains and peered out. The executioner, dressed from head to toe in red leather, held his axe in the air and took practice swings on a stump. Alice bit her fist to keep from screaming as fear churned in her belly. She thought for certain she'd vomit, but since she'd had nothing to eat, there was nothing to expel.

Thump. Thump. Thump. Thump.

Alice covered her ears with her hands and turned away, crawling into the farthest corner to get away from the sound. An hour passed, maybe two. She heard a crowd start to gather outside and the growing swell drowned out the sharp crack of the axe. She took a breath and forced herself to go back and see for herself what was happening. Outside, both peasants and gentry were gathering to watch her die. Some had even brought picnics.

It wouldn't be much longer now. Soon, they'd come for her and she'd be no more. She thought of her parents again. They would never know what had become of her. She wondered what they were doing right now. Reading the morning paper, having tea, being merry? Despite it all, Alice would miss them—even if they had left her at the asylum.

A Ten of Hearts unlocked the door and came inside her room. "Good morning," he said. "I'm here to escort you to your beheading."

Alice dropped the blanket on the floor; she'd added a few holes of her own to it. She glanced outside at the crowd. The prince was sure to be among them, and she found herself thinking about what she looked like. She must be a mess. She smoothed down her hair and rubbed the wrinkles from her gown. She didn't want his last memory of her being one where she was wretched.

Alice faced the Ten of Hearts and said, "I'm ready."

More guards waited outside the door. They stayed to the front and back of her as they guided her to the block. She savored every step down the stairs—the shift of her weight, the movement of her arms, the dip of her knee. She sucked in air and held it—not once but three times—until her lungs were about to burst. Alice couldn't remember if she'd ever actually done that before, but it hurt a little.

She stepped onto the palace green and allowed her feet to sink down into the grass. She was overcome with the beauty of it all—every emerald blade, every hidden wildflower. A rosebush bloomed next to the path, and she studied the dew-misted petals as she walked past, fixing them to memory.

The guards pushed Alice along until she stood at the chopping block, darkened with dried blood and scarred grooves. She looked up and saw the Queen on her balcony, rubbing her hands, clearly excited for her death. Thomas stood next to the Queen. He appeared as miserable as Alice, and that brought her comfort. It meant he didn't believe the accusations against her and at least she could die knowing Thomas thought she was innocent.

One of the guards poked Alice in the back. She sank to her knees and prayed—or she tried. She wasn't a religious person. She remembered her mother and father kept a Bible somewhere, but it didn't have pictures, so she never bothered to read it. Even so, praying seemed the right thing to do at one's death, and she prayed it wouldn't hurt.

Alice placed her chin on the block and closed her eyes.

Chapter 35
Rosamund
House of Hearts, Wonderland
Calla Lilly 61, Year of the Queen

Rosamund watched Alice's procession from the balcony. She couldn't wait to see the murdering thief's head drop. Her sole regret was that beheadings always happened so fast. She must work out a way to slow them down.

Thomas stood next to her, sighing and shaking his head. Every so often, he'd utter, "Please, Queen Mum, please…" and bounce from foot to foot. She refused to speak to him, still angry about how he'd destroyed her crystal cabbage—and that look he'd given her—but all his fidgeting and pleading was simply ruining the show. Sooner or later, Rosamund told herself, he'd forget all about that girl.

It was a perfect blasé day with the scent of damp clothes on the breeze. She loved when the weather matched the mood of the occasion.

Bess leaned towards her. "Would you like to behead Sabrina today?" she asked.

Rosamund gritted her teeth. "Honestly, Bess, can't you see I'm already beheading Alice?"

"Maybe you'd like to behead them both. It would be like killing two ferrets with one axe."

"No, Bess. It wouldn't. I'm making an example out of Alice, and if I execute her and Sabrina, then it wouldn't really make a point, now would it? It would be like any other execution, and

I want this one to be special."

"Yes, Your Majesty."

Rosamund turned back to the palace green. Quite a crowd had gathered, as she had expected. They did love their beheadings—almost as much as she did. Most camped out the night before, eager to get their hands on the commemorative goblets and other merchandise for the first fifty spectators through the gates.

"Your Majesty," Ralph said. "I have something to say of utter unimportance."

"Tell me later," Rosamund snapped over her shoulder. "We're finally getting to the good part."

Ralph cleared his throat. "I must confess that I stole your jewels and pushed Mary Lou out the window. Alice is innocent."

Rosamund froze. "What did you say?"

"I'm confessing, Your Majesty."

Rosamund pried her fingers from the ledge and whirled around. Thomas was already sprinting out of the balcony. She thought of calling after him, but she knew it would be useless. Instead, she focused on Ralph, the cause of this inappropriate interruption. She stepped closer to him, drawing herself up so she towered well above him. He was wearing his best suit and had neatly fluffed fur.

Ralph cleared his throat. "As I said, Your Majesty, I stole your jewels and hid them in Alice's room. I was hoping to sell them for a nice little holiday cottage someday, but Mary Lou caught me, so I had to get rid of her. I have made a full confession. So..." He pulled out a slip of paper from the inside of his breast pocket. "I believe this is in order."

He gave her his death warrant.

Rosamund crumpled it in her hand. Alice's fate had already been settled. Her face had been etched on the goblets and painted on the tunics, toasting the Queen's 338th beheading. Her people expected the girl to die, and nothing that ridiculous rabbit could do would stop it. She said, "I already have a perfectly good head on the chopping block. I will deal with yours later."

"If you continue with the execution," Ralph said, "then everyone will know that you sentenced an innocent person to death. I have letters ready to be dispatched across the Houses of Wonderland, including to Cecil de Berg. I doubt even the Clubs could feign an alliance with the Hearts after that. You'll never get the Papal Bull removed, and, if that doesn't work to get rid of you, then Cecil will do it the old-fashioned way and send his troops from Clickity-Clack to take your house by force."

Ralph straightened his waistcoat. "As you can see," he said. "You don't have a choice."

Rosamund's cheeks trembled with rage. "Oh, bloody hell," she growled.

Chapter 36
Alice
Executioner's Block, Wonderland
Calla Lilly 61, Year of the Queen

Alice felt the air shift above her.

The executioner must have lifted the axe. She could feel it—there was no need to see—and she knew it hovered over her head. Alice bit her lip as she did before the sting of the doctor's needle. It would hurt for a moment, she told herself, and then it would be over.

"Stop!" she heard Thomas yell. "I order you to stop at once."

Alice sensed herself being pulled off the block. It must be her head falling, she decided. She sighed inwardly. She hadn't felt a thing. It had been painless and now she only had to wait for herself to die properly. Just then, she heard the loud clunk of the axe as it dug into the stump, and she realized she was lying in the grass—all of her, not just her head. She opened her eyes and saw Thomas's face. He was so close the locks of his hair tickled her cheek.

"Am I dead?" Alice asked him.

"No." Thomas smiled. "Not even a little bit."

The executioner grunted as he pulled the axe from the wood. "Put her back on there, Your Grace," he said. "I haves a job to do and I means to do it."

Thomas got to his feet and pulled Alice up with him. He wrapped his arms around her, bringing with his embrace the comforting odor of cinnamon. Thomas faced the executioner. "Alice is not to be put to death," he said, and nodded up towards the Queen. "See for yourself."

Alice leaned against Thomas as they squinted towards the balcony, where the Queen stood, staring down at them. They waited for what felt like an awfully long time for the Queen to do something, anything, other than return their gaze with a level of hatred that Alice had yet to experience. Whatever had transpired to save her life, the Queen had not approved. Alice felt each beat of her heart in her chest, grateful that it hadn't stopped—yet.

The Queen reached out her hand, palm down. The crowd was silent as all eyes watched to see what the Queen's decision would be. Then she shot her thumb up, which was immediately followed by the booing and cursing of the crowd.

"Cats," the executioner said, dropping his axe. "She pays me per head, you know, and little Jimmy wants a new train set for his birthday."

"I'll see to it he gets his train set," Thomas said.

"Thank you, Your Grace," the executioner said. "That's kind of you."

"Come," Thomas said to Alice, "let's get back to the palace."

They wove through the feverish crowd; they had been denied their spectacle of blood, and they fussed like children. Thomas tried to shield her, but it didn't stop the mob from yelling in her face and stamping their hats on the ground. Someone threw a rotten squash. It exploded on Alice shoulder, covering her with goo.

They made it inside. Thomas ordered the guards to lock the doors. The crowd's frustration and resentment was growing. Alice wiped the squash innards onto the floor. Thomas helped her.

"There," he said when it was gone. "All better."

"No, it's not."

"The squash? You can't even tell anymore."

"I don't mean that," Alice said, glancing at the door. "I think I need to leave, get out of Gardenia City. I can't go out the front, not with them out there. Maybe there's another way, another door somewhere?"

"No, Alice," Thomas said. "You're innocent. You don't have to run away. She's not going to hurt you, I promise."

Alice wasn't reassured. The Queen was unpredictable. Alice might have her head today, but the Queen would remove it eventually.

Thomas took her hand and started to lead her towards the stairs.

"Where are we going?" she asked.

"To see Queen Mum."

"No," Alice said, shaking her head. "I can't."

"You must." Thomas gripped her shoulders. "You have to show her you're not afraid."

Alice still didn't want to, but Thomas was so adamant, so insistent. She didn't know quite what to do except to nod and let him take her by the arm. They made their way to the balcony, where the Queen was waiting. As soon as Alice saw her, her stomach recoiled. She didn't want to be anywhere near the Queen. Every part of her wanted to run the other way.

The Queen glanced at her as if she were merely a vase somebody was placing in the corner. "It's nice to see you with your head," she said.

Alice trembled. "Thank you, Your Majesty," she said.

"You'll be pleased to know we've caught the true culprit—in the nick of time it seems. See for yourself." The Queen turned.

Despite everything, Alice's curiosity got the better of her and she came closer. Guards were dragging the White Rabbit towards the block. Alice covered her mouth and stared, frozen.

"No," Alice cried. "There must be some mistake. Ralph had nothing to do with it."

"Of course he did," the Queen huffed. "He admitted it all—even Thomas heard."

Thomas nodded and took Alice hand. "He did, I'm afraid."

Alice shivered as she gazed down at the White Rabbit. The mob cheered when they realized they were going to get a show after all. She wanted to scream. Scream at the murderous crowd, the murderous Queen. How easy it would be to push the Queen over the balcony railing or plunge a knife in her rancid heart and be done with it all, but she did nothing except watch helplessly.

"Look at him," the Queen smirked. "Not so high and mighty now, is he?"

Ralph was biting the guards and kicking them. He'd almost got away at one point, but then they grabbed Ralph by the ears and slammed him down on the block. Even from the balcony, Alice could see his chest rising and falling in terror. Her eyes glistened with tears. Ralph hadn't taken the jewels or killed Mary Lou any more than she had. He had done this for her. He had taken her place.

The guards held Ralph down while the executioner rubbed his hands together and lifted the axe. Alice wanted to cover her eyes, but she wasn't given a chance. In a flash, a blink—no more than a batting of eyelashes—the axe dropped, and Ralph's head rolled into the basket.

The White Rabbit was dead.

Chapter 37
Rosamund
House of Hearts, Wonderland
Calla Lilly 61, Year of the Queen

Rosamund clapped her hands when the executioner chopped off Ralph's head, but she didn't feel as elated as she usually did. She had generally liked Ralph, even if she had her suspicions about him. Good help was so hard to find, but she supposed she would have beheaded him sooner or later.

Except, it bothered her that his confession seemed a little too convenient. Had he been willing to die to save Alice? Was that it? She wasn't sure what that could mean, only that something needled her deep inside her belly, something that said to be cautious and to behead Alice as soon as possible.

Rosamund took one last look at the headless rabbit before turning to Marco Polo, who was puffing on a cigar. She had insisted he watch the execution, but he had refused to step even one eggy little foot onto the balcony.

He had asked her, "I don't suppose you've heard of my late cousin, Humpty Dumpty?"

"As I already assured you," Rosamund said, "you are perfectly safe."

"Maybe so, but I've made it a general rule not to stand on any balconies, decks, galleries, terraces, precipices, or anything that includes any sort of a ledge."

Rosamund stopped before him. Marco Polo bowed, which wasn't so much of a proper bow, but more of him rolling towards her and closing his eyes. She supposed it couldn't be helped, being oblong and all. "You missed a good show."

"Not entirely," he said, glancing at Alice, who was snuggling close to Thomas.

Rosamund narrowed her eyes. She didn't approve of how taken her son was with the girl. How he'd defended her, fought for her life. If it hadn't been for Ralph, Alice would be dead and Thomas would be back to being Thomas. Something about the girl had changed him, and she didn't like it.

"With that business done," Marco Polo said, "I'd like to have a word with you."

"If this is about the contract," Rosamund snapped, "then I must tell you that I refuse to agree to all of it. I plan to draft a counteroffer, and I am confident that we can come to some sort of an agreement."

"That is all well and good, but it has come to my attention," he said, "that the House of Diamonds put in an offer."

Rosamund rounded on him. "What offer? What could the House of Diamonds possibly want?"

"The Princess of Clubs, of course. From what I hear, it's a very nice one. The House of Clubs, naturally, is holding off on responding, pending your answer, but they don't want to dally much longer."

Those blasted Diamonds were doing this on purpose. All they did was sit in their snow palace with nothing better to do than pick on her. What would those Diamonds want with the Princess of Clubs? Why, she'd freeze into a froggy statue if she went up north. Not only that, the Diamonds only had daughters. How many princesses did they want up there? Where they trying to run a monopoly on them?

"Very well," Rosamund groaned. "I'll make sure that my counteroffer is sent post haste."

"That won't be necessary. The offer is not up for negotiation. If you don't agree, then I've been instructed to go to the House of Diamonds. They've offered Whipwhirl Wood and Jellyfawn Village—very nice prospects indeed. I've hunted in Whipwhirl myself."

Rosamund swallowed the lump in her throat. "I will have my answer first thing tomorrow. Satisfied?"

"Very," he said and bowed. "I'll wait with hard-boiled breath."

"I'm sure you will."

Rosamund left Marco Polo and dismissed her lady's maids: Bess, Sabrina, and Alice—since she was alive and, technically, still in her employ. She wanted to keep Alice close, where she could keep an ear on her. She didn't believe for one moment that Ralph was completely to blame. Alice had a hand in it in some way.

She went on the hunt for a new bedchamber on her own. She wanted to think, and there were always far too many distractions when others were around. She wandered through the palace. When she first became queen, she'd made many modifications to the place. Something in her head had told her to build, and she had. For years, there wasn't a day when carpenters weren't running around the grounds, and it didn't stop until she could boast that she had the largest palace of all four houses. Many had found themselves lost for good in her labyrinthine maze of hallways, stairs, and doors. Some even said the walls moved when they weren't paying attention, but she found that ridiculous. She'd never been lost; she knew the palace like the bottom of her foot. Its design made perfect sense to her.

Rosamund found a suitable bedchamber and locked the door behind her. She didn't like the room—not enough red for her taste, and the skeleton in the corner wasn't doing much for the décor. Judging by the pail of coal at its feet and the pink ruff and livery, it was her missing royal fire starter. Why, that wallaby had been gone at least ten years. She had wondered where he'd hopped off to. By the looks of the dried stalks of flowers next to him, he'd nabbed his furry paws on some poppies and had completely lost his head. Served him right.

Rosamund turned from the dead wallaby. She was about to ring for a servant to clean up the mess when she saw another ball of white, except this time it wasn't a pile of bones but Madame Diamond.

Madame Diamond opened her mouth, but Rosamund held up her hand, silencing her.

"Don't tell me," Rosamund said, "the spirits told you?"

"They did."

"Lucky guess," Rosamund grumbled and headed towards a table in the corner of the room. "Let's see what the spirits have to say this time."

"What about him?" Madame Diamond motioned towards the skeleton.

"He's not going anywhere."

"As you wish, Your Majesty." Madame Diamond set a teacup before Rosamund. She removed a pot from inside the folds of her dress and filled it. "Drink."

"I'm not much in the mood," Rosamund said, pushing the cup away. "Besides it's not teatime."

"You must," Madame Diamond urged. "It's for the reading."

"Well, if you insist." Rosamund took two gulps. It tasted like moldy bread with a hint of sour milk—an excellent blend. She must find out where Madame Diamond got it. Rosamund burped and wiped her chin.

"Leave a little at the bottom," Madame Diamond said.

Rosamund did so and gave the cup back to the madame, who rotated it in her hands.

"I see..." she said. "I see..."

"Yes?" Rosamund leaned over. "What do you see?"

"A party."

"Oh? Anyone I know?" Rosamund asked. "I hope I get invited."

Madame Diamond turned the cup. "But there's also a funeral."

Rosamund shrugged. "That's probably for Mary Lou. Did you hear that Alice—I mean, Ralph pushed her right out the window?"

Madame Diamond peered closer at the tea leaves. "This isn't a commoner's funeral," she said, concentrating on the cup. "It's a royal funeral."

An icy chill swept down her back. "Is it...is it *my* funeral?"

"The leaves don't say."

"They don't have to say, you nitwit," Rosamund sneered. "Who else could it possibly be if *not* me, huh? I suppose there's Thomas, but I wouldn't say he'd exactly get a *royal* funeral as an insignificant prince. Royal funerals are for kings and..." Rosamund paused "... queens."

Then she realized. It was so obvious. Rosamund's face lit up like unbirthday glitter and she smiled a large crescent-moon smile. "Don't you see what this means?"

Madame Diamond blinked at her.

"It's the Queen of Spades. I'll finally get her head. The party is what I'll be doing beforehand, and then...and then, we'll have a most glorious funeral unlike anything Gardenia City has ever seen. Oh yes, I'll make quite a show of it. Something everyone will be talking about. You know,"Rosamund said, sitting back, "for a fortune-teller, you're not very perceptive."

Madame Diamond bristled. "All interpretations are interpreted by those hearing the interpretations—as a matter of interpretation."

Rosamund ignored her and kept talking. "But if I am to have a royal funeral, that would mean I gave up Milkyam and Peatown. I suppose I must have, if the spirits are showing it."

"The future isn't set in dough," Madame Diamond said, putting the teacup away.

Rosamund snapped her fingers. "I know what I'll do. I'll *pretend* to give that arrogant House of Clubs Milkyam and Peatown and, when they're not looking, I'll snatch them back up again. All's fair in games and politics, they say."

"If you say so, Your Majesty."

"I do say so. Sometimes, my own brilliance surprises me," she said, standing up.

Rosamund rushed over to the contract and dipped her quill in ink. She scrawled her signature with three hearts over the top. When she had finished, she hurried to the door, forgetting all about Madame Diamond and the skeleton, and ran down the hall.

She found Marco Polo canoodling with two young female eggs, clanking their shells against him in a nook. He licked his lips as he eyed them—no doubt with inappropriate thoughts of scrambling on his mind.

Rosamund cleared her throat. "Ahem."

Marco Polo glanced up and nearly cracked himself as he rolled upwards.

"Your Majesty," he said. "I didn't see you there."

She shoved the contract underneath his nose. "It's signed."

Marco Polo reached out for it, but she held it over his head. "Now wait a minute. You'll have to promise me something first."

"Anything ... and what I mean by anything is anything I can do within the limited powers given to me by the House of Clubs."

"I want the Queen of Spades' head."

Marco Polo took the contract out of Rosamund's hands. "Oh, well then, in that case you will have it." He chuckled a deep, yoke-curdling laugh. "You most certainly will."

Chapter 38
Alice
House of Hearts, Wonderland
Calla Lilly 61, Year of the Queen

Something snapped in Alice's head the moment the White Rabbit died—although it wasn't so much of a snap, but more like a bubblegum pop.

Alice didn't move, not even when the Queen turned to leave. All she could do was stare down at the White Rabbit's headless body. Her stomach twisted, but she didn't feel sick. Her eyes watered, but she didn't cry. Her heart thumped, but it didn't break.

Something was missing deep inside, something that made Alice…Alice.

Thomas hugged her and she folded into his embrace. This time though, she was the first one to pull away. A part of her did want to stay with him, but another part wanted to go. She wasn't ready to share her grief. She needed to be alone with it first.

"Are you going to be alright?" Thomas asked.

"I think so," she said, giving him a brave smile. "I should go and change."

"I understand," Thomas said, rubbing her shoulder. "Will I see you at supper?"

"Yes," Alice said. "I'll see you then."

Alice somehow made it to her room and slid into bed. The lumpy mattress molded around her body, and she buried herself under the covers. Sleep begged to take her, and she wandered in and out of consciousness as images bounced behind her closed eyelids. Over and over, she saw the White Rabbit place his head on the block, the executioner raise his axe, and then the White Rabbit's head tumbling down. It replayed in that sequence as if stuck on some perverse loop.

Ralph hadn't stolen the jewels or murdered Mary Lou, so why would he say he did? She could think of only one thing: he had wanted to save her. He gave his life to protect her as he'd promised he'd do. Alice's heart cracked into a million pieces like a shattered stick of rock candy. How could she ever repay him? What could she possibly do for Ralph after what he had ultimately done for her?

Alice sniffed, blinked, and then blinked again.

There was *one* thing he'd wanted above all else: the death of the Queen of Hearts. If Ralph could give his life for Alice, then there was only one way to make sure he didn't die in vain. Alice would kill the Queen herself. This time, there would be no shying away from it, no doubts, no wondering, and no what ifs.

She'd need to let Bill and Lillian in on her decision so that they could get a plan in motion. Alice pulled back the covers, shocked to see that dusk had already fallen. She must have slept, although she couldn't remember doing so. Her back ached, and her eyes felt as if pebbles dangled from her eyelashes, but she forced herself to get up. The Queen was probably wondering where she was, but she didn't care. She had plans to plot. Alice called for Lillian, but she wasn't in the bedchamber. By now, everyone was probably in the dining hall. Lillian included.

Alice quickly washed and dressed. She opened the door and stepped out as if she didn't have a care in the world, as if it didn't matter to her that the White Rabbit had died. Alice headed down the hall and was passing the Queen's old bedchambers, when she heard:

"Psst."

Alice stopped, her heart racing. She hadn't expected anyone to be in the hallway, not when the entire palace was feasting. A white-gloved hand beckoned her from the Queen's door.

A voice whispered, "Over here."

Alice glanced over her shoulder. She felt uneasy, as if she were being watched by hidden eyes. Was she being set up? She moved towards the figure.

"Alice?" a woman's voice asked. "You're Alice, right?"

"Yes," Alice said, curious. "I'm she. Do I know you?"

The gloved hand coiled around Alice's wrist and yanked her inside. Alice didn't have time to gasp before the door shut behind her. Everything in the Queen's room was the same: the fireplace, the poker, and the Queen's chair where she'd been cowering that night when Alice had heard her screams.

The woman took off her cloak, revealing a gown of sparkling white with a single rose pinned on her breast. Her brown hair was pulled back into a knot at the base of her neck. Familiar green eyes bore into Alice with a gentle firmness.

"I've seen you before," Alice said. "I saw you with the Queen the night of the bomb."

"I am Madame Diamond," she said, bowing her head. "I am the Queen's secret advisor. You must come with me quickly; the windows have ears here."

Madame Diamond turned, but Alice remained motionless. She didn't know if she should run out the door or follow her. What could the Queen's secret advisor want with *her?* Did she know what Alice was planning? She was a fortune-teller after all. It all seemed so suspicious, and after the morning Alice had, she had a right to be skittish.

"If you cared for Ralph," Madame Diamond said, "you'll come with me now."

The mention of the White Rabbit's name sent a jolt through Alice. Despite her misgivings, her feet trailed behind Madame Diamond, her loyalty to Ralph pushing her to act.

Madame Diamond went into the Queen's closet and disappeared inside. Alice heard the jingle of keys and the creak of wood. When the madame reappeared, she was holding a lantern. "Here, take this," she said and gave the light to Alice. "There's a staircase in the back. You need to go in first, so I can lock the door behind us."

Alice tried to peer around Madame Diamond to see the door, but it was frightfully dark in the closet. What if there wasn't a staircase, but a giant hole, and Madame Diamond planned to push her in? Alice didn't know anything about her. Maybe the madame was using Ralph in order to ambush her and this wasn't about him at all.

Madame Diamond motioned her forwards. "We can't linger," she said, looking around. "Especially not here."

Alice took a breath and slipped inside the closet, holding the lantern up. She hadn't gone far when she found the door and right behind it was a staircase, just as Madame Diamond said. She had only taken a few steps down before she heard the door lock behind her. Her stomach dropped. It had been a trap. Alice turned to go pounding to be let out and nearly collided into Madame Diamond.

"Allow me," she said and took the lantern.

They circled down a spiraling staircase until they stopped at another door. This one was covered in locks. Regular ones, some in the shape of triangles, and others that didn't look like locks at all. Madame Diamond went through each one until the door finally opened.

Madame Diamond set the lantern down on a table and went around the room, lighting candles until the space was ablaze in light. As Alice's eyes adjusted, shelves stuffed with cakes, cookies, and vials materialized along every inch of wall space and filled every table and chair. She stepped closer to one of the shelves and glanced at a nearly empty bottle labeled "Disappearing Juice" in an elegant, uppercase script. She recognized the writing immediately. Alice gasped and turned to Madame Diamond. "It was you."

Madame Diamond raised an eyebrow. "Me? Whatever do you mean?"

"You're the one who left the 'drink me' bottle on the table when I first came to Wonderland and"—Alice gazed about the room—"and the cake and the mushroom, they're all here."

Madame Diamond grinned. "Those were from my early days. The concoctions I have now are much better—although the classics are still effective."

"You gave Ralph the potion to shrink me, to help me get back to Wonderland."

"Is that what he used it for?" she asked. "He never did tell me."

Alice shook her head. She didn't understand. Why would Madame Diamond be helping Ralph? Did she know what he was really doing?

Madame Diamond moved a box of chocolates from a chair and directed Alice to sit. She went to a cupboard and took out two teacups and a teapot. She set one of the cups before Alice. It had flakes of diamonds embedded in the silver porcelain that twinkled in the candlelight. It was nothing like the usual hearts-and-roses design she'd grown so accustomed to seeing.

Alice picked it up. "How beautiful."

"You like it?" Madame Diamond asked. "It's a traditional set from the House of Diamonds. Every household has one like it, and the tea isn't so bad either. The House of Hearts has the most dreadful brew. It's a wonder they're not all sick. Granted, some would argue that they are."

She poured Alice some tea and her nose filled with the scent of blackberries and spices. She took a sip and closed her eyes, savoring the richness over her tongue.

"Sugar?" Madame Diamond asked.

"Yes, thank you."

Madame Diamond dropped a sugar cube in Alice's cup. Alice stirred and asked, "Is that where you're from? The House of Diamonds?"

"I'm going to let you in on a secret, Alice," she said. "I'm a *spy* from the House of Diamonds under order to dethrone the Queen of Hearts in any way possible. Ralph was my contact."

"You can't be serious."

"Very," she said. "I know all about the Aboveground Organization and their mission. Ralph and I had similar interests, but he didn't always tell me everything. He didn't tell me he was bringing you to Wonderland, for instance. I suppose you were Plan Y if the Papal Bull didn't do the job. He was such a clever rabbit."

Madame Diamond's chin quivered a moment. She stared down at her cup and took a breath as if to steady herself. "Anyway, I have other ways of summoning information."

She got up and brought back a stack of cards. She slowly fanned them across the table in an arc. "I read the Queen's cards the night before you came and something peculiar happened. They turned blank, but this afternoon, they've changed. Here, see for yourself."

She plucked a card and held it up for Alice to see. Alice jerked backwards, unable to believe what Madame Diamond was showing her, but there it was. It was a picture of herself. In it, she was standing before the Queen, holding something behind her back.

"Before," Madame Diamond said, "you were a shadow. Now, I can see you as clear as a frozen dewdrop. I need to know why."

Her eyes fixed on Alice, waiting for a response.

Madame Diamond leaned towards her. "Ralph isn't here anymore, Alice," she said. "You need to trust someone."

Could she trust Madame Diamond? She wanted to. She had such lovely tea, but she'd just met her. What if this was all an act, and she was really working for the Queen, and once Alice opened her mouth, she could be right back in the tower, awaiting execution?

But she knew if she was going to kill the Queen, she'd need help. There was Lillian, but she clearly despised Alice and thought her useless. Lillian might even blame Alice for what had happened to Ralph. That might explain why she was nowhere to be found. What if Alice was utterly on her own in the House of Hearts?

"I think I know why." Alice glanced at the card. "After Ralph was beheaded, I made up my mind to kill the Queen."

"I see," Madame Diamond said, placing her fingertips together. She didn't bat an eye or shift in her seat. Instead, she got up quietly, went to one of her shelves, and came back carrying something. "May I ask you an unimportant question?"

Alice nodded.

"I assume when Ralph brought you here you pledged an allegiance to the true queen—the Queen of Spades. Have you remained loyal?"

Alice sat straight in her chair. "More now than ever."

"That's good." Madame Diamond smiled. "That's good, indeed. I knew the stars hadn't gone astray when you arrived at court. I had this feeling about you and I've never been wrong. Here." She handed Alice a small red vial with a heart-shaped sticker on it. "If you want to avenge Ralph, you'll need this."

A tiny note attached to the bottle read "Mix me."

"When it's time," Madame Diamond instructed, "make sure you plug your nose because even the smallest of sniffs will cause instant death."

Alice gazed up at her. "It's poison?"

"One of the deadliest," she said, "and if you put it in the Queen's tea, she won't know what happened until she's already placed her slipper in the Undying Lands."

Alice clutched the small bottle. "What will happen to me after she's dead? Ralph said that I'd have everything I wanted when the Queen of Hearts was gone. I want to go home."

"Just leave that to me, Alice," Madame Diamond said. "All you need to concern yourself with is killing the Queen. Once she's gone, Wonderland will finally be free, and yes, my dear, you will have everything you've always wanted. Just like Ralph said you would."

Chapter 39
Rosamund
House of Hearts, Wonderland
Clematis 71, Year of the Queen

Rosamund went into the courtyard to see Marco Polo off. She stood next to him on the palace steps while servants ran to and fro, carrying umbrellas, rugs, and striped inner tubes onto various carts. When everything had been thoroughly packed, including—she happened to notice—several of her royal towels and soaps, Marco Polo's horse was brought before them.

"It looks like it's time for me to depart your lovely house," he said, putting on his fedora. He offered Rosamund his jellied arm. "Would you mind, Your Majesty, assisting me down these stairs?"

She obliged him, expecting it would only be for a moment. They took one cautious step after another and what should have taken a few seconds ballooned into ten minutes. When they finally made it to the last step, he had the audacity to ask for a boost into his egg-carton-shaped saddle.

Once the ambassador was finally settled, Rosamund asked, "How soon will I be notified that all is well and the Queen of Spades is mine?"

Marco Polo wrapped the reins of his horse in his gloved hand and said, "I was informed this morning that the King of Clubs has already petitioned Cecil to lift the Papal Bull. As a show of good faith, I will personally inform you when it's completed and escort the princess into your care."

"Very good," Rosamund said, beaming. "I will watch every day for your banners on the horizon."

Marco Polo took off his fedora. "Until that time, I bid you adieu, Your Majesty."

Rosamund watched the ambassador's procession leave until the very last banner and flag of the House of Clubs disappeared behind the gate—where they belonged. She hummed to herself as she returned to her latest bedchamber, where she had left her lady's maids earlier that morning to arrange her things.

A guard was standing outside the door as she approached, and she ordered, "Fetch the Prince of Hearts. I wish to speak with him immediately."

He bowed his head. "As you wish, Your Majesty."

Rosamund entered the room and sat on her receiving chair, barking directions to Bess, Sabrina, and Alice. No matter how many times she'd changed rooms, she still had to tell them where to put her special things: a framed picture of the first death warrant Rosamund had ever signed, a painting of her posing in her croquet outfit—after all, she was the reigning champion, and a marble statue of her elbow that was done by the famed Monsieur Jacques Lefevre.

Just as she was yelling at Alice, once again, that she liked her headless dolly with the red-gingham dress under her pillow, not on top of it, Thomas entered the room. It didn't escape her notice that Thomas and Alice exchanged a glance.

"There you are," Rosamund said, getting his attention. "I have news for you, Thomas. Oh, I certainly do. But first"—she clapped her hands—"everyone out. That includes you, Bess."

"Me, Your Majesty?" Bess asked, pausing her organization of Rosamund's fork and spoon collection. "But you've never asked me to leave the room. You know how quiet I am. Why, you'd hardly notice I was even here."

Rosamund pointed towards the door. "Out, I say."

"Very well," Bess huffed, dropping a handful of spoons with a clatter before skipping away.

Once the door was closed, Thomas studied Rosamund as if she had inconvenienced him in some way. The boy was certainly getting too big for his britches. As soon as this matter with the Clubs was over, she decided she'd send Thomas on another Wonderland Excursion, maybe a permanent one.

"Yes, Queen Mum?" he asked. "What can be of such unimportance?"

"You are to be married."

Thomas's eyes widened. "Married?"'

"Yes," Rosamund said, "to the Princess of Clubs. It's all settled."

He shook his head. "No. I won't do it. I can't marry her. I—"

"We made a deal," Rosamund said, interrupting him. "You better not be getting hot feet on me now. This was all your brilliant idea after all. You're the one who gave me the letter from the House of Clubs."

"Only because I thought you'd already received it, not because I was serious about marrying the Princess of Clubs."

"It's a little too late to be splitting peas, Thomas," Rosamund snapped. "Don't forget, you said you'd marry the princess if I pardoned Alice."

"You pardoned her because Ralph confessed. Besides, I didn't promise I would marry the Princess of Clubs. I said that I definitely *wouldn't* marry her if you didn't pardon Alice."

Rosamund waved her hands. "That's neither here nor there nor anywhere. The point is, Alice has her head, thanks to me. I could have still done it, you know. I could *still* do it."

Thomas stared at her. She believed she detected genuine fear behind his eyes. Good. Let him be afraid. She'd rather him be afraid than obstinate. Fear made followers, and she needed him to do his part, so she could do hers: execute the Queen of Spades.

"You wouldn't," he said.

Rosamund chuckled. "My goodness, it's as if you don't know me at all. Of course I would."

Thomas held his head in his hands and groaned. "You're not going to give me any sort of a choice, are you?"

"Don't ask such rhetorical questions, Thomas. It's annoying. You know I won't."

"Very well," he said. "Do whatever you like. Just leave Alice out of it. You're not to touch her."

Not to touch her? Why was Thomas so devoted to the girl? If Rosamund hadn't known any better, she would have thought he was in love with her. It couldn't be true, naturally. Thomas always had some new tart on his arm. They came and went so quickly that Rosamund could hardly remember their names. But something was different this time. Red blotches crept along Thomas's cheeks, his downcast eyes stared at nothing, and he rubbed his hand along his lips in a way that made her believe maybe he *did* love Alice.

Rosamund wouldn't allow it. Alice was worse than a tart. She wasn't highborn, lowborn, or any born. The girl wasn't one of them, and she certainly didn't belong with Rosamund's son, and she was going to make sure it stayed that way.

"I wouldn't dream of it, my dear Thomas," Rosamund said, forcing herself to smile. "Now, stop being so glum. The ambassador will be bringing Princess Penelope soon, and I want you to treat her in a manner befitting a princess, not like one of your tarts. You understand?"

"Yes, Queen Mum."

"Good. Now run along and mind yourself. You have a fiancée after all."

Thomas skipped out of the room. When he left, her lady's maids shuffled to their places, including Alice. The girl was a wisp of a thing—lanky hair, lanky bones, lanky look about the face. Nothing worthy of her son. How the girl had even caught Thomas's eye was beyond her. No matter—that was all over now.

As Rosamund daydreamed about Constance's execution, Bess kept glancing up at her, probably expecting Rosamund to tell them all about the conversation with Thomas. Only she wouldn't. She'd let them chew on it for a while. Besides, they'd find out soon enough when Princess Penelope arrived at the palace. She couldn't wait to see Alice crumble when it was announced that Penelope was to be Thomas's bride. The thought warmed her like freshly toasted pinecones. Rosamund had agreed to not behead Alice; she hadn't said anything about not hurting her feelings.

Rosamund gazed about the room. She needed a change, and not simply another bedchamber. She needed something bigger, something to distract her and keep her occupied while she waited for Marco Polo's return. "I've changed my mind," she announced. "I want this all packed up."

Bess's mouth fell open. "We've just brought everything in, Your Majesty. Is the chamber not to your liking? Is there something we can do to make it more comfortable? Maybe a few cobwebs or some rocks under the rug?"

"No," Rosamund scolded. "I don't want anything to make it more comfortable. I want it packed up. I've decided it's time I went on my summer tour."

Sabrina clapped her hands and jumped up and down, squealing like a hamster in a death grip. "Oh, goody, goody."

Bess stared at Rosamund. "The tour?" she asked. "Is it safe, Your Majesty?"

"Yes, perfectly," Rosamund said, eyeing Sabrina, whose legs continued to bounce underneath her in a most unflattering display. "I expect the Papal Bull to be lifted any moment. Come along, let's not dally. I want this all ready to go second thing tomorrow."

"Oh, yes." Sabrina nodded. "Let's get started right away." The girl reached down to pick up a pair of Rosamund's knickers when she suddenly stopped and covered her mouth, eyes wide with astonishment.

Rosamund studied the girl. "Whatever is the matter with you? Don't say it's my knickers because Mary Anne had them freshly laundered."

Instead of answering, Sabrina dropped the undergarment and ran to the privy, where Rosamund could hear the girl retching into the royal chamber pot.

"I never!" She gaped after Sabrina, not sure whether to be stunned or offended. Bess and Alice stood there, watching this all occur and doing little more than twiddling their thumbs. "Open the windows, you dolts," she roared, "and for the love of all that is roses, change that pot. Wasn't there a rat in my employ? That would be a good job for such a repulsive creature." She turned to Alice. "Where is the rat?"

Alice bowed her head. "I'm not sure, Your Majesty."

"Why am I not surprised?" she grumbled. "Don't stand there with your fingers in your ears. Get moving."

While Bess was busy with the windows and Alice with the pot, Rosamund picked up the knickers that had been discarded and gave them a whiff. All she could detect was the intoxicating scent of vinegar and onion slices. She was shoving the undergarment under her arm when Sabrina staggered towards her, holding a cloth at her mouth.

"I should let you know," Rosamund said, "that it is not proper for you to be ill when I haven't given you permission. It's especially inappropriate to be sick and use the queen's chamber pot. My potty is sacred."

Beads of sweat glistened along the girl's forehead. "May I go and rest a while, Your Majesty?" Sabrina asked.

"You can't be sick unless I tell you to be sick and not a second before or after. Have you heard anything I said?"

Sabrina swallowed. "May I be sick?"

Rosamund shrugged. "I suppose, but you can't be too ill. I still need you to help me pack."

Sabrina closed her eyes and swooned. Alice raced to the girl's side, fawning and fretting over her in a way that made Rosamund's stomach gurgle as if she'd drunk too much syrup. She thought she might retch a little too.

"Your Majesty," Alice said. "I think Sabrina is very unwell."

Something in Alice's voice gave her pause. It wasn't so much what she said, but *how* she said it. Ever since Alice arrived at her court, she had been the timid Tina, but none of that was present today. She had become a brand-new Alice who didn't piddle herself every time she came into a room. Rosamund wasn't sure if she liked the change.

"Oh, very well." Rosamund sighed. "I wouldn't want to catch it anyway. Getting the Queen sick is grounds for treason, you know."

Rosamund watched Alice lead Sabrina out the door—Sabrina did, indeed, appear unwell. Perhaps she shouldn't have been so harsh, but Sabrina vexed her. Or was it the memory of Sabrina's mother that made her so vexed? The woman Pedro had chosen over her, whom he'd married in secret while pretending to love her, calling her Rosebud when no one was listening. The whole while, he had a wife and child tucked away in Lake Town. As far as Rosamund was concerned, vexed was vexed when it came to Sabrina, and that was a good enough reason to not be pleasant.

"I bet it's nothing but a toe ache," Bess said. "It serves her right. Every time I see Lady Sabrina, she's always stuffing her face with something—tarts, cakes, bread, and jam. Quite the little oinker she's become. Why, if I didn't know any better..."

"What?" Rosamund asked.

"Nothing," Bess said, narrowing her eyes. "Just me thinking without being told to."

Chapter 40
Alice
House of Hearts, Wonderland
Clematis 71, Year of the Queen

Alice thought of Lillian as she helped Sabrina back to the room. Where had she gone off to? It didn't matter, she supposed, since she didn't need her anymore. Madame Diamond had given her everything she needed to finish what Ralph had started, and the fewer who knew, the better. But, still, it was as if Lillian had disappeared.

Sabrina clung to Alice as they walked along the halls. It was the first time they'd been alone since Alice had been pardoned and Ralph executed. When Alice had returned from her meeting with Madame Diamond, she'd seen the faint glow of candlelight coming from under Sabrina's door and thought about knocking. She nearly had, but she hadn't been ready to talk to Sabrina. She hadn't forgotten her silence when the Queen accused her. At the time, Alice had thought it was because Sabrina had something to do with it. A part of her still wondered—since it must be somebody who'd done it—but the idea of Sabrina setting her up didn't feel right. Perhaps Sabrina had been too frightened to speak, only it hadn't stopped her from coming to Alice's defense before. These were all questions that Alice hadn't been ready to hear the answers to yet. So she had tiptoed away, deciding it would be best if Sabrina assumed she'd been sleeping in her room the entire time.

Now, Sabrina rolled her head against Alice's shoulder. "I'm so glad you're here," she said. "These last two days have been dreadful. When those horrible guards led you away, I couldn't stop crying. I think I might have cried myself sick."

"Everything is going to be alright," Alice said, reassuring her as they made their way down the hallway. "We're almost there."

After opening the door to their chamber, they veered to the left towards Sabrina's bedroom. The air inside was stale with old breath and spoiled food. Gowns and petticoats had been abandoned on the floor in mountainous heaps and tossed over chairs and hung lopsided from hangers in the closet. Empty and half-empty perfume bottles, pieces of crumpled paper, and goblets with crusted rims lay strewn across her dressing table and the floor.

Alice stepped over a blackened banana peel as she helped Sabrina into bed, where autographed portraits of a group called Mice to Men were pinned to the wall directly above it. As soon as Sabrina was settled, Alice opened the window, feeling the cool air against her cheeks and inhaling the scent of roses from the garden. She involuntarily glanced down. Over to the right, she found the spot where the bushes had been hacked away to expose Mary Lou's body—right under Alice's window, as they had said.

Sabrina moaned behind her, and Alice found a jug of water and a glass. She held up the glass to the light; it looked clean enough.

"No water," Sabrina said. "I need to eat something. I'll feel better when I do."

"I'll grab you something from the kitchen."

"There's no need. I have some jam in the cupboard over there," Sabrina said, pointing to the corner.

Alice stumbled over a cloak and a few pillows but managed to find the cupboard. She retrieved the jar and handed it to Sabrina, who flung off the lid. Sabrina dug her fingers into the strawberry preserves and plopped them into her mouth in loose dollops. Bits of jelly slid down her jaw and onto her pillow. When she had finished, Sabrina dropped the jar and closed her eyes, sighing under her breath. Alice reached over and touched Sabrina's forehead; it was clammy and feverish.

"I'm going to get a doctor," Alice said, getting up.

Sabrina gripped Alice's hand. "No, please don't."

"Whyever not? You're not well. What if there's something wrong?"

Sabrina loosened the sash around her middle. "I don't have anything I won't recover from eventually."

"Don't be silly," Alice said. "I'll be gone but a minute. It's better to be safe than sorry."

"You can't get the doctor," Sabrina said, struggling to get up. "He'll tell her. He'll tell the Queen..."

Alice turned back to Sabrina. "Tell her what?"

"He'll tell her I'm with child."

Alice's mouth opened. "With child? How?"

Sabrina groaned. "Oh, you know *how*."

"That's not what I meant," Alice said, a little annoyed. "How could this happen?"

"It's a little too late to worry about that." Sabrina leaned her head against the cushioned bed frame. "It's the Queen I worry about. If she finds out, she'll behead me for sure this time."

Alice touched the vial of poison that she kept hidden in her bodice. "I won't let that happen, Sabrina."

"How would you stop it?" she wailed. "There is no reasoning with the Queen, and she already hates me. This is all she needs—it'll be the needle that broke the record stack. I don't care so much for myself." She ran her hand across her belly. "I care for my wee one. My babe is innocent. Just like I was."

Alice stared at Sabrina, imagining her belly growing bigger and the Queen's temper growing with it. Maybe with enough gowns and undergarments, Sabrina could hide her condition. But for how long? She couldn't hide a crying baby. "You have to leave the House of Hearts. You should go immediately."

"I've thought of that," Sabrina said, wiping her eyes with a lacy sock. "I thought of going to my mother in the House of Diamonds, but if the Queen of Hearts catches me, or the Queen of Diamonds doesn't let me stay, then I'll be beheaded for treason on the spot, whether or not I'm with child."

Alice wondered if Madame Diamond could help Sabrina escape. Maybe she would do it as a favor to Alice. Next chance she had, she'd find out, but she didn't want to tell Sabrina about Madame Diamond and get her hopes up.

Sabrina whimpered.

"What about the father?" Alice asked. "Can he help protect you?"

"Him?" Sabrina snorted. "That worm. He's too worried about ruining his chances with the Queen. The whole time... the whole time I thought he loved me. That stupid, STUPID William de Fleur!"

Alice's mouth gaped. "William de Fleur? The Mad Hatter? No..."

"He hates it when people call him that, but that's what he is," she said, smiling. "A mad hatter."

"What were you thinking? Of all the men, why *him?*"

Sabrina shrugged. "I didn't care for William at first, but he was sweet and kind, and I thought he was different. But why does it matter? He was only using me to get...to get... Oh, I'm not supposed to tell."

"To get what?"

"He'd get frightfully angry if he found out you knew," Sabrina said, chewing her lip, "especially since you ended up in the tower because of it."

Alice grabbed Sabrina's wrist and squeezed until the girl flinched. "I didn't *just* end up in the tower. I was also nearly beheaded. Whatever it is, tell me. Right now."

Sabrina pulled her hand away and rubbed it. "If I do, you mustn't get upset."

Alice crossed her arms, not saying a word.

"Very well. I suppose I deserve that." Sabrina took a breath. "Willy... he...well, he asked me to steal the Queen's jewels."

Alice stared at Sabrina with both surprise and horror. "*You* took the Queen's jewels?"

"Only for him. I would never have done so if I had known what he was going to do with them, I swear it."

It was too much. Not only had the Mad Hatter tried and almost succeeded in getting her executed, but he'd done so with the aid of her friend. Now she knew why Sabrina wouldn't look at her. She had known the whole time that Alice was innocent and said nothing. Not even when the guards had led Alice away to be executed. Or when she was being taken down to the block. If it hadn't been for Ralph, Sabrina would have kept silent even after Alice was dead.

"How could you?" Alice seethed.

Sabrina's eyes filled with tears. "I said you mustn't get upset."

"I don't care what you said." Alice pushed over a stack of leaflets with *Gardenia Daily Gossip* splashed across the front. She marched over discarded shoes and boxes of tarts as she made her way to the door. "I never want to speak to you again."

"Wait," Sabrina called. "Please don't go. I didn't know he'd put them in your room. Honest I didn't."

Alice brought her hand to the doorknob. "But you didn't say anything either. You could have told them I was innocent. You could have stopped..." Now it was Alice's turn to feel the sting of tears, but she refused to cry.

"Please, Alice," Sabrina begged. "I was scared. I went to Willy as soon as you were taken away. I told him I'd tell the Queen what he'd done, what we had done, but he said the Queen would never believe me over her own cousin. He said he'd make sure I was beheaded too, if I told. I was frantic. So... so..."

"What did you do, Sabrina?" Alice growled.

She swallowed. "I went to Ralph. I knew that you two were friends. I thought he could help, and I told him about Willy and what he made me do. Ralph told me not to worry, that he'd take care of everything. He'd make sure we were both safe. I didn't think he'd take the blame for it."

"Well, he did," Alice said. She thought of the vial. Maybe she'd save some for the Hatter. She could think of no other person who deserved it more at that moment, not even the Queen. "And now Ralph's dead," she continued, "and I'm sure your sweet William also was the one who killed Mary Lou."

"Oh no," Sabrina said and shook her head. "He wouldn't have done that. Willy couldn't actually hurt anyone."

"Stop defending him," Alice growled. "He's the reason Ralph is dead. He's the reason *I* almost died. Not hurt anyone? He already has."

Sabrina fell silent and wrapped her fingers in the tassels of a pillow. "You're right. I'm sorry. I truly am. Please tell me you'll still be my friend. I would never have done that to you on purpose. He was using me. I see that now. He never cared for me, and I wish I'd never given him the time of night."

Alice still stood next to the door, ready to walk out and leave Sabrina behind, never to talk to her again. She didn't know why she was hesitating. Maybe it was because Sabrina stared up at her with the sorriest face: cheeks glistening with tears, eyes red from shedding them. Alice knew she hadn't done it intentionally, and if it hadn't been for Sabrina, Ralph would never have come in time to save her. "I'm not sure if I forgive you," Alice said, "but I won't leave. Not yet anyway."

Sabrina sighed. "I'll prove to you that you can trust me. You'll see. You're my only friend here."

For better or for worse, she was Alice's only friend too.

Alice said, "If we are to remain friends, then you have to tell me why William wanted me beheaded. No more secrets. We must trust each other."

"You're right. No more secrets," Sabrina said as she wiped her nose on her sheet. "Except I don't know why. Willy's always talking about the throne and how much he wants it. He's obsessed, really. What in Wonderland could possibly be so amazing about that chair?"

Alice stopped and looked at Sabrina, her eyes wide. "Isn't it obvious? It's not the throne itself. He wants to be the King of Hearts."

"Willy?" Sabrina sniffed. "You think so?"

"What other reason could there be? He must have a claim to it in some way, some right to succession. Unless things are different here in Wonderland?"

"Let me see." Sabrina tapped her chin. "If the Queen of Hearts was no longer the Queen of Hearts, then the throne would go to the Prince of Hearts, as long as he can recite the alphabet backwards. I've heard he practices every morning, so that shouldn't be an issue. If he couldn't though, then it would go to the Queen of Spades, but she's going to get beheaded any second, they say."

"And if she's no longer around?"

"Well." Sabrina let out a long breath. "I suppose Willy, as the Queen's cousin, would be next in line, although I can't be certain. There could be some sort of rule I don't know about. Throne-ology was never my strongest subject."

Alice felt the hairs on her arm stand up. It was starting to make sense. She could hardly believe that anything in Wonderland would, but this did. The Hatter was after the throne, that much was certain, but why have Alice executed? If the Hatter knew what she was up to—that she was there to kill the Queen—he would be helping Alice, not trying to get her out of the way.

There must be a reason. As she thought about it, Alice paced about the room, sidestepping gowns, cushions, and empty goblets with Mice to Men etched on them. The Hatter must think she had some claim to the throne, but she didn't. None whatsoever. Unless she married into it.

If she married the prince.

Alice's pulse raced. Was that it? Did the Hatter honestly think that Alice had a chance of marriage to the prince? It was absurd. The most ridiculous notion ever. Thomas had wanted to be friends, nothing more, and the Hatter was *mad* after all, but the thought of it...the thought of something more with the prince made Alice dizzy.

No. She shook her head. She couldn't let her emotions get the better of her. She had to be reasonable, and thinking that Thomas would want to marry her was far from that. Besides, the Hatter hadn't wanted Alice anywhere close to the Queen the moment she came back to Wonderland; he'd objected straightaway to her becoming a lady's maid. There must be another reason he wanted her dead.

Then she had a thought.

Alice took a step towards Sabrina. "I need you to tell me what happened to the last lady's maid who stole the Queen's jewels *before* she was beheaded."

"Oh, her?" Sabrina leaned back into her pillow. "Her name was Lady Godiva. She had a funny thing about clothes—she never wanted to wear them. Nobody knew where Godiva came from. Some say she stepped out of the fog one day and there she was. The oystermen who found her didn't know what to do with her, so they brought her to court. The Queen wanted Godiva out of her sight; she found her refusal for clothing undignified, but..." Sabrina paused, her eyes widening. "You know, it was Ralph who proposed the idea of her staying on as a lady's maid. Just as he did with you. Isn't that odd?"

Alice's chest tightened as if there weren't enough air in the room. It could have been a coincidence, but it was too similar—Godiva's sudden appearance in Wonderland and Ralph helping her get into the Queen's court. Had Ralph recruited her and brought her here? Was Godiva in the Aboveground too? Alice's thoughts swam, drowning in one horrible realization: she hadn't been the first. How many others had there been? What happened to them?

"Was Thomas here when Lady Godiva was beheaded?" Alice asked in almost a whisper.

"Actually"—Sabrina pursed her lips—"he was sent away before that. There were some rumors that he fancied Lady Godiva, but then again, so did a lot of men."

"Fancied her?" Alice's heart dropped into her stomach like a stone in a pond. She shouldn't be upset about who Thomas desired. She had no right to be, but she couldn't help it.

Sabrina shrugged. "I don't know if it was true or not. They'd been seen in the garden together, but that doesn't mean anything. Lots of people go in the garden."

Alice knew Sabrina was trying to make her feel better, but she had no doubt that Thomas had led Lady Godiva to the same secret place he'd taken Alice. She could see it all in her mind: them sitting on the bench under the cherry blossom tree, talking about wherever Godiva was from, and Thomas asking if they could be friends—as he'd done with her. Alice felt like a half-wit for believing she was special, as if maybe she were different.

Sabrina said, "It was a rumor, nothing more."

"It's fine, honestly. Just tell me about the stolen jewels. Did you take them for the Hatter then too?"

Sabrina shook her head. "We barely even spoke to each other back then. He must have been doing it himself. Come to think of it, he was spending a lot of time in the Queen's rooms, but I thought it was because he also fancied Lady Godiva."

"Where were the jewels found?"

"Oh my goodness," Sabrina gasped, bringing her hands to her cheeks. "They were discovered in Lady Godiva's room. You don't think Willy had anything to do with that as well, do you?"

Alice nodded. "I'm certain of it."

"I always thought there was something strange about what happened," Sabrina said. "I mean why wear jewelry and not clothes?"

Because it wasn't about that. The Mad Hatter had disposed of Lady Godiva in the same way he'd tried to do with Alice. He must know about the Aboveground. Why else would he scheme to rid the palace of its members? It would have made complete sense except for one thing: the Queen was the biggest obstacle to the throne. Wouldn't the Hatter want the Aboveground to get rid of her, so he could be one step closer to taking it?

Alice sighed. No matter how close she felt she was getting to the truth, it always seemed further away. Something was missing—some crucial piece. Did the Hatter want the throne, or was he protecting the Queen? It couldn't be both, could it? She wondered what Madame Diamond would think, and at her next opportunity, she was going to discuss it with her. Maybe the cards had the answer.

Until then, there were only two things Alice knew. Either, one she was in danger because she was still a member of the Aboveground, or two, Thomas was in danger because he was next in line for the throne. The Hatter had already tried to get rid of Alice. Was Thomas next?

Chapter 41
Rosamund
House of Hearts, Wonderland
Hydrangea 81, Year of the Queen

Rosamund couldn't sleep that night. She had too many things to be excited about. First, the tour and, second, the Queen of Spade's head—though not necessarily in that particular order. Whenever she thought of tomorrow and then the next tomorrow and then the next, her legs jumped under the covers like a child on the Eve of Heartsmas.

As the hours marched by, Rosamund tossed and turned. She flopped and flapped. She counted chickens, then fish, and then elephants, but nothing worked. She rang for Bess at least twenty times: to get her pillow flattened, her blankets retucked and then untucked, and finally after Bess had brought her a warm glass of salt water, she started to drift off. Just as she was nearly good and asleep, she felt something cold press into her cheek.

Her eyes snapped open.

Pedro's bloody stump hovered inches away from her. "Hullo, Rosebud," he said. "Did you think you could hide from us forever?"

Rosamund shrieked and pushed his head away. It whirled in the air, slamming into Thomas. "How'd you find me?" she demanded. "I've been careful. I've changed rooms."

Thomas glanced over at Pedro. "Let's say a little grasshopper told us."

"Which little grasshopper?" Rosamund demanded. "You must tell me at once so I can have it beheaded."

Thomas ignored her request and, instead, shook his stump at her. "Honestly, Rosie, *hiding?* That would hurt my feelings—if I could feel anything, that is."

"What do you want?" she asked them. "Revenge? Well, you're not going to get it." Rosamund grabbed the mallet for her gong. "I'm leaving this instant, and this time, I'm going to make certain that you never find me again."

Pedro said, "I wouldn't do that if I were you."

"And whyever not?"

"Because you might be able to run away from us, but you can't run from them."

Rosamund stopped. "Them? What sort of nonsense are you talking about?"

Thomas jerked his head towards the curtain. "See for yourself."

Rosamund slowly sat up, still gripping the mallet, and moved the fabric aside. Her eyes bulged as a sea of heads swam through her room, bouncing into each other. As soon as they saw her, they began moaning in a cacophony that sounded as if they were calling her name. Hundreds of bloody stumps, hundreds of vacant eyes searching for her. Her hand trembled as she covered her mouth and stared at faces both strange and familiar. "Is that...is that...Colonel Mustard of Custard Cathedral? I haven't seen him for ages—"

"And Bishop Newmark," Thomas said, "and the Sire of Pemberknee and everyone else you've beheaded. They are all here and accounted for."

Rosamund shut the curtain, silencing the howling. She crossed her arms and glared at Thomas and Pedro. "You two are behind this, aren't you? Are they going to hover there all night? Because I need my rest. I doubt I'll get a blink of sleep while they wail and carry on, so tell them to shove off."

Pedro smiled. "Not this time, Rosebud. Like you said, it's revenge we are all after. Our blood is on your feet, and we're not going to rest until your head is with us."

Rosamund pulled her blankets up to her chin. "You wouldn't dare."

"We would," Thomas said, "and, just now, the only thing stopping those heads from coming to claim yours is us. Come to think of it, we should probably scurry out of their way, don't you think, Pedro?"

Pedro puckered his bruised lips. "I suppose we could wait a tad longer if..."

Rosamund sat up. "If what?"

"If you do something for us," he said.

"What can you possibly want? You're both dead."

A lock of Thomas's white hair fell over his eye as he turned towards her. Out of habit, she wanted to flick it out of the way. "We want you to clear our names," Thomas said to her. "We want you to tell everyone we weren't traitors."

Rosamund's mouth dropped. "I can't do that. That's impossible."

"Then I suppose you haven't given us much choice."

Thomas whistled.

Rosamund felt a shift in the air. Something was happening outside her bed curtains, and she was too terrified to discover what it was. She stared at the embroidered roses and hearts on the canopy above her. She held her breath. The curtains bulged—they were small bumps at first, like the bubbles in a pot being brought to boil, but then they grew into chins, noses, and gaping mouths pummeling and pressing against the fabric. Rosamund screamed and brought her knees to her chest, trying to make herself as small as possible. The heads surrounded her, throwing themselves against the curtains. As long as they held, she'd be safe, but then she heard fabric tearing. They were chewing through the canopy.

"Make them stop," Rosamund shrieked. "I'll consider your request if you make those dreadful heads stop."

Just like that, everything became silent. No moaning, no thumping. The curtains settled as if nothing had happened. If Thomas and Pedro weren't still hovering above her, she might have thought she'd imagined it.

"Are you ready to agree to our terms?" Thomas asked.

Rosamund grasped for something to say—something to argue—if merely to stall another onslaught of bloody stumps. "Why all this bother?" she asked with a nervous laugh. "What does it really matter if I tell everyone you weren't traitors? It won't change anything."

"It changes everything," Thomas said. "I don't want my son thinking his father was a traitor."

Rosamund waved her hand. "Come now, Thomas. Are we really going to split peas over a label?"

Pedro faced her. "What about me? You took my property along with my head when you convicted me of treason, under the Being-a-Traitor Fee and Subsequent Penalties clause."

"Well, that isn't my rule," Rosamund said. "That's been around since the House of Hearts first existed. You can't very well hold that against me."

Pedro said, "But my lands in Lake Town would be reinstated if I didn't have *Traitor* over my gravestone, and my wife and daughter, who is no better than one of your prisoners, wouldn't be without home or hearth, now would they?"

"Prisoner?" Rosamund laughed. "That girl has nowhere to go. Her own mother doesn't want her. Believe me, I've tried to send her to the Diamonds. She'd be one less weight around my ankle if she did go, but that woman refuses to claim her. So what did I do? I gave Sabrina a home and a station, not that she much deserves it."

Pedro was silent.

"And, yes, let's talk about that property of yours," she glared up at him. "Who gave you those lands? That's right. I did. It was supposed to be our… Oh, what does the past matter now? Besides, this isn't about your wife and daughter. This is about you. It was always about you, so don't try getting noble on me now."

"How can I be noble?" he asked. "I'm a head."

"See, what did I say? *All* about you."

"Rosebud—"

"Stop calling me that, Pedro!" Rosamund yelled. "You may never call me that again."

"Don't pretend you don't still care for me," he said. "You're still wearing the locket I got for you."

Rosamund yanked the necklace off and threw it.

Even after all that time, the sting of Pedro's betrayal felt as raw as the day she'd received the anonymous letter saying that her faithful Pedro hadn't been so faithful. When she first met Pedro, she was a new queen. He had come to her requesting to become a knight for the House of Hearts. A true knight, as in the days of old, defending the strong and tossing the weak. He had holes in his breeches and two crumpets to his name. When he went on one knee, swearing that she'd always be his one true lady, she knighted him right then and called him Pedro the Faithful.

As time passed, something of a love grew between them. Slowly, at first. Rosamund had been engaged to Thomas, after all, but it didn't stop Pedro from leaving her little notes wrapped around rose stems or lightly brushing her hand with his thumb when they were close. She found herself thinking more and more of Pedro and making excuses to be in his company, until they became inseparable.

She stopped hiding her feelings for Pedro from her advisors and even from Thomas, who fought for her attentions. He didn't stand a chance though—Pedro had her wrapped around his finger as tight as a fiddler's string. It was Pedro's guidance that helped her be the queen she was today. He encouraged her to be severe, to take on her oppressors with no mercy. She didn't have the stomach back then for beheadings, but he taught her how to use other means to get rid of plotters, usurpers, and general no-gooders. The Lost Woods was his favorite method, but then Pedro always had a flair for getting rid of people and creatures that Rosamund never wanted to see again.

Her advisors hated him. They did everything they could to drive a wedge between her and Pedro, but Rosamund had been blinded by passion, even willing to give up the throne to be with him. What did she care about ruling the Hearts when her own led her in another direction? Then one afternoon, as she was packing her things for Lake Town, she received the letter about his little side dish. Instead of running away with Pedro, she had him beheaded. He was her first, and Rosamund kept his death warrant as a reminder of what happened when she let her guard down.

Tonight would be no exception.

"What's your decision?" Thomas asked. "We need to know. Will you clear our names?"

Rosamund put her nose in the air. "I'll have to think about it. It isn't that simple. How can my people trust me if they think I've beheaded innocent people?"

"But you have," Thomas said.

"That is a matter of interpretation," she said, "especially in his case." She jutted her chin towards Pedro.

"But I wasn't a traitor," Thomas said, coming closer. "You know I wasn't. I was loyal to you—"

"Certainly you were," Rosamund said, interrupting him. "Don't think I've forgotten all those tarts you had before me. Your son is like you, you know. Chasing tarts wherever he goes."

Thomas puffed out his cheeks. "It's always been you. From the first moment I saw you. Always. What would it take to prove that to you once and for all?"

"It's simple, really." Rosamund shrugged. "Keep the heads away and I'll know you're loyal."

"You know I can't do that," he said, "but what if we could sour the deal a little?"

Rosamund gazed up at him. "Go on..."

"How about this?" Thomas glanced over at Pedro. "You tell everyone we weren't traitors, and we'll tell you who the real traitors are. How's that for loyalty?"

"You're heads," she said with a shrug. "What do *you* know about anything? I bet you're just trying to trick me."

"Is that so?" Thomas raised his eyebrows or tried to anyway. "Hickory Dickory Dock."

Rosamund nearly tumbled out of bed at the sound of those words.

"See?" Pedro said. "We know a lot more than you think."

Rosamund argued with Thomas and Pedro almost all night. No matter how much she insisted that, even in death, it was their duty to tell her who the traitors were, they refused to do so until she cleared their names.

She must have fallen asleep mid-argument, because she woke to broad daylight, with someone pushing her.

"You swore an oath," Rosamund grumbled.

"I did, Your Majesty," she heard Bess say, "but you still must get up. It's already 7:37 am."

"I don't give one tickly feather what time it is," she groaned, turning back on her pillow. "Come back later."

"Everyone is getting ready to leave."

"Leave?" Rosamund's eyes popped open. "Leave where?"

"On the summer tour."

"They can't leave without me," Rosamund said, throwing the covers aside. "It's my tour."

"I am aware, Your Majesty," she said. "I tried telling them."

Rosamund got out of bed, feeling an ache in her knees and back. "Well, why are you standing there, gawking at me? Get me my gown, wig, and powder. Where are Sabrina and Alice?"

"Here, Your Majesty," Sabrina said, coming into the room with the morning grounds. "Mary Anne is busy loading your pet porcupine, so I thought I'd bring your breakfast."

"And Alice?" Rosamund asked.

"She's collecting your wigs. All the auburn ones. I know they're your favorite when you're on a tour."

Sabrina set the tray before her. Rosamund thought of Pedro's ridiculous comment. His daughter a prisoner? Please. She stuffed a forkful of jellied tuna and gravy into her mouth. "I see you're looking better today," she said to Sabrina. "I must say, yesterday, you were quite ghastly."

"Thank you, Your Majesty," Sabrina said. "I do feel better. Right as sleet, I'd say."

Rosamund eyed the girl as she chewed. "Bess is right… You have put on a pat of weight, now haven't you? Lose it immediately. I can't have a whale in my company, now can I? If I did, there'd be plenty to choose from at Redwater Harbor."

Sabrina bowed her head. "Yes, Your Majesty."

"With all that weight," Rosamund said, nodding, "I'd say you were positively glowing. Shameful."

Sabrina's face was awash with pink as she skipped away. It served the girl right. She should be embarrassed for letting herself go like that. The nerve of it. After all, Rosamund had to be seen with her. Didn't Sabrina even think about that?

Rosamund pushed aside the rest of her breakfast and shoved a handful of her morning grounds under her lip. As Bess and Sabrina busied themselves around the room, she kept glancing over at the bed where she'd spent the night with Thomas and Pedro. With the sunlight shining on the carpet and the bustle of activity, it felt almost as if it had been a dream, something she'd made up. Only the dangling threads from the hole chewed in the canopy told her it wasn't. If that was real, then what Thomas and Pedro knew about the traitors in her house was as well.

It bothered her not knowing who the traitors were. Bothered her to the core. Almost enough to give in to their request—almost, but not quite yet.

Alice came in with her wig—her least favorite—and she wondered if the girl had done it on purpose, but it was too late to do anything about it now. Rosamund stood as she was pinched and crimped and pulled into a corset. They tucked her into her gown, and like a pickle atop a cake, they placed her wig on her head, powdered it a bit, and she was ready.

She grabbed a gumball and left Bess, Sabrina, and Alice to deal with her fifteen trunks, twenty-one bags, and thirty hatboxes. It was their duty to deal with her baggage, and who was she to interfere with the work of lady's maids? Not everything was tea parties and balls.

Rosamund sprang down the palace steps, the pain in her joints gone with the fresh air, and stood on the palace green, shielding her eyes from the sun. Servants ran in every direction, carrying picnic dishes, hedgehog and flamingo cages, barrels of cordial, rugs and tents, and, of course, her summer tour throne. Everything she would need for her holiday in the countryside.

Rosamund made her way to her carriage. It was the biggest and reddest one in the entire procession with a custom design of rubies and garnets on the back that read "All Ways are the Queen's Way." Just so Scarlet didn't have to travel with the lowly palace horses, Rosamund had a carriage specially built that hitched right to the back, so she could have her prized steed with her at all times.

A guard bowed as she approached. "Your Majesty."

She walked past him. "Bad weather we're having. I couldn't have asked for any worse for the first day of the tour."

"Indeed, Your Majesty," he said. "Indeed."

A page opened the door to her carriage while another waited to give her a boost. She grabbed on to the handles, put her dainty foot in the page's hands, and then in one swoop, she was lifted inside. She had barely settled onto her seat when she looked up and nearly choked on her gumball.

Sitting next to Mr. Snuggle-Gus, her pet porcupine, was the Queen of Spades. "Good to see you, Rosamund," she said. "Glorious day, don't you think?"

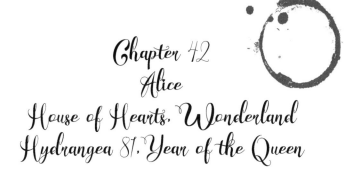

Chapter 42
Alice
House of Hearts, Wonderland
Hydrangea 81, Year of the Queen

Alice slammed the top of the Queen's trunk down. She needed to warn Thomas. Until she could work out what the Mad Hatter was truly after, she had to assume that Thomas was in as much danger as she was.

As soon as Alice helped the servants tuck away the last of the Queen's belongings, she went in search of the prince. He must be somewhere close, with all the packing and preparation for the tour nearly completed. As she hunted for him among all the bustling servants and guards and carriages, she almost ran face-first into the Mad Hatter. He was arguing with a hippo over the paradoxical nature of cheese. She managed to hide behind a Seven of Hearts until he passed. Just as Alice was about to give up, she caught sight of Thomas passing through the hedged archway of the garden.

She rushed over and found Thomas walking down the path with his back towards her. Alice opened her mouth to call out his name, but the sound of a giggle silenced her. Marilyn Montague sashayed out of an arbor in a ruffled pink dress, twirling a lacy parasol. Alice stood, rooted to the ground, as Marilyn leaned forwards and kissed Thomas's nose.

Alice staggered. She reached out, needing something to hold on to, something to steady herself. Without realizing it, her hand wrapped around a rosebush vine, thickened by age.

She stared at Thomas and Marilyn, her eyes watering, her hand tightening on the vine. Thorns bit into Alice's skin, but she didn't notice. All she saw was the way Thomas fluttered around Marilyn as if he were a moth and she a burning candle. He tucked Marilyn's hand in his arm, no doubt getting ready to lead her to his secret alcove where they'd sit under the cherry blossom tree and do more than talk. Thomas had run to save her from the executioner's axe. She'd thought his act of bravery and concern for her wellbeing had drawn them closer together, but by the looks of things, coming to Alice's rescue was just another day in the life of the Prince of Hearts.

Alice released the vine, leaving blood on the gnarled thorns. She wiped her hand on her gown and backed away on tiptoes. She didn't want Thomas to know she was there and had seen him act like a sheepish schoolboy around a pretty girl. But mostly, she didn't want him to see the pain it had caused her. She had almost made it to the entrance, where the bustle of palace activity lay outside, when she heard Thomas call:

"Lady Alice?"

Alice stopped in midstep.

Thomas hurried over to her. He took her hand, the one that had been holding the vine, and despite the aching in her palm, his touch felt warm and soft. She wanted to slap him away. She wanted to tell him that she'd changed her mind and decided not to be his friend after all, since she was sure he was *friends* with every attractive female in the House of Hearts. Instead, she stayed still and forced a smile.

Thomas studied her. "Where have you been? You never came to supper."

Alice glanced over at Marilyn. "I...uh..."

"You're angry," Thomas said, searching her eyes. "You are, aren't you? You can't be, because I should be angry with you. I have half a mind to believe you've been avoiding me."

Before Alice could answer, Marilyn came up from behind Thomas and laid her head on his shoulder. She was so close that Alice could smell her rose perfume and see the shimmer of her lipstick. "Oh, Tommy," Marilyn said. "She's probably been hiding that head of hers. I would too if I had all but lost mine." Marilyn uttered a lighthearted laugh as if Alice getting dragged to the execution block was the silliest thing ever.

"I should go," Alice said, glaring at Marilyn.

"No, stay," Thomas insisted. "Walk with us."

Alice shook her head.

Marilyn ran her finger along Thomas's shoulder. "The child said she wanted to go, so let her."

Child? Alice felt her cheeks burning hot. Compared to the voluptuous Marilyn Montague, she did feel like one, even at fifteen years old. If she had her old headband and wore her blue smock, she wondered if anyone would think she'd aged at all.

Alice gazed over her shoulder. She had wanted so much to find Thomas. Now all she wanted was to get away and she wished she hadn't gone searching for him. Even if he was in danger, he had Marilyn. He didn't need her.

Thomas kept his eyes locked on Alice. "I am the Prince of Hearts," he said, "and I order you to stay and take a stroll with us."

"Very well."

Thomas put Alice's hand on his arm and then did the same with Marilyn, delighted with his trio.

"I'm glad to see you, Alice," Thomas said. "Where have you been?"

Alice questioned if he truly cared or if he was being polite. She wasn't sure anymore. "I've been busy with the Queen," she said.

Marilyn snorted. "I'm glad I don't attend to the Queen. It would be dreadful having to jump whenever Her Majesty wishes."

Alice took a breath, feeling irritation prickle her spine. "It can be difficult at times," she said. "I suppose that's why only *ladies* can manage it."

Marilyn shot Alice a nasty look as she pulled out a handkerchief from the top of her dress. It had glittery hearts on it and she couldn't help but notice that there was an embroidered *T* in the corner. "My, my…isn't it warm today?"

"Really?" Thomas asked. "I thought it more humid."

Marilyn dabbed her chest and Thomas's eyes followed her movements. Alice turned and studied a bush of rhododendrons, refusing to watch Marilyn make a show of herself and Thomas play the avid spectator.

"Oh, dear." Marilyn's handkerchief fluttered away on the breeze. "My favorite hanky," she cried and stuck out her lower lip. "Tommy, will you fetch it for me? I don't know what I'll do without it."

Thomas went to do as Marilyn had asked, but Alice gripped his arm and said to Marilyn, "Why don't you get it yourself since you let it go in the first place?"

Marilyn jutted her chin. "I did no such thing."

"Is that so?" Alice asked, raising her eyebrows.

"Don't listen to her, Tommy," Marilyn said.

Thomas gazed at Alice for a moment before he turned to Marilyn. "It's right over there on the ladybird bush," he said. "It isn't far."

"Very well," Marilyn huffed. "I'll have to dirty my fingers, but I can see nobody cares about me."

Marilyn marched away. As soon as she was out of earshot, Alice said to Thomas, "I have to talk to you about something."

"I have to talk to you about something too," he said, and paused a moment. "I'm getting married. Queen Mum arranged it. I'm to marry the Princess of Clubs as soon as she arrives with the ambassador."

Alice's mouth opened, but no words came out. Married? The word felt so final, and she supposed it was. All the jealousy and hurt over Lady Godiva and Marilyn Montague seemed so trivial and unimportant. Thomas was to be someone else's love forever, and no matter how much Alice had wanted more, was willing to vie for more, it would never happen. Alice would simply finish her mission and go home to her cat and her chess set. She'd spend her nights dreaming of Thomas while he lived happily ever after, and Alice would simply live after.

"So..." Thomas said quietly. "What were you going to tell me?"

Alice couldn't think. "Oh...well, it was...it, uh..."

"Yes?" Thomas asked, leaning towards her. She could smell the scent of clover coming from his skin.

"Found it," Marilyn announced and skipped over to them. "Aren't you proud of me, Tommy? I did it all by myself."

"I can't," Alice said. "Not here. Not with—"

"I understand," he said, nodding. "Very well then. I'll arrange a time for us to talk in private when we're on the tour." He winked at her. "It'll be a secret."

Alice swallowed, feeling sick and unable to concentrate, unable to even be annoyed by Marilyn Montague.

"I really should go," Alice said. "The Queen must be ready to leave by now."

"You're right," Thomas said. "We should all go."

He smiled as he relinked their arms—Alice on one side, Marilyn on the other. As they strolled back out of the garden, Marilyn cooed and sighed the entire time, and Alice wondered how Marilyn would react when he told her about his engagement. Alice almost felt sorry for her in a way. They were both placeholders until his bride came.

When they came out of the garden, the palace gates were open and a troop of guards on horseback was moving to the front of the procession. A bear in a toga leaned out of his carriage window and banged on the side. "Oy. We going to be here all day or what?"

Alice turned to Thomas to say goodbye, but Marilyn's handkerchief had unwittingly managed to slip from her grasp once more. Instead of waiting, Alice headed towards the train of carriages that couldn't be more dissimilar and hodgepodge if they were rocks along the riverbed. Those in the front had inlays of rubies and gold in the wood and were twice the size of the carriages at the back, which were barely passable as carriages at all, since most were simply wagons with tents erected on them. But Alice didn't have time to think about where she'd fall in the line as she jogged up and down, calling for Sabrina and feeling panic rise up her throat. She'd been so eager to find Thomas that she hadn't paid attention to which carriage she'd been assigned to, and if she didn't find it soon, she'd be left behind.

Just as Alice was about to double back from the middle of the procession, Sabrina popped her head out of a carriage window and waved. "Alice, over here. Alice."

Breathing hard, Alice climbed inside and collapsed on the red velvet seat. The news of Thomas's engagement settled like a weight on her chest. She wanted to cry and scream that she hated everything about Wonderland and wished she'd never seen the White Rabbit or followed him down his stupid rabbit hole all those years ago, but she couldn't. Not in front of Sabrina.

"There you are," Sabrina said as she sat surrounded by cakes and puddings. "I was getting so nervous that you weren't going to make it in time and the thought of it made me hungry. You scared me. Where did you sneak off to?"

Alice didn't want to tell her she'd been with Thomas. Sabrina would ask what they'd spoken about, and she wasn't ready to tell her that he was to be married. It was already hard enough for her to hear the words in her mind; saying them aloud would somehow make it worse. "I had to gather some final things the Queen wanted."

Sabrina took a bite of a biscuit; crumbs stuck to her lips as she chewed. "I wish you'd seen how she had stared at me earlier," she said. "I think she knows."

Alice sighed. She wasn't in the mood to deal with Sabrina's troubles, not when she had plenty of her own, but if she didn't want her friend to press her, then she had to act as if nothing were the matter.

"How could she?" Alice asked. "You certainly aren't showing yet."

Sabrina lifted a platter of pink-and-white macaroons. "How do you know? You've never been with child. Maybe this is how you're supposed to be. Macaroon?"

"Oh, very well," Alice said. She leaned over to take one of the cookies and then decided two or three would be better. "Just because I've never been with child doesn't mean I don't know what it looks like. You're not showing. You will, eventually, but not yet. Don't worry. The Queen doesn't know."

"Well, still."

Just as Alice was about to take a bite, something bumped up against the carriage.

Sabrina paled. "Someone is listening to us," she whispered, and nodded to the outside.

Alice followed her gaze towards the window. With the macaroons still in her hand, she flung back the curtain, expecting it to be nothing except for the jostle of the carriage as they finally started to get moving. Instead, she found Mary Anne standing on the other side with her ear pressed to the etched glass.

Mary Anne's eyes widened for a moment when she realized she'd been caught, but then her face contorted into a smirk. She stuck her tongue out at Alice before she ran away.

Sabrina grabbed Alice's arm. "Do you think she was there the whole time?"

Alice stared after Mary Anne and shook her head. "I...I don't think so."

But Alice knew better: Mary Anne had heard everything.

Chapter 43
Rosamund
House of Hearts, Wonderland
Hydrangea 87, Year of the Queen

Rosamund threw open the door of her carriage. The page scrambled underneath her as she stepped over the edge and planted both feet on his back. "Guards," she roared. "Guards, GUARDS."

Captain Juker rushed over, unsheathing his sword. "Are you in danger, Your Majesty? Is there a plot above foot?"

"I'll very well say there is," she said, and jutted her thumb behind her. "The prisoner is sitting, as pretty as she pleases, in my carriage. Remove her at once and take her back to the tower where she belongs."

"I see," he said, putting his sword back. "You're speaking about the Queen of Spades."

Rosamund raised her eyebrows. "You knew she was there?"

"Of course, Your Majesty. I was given orders to have her taken from her cell and placed in your carriage. You were not informed of this?"

"I most certainly was not," Rosamund snapped. "And who gave this order?"

"Your advisors, Your Majesty."

Rosamund sucked in air. "My advisors. *They* decided." She puffed out her cheeks. "They've gone far too far this time. Far too far, I say." She looked around. "Where are they? Bring them to me at once."

"As you wish," Captain Juker said and turned on his heel.

The page groaned underneath her as she tapped her foot and waited. Finally, she saw William and Charles emerge from the throng and make their way towards her; neither one acted as if anything were the matter, as if it were perfectly acceptable to put a prisoner in the Queen's carriage. What was next? A chain gang hooked to the back? She fumed under her powdered wig as William laughed with Captain Juker and Charles spun his walking stick between his feathers, sucking on his pipe. Rosamund questioned the use of having advisors when she could make decisions on her own—better ones, in fact. She should behead them both and wipe her hands of the whole ridiculous practice for good.

Charles and William stopped before her and bowed.

Rosamund put her hands on her hips. "Whose brilliant idea was it to put the Queen of Spades in my carriage?"

William glanced at Charles. "It was both our brilliant ideas, and what a brilliant idea it was. We didn't know where else to put her."

"How about in the tower, and NOT IN MY CARRIAGE, you half-wits. She doesn't get to enjoy herself on my tour. It's *mine*. Since when did we ever bring prisoners anyway?"

"We haven't, Your Majesty," Charles said, "but how can we make sure the Queen of Spades doesn't escape when nearly all the guards are in your train? Matter of fact, we've already heard rumblings of a Proverbial coup just this morning. Didn't we, William?"

"Yes, indeed." He nodded. "A most sinister one."

Rosamund paused. A Proverbial coup. "What sort of rumblings?" she asked.

Charles dumped the contents of his pipe on the ground and patted the bottom of it. "Oh, it was nothing we thought to concern you with, this being your holiday, but if you must know, it was a plot to storm the tower, free the Queen of Spades, and place her upon your throne—all while you were sipping your cherry cordial far away. You know, the usual. So you see, Your Majesty, we didn't have much of a choice other than to take the prisoner with us."

Rosamund balled her hands into fists. When would all these plots end? All she wanted was to rule in peace, maybe do a few public projects, some painting, build a pyramid, but these plotters never gave her a moment's rest. As soon as she got the Queen of Spades' head, she'd better not hear whisper or croak of another plot again, or she might have to behead every living creature in her Queendom. Maybe all of Wonderland.

She stared at Charles and William. For once, her advisors had proved their usefulness. Perhaps she'd keep them around for a bit longer. The page whimpered underneath her as she shifted her weight.

"Quiet, you," she growled at him. "Or it's off with your head."

The page went silent.

Rosamund faced her advisors. "Very well," she said. "We shall take her, but move her immediately—strap her to the top of one of your carriages for all I care, just get her out of mine."

"Unfortunately, Your Majesty," William said. "All the others are full, including the tops."

Rosamund scanned the train of carriages. Claw-foot tubs and chandeliers and serving sets had been heaped in lopsided mountains on the carriages closest to her own. Farther down, she could make out piles of mattresses and bundles of chicken wire and even a whole family of jackalopes sitting around a campfire, cooking sausages. Her stomach rumbled as the aroma of the food wafted in her direction.

"As you can see," Charles said, "we wouldn't want to shove her somewhere she might escape, not when we're so close to having the Papal Bull removed. Your carriage, on the other hand, is the most heavily guarded."

Rosamund glared at Charles and William. "Very well, have it *your* way. But if I must endure the insufferable Queen of Spades for my entire tour, then somebody had better march over to those jackalopes and get me a sausage."

She slammed the carriage door shut behind her and plopped on the seat opposite Constance. She stared out the window, pretending to be interested in watching the page be carried away by two servants. He moaned and made a general fuss as they did, crying that he'd couldn't feel his legs or some such nonsense.

Constance said, "Thank you for inviting me on the tour."

"I didn't."

"Well, thank you all the same. It's so pleasant to be out of the tower. I'm afraid my bones will never dry out from the damp in the air."

Rosamund gave Constance a sideways glance. Her gown was a bit moth-eaten in some parts and her hair grayer near the temples. Damp or no damp, Rosamund quite liked Constance's tower look; it made Rosamund appear more put together, more like a queen, while Constance was no better than some old beggar. If those ridiculous Proverbials got so much as a glimpse of Constance now, they'd never want her to rule.

Constance ran her hand along the velvet seat. "Is this hand-crushed triple plush?"

Rosamund sniffed. "Is there any other fabric for a carriage?"

"You always liked having the best."

"That's because I am the best."

Constance tapped her hands together, her eyes brightening. "Oh, I would so love some tea."

"Of course you would." Rosamund reached for the blow horn. "Oh, very well, but only because I would like some too." She gave the horn three blasts and a servant immediately opened the carriage door. "Yes, Your Majesty?"

"Bring us tea."

Within a minute, a table and a tea set had been assembled along with bacon éclairs, strawberry and salami club sandwiches, a stack of extra crumbly biscuits, and a platter of sausages.

"Oh, this is delightful," Constance said. "Such a treat."

Constance placed a napkin on her lap and reached for a weenie, but Rosamund slapped her hand away. "Keep off. Those are mine."

Constance recoiled and held on to her hand. "I beg your pardon."

"You're not pardoned," Rosamund said, "not in any sense of the word, but you may pour the tea. As you know, the Queen never pours her own tea."

Constance picked up the teapot. "I suppose when there are two queens, one of them must pour."

Rosamund sneered, "I'm a queen. All you have is a title. Matter of fact, you shouldn't have it at all. It's a disgrace to all royalty."

Constance pinched her lips together, saying nothing. What could she really say? The truth hurt sometimes, but Rosamund prided herself on always being very punctual with the truth. It was one of her many virtues.

After placing a pat of butter in each cup, Constance set the butter dish down and said, "There you are, *Your Majesty*. Your tea is served."

"Aren't you going to offer me two pats?"

Constance shrugged. "I didn't think you needed two."

Rosamund burned. The insolence, the downright uncouthness—the *gall*. Is this what she got for bringing Constance into her carriage? To have her kindness abused? She sucked in her gut. "For your information, I wouldn't have accepted two anyway."

The carriage jostled forwards, and Rosamund's stomach bounced back out. She turned from Constance, leaving her tea untouched. She was suddenly too disgusted for any of it: the tea or the dainties on the table. Not that she couldn't eat them if she'd wanted to. It wasn't as if Constance had Wonderland's most glamorous figure. She wasn't anything more than a broom in a gown. Certainly, nothing worth bragging about.

Rosamund perked up when she heard her name being chanted by her people from down the road. Of course, it was a law that they drop everything when the Queen decided to grace them with her presence, but it charmed her nonetheless.

"Oh my," Rosamund said, pulling back the curtain and grinning as widely as an orangutan. "They can't get enough of me. It's almost scandalous, don't you think?"

Rosamund waved as they approached the crowd lining the street. Everyone was there, from the milkmaids to the bird-poop scrapers. They blew raspberries and pummeled her carriage with roses. A few of the blooms smacked her in the forehead and a stem nearly went into her eye, but she pretended it was all in good fun since she knew Constance was watching—probably as glum as a blobfish in a beauty pageant.

Then she heard: "Hullo. Oh, hullo there, hullo."

Constance was leaning over her and waving frantically. She pushed her away. "What are you doing, you fool? Get back. They don't care about you."

"It's a custom for royalty to greet the crowd as they progress through the city. I'm still royalty, you know."

"Not for long," Rosamund grumbled under her breath. She forced a smile and went back to the window. She didn't feel much like waving anymore, now that Constance had ruined it. Just like she'd ruined teatime and would most likely ruin her entire tour. It was all the fault of those ridiculous Proverbials that she was even there in the first place. Once this was over, she'd snuff them out, and in twenty years, nobody would even remember what a Proverbial was. It would be as if they'd never existed, like jubjub birds and bandersnatches.

The carriage finally crossed the bridge out of Gardenia City. Rosamund still heard her people calling her name, but she was getting a terrible wrist cramp, and it was only poor folk at that point anyway, who were always a little overzealous for her tastes. She shut the curtain and leaned against the cushioned backrest and rubbed her temples. All she wanted was quiet, but she couldn't even get that with Constance's endless sipping.

"Dear me," Constance said, brushing aside the curtain. "It's been ages since I've seen the country. It's going to be so refreshing, don't you think? Remember when we'd go with Daddy and Mummy? How excited we'd get the night before? Neither one of us could ever sleep. I loved all the picnics and the long walks by the river—"

"It's not going to be parties and plays for you," Rosamund snapped. "You will be under lock and key wherever you go. I don't need you to come and bludgeon me in my sleep."

Constance gasped. "I would never."

"Oh, yes you would," Rosamund snorted. "In one shake of a mouse's tail, if you were given half the chance. You *want* me dead. Don't try and deny it."

Constance placed her hand over her heart. "I have no idea what you're talking about, truly."

"No idea?" Rosamund said with almost a laugh. "I heard you say those words when I ordered you to the tower. You said, 'Hickory, dickory, dock.'"

"'Hickory, dickory, dock'?" Constance repeated with an amused smile. "Is that what this is about? I always say *hickory, dickory, dock* whenever something surprises me, as some say *stickfiddles* or *wiggly-piggly* or other such nonsense."

"Lies," Rosamund roared. "You are trying to hoodwink me. *Hickory, dickory, dock* is your code word."

"Where did you get that idea?" Constance asked.

Rosamund huffed. "I just *know* it."

"It wasn't one of your half-wit advisors?"

"Don't call my advisors half-wits," Rosamund said. "Only *I* can call them that."

"Well, at least you finally agree that they are. It's about time you started thinking for yourself. Bravo."

"How dare you?" Rosamund said, chewing on her next words. "I've always ruled, not them. I make my own decisions. Why the other day, I..."

Actually, Rosamund couldn't think of a single time that she did something on her own. Her advisors were always present, always giving her advice, always telling her what to do—and she was always doing what they said. She stared at Constance and crossed her arms.

"Well?" Constance asked. "Just the other day what?"

"Mind your own shoe wax, would you? What would you know about it? You don't even have a queendom. You're nothing but a used-up mome rath. That's all you are. A nobody."

Constance shook her head. "What happened to you, Rosamund? Why are you like this? You were such a sweet child. Remember how you used to trail after me with a ball of string wrapped around your fingers, wanting to play that game. What was it? Rat's cradle? Do you remember that? Where did that little girl go?"

"Where do you think?" Rosamund snorted. "She disappeared when I became the Queen of Hearts. You think it's been easy? I've had to fight every moment against plots and plotters since I became queen. Even you came to plot against me. My own sister. You should be ashamed of yourself."

"You have it all wrong, Rosamund."

"Wrong? Hardly. You're a no-good plotter like all the rest of them. If it wasn't for that absurd Cecil de Burg and his Papal Bull, your head would already be on a spike. But he won't be able to protect you much longer. Any day now, it will be lifted. Once it is, I'll finally get what I've always wanted: to be an only child."

Chapter 44
Alice
Longshoot Castle, Wonderland
Hydrangea 81, Year of the Queen

Alice stared out the carriage window. Moonlight reflected off a lake. Its ripples matched the tremors in her heart. In the distance, lights flickered from the windows of a castle. She wondered whose home they were inching towards and if it belonged to someone she had met at court.

Sabrina snored on the opposite seat cushion. She'd fallen asleep hours before, surrounded by crumbs and empty wrappers. Alice couldn't sleep. She couldn't stop wondering what Thomas was doing and if he were thinking of her too. She knew those thoughts were useless. Thomas was betrothed to the Princess of Clubs now. She had to accept it. She didn't really have a choice.

The carriages rumbled to a stop.

Sabrina yawned and stretched her arms. "Where are we?"

Alice shrugged. "I was hoping you could tell me."

Sabrina parted the curtain and looked outside. "Oh, that's Longshoot Castle," she said. "I'm surprised the Queen would want to come. It was Ralph's home, after all. Creepy, isn't it? It's like a giant rabbit hole. I despise rabbit holes, even though they're the quickest way from point A to point F."

Alice gazed up at the gnarled turrets, twisted spirals, and widened windows that grinned like rows of teeth. She shuddered. It seemed too dark and frightening a place for Ralph to call home—rabbit hole or not. She remembered his cottage and little garden from when she had first come to Wonderland. It was cozy, inviting, with its charming little trinkets. But this... this was like something out of a nightmare.

Sabrina sighed. "Now that Ralph is dead, I suppose the Queen has already given it to someone else or we wouldn't be here. Speaking of Her Majesty, we should go. She might be on her summer tour, but that won't mean her mood will be any better if she sees were not in attendance."

Alice and Sabrina hurried towards the front of the train. As they passed one of the carriages, Alice's breath caught in her throat when she heard Thomas's voice inside. She stopped and edged closer to the carriage's window, knowing it was wrong to snoop but unable to help herself. Someone was crying. She didn't need to guess who that was.

She heard Thomas say, "I'm so sorry. It wasn't my decision."

"But you promised me," Marilyn wailed.

"I don't remember promising, sweetgums."

"Yes, you did. You promised me with your eyes."

Sabrina grabbed Alice's arm. "What are you doing?" she whispered. "If we're not right there when the Queen steps a pinky toe on the ground, we'll be done for."

Alice forced herself to move on even though she longed to keep listening to Thomas and Marilyn's conversation. It did make her feel better knowing that Marilyn was taking the news worse than she had.

They pressed forwards, leaving Thomas and Marilyn behind. Walking became jogging, and when it seemed as if they'd never make it, they both started running. No matter how many carriages Alice and Sabrina passed, they weren't any closer to the front. By the time they arrived, Alice had to lean against the Queen's carriage, trying to stop herself from vomiting. Alice expected the Queen to say something, but she simply fanned herself as she stood upon the back of a page, strangely uninterested. Perhaps she was distracted by something else.

Bess growled, "About time. I've already been here a full minute."

Sabrina gripped her sides and panted. "We're...we're...sorry. If we were closer, we wouldn't have had to run so far to get here. I think it's made me a bit winded."

"Excuses, excuses," Bess said and crossed her arms. "As a lady's maid, you're always supposed to be waiting, precisely where you must be waiting, which in this case—"

"Do you ladies mind?" the page asked, shifting his weight under the Queen. "Do you think you can take this chitchat down the way a bit or would you rather wait until my back splits in two?"

Bess's mouth dropped. "How dare you make suggestions. You lowly of the lowest rung."

The Queen smacked Bess on the back of the head. "Stop blabbering," she snarled. "Are we going to stand here all night? There could be a dangerous fever in the air, you know. Matter of fact, I think I feel one coming."

Bess bowed. "Yes, Your Majesty. You're quite right, as always."

Alice took her position on one side of the Queen with Sabrina on the other. As Alice offered her arm up, she felt the Queen plant her spongy palm on the top of her head. Alice tried hard not to wobble while the Queen used her for balance as she stepped off the page's back and onto the ground.

The Queen said. "Let's not forget Mr. Snuggle-Gus."

"Certainly not," Bess said and nodded at Alice. "Go on. Be quick about it."

Alice moved towards the carriage, not knowing what to expect from a name like Mr. Snuggle-Gus. With the Queen, it was liable to be anything.

"He's right here," she heard a familiar voice say. Alice gazed up at Constance in amazement.

"You?" Alice's heart thudded in her chest. "But how?"

Constance shot a glance at the Queen. "Not here," she whispered as she handed Alice a leash. "Come, come, Mr. Snuggle-Gus," she said, loudly. "It wouldn't do to dawdle. You know how Her Majesty feels about dawdlers."

From the back of the carriage, a porcupine shuffled forwards with a ruby-inlaid collar and paper hearts stuck to its quills.

Cringing, the page positioned himself under Mr. Snuggle-Gus as Alice gave the leash a little tug and the porcupine jumped down and shuffled towards her.

Next was Constance's turn. She attempted to place her foot on the page's back, but he scrambled out of the way.

"Sorry, ma'am," he said to her. "You-know-who would have my head."

Constance nodded. Alice wanted to help her, but she knew she couldn't. Not with the Queen watching. All she could do was stay close by and at least make sure she got out of the carriage safely. After some finagling, Constance managed to drop down. The moment her feet hit the ground, guards surrounded her.

The Queen yanked Mr. Snuggle-Gus's leash out of Alice's hand and said to one of the guards, "Make sure the Queen of Spades has the draftiest room in the entire castle."

The guard bowed. "Yes, Your Majesty," he said before leading Constance away. Alice had to fight the urge to watch her go.

The Queen sniffed and marched in the opposite direction of the Queen of Spades. Alice, Sabrina, Bess, and Mr. Snuggle-Gus fell in line like a string of newly hatched ducklings. They hiked up a series of coiling steps. At first, it didn't seem any trouble at all, but by the time they made it to the entrance of the castle, Alice's brow dripped with sweat and her legs burned. Even Mr. Snuggle-Gus had to be carried. Bess held him on a cushion, keeping the porcupine as far out in front of her as possible.

The Queen slammed the knocker; it was shaped like a rabbit's leg.

The lock slid out of place. Alice waited to see who was on the other side—the new owner of her beloved White Rabbit's home. She bit her lip, steadying herself, and not merely because of nerves, but because her body could barely remain upright.

The Mad Hatter flung the door open and twirled his arm in sweeping loops. "You are not welcome here," he said.

"Don't be so grandiose, William," the Queen huffed. "Nobody likes a show-off."

Of course, he had taken Ralph's house. Alice burned as she stared at the top of the Hatter's head. Here he was. The person responsible for almost having her killed. If she'd had the executioner's axe, she would have dropped it right on his neck.

Alice glanced over at Sabrina, wanting to see her reaction. Her friend kept her nose upturned as if to ignore the Hatter completely. Only, Sabrina couldn't hide the smile twitching on her lips or blush spreading across her cheeks the moment the Hatter's eyes fell on her. Alice groaned. So much for loyalty.

"Please, do come in, Your Majesty," he said. "Your royal supper awaits."

"Then stop blocking the door," the Queen said, and pushed the Hatter out of the way.

They entered a massive hall that had been carved out of an old tree. Alice studied the interwoven branches and vines that wound and knotted around each other on the ceiling. Within each nook and cranny, candles burned and dripped wax along the bark.

In the middle of the room, a long table had been set up with candelabras every few place settings.

"Remodeling will be necessary, of course," the Hatter said, falling in step with the Queen. "It's going to be a nightmare getting all the wood paneling out, and don't even get me started on that tacky wallpaper."

The Queen pointed to the front of the room, where there was a giant portrait of the White Rabbit. "Take that dreadful thing down. I won't be able to enjoy my supper with that thieving, murderous traitor eyeballing me."

Servants quickly ripped it to pieces in a frenzy to get it out of the Queen's sight. All that was left was a spot on the wall that had been shielded from years of dust and smoke from the fire. Even with it gone, Longshoot Castle still held too many reminders of Ralph: the carrot engravings, the jeweled eggs, the bunny-ear artwork, including one listed as a "Self-Portrait," and the clocks of all shapes and sizes but all resembling pocket watches. It made Alice want to crumple onto the floor in tears, but she had to stay focused on her revenge and shut everything else out.

The Hatter snapped his fingers and servants ran to the table carrying silver platters of prune cobbler, strawberry marsala, and sausage crème pie. Minstrels started playing a lively rendition of "Pat-a-Cake" while everyone gathered around the table.

Alice hadn't eaten much on the trip from the palace to the castle, and after all the running and climbing for the Queen, she was absolutely famished. A servant had barely put a helping of strawberry marsala on her plate before she took a giant bite. Either Wonderland food was growing on her, or she was too hungry to care.

As the dishes were served, the Mad Hatter said to the Queen, "I did the best I could, but my dining options were limited. All Ralph had in the pantry were carrots and lettuce. Why he spent any time here at all is a mystery. It's like being sentenced to the dungeon."

Alice brushed her fingers along the vial of poison in her bodice. If it wouldn't have been too obvious, she would have used it on the Hatter that very instant, if merely to get him to stop talking in that way about the White Rabbit.

She felt a tap on her shoulder and jumped. Thomas stood behind her.

"Mind if I have a seat?" he asked.

Alice turned and pretended as if she were more interested in her yam soufflé. "What about Marilyn?"

"She's off somewhere despising me," he said and sat in the chair next to her, clearly unbothered by her snotty attitude. "What were you going to tell me back in the garden?"

Alice looked down at her plate. Now that she'd had some time to think, she didn't know if she should tell Thomas about the Hatter. What if he thought she was overreacting? She could be wrong, she supposed. But even if there were only the slightest possibility that Thomas's life was in danger, she had to warn him. No matter how broken her heart was, she'd be dead without Thomas. He had pulled her out of harm's way. She owed it to him.

"There is something..." Alice started to say. "I'm not sure how to tell you. I'm worried you might think I'm being ridiculous."

Thomas clutched her hand. " Tell me."

Alice turned to him. His blue eyes sparkled in the candlelight. "I think Lord William is plotting to kill you."

He laughed, and Alice felt her face grow warm. She was sure it was the color of ripened tomatoes.

"My goodness," he said. "That *is* ridiculous. You sound like my mother."

Alice's embarrassment warped into hot anger. She gritted her teeth. She dropped her napkin and stood to walk away, but Thomas held on to her.

"Don't be so cross, Alice," he said, continuing to chuckle. "A plot involving William? That poor fool couldn't swim himself out of a teapot, let alone come up with some plot."

"But—"

"No buts," he said, interrupting her. "There's nothing to worry about, I promise you."

The minstrels started playing a melancholy "Oh Clementine."

"You hear that?" he asked her, swaying in time to the music. "I couldn't possibly let such a beautiful song go by and not waltz to it." He held out his hand. "Speaking of, I believe I owe you a dance."

Thomas took her hand and she rose out of the chair. Her heart began to race. For the moment, the Hatter and his plot evaporated from her thoughts like the blistering sun bearing down on a droplet of water. It was as if Thomas's touch were a forgetting salve and all that mattered was the dance.

Thomas placed his hand around Alice's waist and drew her close. He swept her around the dance floor, and Alice was certain she'd stumble and make an utter fool of herself. Somehow, her feet kept up with Thomas's, and they moved together like two ribbons, floating on the wind.

Alice wished the music would go on forever, but when the melody faded, Thomas released her. Alice gazed into his eyes, waiting for something, anything, to make this moment last a little longer.

The spell though, if there had been one, was broken by Marilyn Montague's voice.

"My turn," Marilyn said. "I want to dance next, Tommy."

Alice stepped aside as Thomas took Marilyn's hand. "Shall we dance again later?" he asked Alice, but she didn't get a chance to reply before Marilyn whisked him away. It wasn't as if he really wanted another dance, Alice told herself. He was merely being polite so it wasn't completely obvious he was setting her aside for Marilyn. Again. What was so magnificent about her anyway that, whenever she was around, all Thomas could see was her?

Alice's way was blocked by a line of dancers. She dodged twirling couples until she was at the far end of the room where Madame Diamond sat in the corner, doing palm readings. Alice moved in her direction, eager to tell her about the Queen of Spades, but Madame Diamond looked up and shook her head, signaling for Alice to stop. She supposed that was wise. It would be better if the Queen didn't see them speaking to one other. She'd have to tell the madam about the Queen of Spades another time, if she didn't know already.

Alice thought about going back to the table, but Sabrina was busying herself with the Hatter, who busied himself with the Queen, and the Queen, well, she busied herself with her own amusement, namely ignoring the Hatter. With everyone preoccupied, Alice decided nobody would notice if she went to bed early. Her heart was still sore from Thomas's news, and watching him enjoy himself with Marilyn Montague made it worse.

A servant led Alice to her room. She had to climb another winding staircase, slide down a loop-de-loop, and scramble over a rock wall. By the time the servant opened one of the hundreds of doors and ushered her inside, Alice's body felt like jelly. She tossed off her slippers and had started to peel away her gown when she heard something rustle in the closet.

Alice held her breath as she listened. Just when she thought she'd imagined it, she heard it again. Something was in her room. She searched for a weapon—anything to protect herself—when the closet door cracked open and two black eyes stared back at her.

Chapter 45
Rosamund
Longshoot Castle, Wonderland
Hydrangea 87, Year of the Queen

Rosamund was in a temper all night long, which was the Queen of Spades' doing, and it didn't help that William wouldn't stop chattering her nose off.

"Be QUIET," Rosamund roared. "I am on holiday, and that means I get a break from your blabbering. Shoo. Go on, get."

William scooted his chair away. "My shallowest, most duplicitous, most egregious apologies."

Sabrina livened up at William's dismissal and shoveled three tarts, a slice of plum pie, and a powdered potato in her mouth and swallowed it all in one gulp. Nearly about to gag, Rosamund averted her gaze and found herself watching Madame Diamond, who was sitting at a table in the corner entertaining a herd of gentry with palm readings.

It wouldn't be much fun if everyone else got their palm read and she didn't. She glanced at the etched lines in her hand. If she connected them all together, it rather resembled a squirrel holding a block of cheese. Having such a palm meant that she was the smartest, most beautiful in all of Wonderland. Still, it wouldn't hurt to have it confirmed.

While Sabrina guzzled strawberry cream, Rosamund stood and said, "You'll have to excuse me," to a family of raccoons sitting to her left. Not that she really had to excuse herself. It was technically *her* table in *her* castle, even if it was newly bequeathed to William. But sometimes on holiday, she thought it good to be polite.

Madame Diamond bowed her head as Rosamund approached and said, “Let’s say that a little spirit whispered in my ear that you—”

“Want a palm reading,” Rosamund finished for her and pushed a kangaroo out of the seat. “Really, Madame Diamond, these spirits of yours are getting awfully predictable.”

Rosamund held out her hand. A crowd gathered around them—curious nobodies, anxious to know what the Queen’s palm had to say. She supposed she was doing them a service, letting them see what it was like to have the palm of a very unimportant person.

Madame Diamond traced the lines in her hand. “Oh yes…I see…I see. This one here”—she pointed to a line that stretched from the top of Rosamund’s index finger down to her wrist—“indicates long life.”

“Naturally.” Rosamund nodded to the onlookers.

“And this one shows that you are well loved.”

“Tell me something I don’t know, would you?” Rosamund chided.

Madame Diamond circled the flesh under her ring finger. “This means that you will get everything you want.”

“I *am* the Queen and that’s the general idea.”

“But this line.” Madame Diamond’s eyes widened. “This line is very concerning. Oh yes, very concerning indeed. It says you must be wary of strangers.”

Rosamund squinted at the crowd. She could have sworn it had grown bigger since the last time she noticed. The ostrich in the bowler hat wasn’t there before, nor was the polar bear with the handlebar mustache, she was certain of it. She didn’t like the way they murmured to each other. What if one of them were this stranger? If they were, she needed to not let them see she was scared.

“Strangers, you say?” Rosamund snickered. “As a rule, I never talk to or take sweets from strangers, so I suppose I have nothing to worry about there. Besides, I know everyone who’s anyone, and those are the only strangers I’m around, who aren't strangers at all in my opinion."

Madame Diamond tried to jump in with something else to say but Rosamund cut her off.

"I think that's enough," she said, silencing her. "I'm sure someone else would like to get their palm read, although I doubt it will be as good as mine."

Rosamund skipped away to the accompaniment of their bravos and applause. She returned to her table, her mood sorely worsened. The palm reading was meant to be a fun distraction, but the comment about strangers bothered her. She watched Madame Diamond give the ostrich a talon reading while the polar bear took notes. It seemed they hadn't been the strangers after all, so who was? She peered at her hand, trying to see for herself what it said, but nothing seemed out of the ordinary. She'd have to talk more about it with Madame Diamond when they're weren't so many looky-loos around.

Bess came over. "Are you ready for bed, Your Majesty? You don't want to be a cranky crab dragon tomorrow, now do you?"

Rosamund yawned. "No, I suppose I don't, though there's nothing cranky about crab dragons. I find them a complimentary sort, for the most part."

Bess gazed around. "I don't know where Alice has gone off to. Shall I get Sabrina?"

Sabrina was licking apricot gravy off her fingers.

"No." Rosamund grimaced. "That will not be necessary."

Bess took Rosamund to the temporary lodgings she'd be staying in while at Longshoot. They were Ralph's old rooms, and they were the best in the castle. With all her things, it did feel somewhat comfy, but it certainly wasn't home. For one thing, the fireplace was far too small, the couches and chairs barely big enough, and her legs were certain to dangle over the edge of the bed all night. At least the mattress was a good, solid, lumpy one, and the pillows were extra scratchy.

Bess tucked Rosamund into bed.

"What should I do tomorrow?" Rosamund asked her.

"How about a game of skittles?" she replied. "Wouldn't that be delightful?"

"Oh yes. Tell William to arrange a game tomorrow—something fitting for a queen. Nothing more will do."

"Yes, Your Majesty. Good night." Bess bowed and skipped out of the bedchamber.

Rosamund shoved her pillow under her head. As soon as she closed her eyes, she heard Pedro's voice in her ear.

"Hullo, Rosebud."

"Go away," Rosamund groaned. "I haven't made up my mind yet, and you know very well that the Queen doesn't conduct any business on the tour. It's supposed to be a holiday, you know." She pulled the blankets over her head and squeezed her eyes shut.

"We didn't come for that," he said.

"Oh? Then what did you come for?" Rosamund asked. "To tell me who the real traitors are?"

"Not quite," he said, "but we do feel bad about how we left things last time."

"And to make up for it," Thomas added, "we wanted to offer you a show of good faith."

Rosamund lowered the blankets. "What might that be?"

Pedro smiled. "We brought an extra special guest with us." He nodded to Thomas. "Bring him in."

After quite a kerfuffle of pots banging and the cuckoo of a cuckoo bird, Thomas returned with his teeth clamped on a certain traitor's ear as he dragged the newcomer before Rosamund. It was a most unwanted and very unwelcome guest.

Ralph.

Compared to Pedro and Thomas, Ralph was looking much worse for wear. His white fur had browned in several spots and his pointy ears drooped around his face. Maybe rabbit heads beheaded badly.

"What's *he* doing here?" Rosamund pointed at him.

"Hickory, dickory, dock," Ralph sang as he twisted in a circle. "Hickory, dickory, dock."

Rosamund ground her teeth. "Quiet him this instant."

"That's the problem," Thomas said, spitting out bits of fur. "He's barely said much of anything else. Matter of fact, he's been repeating the same phrase ever since...well, ever since you beheaded him."

"Hickory, dickory, dock..."

"Get him out of here, NOW!" Rosamund yelled with such force that her voice flattened the ruffles of her nightgown. "I never want him in my sight again. If this is a show of good faith, then I don't know how I'll ever be able to trust that you will tell me who the traitors are. You might as well unleash the horde of heads on me now. How can I possibly clear your names with this type of reassurance? Leave me be, both of you, and take Ralph with you."

The rabbit's head swiveled towards her. Its eyes rolled in two different directions. "Ralph? Who's Ralph?"

"*You're* Ralph, you idiot."

"Is he?" Pedro asked.

"Of course he is," Rosamund snapped. "Honestly, did you lose your senses when you lost your body? Don't hover there and tell me you don't recognize my old advisor."

"Oh, Rosamund," Thomas said with a sigh. "You only see what you want to see."

A voice purred in her ear. "Hasn't that always been the problem though?"

Chapter 46
Alice
Longshoot Castle, Wonderland
Hydrangea 81, Year of the Queen

A voice whispered, "Don't scream."

Alice stood, staring at the closet door with her heart banging away in her chest and her hands shaking so badly that she didn't know if they'd ever be still again. "Who's there?"

"Promise, you won't scream first."

"Tell me who you are," Alice said, stumbling away, "or I *will* scream. I swear it."

"We don't have *time* for this. No time. NO TIME."

Alice froze. "White Rabbit? Is that you?"

She shook her head as if to shake the thought away. It couldn't possibly be him. Ralph was gone. He was never coming back. She clenched her fists and faced the closet, feeling anger shred her insides at whoever was trying to impersonate her beloved friend. "Who's in there? What do you want? If you don't tell me right now, I'll get the guards."

The closet door swung open and Ralph stepped out, brushing cobwebs off his shoulders. "I see nobody has dusted for a while."

"Impossible." Alice gasped and backed away. "Are you a ghost? Have you come to haunt me?"

"Don't be ridiculous. I'd have to be dead to be a ghost, which as you can see, I'm not."

"But I watched you die." Tears welled in Alice's eyes. "You have no idea what that did to me. And to see you come in here...acting as if it were nothing at all. Was it some trick you played on the Queen? What about me? How could you do that to me?"

"I'm so sorry," he said, reaching towards her.

Alice flinched. "Don't touch me."

She'd mourned for him and it had been a lie. She remembered that moment in her room after she thought Ralph had died. The wretched despair. A darkness she'd never experienced before and Ralph, here, alive, proved he hadn't cared how she'd feel. How it would affect her. He didn't care about anyone but himself.

"You should have told me your plan."

"I couldn't," he said. "I needed the Queen to believe it. Your reaction made her believe. I wasn't trying to hurt you. I promise, Alice."

"If it wasn't you on the block"—she wiped her eyes—"whose head did the Queen take?"

Ralph motioned to a nearby table where a pot of tea waited. Alice wondered how she hadn't noticed it before.

"It should still be warm," he said. "Would you like to sit?"

Alice nodded. Ralph poured them each a cup. He took a sip and droplets of tea ran down his whiskers, staining his fur collar. Alice couldn't touch her tea. Not because it smelled of rotting prunes, but because she felt ill and relieved all at once. A part of her was happy that the White Rabbit was alive, despite feeling she'd been deceived, but she was also terrified to discover who had died instead. Alice recalled how Ralph, or who she thought was Ralph, had fought all the way to the executioner's block. Clearly whoever did take his place, didn't do so consensually.

"Who?" Alice asked again. "Who was it?"

"You probably don't even know him," Ralph said, and twitched his nose. "It was the March Hare. He'd been disguised to look like me. Simply amazing what a little white paint could do."

"The March Hare..." Alice's voice grew louder. "Yes, I *do* know him. I—"

"Shush," Ralph said, glancing around. "No one can know I'm here. Please. Be more careful."

Alice leaned forwards and lowered her voice. "I had tea with him the first time I came to Wonderland. It was a tea party with the March Hare, the Mad Hatter, and the Dormouse."

"That was probably a different March Hare," Ralph said with a shrug. "There are so many of them. They breed like... they breed like...well, you know. And they are all mad—especially during Carnation. It was likely he didn't even know what was happening."

Alice wrapped her hands around the tea cup. The warmth did nothing to thaw the chill she felt. "Not from where I was standing. It seemed as if he knew a great deal."

Ralph waved her off. "That's not the point."

"Not the point?" Alice repeated. "You sent an innocent creature to his death."

"Would you have preferred I died? Or you died?" Ralph asked, putting his teacup down. "I did it for you, Alice."

Back when she thought Ralph had sacrificed himself for her, she'd have given anything to have brought him back. Anything. Even sacrificing another. But if that was true, then why did she feel sick to her stomach as she sat across the table from him?

Ralph opened his watch and closed it. "There's something I need to tell you—"

Someone tapped on the door. Ralph's hindleg thumped.

"Burnt butter," he muttered as he stood up. "I must go."

"Wait," Alice said. "What did you want to tell me?"

"No time." He hopped towards the closet. Before disappearing inside, he turned to Alice with his finger over his mouth. "Remember," he whispered. "No one."

The tapping came again, more urgent this time.

Ever since Alice had arrived in Wonderland, she had felt as if she knew about half of what was really going on. She was growing tired of it and wanted to know what the White Rabbit had to say, especially now that he'd come back from the dead.

Alice tiptoed to the door and pressed her ear against the wood. She didn't know who it could be. Sabrina, most likely. Alice wasn't in the mood to deal with her just then. She still needed to process it all, not nurse her friend's pregnancy fears. If she stayed quiet enough, she hoped Sabrina would go away.

"Alice?" she heard Madame Diamond call from the other side. "Alice, are you there?"

Alice opened the door. Madame Diamond hurried in and gazed around.

"Is someone here?" she asked. "I thought I heard voices."

Alice wondered if she already knew about Ralph, but then remembered Madame Diamond said he didn't always tell her everything. Perhaps the fact that he wasn't dead was one of them.

"No, no one. It's just me."

Madame Diamond picked up one of the teacups and sniffed. "It smells of grilled onions and oranges."

"I thought it had more of a prune aroma." Alice laughed nervously and glanced at the closet. She wondered if Ralph were there, listening to the whole thing. "It smells worse than it tastes."

"And two cups?"

"They boil the water so dreadfully hot that I pour another to allow it to cool down."

Madame Diamond nodded. "I do that sometimes too."

Alice inwardly sighed as Madame Diamond took a seat, appearing satisfied with the answers.

Madame Diamond said, "You need to prepare yourself for quite a shock." She took out her cards and placed them side by side.

"See for yourself," she said.

Alice was certain they'd show that Ralph was alive. She didn't know how she'd be able to keep it a secret from Madame Diamond after that. Except when she looked at the cards, the blood drained from her cheeks.

They weren't of Ralph. Instead, they were images of severed heads.

The first one was the Queen of Spades. The second Madame Diamond. The third Lillian. The fourth Bill, who was nearly unrecognizable because his sickness had bleached his entire skin a pasty white. And the fifth...the fifth was Alice's head.

Alice wanted to back away, but she couldn't take her eyes off the picture. The blood-soaked, severed part of her neck, the pale gray of her skin, the dull glaze over her eyes. It didn't seem real, yet it was almost as if she could reach through the card and touch a strand of her hair. It was clear that Ralph wouldn't be able to protect her a second time. This time, she would die. She brought her hand to the soft skin of her throat. The feathery touch gave her the chills.

Madame Diamond said, "The Queen is going to find out we're plotting to kill her. When she does, she'll behead us all."

"Can we stop her from finding out?" Alice asked.

"If I knew how, then maybe. I've checked the crystal ball, I've checked the tea leaves, I've checked palms—even her palm—but I can't work out how she discovers it." Madame Diamond sighed. "It doesn't matter anyhow. Our deaths are close. Recognize the background? That's here. That's Longshoot Hall."

Alice leaned closer to the cards. She could see the outline of the wall where Ralph's portrait had been before the Queen had ordered servants to tear it down. She ran a trembling hand across her forehead. "What should we do?"

"Do you still have the vial?" Madame Diamond asked.

"Yes," Alice said, taking it out from inside her bodice.

"You have to do it tomorrow," Madame Diamond said and gripped Alice's hand; the vial pressed hard into her skin. "She might know about us already. There's no time to waste. Tomorrow, Alice. Tomorrow, you must kill the Queen."

Chapter 47
Rosamund
Longshoot Castle, Wonderland
Hydrangea 81, Year of the Queen

Flashes of purple flickered next to Thomas and Pedro. Ralph, or whoever that rabbit was who resembled her beheaded advisor, didn't notice. Although in his defense, he didn't seem to be aware of much.

"Something smells beefy in here," Rosamund said, sitting up in bed and glancing around the chamber.

A pair of white teeth materialized, grinning in a sardonic way from ear to ear.

"Hullo."

"Chester."

The teeth disappeared.

"You get back here, Chester," Rosamund ordered. She threw the blankets to the side and got on her feet. "I'm going to behead you myself."

Chester emerged high above her as if he had simply walked through an invisible door. He folded his paws, placing one on top of the other. "Testy, testy. Is that how to treat a guest?"

"We've had this conversation before, and once again, you're *not* a guest. Come here, you." Her blood boiled as she lunged for him. She hated the way he stared down at her. She hated his striped tail, his fluffy ears. She hated everything about him—all cats really. Almost nearly as much as she hated traitors, but Chester... She hated that cat most of all. She stood on her tiptoes and tried to grab his tail, but the blasted thing jumped out of the way.

Chester waved a paw at her. "You mustn't lose your temper."

"Pedro. Thomas," Rosamund barked. "Help me catch that dreadful thing."

Rosamund chased Chester around the room, but every time she was about to get him, he'd slip from her fingers. Soon she was gasping for breath and still no closer to capturing that horrid feline. Pedro and Thomas were useless—all they did was stay in their spots and float.

Chester jumped to the farthest corner and stuck his nose in the air. "I can see I'm not wanted."

"You're never wanted, but when has that stopped you?" Rosamund asked as she dragged a chair over. "Don't think you can leave. Not with your head, you can't. I order you to give it to me right this instant. As I am your queen, you must obey."

"And to think," he said with his tail in the air, "I was going to tell you about a plot. Probably the worst one yet. Well, maybe not the worst. What could be worse than doing away with one's own parents?"

Rosamund cringed. Thomas swiveled his head towards her. Even the Ralph-thing did. Only Pedro looked off in another direction and started to whistle. If he thought he was somehow going to escape the blame, he had another *think* coming. He was just as guilty.

"What is he talking about?" Thomas asked.

"Oh, don't be so surprised," Rosamund snapped and set the chair down. "Of course I was behind my parents' accident in the ravine. Pedro helped me plan the whole thing, as usual."

Thomas gazed at Pedro and then at Rosamund, almost as if he were about to cry. She never understood why he was so fond of those old bean pots she called Mummy and Daddy.

"But they were kind," he said, "and they were kind to you, especially. Remember how your mother would bring me curdled cheese pudding and your father would always have some trinket or another from those far-off places they'd visited? Of everyone in Wonderland, why them?"

Rosamund turned away. Thomas was trying to make her regret what she'd done and, maybe if she had to admit it, from time to time, she did feel a little awful about it. But he wasn't the Queen of Hearts and didn't have the kidneys to make the sacrifices it took to stay on top.

"I had to get rid of them," she said. "They wanted Constance on my throne. They were going to make me give it to her."

"You don't know that for certain."

"Yes, I do. They always liked Constance more than me. Daddy would go on and on about how Constance was doing so well in her studies, and Mummy would gush about all her courtships. Don't you see? They wanted her to be queen, not me. I had to stop that from happening."

Thomas opened his mouth, but Rosamund held up her hand.

"Enough is enough. There's no going back now and changing what happened. Accept it, Thomas, because that's not what's unimportant just now. For those of us still alive, what is unimportant is this supposed plot Chester is talking about." She faced the cat, who was bouncing up and down in rhythm with the heads. "The second worst one you say? Is that right?"

Chester purred, "Mmmmhmmmm."

Rosamund jutted her thumb over to the Ralph-thing. Its eyes were circling in two different directions. "I'm guessing it has something to do with him."

"Most definitely."

"Then perhaps," Rosamund said, chuckling a little, "perhaps, I was being a bit too hasty asking for your head. You know me. Temper, temper. Now what is this plot about?"

Thomas and Pedro floated closer. She obviously didn't need them at all. Chester would reveal who the real traitors were, and she wouldn't have to clear Thomas's and Pedro's names. They would be forever known as traitors to the throne, and they could float on out into oblivion for all she cared.

"I don't know if I want to tell you now," Chester said. "Not after how you treated me."

Pedro sneered. "I doubt he even knows anything about a plot. You know how much cats can be trusted."

"I can handle this, thank you very much," Rosamund snarled. "What do you want then, Chester? Mice? Catnip? A manor to place over your litter box?"

"Sounds tempting, but no. I have something else in mind."

"Of course you do. I presume you'll want your death warrant lifted?"

"That would be nice. You have no idea what a damper it puts on one's social life."

"Very well. Against my better judgment, consider it done. Anything else?"

"There is one more thing, but we can discuss the terms later. Much later. In the meantime, Chief Royal Cat of Wonderland will do."

"Absolutely ludicrous. There is no such position."

"You could make one," he said. "You are the Queen of Hearts...at least for now."

"And what is that supposed to mean?" Rosamund's eye twitched. This was why she hated cats. They were such tricky and smug things, always giving themselves airs.

"Make me Chief Royal Cat of Wonderland," he said, "and I'll tell you."

"How can I know that your information is good?"

Chester bounced towards her, getting dangerously close. "Oh, it's good," he said. "I have a way of being everywhere and nowhere when I want to be and even at times I *don't* want to be. I hear the most interesting things when nobody thinks I'm around, as you already know."

Rosamund sat in the chair she'd been dragging and waited for Chester to continue. His green eyes glowed in the dim light. He wasn't a bad-looking cat, she supposed. She used to like cats, even had one as a pet at one point, but something changed. She couldn't put her finger on it, but it was as if, in an instant, she wanted to wring every cat's neck in Wonderland.

And she did.

Only Chester was left. If Rosamund had her way, and she always did, he wouldn't be Chief Royal Cat of Wonderland for long.

"Fine," she said. "Whatever you say. Give yourself five titles. Ten. Twenty. You can have anything you want *if*—and I do mean if—what you say is true. Now, tell me about this plot."

He tapped his paws together. "The plot, well, it's a jolly good one, and let's say it involves a group of your subjects, very hush-hush. You'll absolutely die when I tell you who they are."

"And *who* are they?" Rosamund asked, using her nicest inside voice, except Chester didn't seem to notice.

Instead, he rolled onto his back and laughed. "If they knew I was talking to you—oh my! They'd lose their buttons."

"Yes." Rosamund leaned forwards. "Who would lose their buttons?"

Chester frowned. "I seem to have got ahead of myself. Pity."

Rosamund fell back in the chair and sighed. "You'll want to start from the beginning, I expect."

"No, not at all," he said, surprising her. "There are never beginnings, you know."

"Never beginnings? How absurd."

"Not so absurd actually."

Chester's nonsense was putting her on tacks and thimbles. The cat had grown madder. Beheading him at this point would be putting the creature out of its misery.

Rosamund growled. "Fine, then. Get on with it, would you?"

"The last thing you should know," Chester said as he folded his paws before him, "is that I am a member of the Aboveground Organization. Fake member naturally. We differ on our methodology."

"And what does this Aboveground Organization want?"

"What do they want?" Chester laughed. "Your death, of course."

"Give me their names." Rosamund pointed at him. "A deal's a deal."

"How about, for now, I give you one?" Chester grinned wider and wider until the edges of his mouth stretched up to his ears. "Alice."

Chapter 48
Alice
Longshoot Castle, Wonderland
Azalea 91, Year of the Queen

All night, Alice thought of Madame Diamond's cards, Ralph's sudden resurrection, and of the one person she hadn't seen since they left the palace: Lillian. Where was she? Did she know about Ralph, and was that why she'd gone missing? Even so, it didn't seem like Lillian to shirk her duties to the organization. If she were around, Alice could warn her about the cards, but she supposed the rat was going to find out soon enough anyway.

Alice jumped as Sabrina hurried into the room.

"You're not dressed yet?"

"No." Alice snatched the vial of poison she'd left on the nightstand and tucked it into her nightgown. "Have I overslept?"

"Nearly," Sabrina said and headed for Alice's closet.

"Wait. Don't—"

"What?" Sabrina asked and opened it. All that was inside was Alice's dresses. "Is everything all right? You don't seem yourself."

Alice didn't know what she was expecting. For Ralph to have stayed in her closet all night curled up in a fluffy ball? Of course there must be a secret passage behind the door and he was off hiding somewhere in the castle. It was exactly what she would be doing if she had any sense, but there were others to think about as well.

"Yes," Alice said. "I'm fine."

"Good. You need to be on your tippy-top today." Sabrina grabbed a pink gown with red roses and handed it to Alice. "The Queen wants us out on the lawn this morning."

"Whatever for?"

"I'm not sure, but anything is likely on the summer tour." Sabrina smiled. "Isn't it such fun?"

Alice thought of Madame Diamond's cards and swallowed. "Quite."

Sabrina helped Alice dress and rummaged in her jewelry box for some earrings to match. While Sabrina was distracted, Alice secured the vial in her bodice. The Queen would expect her tea first thing, and she'd have to be ready to mix it in if given the slightest bit of a chance.

"These here," Sabrina said. "They're lovely. You must wear them."

Sabrina held up a pair of earrings shaped into roses. Alice felt herself go cold. She recognized the pair. She was wearing them in the picture in Madame Diamond's card. Alice's eyes widened.

Not already. Not *today*.

"No," Alice whispered.

"But they match perfectly," Sabrina said and frowned. "You must. Here, let me put them on for you."

Alice couldn't move. She tried to open her mouth to protest, but the muscles wouldn't budge. It was as if fate had paralyzed her, forcing her to complete the picture on the card. Alice could barely breathe as Sabrina put on the jewelry she would die wearing.

That was, if she didn't get to the Queen first.

"There," Sabrina said, standing back. "You're all finished."

Alice stumbled as Sabrina pulled her to her feet.

"Are you sure you're all right?" Sabrina asked again. "You seem ill."

"Yes," Alice said, her tongue sticking to the roof of her mouth. "We should go. The Queen is probably waiting for us."

As they sped through the castle, doubt crept into Alice's mind. What if the Queen wanted to meet outside because the executioner's block was already waiting for her? With each staircase they descended, the more Alice convinced herself it was true: she was being led to her death. All she wanted to do was to run and hide. Sabrina seemed to grip Alice's hand even tighter, refusing to let her go anywhere but forwards.

They stepped outside onto a lawn. A scream pushed up Alice's throat when the Queen turned towards them, twirling an umbrella in her hand and grinning. "There you two are. I was starting to wonder."

The Queen barely glanced at Alice and wasn't acting as if anything were amiss. Alice looked around. There was no executioner. No axe. No block. Only an archway draped with flowing red silks, a bright-white line drawn on the grass, and the lake that shimmered just beyond.

Alice swallowed the scream and doubled over in relief. It was all in her head. She'd overreacted, and she still had time to save herself. Once they had tea, all would be well. But a growing number of the gentry trickled out of Longshoot, making the idea of slipping poison in the Queen's cup even more problematic.

"Oh goody," the Queen said. "Everything is almost ready for skittles. Do you play, Alice?"

"A little," Alice said. She didn't see anything for skittles: no pins, no balls, just a colony of penguins waddling single file on the lawn. Alice had played skittles quite a bit back at home. One summer, she played so often she started playing by herself when everyone else refused. She had become fairly good at the sport.

She tried to sound casual as she asked, "Are we to have tea?"

"Not now," the Queen said. "The game is about to start. Where is my royal armadillo?"

Disappointment settled in the pit of Alice's stomach, but she knew the Queen would want tea at some point today, hopefully before she ordered their executions. The one assurance Alice had was that, according to the cards, Lillian would have to be around for it, and she was still nowhere in sight. Whenever it was supposed to happen, it appeared it wouldn't be that morning.

"Armadillo?" Alice asked.

"Of course," the Queen said. "How else do you intend we play?"

Alice gazed over at the penguins. They had placed themselves in a diamond pattern. Just as with the game of croquet she'd played with the Queen on her first visit, this was going to be Wonderland skittles. Alice didn't know what surprised her more: that she still expected normalcy in Wonderland or that the Queen was using armadillos and penguins to play skittles.

Bess called, "I have your royal armadillo right here, Your Majesty."

The duchess wove through the crowd, holding up a bag with "Property of the Queen" written on the side.

The Queen unzipped the top and pulled out a miniature armadillo that had already rolled itself into a ball. As the trickle of gentry became a flood, the Queen marched to the white line and took aim. She swung the armadillo back and forth before shooting the creature towards the penguins. It hit the grass and rolled, veering away from the birds, and was clearly going to miss them altogether. But then, one of the penguins jumped in front of the armadillo and flung itself backwards, pushing the rest of the penguins onto the ground.

The Queen jumped. "Knock!"

Everyone cheered for the Queen as the armadillo scurried to her. The Queen picked it up, and it tightened once more into a ball.

She laughed. "This is so easy for me, I can do it with my eyes closed."

The Queen closed her eyes, pulled the armadillo back, and let it go flying. It landed nowhere close to the birds. The armadillo trotted over to the penguins as they waddled, fell, and waddled some more before crashing together in a heap.

The Queen opened her eyes.

"That's knock two! Now watch me do it with my other hand."

The armadillo scampered over to the Queen's outstretched palm. Without bothering to take her time, she gripped the creature, wound up, and released it. The armadillo was lobbed in the air and plopped before the penguins. The birds scooted forwards until the nose of the armadillo touched the lead penguin's chest, and they all tumbled onto the ground.

"That's a goose," the Queen roared to the accompaniment of applause.

A servant gave Alice an armadillo. She'd never held one before, miniature or not. It snuggled into her hand, tickling her with its snout. She ran her fingers along its armored back; it reminded her of the polished rocks along the river. The creature certainly wasn't Dinah, but she thought it charming all the same. Even though its talons left fiery scratches in her skin, she imagined an armadillo would make a nice pet someday, assuming she managed to make it through the day with her head still attached.

The Queen pirouetted away from the crowd as they lowered the pitch of their tribute to a dull hum of bravos. She smiled at Alice. "Now, your turn."

As if on cue, Alice's armadillo curled into a ball. She swung the creature, feeling awful about having to throw the poor thing but knowing she'd have to do it with the Queen watching. She let it go, and it rolled onto the grass at a perfect angle towards the lead penguin. As it was about to hit, the penguin scooped the armadillo into its mouth and swallowed.

The Queen clucked her tongue. "Right in the gutter. Better luck next time."

Alice stared at the penguin, stunned. It fluffed its feathers a bit and clacked its beak as if it had done nothing at all. "But it...but it *ate* my armadillo."

"Now, now, Alice. Don't be a spoilsport. Your turn is over. If you'd knocked them all down as I did, then you'd get to go again, but there's nobody as good as me, so I'm not really surprised."

The Queen yodeled and a servant promptly handed her another armadillo, but this one wasn't as keen on cuddling into Alice's palm as the last one.

"Move along, Alice," the Queen demanded, and looked around. "Who's next?"

The Hatter stepped up with his armadillo and Alice took the opportunity to walk away. She didn't want to witness another armadillo slide down a penguin's gullet. It felt so senseless and cruel. Not that she should expect anything else from one of the Queen's games.

"That's why I hate playing skittles," Thomas said.

It was as if he had read her mind. Had she been talking aloud? Alice turned. Thomas was behind her. His red hair seemed redder today and his eyes bluer. She felt herself flush as they settled on her. She glanced around for Marilyn, but she wasn't anywhere in sight.

"The penguins only fall for Queen Mum," he continued. "It makes her happy. I suppose that's all that matters."

"But she isn't actually winning."

"She doesn't know that."

"It doesn't seem very fair to the poor armadillos."

"Oh, you shouldn't concern yourself too much with them."

"And whyever not?" Alice balked. "They get *eaten.*"

Thomas laughed. "The penguins cough them up when the game's over. The armadillos are slimy and smell a bit fishy, but they're very much alive and accounted for. When everyone's finished playing, you can see for yourself."

While it made Alice feel better for the armadillos, it wasn't exactly something she wanted to be a spectator of. She shrugged. "Perhaps."

Thomas glanced over at the crowd. They were jeering at the Dodo who was taking aim. "You mind if I stay with you? I always feel uncomfortable at these things."

Alice looked down at her feet and nodded. If today was really her last, then she was happy to spend part of it with the prince. The game continued and Thomas stayed by Alice's side. After a while, no one was keeping track of the score except for the Queen, who proclaimed continually that her score was the highest. Half the time passed with searches for missing armadillos that had fallen asleep or had scurried away from the penguin's beaks.

The Queen decided it was time for the final round. She grabbed her armadillo and marched to the white line.

Alice glimpsed Madame Diamond among the onlookers. She nodded at Alice when their eyes met. Alice had to stop herself from running over and warning the madame that today would be their last day, but she didn't know if someone were watching them. All Alice could do was bow her head in response. The Queen would likely insist on tea after her win. Then she'd have her chance, and if everything went right, it wouldn't matter if their executions were to happen that day or not.

Thomas leaned towards her. "Look at Queen Mum. See what I meant earlier? Doesn't she seem so pleased?"

The Queen had one eye squinted and her tongue stuck out slightly from her mouth. *Pleased* wasn't the word Alice would have used. Focused, perhaps. Alice turned to Thomas. He watched his mother with such pride that guilt ricocheted inside her. The Queen was insane and cruel, but Thomas loved her. He'd never forgive Alice if she succeeded. But maybe, in time, he'd understand that she didn't have a choice.

The Queen coiled her arm back, ready to rocket the armadillo towards the penguins. As she tried to let it go, the armadillo's tail became hooked on the Queen's bracelet. The animal flew upwards in a wide arc, throwing the Queen off balance and sending her tumbling backwards, straight for the edge of the lake. With a splash, the Queen disappeared under the water, leaving a puddle of lace around her head.

Nobody moved, not even when the Queen resurfaced, spluttering, "Help! Someone help me! I can't swim!"

The Hatter pushed through the crowd. "Someone must rescue the Queen," he cried.

"Why don't you?" a turtle asked.

"I can't swim either."

The turtle shrugged. "Neither can I."

The Queen shouted, "I command that someone save me!" She had managed to splash herself away from the edge, getting closer towards the center of the lake.

Alice was the closest to her. She darted forwards out of instinct and then stopped. What if she let the Queen drown? It was not as if anybody else acted as if they wanted to help her. All Alice had to do was stay put and their problems with the cards would be over.

The Queen rolled over on her back. "Help! I can't hold out…much…longer…"

Thomas pushed past Alice, plugged his nose, and jumped. His head emerged from under the water, and he doggy-paddled to the Queen. As he got close, she clutched his neck in her panic and pulled them both under.

Alice put down her armadillo and took off her slippers, ready to rescue Thomas, and the Queen if she must, but he erupted from the lake like a flying fish. Standing in knee-deep water, he pushed his soggy hair out of his eyes.

The Queen continued to flounder nearby. In one swoop, Thomas yanked her up and set her on her feet.

"Oh, oh…" the Queen said and glanced around her. "I suppose there are disappearing sinkholes in this lake. Let's get out before one comes back."

The Queen waddled to the edge with Thomas's assistance. Bess helped them out.

"Damp towels," Bess ordered. "I need damp towels immediately."

Servants rushed over with them. Bess took one and went to drape the cloth around the Queen's shoulders, but the Queen stopped her.

"No," she said, glaring at Alice. "I want Alice to do it. She's *certainly* been standing there long enough, now hasn't she? Why, if I didn't know any better, I'd say she was hoping I'd drown."

Chapter 49
Rosamund
Longshoot Castle, Wonderland
Azalea 91, Year of the Queen

Rosamund had the guards search Longshoot Castle for Ralph while they played skittles.

"Go through every closet, vault, and sink," she told them. "Leave no rabbit hole unturned. He's somewhere in here. Find him."

While Rosamund was out on the lawn, Captain Juker came out of the castle and pantomimed as if he were trapped inside a box. It was the signal. The search was completed. She called the final round of the game and then the horrible incident with the lake occurred. Those disappearing sinkholes could be dangerous. She knew firsthand, having fallen into one as a child. At least, after all that, having Ralph in her clutches would have offered some satisfaction, but Captain Juker had whispered in her ear that he still hadn't been found. Blast it all.

Servants hauled her bathtub into the room and set it before the window, so the sunlight captured every ruby, garnet, and speck of gold. They promptly filled it with cool water and Bess sprinkled the top with rose petals. With help from her lady's maids, Rosamund peeled off her wet clothes from the lake and settled into her tub, but it did nothing to relax her. Instead, she continued to fume whenever she thought of Ralph.

No matter. She might not have that backstabbing rabbit, but she still had one traitor under her watchful gaze.

Alice, the assassin.

It wasn't like Rosamund to ever trust a cat, but Chester had been right about Alice. She had done nothing while she nearly drowned. The girl wanted her to drown, of course. Matter of fact, she wouldn't be surprised if Alice had stuck out her leg and tripped her while she was struggling to remain upright. Rosamund was known all throughout the houses for her grace and poise. In another life, she could have been a great dancer. That was, if she hadn't been destined to be queen, but to lose her balance entirely and go careening into a lake was so unseemly and not like her.

Bess handed Rosamund her rubber ducky. "Here you go, Your Majesty."

Pretending to play with the ducky, she kept her eye on Alice. She was getting the table set up for tea. Organizing the biscuits on the platters, the cakes on another, and folding the napkins. It was so obvious now. Alice had been up to no good the moment she'd smeared her muddy feet on her threshold.

Rosamund sniffed. She couldn't help that she was so trusting. It was all the fault of her delicate disposition, she supposed, but she did know what to do with rubbish. She only needed to wait a little longer. She wanted the finale to be something everyone would remember, something worthy of her reign. According to Chester, she'd have it if she could mind her temper a bit longer. His advice had been sound so far. It almost made her regret her deep-seeded hatred for cats. He would have made an excellent advisor.

The water in the bath had begun to warm. Rosamund had finished anyway. Bess helped her out of the tub, her wet feet sinking into the carpet. Once dry, Rosamund motioned for her robe. Sabrina waddled over with it, holding it in front of her. Rosamund turned and, as Sabrina draped it across her bare shoulders, the girl's stomach brushed against her back.

Rosamund tied the sash and smirked. "Getting a little round, are we?"

"I'm trying to be better, Your Majesty," Sabrina said, blushing. "Honestly, I am. But nobody can take such great care of themselves as you. You're a shining example to us all."

Rosamund poked her in the middle. "While I agree, still, your stomach...it's unreasonably large. It's getting bigger and bigger. I knew it was a matter of time before all that scarfing at the supper table would get you into trouble."

Mary Anne appeared from a side cupboard, holding an armful of towels. Without Mary Lou around, she hardly ever noticed the other Tweedle girl anymore.

"She's in trouble all right, Your Majesty," Mary Anne said, "and that belly of hers won't stop getting bigger until she has her wee one."

Rosamund raised her eyebrows. "*Wee* one?"

Bess no longer fussed with Rosamund's gowns, and Alice stopped arranging the table. Everything in the room grew still, even the ticking of Ralph's infuriating clocks. The only sound Rosamund could hear was Sabrina's ragged breathing.

"Be silent, you Tweedle idiot," Sabrina snarled at Mary Anne. "You don't know what you're talking about."

"Oh, I don't, do I?" Mary Anne faced Rosamund. "I overheard Lady Sabrina and Lady Alice talking about it before we left the palace. Sabrina is with child, Your Majesty, make no mistake."

"You horrid, little busybody," Sabrina said, and lunged at Mary Anne. "I'll teach you to eavesdrop. I'll box you on the ears."

Rosamund jerked Sabrina back by the arm and growled, "Is it true? Are you with child?"

"No, Your Majesty," Sabrina stammered. "I'm...I'm just fat."

"Don't you lie to me." Rosamund squeezed Sabrina's arm until the girl winced and tears shimmied down her cheeks. "Are you with child?" she asked again.

Sabrina hung her head and nodded.

"I, for two, am not the least bit surprised," Bess said, chiming in. "I told you so, Your Majesty. I told you she'd be nothing but trouble all those years ago. Now look. Trouble finally came."

Rage churned in Rosamund's stomach, oozed up her throat, and erupted out of her mouth. "I should have realized it as well," she hissed, releasing Sabrina's hand. "You're no better than your mother. She was a harlot too."

"Don't say that!" Sabrina cried. "Don't say such things about my mother. She was good and kind and so was my father."

Rosamund slapped Sabrina hard. "Don't talk about things you know nothing about. Your father, Pedro, was a no-good rogue, and your mother was worse. Get out of my sight. I never want you in my presence again. You and your child can live the rest of your lives shambling from town to town, street to street. I will issue a royal decree that no one shall take you in, under penalty of death, and believe me, they won't."

Sabrina dropped to her knees and grabbed the hem of Rosamund's robe. "No, Your Majesty. *Please.* I'm sorry."

"Sorry?" Rosamund asked, kicking her off. "I'm sorry I ever let you become a lady's maid. You obviously should have remained in the scullery where you belonged. Good luck finding a suitable husband now. You'll be lucky if the stable boy will have you." Rosamund laughed. "It probably is the stable boy's child, but I doubt even he would be willing to join you in destitution."

Sabrina put her hand on her stomach. "My child is no lowly stable boy's, and the father and I are already married."

"Married?" Rosamund's mouth dropped. "You married without my permission?"

Bess smirked. "Obviously that isn't the only thing she did without your permission."

"Stay out of it, Bess," Rosamund ordered, but then she paused. She stared at Sabrina groveling on the heart-shaped carpet and wiping her nose with the back of her arm. Why should Rosamund have pity on this wretched thing? She should have been rid of her when she'd been rid of the parents. "Or better yet," Rosamund said, addressing Bess. "Make yourself useful and get me a death warrant. It's off with Sabrina's head this instant."

Bess sighed and headed towards the door. "About time, Your Majesty. It's been pending on your to-do list since she practically arrived at the palace."

"You know what?" Rosamund said, causing Bess to pause. "I have an even better idea. Get me two death warrants. I wish to behead both Lady Sabrina *and* her husband." Rosamund turned to Sabrina. "Now be a good girl and tell me who it is. The toilet bowl cleaner? The window pane huffer? Who?"

"Lord William de Fleur," Sabrina said, her eyes watering.

"William?" Rosamund flinched as if the name had bitten her. "My cousin William?"

Sabrina nodded. "We were married last night after you went to bed."

Rosamund gritted her teeth. That fool. That traitorous hatter. If it weren't for her, William would still be off having tea parties, wishing for the titles and the lands he'd always coveted with every unbirthday candle he blew out. He owed her everything, least of all his loyalty. How dare he think he could marry one of her lady's maids behind her back? And of all the maids, why Lady Sabrina of Lake Town? She felt the sting of Pedro's betrayal all over again, except this time it was her own cousin who had betrayed her. She'd show him. She'd show them both.

"Guards!" she called out.

Two Fives of Hearts rushed into the room with their lances drawn. They bumped into each other and into the table Alice had so carefully arranged, sending biscuits and cakes tumbling to the ground. In Rosamund's anger, she'd almost forgotten about her little assassin. She watched as Alice immediately went to work, putting the table back to sorts. It seemed odd that the girl was much more interested in tea than her own friend, Sabrina, quaking before her. But, she supposed, that was what Sabrina deserved for not having enough sense to stay away from a would-be killer.

"Put those lances down," Rosamund demanded, "and bring me William at once."

The cards bowed and left, but not without knocking into each other a final time before exiting the room.

"Would you like me to get the death warrants for Lady Sabrina and Lord William?" Bess asked.

"No, you idiot," Rosamund said. "How am I supposed to execute death warrants while in my robe? Get me dressed."

It took less time for Rosamund to put on her gown, wig, powder, and shoes than for William to come strutting into the room. By then, it felt as if she had spent the last several minutes warming brimstone under her feet.

"You asked for me," William spat. "Whatever you wanted to thank me for, Your Majesty, is most welcome."

"Welcome? WELCOME?" Rosamund stepped towards him with fists clenched. "Are you also welcome for marrying one of my lady's maids without my permission?"

William stumbled backwards. "But...but Your Majesty, it's not what you think. I didn't want to marry her. She forced me. She made me do it."

Sabrina rushed over to William, but he pushed her away. "No, Willy," she cried. "You don't mean that. You said you loved me. Don't you remember?"

"Don't listen to her, Your Majesty. It's all lies."

Rosamund put her hand to her forehead and sighed. "Silence. I've heard enough. All that is left is for my royal decree. Are you ready, Bess?"

Bess held up her quill.

"Now then." Rosamund pointed her finger at William. He darted from side to side as if he could hide from her edict. "William de Fleur, I hereby strip from you your title and your properties."

William sucked on his bottom lip. "But, Rose, I mean... Your Majesty—"

"You're lucky I'm letting you leave with your head, which I'm only doing because you are my second cousin. If you were my first, you'd both be beheaded. Take your bride and be gone." Rosamund waved him off. "Guards. Escort them away."

"But...but," William blubbered as the guards grabbed him by the arms. "This is my castle."

"Not anymore," Rosamund snarled, "and I hereby...I hereby give it to..." Bess straightened in expectation, but Rosamund's gaze fell on Alice. Now *that* was a possibility. It wasn't as if Alice would have it for long, and it would give her time to decide who she really wanted to give Longshoot to—if she wanted to give it away at all "I hereby give Longshoot Castle to Lady Alice."

Alice's mouth opened. "Your Majesty? It's so unexpected. Are you certain that you—"

Rosamund cut her off. "No need to thank me. Where was I? Ah, yes." She nodded to the guards and motioned to William and Sabrina. "Take these two away. Make sure to keep them in your sight until they are far from the castle and are thoroughly miserable. See to it that the musicians play music while they leave. You know how I feel about pomp and circumstance. We have standards that must be maintained."

"Yes, Your Majesty," the guards said and dragged William out of the room.

Sabrina trailed after him like an alpaca that had dribbled all over the carpet, sniveling as she went. "Willy, Willy..."

Once the door closed, Rosamund plopped down on the settee. "Alice. Tea. Now."

Alice jumped as if she'd been bitten on the toe. She turned to the table and started putting together a tray faster than she'd ever seen any lady's maid do before. Why hadn't Alice shown such care with tea before she became an assassin? To think, she might have made it far in Rosamund's house, perhaps even taken over Bess's position one day, but now the sole place for her to go was down.

Bess came over. "What an ordeal. Would you care for a warm rag for your forehead?"

"That would be nice." Rosamund closed her eyes. As soon as Bess placed the rag on her brow, she heard the blow of a horn. "Now what?" she grumbled.

"Sounds like a trumpet," Bess said.

"A trumpet?" Rosamund tossed the rag and sat up.

She rushed to the window. Under a cloud of dust, the green-and-white banners of the House of Clubs waved in the distance as a train of horses and gilded carriages made their way to the castle. It was the ambassador. Finally, sweet milk of magnesium. The Bull had been lifted and he was coming to tell her so. She was free to take the Queen of Spades' head—and a few others along with it.

Alice came over carrying a tray. "I have your tea ready, Your Majesty."

Rosamund pointed out the window. "Can't you see that the ambassador is here? There are so many heads and so little time."

"But the *tea*, Your Majesty," Alice said again.

Rosamund turned towards Alice. She could feel the edges of her mouth stretching up to her cheekbones. She couldn't remember the last time she'd been so happy. "Don't worry your pretty little head. *I* will have tea later. Too bad I can't say the same for some of us."

It didn't escape her attention that the tray trembled in Alice's hands.

Chapter 50
Alice
Longshoot Castle, Wonderland
Azalea 91, Year of the Queen

Alice knew her silence during Sabrina's banishment was no better than when Sabrina kept quiet when the Queen ordered her beheading. Sabrina, no doubt, probably thought it was some sort of revenge, only it wasn't. Alice hated herself for doing nothing, but if she interfered and the Queen banished her too, then she'd lose her chance to be rid of the Queen altogether. Alice thought she could have the royal decree dissolved once she was dead and then Sabrina could come back to court—preferably without the Mad Hatter, but she supposed he'd have to come as well. With the vision of Madame Diamond's cards constantly in her mind, Alice couldn't even gloat when the Hatter finally got his comeuppance. Her need to survive trumped everything.

When the Queen had finally asked for tea, Alice busied herself with the cups and teapot, hardly noticing the brew smelled like pickled eggplant. She felt out of sorts, not quite in her body, almost as if she were watching herself going through the ritual of placing the cups on the saucers, putting a pat of butter in each, and pouring. She set the Queen's cup before her and uncorked the vial, holding the poison above the dark brown liquid. She didn't know why she was hesitating. If she killed the Queen, then she'd save five others, including herself, and yet, she couldn't bring herself to pour.

The sound from a trumpet startled Alice, causing her to spill most of the poison. She managed to save a few drops. It would have to be enough. Without trying to think too much of it, she quickly stirred it in the teacup and carried the tray to the Queen, who was peering out the window. In less than a minute, Alice had thought that all her problems would be over.

But the arrival of the ambassador had ruined everything. He was here to give the Queen what she wanted: Constance's head. If she got that, then she got all their heads, which meant the Queen was going to find out about the Aboveground very soon. Matter of fact, the traitor could be coming into the room any second.

Fear twisted its dry fingers around her throat. Alice didn't know what to do. If she still had some poison, she might have another chance to slip it in the Queen's drink, any drink, but the vial was empty, and she had no idea where to find Madame Diamond. She still had to try something.

The Queen rushed out of the room to meet the ambassador. In her hurry, she didn't bother to check if Alice or Bess were following her. Alice took the opportunity to drop the tray and run to her room. When she got there, she threw back the closet door and tossed aside the heavy gowns of crushed velvet.

"Ralph," she said. "Ralph, are you in there?"

The back of the closet opened. "Yes," he said, and hopped towards her. "I'm here."

"Ralph, thank goodness." Alice sighed. "The ambassador is at the castle. The Queen will take the Queen of Spades' head and ours too. Madame Diamond saw it in the cards."

Ralph twisted the buttons on his jacket. "The Queen is going to find out," he said. "I feared this would happen."

"Why didn't you tell me?"

"I was trying to last night. I wanted to warn you there might be a traitor in the Aboveground. It was a hunch at first, but now—if Madame Diamond's card are correct—then it's certain."

"Lillian." Alice balled her fists. "She's been missing since the day of your fake execution. She's the traitor."

Ralph shook his head. "Lillian's been in hiding, working for me, and sniffing out who the real traitor is. So far, no luck."

"I suppose that would explain why I haven't seen her." Alice collapsed onto one of the chairs. Right above her was a painting of a bowl of carrots and a wedge of cheese. "I suppose it couldn't be Lillian anyhow. Her head was in a basket along with ours. Bill's too. But if it's not either of them, then that only leaves..."

Alice's heart thumped.

Chester.

She bolted out of her seat, nearly knocking over a wooden-stick figurine. "Chester's the traitor. We have to stop him."

"How?" Ralph asked. "Besides, it might already be too late." He held up his pocket watch. It ticked slow and deep, like a fading heartbeat. "Soon, there really will be no time left."

"That's it then?" she asked, staring at him. "After everything, you're giving up? You're not even going to try?"

Ralph had the luxury of keeping his head, at least for now, but she would lose hers soon if she didn't do something. She ran to the door.

"What are you going to do?" Ralph asked.

"The one thing I *can* do," she said. "I must stop Chester from telling the Queen."

Chapter 51
Rosamund
Longshoot Castle, Wonderland
Azalea 91, Year of the Queen

Rosamund came to the grand hall. A castle worker in a yellow jacket held a stop sign at the entrance. Other workers huddled together in clumps, drinking tea and watching as one did all the work.

She waited as her throne was lifted onto a dais using ropes and pulleys. When it was safely set down, the worker at the door changed his sign from "stop" to "skip" and waved her in. She came up to the dais, bounding up the steps two at a time, took her seat, and waited for the Clubs' procession to make it to her threshold.

Ten minutes passed, then twenty…then thirty. Rosamund looked around. "What's taking so bloody long?" she demanded. "You there." She pointed to one of her guards. "Find out what's happening."

The guard bowed and ran out of the room, nearly colliding with Thomas.

"Ah, Thomas," Rosamund said. "Come up here and have a seat with me."

Castle workers brought up another, much smaller, throne and set it next to her. Thomas shuffled up the steps, thumbs shoved into his trouser pockets. He refused to meet her gaze.

"Cheer up," she said. "Your intended will be here any second now. You don't want her to see you acting like sour custard, do you?"

"I don't care what she sees," Thomas said, pouting.

The guard came back and knelt before the Queen. "It's the steps to the castle, Your Majesty," he said. "The ambassador insists he be rolled up out of fear of cracking. It's a slow process."

Two pages entered the room and blew their trumpets.

"Finally," Rosamund grumbled.

The Royal Announcer stepped forwards, wearing a giant heart on his chest and a powdered white wig. It used to be one of Ralph's jobs. She wondered if that rabbit were watching. She hoped he was.

The Royal Announcer said, "I present to Your Highness's audience, the Ambassador of the House of Clubs."

Marco Polo strolled into the hall and bowed before her. "My apologies for making you wait, my most beauteous Queen."

"Ambassador," Rosamund said. "It's good to see you so soon."

"You do have the most welcoming court," he said, gazing over at the same young eggs she'd caught him consorting with at the palace. "But I've also come bearing gifts. Two, in fact." He moved aside. "For the first, I'd like to present Penelope, the Princess of Clubs."

Marco Polo motioned a frog to come closer. The princess wore a green gown, jade slippers, and had an emerald tiara on her slimy head. She kept her giant, bulging eyes fixed on Thomas as she hopped alongside the ambassador. Rosamund had forgotten how ugly the frogs were. The whole lot of them. She glanced over at Thomas. He was staring at the ceiling, biting his fist. If matters weren't so pressing, she might have felt sorry for him, but she had more unimportant things to worry about.

"Go on," Rosamund said. "Don't be rude. Greet your intended."

Thomas went towards the princess and offered her his arm. The frog wrapped her webbed fingers around it and turned her face towards him, batting her eyelashes and puckering her lips. No amount of lace and velvet was going to make that frog a suitable princess of the House of Hearts. Maybe the princess would have a little accident before she made it to the altar.

Once Thomas and the princess settled, Rosamund raised her eyebrows at Marco Polo. "And for the second gift?"

He reached inside his doublet and pulled out a rolled parchment.

"Is that what I think it is?" Rosamund asked, reaching out her hands. "Give it here."

With assistance, Marco Polo was lifted onto the dais. Just as his little eggy feet touched the heart-embroidered rug, Rosamund saw Alice come into the hall and look around as if she were expecting someone. An assassin friend, perhaps? Rosamund wanted to laugh. She was the one in control. Always had been. Unless she wished it, Alice couldn't even get close to her. She was surrounded by the Aces. All Rosamund would have to do was give them a nod, and they'd take her down. Alice was the worst assassin she'd ever encountered.

"Ah, there you are," Rosamund said to Alice. "See to it my best sparkling cider is uncorked—this is a celebration." She chuckled under her breath. "In more ways than one."

Alice stared at her in a funny way. What was that girl up to? She supposed it didn't matter. Whatever it was, would come to nothing. It would all be over soon. She watched Alice go to one of the servants. The cider should keep her busy while Rosamund used these last few moments to finish what needed to be finished.

Marco Polo wiggled his eyebrows as he handed her a pen. "Shall we make it unofficial?"

"I thought you'd never ask." She uncoiled the parchment in a snap.

Marco Polo hovered over her shoulder. He was so close that she smelled butter and salt on his breath. "Cecil's signature is right here at the top, where it should be. That way you know it's not a forgery and here"—he pointed to another line—"this is where you sign."

The Queen whistled and a servant came over and offered his back. Rosamund laid the parchment down and scrawled her name on the line, finishing it with three floating hearts. "There, all done."

Marco Polo took the document from Rosamund. "Very well. You may consider the Bull dissolved, Your Majesty. You're free to do whatever you wish with the Queen of Spades."

"Funny," Rosamund said. "I can only think of one thing."

She nodded to Captain Juker, who ran out of the hall to go and fetch her prize.

"Now, Alice," she said. "Where is that cider?"

Chapter 52
Alice
Longshoot Castle, Wonderland
Azalea 91, Year of the Queen

Just as Alice was about to get the cider, she saw a grin emerge next to the Queen; its crescent-moon shape was unmistakable.

Chester.

She knew it. He was the traitor. Had been this whole time. Alice shook with rage as she stared at his toothy smile. It should have been obvious. Not coming to the palace was clearly a ruse. Chester had probably been there the whole time, hiding in the corners, listening to everything, and he was about to report it all to the Queen, just as Madame Diamond's cards had predicted.

Alice wouldn't give him the chance to betray them. She'd get to him first.

Chester's eyes became visible, then his furry head, and finally his entire body slithered out of midair. He surveyed the room, flicking his puffed tail.

"Your Majesty," Alice said, pointing. "It's that dreadful Cheshire Cat. Didn't you order him beheaded?"

"What?" the Queen turned her head, left and right. "Where is he?"

"Right *there*. Just above you. Can't you see him?"

Chester didn't disappear, didn't vanish like as usually did. Instead, he grinned more widely.

The Queen peered up at him. "Of course I can see the Cheshire Cat, you dimwit. I see everything."

Alice waited for her to scream, *Off with his head!* but instead, she said, "You should remember your manners, Alice. Chester is the Chief Royal Cat of Wonderland, you know."

Chester laughed, jerking his head from side to side. Alice felt as if her bones had dissolved into sand. She leaned against a marbled pillar, steadying herself. The way the Queen responded to Chester meant one thing: he had already told her. The Queen knew about the Aboveground. For how long? All day? This afternoon? Just now? Why hadn't the Queen gone mad and ordered Alice's execution already? It wasn't like her. Nothing was making sense.

The Queen raised her eyebrows. "Is the cider ready to be poured?"

"Not quite yet, Your Majesty," Alice managed to say.

"Then you had better get on with it. You know how I hate waiting." The Queen turned from Alice and resumed her conversation with the ambassador.

Alice's thoughts circled about her in a frantic swarm. She forced herself to head in the direction where the barrel of cider was being rolled into the hall. She passed one of the exits and told herself she should make a run for it, but it was blocked by guards. Alice peered around the room. Guards sat in front of every single doorway, entrance, and opening.

Something was about to happen.

The hallway swirled into a reddish blur—Animals. People. Hearts. Clubs. Alice couldn't catch her breath. She was going to collapse at any second.

A hand gripped her arm and held her upright.

"Steady," Madame Diamond breathed in her ear.

"She knows," Alice blurted. "She knows everything. He… he's told her about us."

"Shush, Alice. You must focus now." Madame Diamond pressed another vial into Alice's palm. "This is our last chance."

"How did you know?"

"A little rabbit told me."

Madame Diamond released her grip and disappeared into

the growing crowd. A nervous buzz hung in the air. It was present in the meaningless chitchat, the fugitive glances. They were all waiting, but for what?

Alice made it to where two servants were pouring the cider.

"Let me," Alice said to them. "You two, go. I've got it."

One of the servants said, "But the Queen wanted us to do it."

Alice grabbed the glass out of the servant's hand. "You must have misheard her. You wouldn't want the Queen to think you're disobeying her orders, would you? You know what she'd do."

The servant shrugged to the other. "No, we wouldn't want that."

"Good. Go and get some more glasses."

"Yes, my lady."

Once the servants had left, Alice glanced over her shoulder. The hallway was so crowded it was impossible to determine if anyone were watching her, but she couldn't worry whether someone was or wasn't. She had to take her chance and be quick about it. She poured the poison into the glass and then mixed it with cider.

The Queen was introducing Chester to the ambassador and the frog-looking princess. Alice would give her the glass now. She probably wouldn't even notice, since she was so engaged with that traitorous Chester. She slipped the empty vial into her bodice.

Bess snarled. "What are you doing?"

Alice jumped at the sound of the duchess's voice. She stammered, "N…nothing."

"Doesn't seem like *nothing* to me—more like lollygagging."

"I was preparing the Queen's cider. If you don't mind," Alice said, holding up the glass, "I'll be on my way."

"Oh, no you don't." Bess took the glass out of Alice's hand. Some of the poisoned cider spilled over the side. "That's my job, and besides, have you noticed there's more than one person up there with the Queen? Are they going to be drinking their cider out of invisible glasses? You're as deaf as a hat, you are."

Bess set the poisoned glass onto a red tray. She grabbed three other glasses, filled them with cider, and shuffled them around the Queen's poisoned glass as if she were a magician performing a shell game. Alice quickly lost track of which was which. She stood back, helpless to do anything about it.

When Bess had finished, she smirked, "That'll do, Alice."

The duchess marched into the crowd with the tray high above her head. Alice turned to watch her go and caught Chester grinning at her, as if he knew what Alice had tried to do and loved that she had failed again and, worse, that an innocent person might die because of it. The Queen, Thomas, the frog princess, or the ambassador—any one of them could get the poisoned glass.

She'd rather be beheaded than murder someone who didn't deserve it.

Alice shouted, "Bess, stop!"

The duchess continued to move closer to the Queen. Alice tried to follow her, but the crowd had swelled. She attempted to slide past an ox in a tweed jacket, but a tiger in a jeweled turban blocked her path and scowled at her when she accidentally stepped on its tail.

She stood on tiptoe, bouncing from foot to foot as she struggled to see above the rumps and horns and hats of those before her. She saw Bess stamp up the stairs and offer the tray to the Queen, who took a glass, and then she went, one by one, to the rest. When Bess had finished, the Queen, Thomas, the ambassador, and the frog princess all held one. Who had picked the poison? Which one of them was about to die? Chester continued to watch her.

As Alice was about to scream, *Don't drink it*, a flurry of black cloth like a raven's wing caught her eye. Guards were dragging Constance into the room. Alice felt herself pale at the sight of her and went cold altogether when she watched the executioner follow them in.

Constance stopped before the Queen. "I suppose this is what you wanted?"

"Of course it is," the Queen said. "And not a moment too

soon either. It's nearly 7:37."

Constance smiled bitterly as the guards forced her to her knees and brought in a block. They were going to execute her right before the Queen, close enough for Constance's blood to spray the Queen's slippers.

Alice stared at the Queen of Hearts, horrified. She'd always known that the Queen was mad, but this was wicked. How could she crave blood in such a way? She could have a pool filled with the amount of blood she'd taken.

The Queen stood and held her glass up to get the crowd's attention. Everyone quieted.

"You are all in for a special treat because for tonight's festivities..." The Queen paused and bit her lip as the excitement in the room began to grow. When the spectators were nearly in a frenzy from the anticipation, she continued. "For tonight's festivities, you will get to witness the execution of the Queen of Spades."

Everyone jumped up and down, clapping and squealing with excitement.

The Queen held up her finger. "But wait..."

The entire room leaned forwards, eager to hear what she had to say.

"She's not the only one getting beheaded tonight." The Queen smiled. "That's right, folks. I have *more* to behead."

All Alice could hear was cheering. Some held on to one another, others cried, and a few fainted. From the back of the room, guards dragged Lillian and Madame Diamond to the front. Bill had to be carried; he had wasted away so much that he was nothing more than a lizard skeleton. The prediction from the cards was coming true. Alice spun around to run, but she was surrounded by the Queen's overenthusiastic audience.

Guards grabbed her and the spectators parted, offering a direct pathway from her to the Queen. The guards pushed her forwards.

The Queen smirked at her. "Don't think I've forgotten about you, Alice. You little assassin."

"Mum, no!" Thomas cried. He dropped the glass of cider

and lunged forwards. As the liquid soaked into the rug, Alice thought of the poison. She felt relief knowing that at least it wouldn't be Thomas who drank from the poisoned glass.

The Queen nodded to some more guards. "Hold him."

Thomas tried to fight them off, but there were too many. The guards had him restrained within seconds.

"Rest assured," the Queen said, returning her gaze to Alice, "there won't be any white rabbits or handsome princes to save you this time."

Four more executioners dressed in scarlet robes entered the hall with axes in their hands. Alice was taken to a block and forced to her knees. On one side of her was Lillian. She gave Alice a weak smile; the fur around the rat's eyes was damp with tears. Seeing Lillian this way made Alice feel sorry for thinking she was the traitor. On the other side of her was the Queen of Spades. She held out her hand to Alice.

"It'll be for the best," Constance said. "You'll see."

Alice took her hand. She shook so hard that her shoulders knocked against the wood. She didn't understand. On the outside, her body was quaking as if electricity raced through her. But on the inside, she was calm, almost at peace—as if she knew somehow that this was what everything was leading up to, this moment right here, ever since she took the White Rabbit's paw and left the asylum.

If she were to die, she was happy it would be here in Wonderland. Here, where she was accepted as she'd never been at home, despite the madness that permeated every corner of it. Ralph had told her when she'd first come back to Wonderland that she should be wherever she belonged. That was here. This was where she belonged.

Drums rolled.

Brrrrrrrrrruuuuuuuuummmmm...

From the corner of her eye, she saw the executioners raise their axes.

Brrrrrrrrrruuuuuuuuummmmm...

The Queen said, "We shall drink to their deaths."

Glasses shot in the air. Alice winced. If it wasn't Thomas

who'd been holding the poisoned cider, then either the Queen, the ambassador, or the frog princess was about to die along with them. At least Alice would already be dead, and she wouldn't have to live knowing she'd killed an innocent person.

"And now," the Queen shouted, "off with their heads!"

The rest of the room echoed it back, except to Alice it sounded different, shifting in a way, but she supposed it had something to do with the blade slicing through her neck.

"Off with their heads!"

"Off with their heads!"

"Off with HER head!"

Chapter 53
Rosamund
Longshoot Castle, Wonderland
Azalea 91, Year of the Queen

Rosamund brought the glass to her lips and poured the contents down her throat. As it went down, a curious thing happened: she couldn't swallow. It was as if she'd drunk hair instead of cider. She turned towards Chester. He was watching her closely. He must have done this. He'd slipped a hairball into her drink. She knew she shouldn't have trusted him, shouldn't have trusted a cat, but it was too late.

The glass slipped from her grasp, shattering into a thousand pieces. She brought her fingers to her throat and tried to say, "Off with his head," but no sound came out except a couple of hoarse grunts.

Rosamund dropped to her knees, arching her back and coughing, but the wad of hair wouldn't budge. Her throat burned, and every inch of her lungs longed for the tiniest sip of air. She struggled to get up, but she slipped on something and banged her head. The room became fuzzy, reminding her of the wisps of mold on a piece of bread. Something stung her in the back; she couldn't recall if she'd invited bees on her tour. She tried to scoot away, but it was as if her legs had been submerged in pudding.

She heard her name. Her old name: *Ecila*. Yes, that was it. How could she have forgotten? Ecila. There it was again. Someone was calling her: Ecila, Ecila, Ecila … Who was that?

The voice sounded familiar. Like someone she'd known her whole life or maybe for all time.

Just as she was about to place it, Constance's voice drowned it out. It was so like her to butt in when she wasn't wanted

"Rose? Can you hear me?"

Rosamund tried to say something, but every piece of her withered like the petals of a plucked flower. Her eyes rolled upwards. The face of a clock smiled down at her.

7:37.

"Goodbye for now, my dear sister," Constance said. "Goodbye."

Rosamund sniffed one last sniff and was no more.

Chapter 54
Alice
Longshoot Castle, Wonderland
Daisy 00, Year of the New Queen

Alice was blinded.

It was as if the whitest of lights had filled the room and erased everyone with it. She squeezed her eyes shut, but the light pierced her lids and buried itself deep into her mind.

She heard a thud.

That must have been the axe slicing through her neck and fixing itself into the wood underneath. She was surprised how painless it was, as if it were the most natural thing in the world to have one's head cut off. It didn't even hurt.

Something scratched her cheek, and she was overwhelmed with the scent of pine; its earthy smell lingered in her nostrils. She opened her eyes. She didn't know what she expected next, but it certainly wasn't finding out that her head was safely connected to the rest of her body and not in a basket.

The brightness faded. Alice blinked, and the room came back into focus. Madame Diamond laughed as she ran her fingers along her throat. Lillian looked around, eyes wide. Perhaps she was as surprised as Alice to realize she wasn't dead. Bill lifted his head up and down on the block as if he weren't sure what to do.

They were all there except Constance, who was not beheaded, Alice was relieved to discover. Just gone.

The Queen of Hearts, however, was another matter. She saw the Queen's red slipper between a cluster of bodies. Someone was sobbing. Was it Thomas? Bess? Everything felt so hazy. Then she remembered the poisoned glass. The Queen must have chosen it after all.

Alice moved towards the Queen. She had to see for herself, see what she had done. The Queen had wanted to kill her—twice. She should have a sense of relief that the woman was dead, but instead, she had a pit in her stomach that ached with guilt. She stumbled through the crowd, sluggishly, as if her feet were tangled in watercress.

Everyone in the hall ogled at the Queen. She didn't like them staring in that way. They should show some respect and avert their eyes. Perhaps get a blanket to cover her. She was their Queen, after all, even if she wasn't a very good one.

Alice managed to push her way through. Constance was on the ground, weeping, as she held the Queen to her. The Queen's head flopped over Constance's arm and Alice stopped suddenly, feeling as if she were about to be ill. A cube of butter was stuck in the Queen's throat and a dagger handle glinted from her back where it had been plunged. The glass of cider was shattered into a hundred pieces next to the Queen's foot where a banana peel had been stuck. Alice had to blink a few times to make sure she wasn't imagining it all.

Perhaps it *wasn't* the poison that had killed the Queen. It could have been any one of the other things that did it. If it wasn't for the empty glass—and the fact that the frog princess and ambassador were very much alive—she could almost make herself believe she hadn't had anything to do with the Queen's current state.

Thomas knelt by the Queen in silence as melted butter dribbled down her chin. He stood and addressed the crowd. "Who's guilty of this treachery?" he demanded. "Who?"

Everyone began talking among themselves, peering over their shoulders and eyeing each other with suspicion. Alice backed away. She hoped to disappear into the throng, maybe disappear altogether if she could find Ralph. She'd done what she'd come to do. Now it was time for her to go.

"It was her," Marilyn Montague said, pointing at Alice. "She poisoned the Queen's glass. I saw her."

The crowd shied away from Alice, leaving her with no place to hide from Thomas's tortured gaze. She shook her head, more out of instinct than anything else. She didn't want to lie to Thomas, but she didn't want to tell him the whole truth either. She stammered, "Wh-wha-what about the dagger? Or the butter? Or the banana peel? How could I have done all that with my head on the block?"

Bess stepped forwards. "Alice killed the Queen. All these things must be side effects of the poison. Completely natural side effects."

Tears watered in Thomas's eyes. "How could you? She was my mummy and you killed her. I thought you cared for me. I thought you were my friend. Why?"

This was it, the moment she'd been dreading. Thomas would never be able to forgive her and nothing she could say was going to erase the pain she'd caused. She looked up at him and flinched at the anguish in his face.

"Thomas," Alice started. "You don't understand. I didn't have a choice."

"You did have a choice," he said. "You didn't have to do that to her."

"I didn't." She glanced at the Queen's body. "Not *all* of it anyway."

"Look at her!" Thomas yelled, startling Alice. "Look at what you did to your queen. There's but one thing good enough for traitors like you."

Alice stared at him. "Don't!" she said. "It weren't all me. Can't you see that?"

"Guards," Thomas commanded. "Take Lady Alice away. Make sure she's constantly watched. She is not to escape to her Land of Eng—not when her head belongs to the House of Hearts."

Chapter 55
Rosamund
Royal Cemetery, Wonderland
Daisy 10, Year of the New Queen

It rained the day Rosamund was buried.

They sang her favorite songs and recited her favorite ballads. If Rosamund had been there, she would have thought it very appropriate.

Very appropriate, indeed.

Chapter 56
Alice
House of Hearts, Wonderland
Daisy 20, Year of the New Queen

Alice traveled back to Gardenia City in the queen's carriage. It should have been a pleasant journey, with the carriage's luxurious seats, servant fanning system, and built-in puppet show, but every time she peeked out the window, all she saw was an escort of guards—put there by Thomas. Their presence was a constant reminder that she was a murderer and must be treated as such.

When they arrived, more guards ushered her into a wing of the palace she'd never seen before. The red paint bled down the sides of the walls, and the little light that crept in was quickly trapped and slaughtered. A strange medicinal scent hung in the air, making the entire wing feel sterilized.

They shoved Alice into a room and locked the door behind her. Inside was a seating area, and beyond that was another door that opened to a giant canopy bed with hand-engraved hearts in the wood. One of the hearts had the word "rose" scratched within it.

Before she got a chance to inspect further, she heard the door open. Mary Anne hummed to herself as she brought in a tray. "I was told to bring you this," she said and set it down. "I didn't want to, but they made me."

On the tray was a note with Alice's name scrawled across the front.

Mary Anne skipped out of the room. Once the door had closed, Alice opened the note.

Be ready soon. This doesn't mean noon.

Ready? Alice flipped the note over, but there was nothing written on the other side. Ready for what?

Alice examined the rest of the tray's contents: some soap, a dab of perfume, and a little red bottle with a label attached that read: Queen Me. She pulled the topper off and sniffed: roses and daisies. She held the bottle to the light to examine the contents. It was goopy on the inside, and she thought it must be to clean her hair. She took the tray to where there was a basin and a water jug. She stripped down to her undergarments and—as best as she could—washed her hair with the Queen Me shampoo and soaped her skin.

When she had finished, Alice grabbed the brush and peered into the mirror. Her eyes widened; the brush tumbled from her fingertips. Her hair had turned red—the same color as the Queen of Hearts. Her hands shook as she poured more water in the basin. She scrubbed every strand with the soap to wash out the dye. Water had drenched her undergarments and dampened the carpet around her feet by the time she'd finished. She examined herself in the mirror. The color hadn't changed one bit. If anything, it had become brighter.

She heard the door in the other room open. Alice whirled around.

"Alice?" Ralph called. "Are you in there?"

"Just a minute."

She wished she had a hat or a bonnet—anything to hide that her hair was practically glowing on her scalp. All she could do was wrap it into a knot, pin it at the base of her neck, and hope it wasn't as noticeable as she feared. She slipped on her gown and took one last glimpse at herself in the mirror. She froze as a jolt of horror went down her spine, causing her knees to nearly buckle. For a second, she thought she was looking at the Queen of Hearts, but then realized she'd been mistaken. It was her own reflection.

Alice came out into the seating area. Ralph was examining his watch. It wasn't ticking slowly as it had at Longshoot. Instead, it did the opposite, racing as if it were keeping time to a pair of hummingbird wings in midflight. The sound of it did nothing to calm Alice's nerves about her hair.

Ralph glanced over at her and did a double take. "My goodness," he said, his nose twitching. "What happened?"

"Is it that awful?" Alice asked, tucking a loose strand back in place. "I tried to fix it."

Ralph shut his pocket watch and put it inside his coat. "Just now, we have more unimportant things to worry about than your hair. Guards will be here any minute to take you to Tart Court. You are to be tried for killing the Queen."

Alice took a breath and nodded. "I've been thinking about it, and I believe I should accept my punishment. That would be the right thing to do. I'm guilty. I put the poison in her glass. I don't think I can go on, knowing what I've done."

"And what of the butter, the dagger, and the banana peel? Did you do all that as well?"

"No, but I—"

Ralph cut her off. "You're not solely to blame, and I refuse to let them put it all circularly on your shoulders."

Alice shrugged. "But what am I to do?"

"Leave," Ralph said and stood up. "You did your part, and now it's time I do mine."

He went over to the far side of the room and moved a curtain. Alice expected to see a window behind it. Instead there was a secret passageway. Evenly-spaced sconces lit the dark walls that led to who knows where. Ralph motioned Alice over. Once she was inside, he rearranged the curtains behind her, making the space feel cramped and heavy, as if there weren't a bedchamber within a finger's reach behind the thick velvet. He took her hand, and they followed the corridor until they came to a life-size painting of a door.

"Here we are," Ralph said.

Before Alice could question it, Ralph tilted the painting, revealing a real door underneath. She could only guess what was on the other side. Her home? Ralph had promised, but then again, she wasn't sure if she could fully trust him after he'd had the March Hare executed in his place. The only other option was the asylum. If it was the asylum, then what? Once Nurse Hart or Nurse Glass found her, they'd have her questioned by the doctors, and it wouldn't matter whether she kept silent about Wonderland or not: they'd still want to continue with their procedure. In her mind's eye, she remembered the look of that girl, Sarah BreeAnn, who she'd seen on her way to the operating room. Alice shivered. She didn't know how, but she wouldn't let them do the same to her. She had almost lost her head twice this time in Wonderland and she'd managed to survive. She would again. There was one thing that confused her though. It was that second time on the block. When the Queen was poisoned, Alice's head was about to be cut off. She should have died right along with the Queen. What stopped the executioner's axe that time?

Ralph pulled a ring from his coat pocket and fumbled through the keys. Finally, he held a gnarled one in his hand. "At last," he said. "For a moment there, I thought I'd lost it in a rabbit hole." He ran his paw across the top, and a tiny chamber opened, revealing another key inside. Ralph took that one, put it in the lock, and turned.

Alice realized she hadn't said goodbye—not to Constance or Madame Diamond or Sabrina, and not to Thomas. She ached with hurt when she remembered the hatred in his eyes at Longshoot. She meant nothing to him now, except for a head that belonged on a spike.

Ralph swung the door open. Alice held her breath, wondering what she'd see on the other side—the room she had escaped from at Préfargier or somewhere else entirely? If she had a choice, which she doubted she did, she hoped it would open to a spot next to the river by her old house.

But it wasn't any of those places. Instead, there was a brick wall.

"Impossible," Ralph said.

Alice faced him. "What does it mean?"

"Nothing" He shook his head. "It means nothing. Besides, there are other doors. Come."

Ralph took Alice through several hidden corridors with secret doors to her world. Every time he slipped the key into their locks and opened them, the results were always the same—bricked from top to bottom.

At the last door, Alice said, "Thomas must have done this. He said I wasn't to escape, remember? He must have known about the doors and had them bricked up."

Ralph appeared puzzled. "He can't. This isn't us. It has to be from the other side."

"What's from the other side?" Alice asked, her voice rising. "What's happening?"

"I don't know." Ralph shook his head. "We'll have to get you out of the palace somehow. Get you into hiding, maybe with one of the other Houses. That's what we'll do. We have less than a second and not a minute more."

They ran back to the room. Alice struggled to get through the curtains. They wrapped around her, constricting and sucking the air out of her lungs. Finally, she stumbled into the room, landing next to the polished boots of a guard.

The guard eyed Alice. She'd seen him several times with the Queen. His amber eyes bore down on her. "Playing in the curtains?" he asked her.

"I...I..."

"It's alright. I do it all the time." He held out his hand to help her up. The guard's uniform twinkled from all the light bouncing off his medals. "I'm the Captain of the Aces, Captain Juker. I'm here to escort you. Now if you're ready...after me, please." He clicked his heels together and marched out of the room.

Alice glanced over at Ralph. He nodded for her to go. With her legs shaking underneath her, she ran to catch up with the captain. This wouldn't be her first time at Tart Court. It was where the Queen had first ordered her beheaded, but she'd escaped before it could happen. She suspected that, this time, it wouldn't be that easy.

The giant heart doors of the court were already open when they arrived. She followed Captain Juker inside, hiding her face from all the stares she attracted. It felt as if everyone in Wonderland had come to witness her trial, including the other houses. Frogs and lizards in green gowns and breeches from the House of Clubs watched her with bulging eyes. Opposite them were members of the House of Diamonds with pale eyes, bluish hair, and white robes. The front rows were all taken up by scowling hawks and vultures from the House of Spades, covered from neck to claw in stiff, black clothing.

Alice wished she could hide, but all she could do was bring herself to the front of the room, where Thomas watched her progress. He sat on a throne seated high on a stage. To his left was Constance. Somehow, Alice continued to move forwards, putting one foot before the other, until she was standing before them. Thomas stared at her with a confused expression as if he didn't recognize her. Simply changing the color of her hair couldn't have changed her appearance that much, could it?

Captain Juker stopped before them. "I have brought the prisoner."

"Thank you, Captain," Constance said and waited until every murmur, whisper, and mutter had stopped. "Lady Alice, you have been pardoned by the House of Spades, the House of Diamonds, the House of Clubs, and by Cecil de Burg of the Holy of Holies of the Holiest Church of Wonderland." She nodded to a walrus in a tall jeweled hat and cloak. He raised a fin at her in response. "Everyone," Constance added and returned her gaze to Alice, "but the Great House of Hearts. Today, your guilt will be determined in the murder of its Queen."

Thomas continued to watch Alice with a perplexed expression. Constance gave Thomas a nudge, and he jerked backwards as if she had woken him from a deep sleep. "Yes...yes," he said. "Let the trial begin."

Another throne was brought in and positioned next to the Queen of Spades. She patted the cushion. "Come here, my sweet."

Alice felt all eyes on her as she climbed the steps and sat. From her new vantage point, she could see the jury box and the jurors within. Her heart fluttered when she saw the faces of Bill, Marco Polo, Bess, Marilyn Montague, and Lillian. They were busy scrawling away on their slates. She didn't know if it was good or bad that they were her jurors. Some of them would most certainly be against her, but a few of the others, like Bill and Lillian, she hoped would be on her side.

Ralph entered the room and came before them. He'd changed his clothing and wore a red jacket and ruff around his neck. "Sorry I'm late. All sit," he announced. "The Honorable Earl Charles LeMarque presiding."

The Dodo sauntered into the courtroom in a robe and a white wig. They all waited as he climbed a long, winding staircase up to a bench that surveyed the room. With each step the Dodo took, the stuffier the air became and sweat trickled down Alice's temples.

Once the Dodo arrived, he said, "You may all tap your foot."

The spectators did as they were told. Alice followed along when she saw that Constance and Thomas did it too.

"Now for the accusation." The Dodo cleared his throat. "Who among you accuses Lady Alice of killing the Queen of Hearts?"

Alice expected Thomas to accuse her, but he stayed silent. She glanced around at the people and animals seated in the courtroom. She looked at them, and they looked at her, but none said a word. Perhaps she was supposed to accuse herself. She had poisoned the Queen after all. Maybe she could explain that she was sent to help the people of the House of Hearts, that if she hadn't killed the Queen, then the Queen was surely going to have her executed and who knows how many others after her.

The Dodo said again, "Is there anyone here that accuses Lady Alice?" He studied the room. "Very well. Going once. Going twice..."

"I do," a familiar voice said. "I accuse Lady Alice of killing the Queen."

Chapter 57
Alice
House of Hearts, Wonderland
Daisy 20, Year of the New Queen

The Mad Hatter sauntered forwards. The top of his hat was taller than usual. Alice looked around for Sabrina and found her seated between a leopard and a prairie dog. Sabrina waved at her when their eyes met.

The Dodo leaned over the desk. "On what grounds?"

"A witness saw her put poison in the Queen's cup," he said, and stuck his hand inside his doublet. "And I have it on good authority—namely, my own—that she wanted the Queen's throne. Wanted it since the moment she came to Wonderland. That's why she killed her."

There was a gasp in the courtroom. The jurors hunched over, etching furiously on their slates.

"Me?" Alice raised her eyebrows. She knew the Hatter was mad, but this was beyond. "I wanted the Queen's throne? I might be guilty of a lot of things, but not that. *You're* the one who wanted the throne."

"Shush, Alice," Constance said, leaning towards her. "You mustn't interrupt an accuser in the middle of an accusation."

The Hatter stuck his nose in the air. "I don't care who knows. I've wanted that throne since the moment I set eyes on it."

"See?" Alice said to Constance. "He admits it."

"Of course I admit it," the Hatter said, spraying a fountain of spittle. "Have you sat on that throne? It's to die for, no pun intended. It has cushioning in all the right places, excellent lumbar support. And here's a secret for you. Not too many know this but"—he leaned forwards and put his hand to the side of his mouth—"the fabric was imported all the way from the Far Crest. It's fabulous."

"So you didn't want to be King of Hearts?" Alice asked him.

"Heavens no. Who would want that job?"

Many of the onlookers laughed while Alice's face burned. The Hatter had managed to spin everything around and make her look like a fool in the process. But wanting the throne wasn't the only thing he had to answer for. Alice took a breath. "Then admit," she said to him, "you tried to have me killed. You put the Queen's stolen jewels in my room."

"I didn't do it to get rid of you," he said and jutted his thumb towards Sabrina. "It was to get rid of *her*. I was hoping Sabrina would get caught in the act and the Queen, well, you know what she'd do, obviously. I panicked when I heard guards coming after they found Mary Lou in the hedges, and I threw the jewels in your room. But see, it all worked out so swimmingly. You still have your head, and"—he turned to Sabrina, whose bottom lip was trembling—"we're married now, aren't we dear? Isn't it splendid?"

"But you did the same thing to Lady Godiva," Alice said, "and she was beheaded."

"Lady Godiva?" The Hatter laughed. "Lady Godiva was nothing but a petty jewel thief. She had warrants out for her arrest in the other three houses, including Panoply City, under her aliases Wendy Darling, Cleopatra, and Mary Mack, before stepping one bare foot in the House of Hearts. Where do you think I got the idea for stealing jewels in the first place?"

Alice shifted in her chair. The Hatter had an explanation for everything, reasonable ones even, especially by Wonderland standards. But then again, how else had he been able to get away with his crimes without ready-made excuses? She wondered how long he could keep it up.

"What of Mary Lou?" she asked, raising her eyebrows. "What reason do you have for pushing her out of my window? Don't say that you weren't there. You already said you were in my room with the jewels."

The Hatter stamped his foot. "Of all the offensive things to accuse me of, that one takes the pie. I would never taint my good reputation by killing some chambermaid. That's just tacky."

"Stop lying." Alice glared at him. "You pushed her out the window. Admit it."

"He didn't." Mary Anne came forwards, wringing a tissue in her hands. "I did it. I pushed Mary Lou out the window. I'm as guilty as a parrot in a pudding." She glanced to each side before continuing. "You see...you see...we were in Lady Alice's room tidying up, and Mary Lou said that I stitched like an old billy goat, and I told her that she sewed like a skinny toe-slug, and then she said I looked like a toe-slug, but then I said I might look like a toe-slug, but she was a toe-slug, so she boxed me on the ears and I…I didn't even think. Next thing I knew, I'd pushed her out the window."

Alice looked at the Hatter. He shrugged.

Mary Anne wiped her eyes with the back of her hand. "It's all our fathers' fault," she cried. "They passed on the Fighting Fever. What was in them was in us too, and now Mary Lou's dead, and it's all my fault, and I don't care who knows. I DON'T CARE!"

She ran out of the room, wailing, "Mary Lou, Mary Lou…"

Everyone turned in their seats to watch Mary Anne leave and stayed there until her howling grew fainter and was gone altogether. Only then did the spectators collectively twist forwards.

The Dodo cleared his throat. "Now that's settled. Let's get back to the accusation, shall we?"

The Hatter asked Alice, "Are you satisfied?"

"Yes." Alice sighed. "I suppose so. For now."

"Very good." The Dodo put on a pair of spectacles. "The accusation has been entered and Lady Alice has been accused. Who has the evidence?"

"We do," Bess said, standing up. Marilyn Montague slid next to the duchess.

"They can't do that," Alice said to the Dodo. "They're on the jury."

"The accused will remain silent," the Dodo snapped before returning his gaze to Bess. "What is your evidence?"

"I watched Alice pour the cider, and Marilyn saw her put poison in the glass," Bess said.

The Dodo took notes, and the rest of the jurors followed suit. "Are you both willing to swear by this information?"

They nodded.

"Very well, raise your right leg and wobble."

They both did as the Dodo asked.

"Do you solemnly swear that you saw Alice pour the poison and the cider, but not at once and not in that order?"

In unison, they said, "We swear."

"You both may be seated." The Dodo took out a quill and dipped it in ink. "I believe that's enough for eyewitnesses. Now for the royal physician. Can someone please call for the royal physician?"

An otter entered through the doors. Compared to all the colors of the other houses, his dark gray clothes reminded Alice of a raincloud coming into the room. She didn't think it boded well for her.

Once the otter appeared settled in the witness box, the Dodo said, "For the final straw, what did you find in your examination? Poison, I presume?"

The otter took out a parchment and opened it. He scanned the document while his whiskers flicked back and forth. "The Queen *did* ingest poison."

Alice felt as if a bag of stones had settled in the bottom of her stomach. She slumped in her seat. It was undeniable. The Queen was holding the poisoned glass. She drank it. It was Alice's fault she was dead. She couldn't fool herself into pretending that maybe she didn't have a part in it because she'd played the biggest role of all.

"There you have it," the Dodo said, banging on his gavel. "Alice is guilty."

The courtroom erupted into a symphony of gasping, shrieking, clapping, and a few "I told you so's."

The Dodo leaned over the bench and asked the royal physician, "Do you concur with the verdict that Alice is guilty?"

The otter said, "She could be."

"Could be?" The Dodo fumbled with his spectacles. "Could be is better than couldn't be, wouldn't you say?"

"I couldn't. I'm not an expert in that field."

The Dodo's feathers ruffled around his neck. "Then what can you say?"

The otter checked his notes. "Only that I couldn't determine how the Queen died. She could have also suffocated on the cube of butter. Or bled to death from the stab wound from the dagger. Or died from a broken neck from slipping on the banana peel found on her shoe." The otter folded the parchment into the shape of a hat. "The results are inconclusive."

The Dodo looked around the courtroom. "If it wasn't Alice, then who killed the Queen?"

The room rumbled with accusations. Fingers pointed, words flew, eyes glared, and fists shook. The Dodo slammed the gavel on the bench, but nobody paid attention.

Alice couldn't take the shame that burned within her. "I did it," she said, standing. "I put the poison in the Queen's cider."

Constance grabbed Alice's hand. "You've said enough. No more."

Bess shouted, "It was me! I killed the Queen!"

Everyone's attention shifted to the duchess, who stood, gripping the edges of the jury box. "That's right," she said. "I did it. I shoved that butter cube down the Queen's throat until I couldn't cram it in any farther. She had it coming. I tell you. It was always *Bess, do this* and *Bess, do that*. I couldn't take it anymore." She held out her hands. "Go ahead. Take me away. Do what you wish."

The Hatter approached the podium and wagged his finger at the duchess. "I think not, madam. I won't let you take all the credit." He stared up at the Dodo. "She's not guilty. *I'm* guilty. I stabbed the Queen in the back with the dagger. She kicked me out of my own castle. She got what she deserved."

"Oh no, no, no," Marilyn Montague said, chiming in. "It wasn't either one of you two. I am the guilty one. The Queen was going to rip me and Tommy apart. I couldn't let her do that, so I slipped her the ol' banana peel when she wasn't paying attention."

The Dodo rubbed his head before taking out his pipe, tapping the bottom, and lighting it. "Is there anyone here who didn't try to kill the Queen?"

People ducked their heads to avoid eye contact; a few squinted up at the ceiling and whistled while others seemed interested in the floor's tile arrangements.

The Hatter pointed up at the Dodo. "What? As if you didn't?"

"On several occasions, certainly, but this trial isn't about me," he said, and addressed the jury. "Has the jury come to a decision?'

One by one, each juror stood and held up their slates. Lillian's had swirl marks. Marco Polo had written: "All the King's Horses and all the King's Men." Bess's had a whole lot of exclamation marks. Marilyn's slate wasn't a slate at all, but a mirror so she could stare at herself, and Bill had drawn a smiley face.

The Dodo took a puff of his pipe. "The decision is unanimously undecided. I have no choice but to clear Alice of all charges." He chucked the gavel behind him. "The court will adjourn."

Women tossed their bonnets and men threw their shoes.

Thomas headed in her direction, dodging a few boots on the way. She never would have thought he'd look at her again, let alone speak to her. Her stomach coiled into knots. Was he coming to accuse her of purposely getting away with the Queen's murder? She'd tried to make amends and take responsibility, except it hadn't turned out the way she'd expected.

When he was standing right before her, Alice began to say, "I'm sorry," but Thomas shushed her.

"No," he said. "You don't owe me an apology. I owe you one."

"*You?*" Alice asked.

"Yes." He took her hand. "You weren't the only one who killed my mother. I'm sorry I accused you."

"But—"

"It was wrong of me. I jumped to conclusions. I was so angry and hurt at the time. I wasn't thinking straight, but after today...hearing all that testimony from you, from William, Bess, and Marilyn...well, it made me feel better in a way."

"Feel better?" Alice asked, stunned. "Feel better to hear how many people wanted the Queen dead?"

"It sounds absurd, mad even, but yes. Her death made so many happy, and Mum was always keen about putting others first."

Alice didn't have the heart to correct him, not while she was part of the reason for his grief. Instead, she nodded. "She was like that, wasn't she?"

"Yes," Thomas said, his eyes watering. "She was."

A group of cards marched into the courtroom. Emblazoned on their tunics was the insignia of the House of Spades. They came up to the platform and stopped. "Your Majesty," they said and bowed.

Constance clapped her hands. "Well then," she said to Alice. "That's my cue. I must be off."

"What about Gardenia City?" Alice asked. "What about the House of Hearts? You are supposed to be the new queen."

"Me?" Constance looked surprised. "This was never about me."

"How can you say that? Of course it is, this whole thing has been about you."

"Was it? It's so hard to keep track anymore."

Alice said, "But I took an oath to the true queen."

"And that's you, dear," she said. "You're the Queen of Hearts. But don't worry..." She winked. "I might be back someday to steal it from you. After all, we're sisters by crown."

Alice could hear several chuckles in the courtroom.

"What are you talking about?" Alice asked her. "I'm not the Queen of Hearts."

"My goodness, didn't they tell you?"

Alice felt her chest tighten. "Tell me what?"

"The old rule. Why, I think it goes back to the very first Wonderland book of bylaws and mylaws, which reads exactly this way:

KILL THE QUEEN, BECOME THE QUEEN

Translated by Looking Glass Mirror, it says: *Kill the Queen, Become the Queen.*"

"There is no such rule," Alice said, her voice nearly at a shrill from the panic coursing through her. "At least not where I'm from. I'm not the Queen. I'm supposed to go home. The White Rabbit, he said—"

"Home?" Constance was taken aback. "But you are at home. Don't you see?"

Alice glanced at the faces in the courtroom. She hadn't realized they'd been watching her—everyone, even the Dodo. It was as if they were waiting for what she was going to say, what she was going to do, what she was going to *command*. It seemed so ridiculous, silly even, but the more the idea settled on her, the more enticing it became. Was it possible? Was this real?

She shook her head. She had to go home. She couldn't leave her mother and father. Not like this, not forever. But, when she thought about it, she didn't know *why* she wanted to. Her parents had thrown her away, dropping her off at the asylum for the doctors and the nurses to do whatever they wanted to her. They would never have done that to her sister, Katherine. No matter if Katherine talked about Wonderland or men on the moon or creatures in the attic. They cared for Katherine. They didn't care for Alice. But here everything was different.

Thomas wrapped his arm around her. "I knew you were a princess," he said. "Only a princess can become a queen."

Queen Alice.

The Queen of Hearts.

Curiouser and curiouser.

Chapter 58
Dr. Gottlieb Burckhardt
Préfargier Asylum, Switzerland
January 12, 1889
Alice in Wonderland

Dr. Burckhardt watched Alice through the plate of glass. She sat in front of a window that looked out to where snow sat heavy on tree branches, threatening to snap them like breaking bones. It had been one of the worst storms in ten years, and the whiteness overpowered everything.

Alice didn't notice the snow outside. She didn't notice anything. Her mind was numb to the world, lost in its own blizzard. He hadn't seen a patient react this way before. Alice was a first. Blood spotted through her bandages, staining her hair red. It would need to be changed soon.

Dr. Longfellow had wanted to take Alice back to Oxford to be closer to her parents. He thought it might be helpful, and maybe it would have been, but Dr. Burckhardt couldn't let her leave. Dr. Longfellow was a competent enough doctor, but he had no expertise with cases like this, and Alice had become his special case, a mystery he needed to solve. He had hoped to have some progress to report at the medical conference this year in Berlin, but it didn't matter what he tried; he couldn't bring Alice out of her catatonic state.

Still, Dr. Burckhardt believed that there was something left of her. He wasn't about to give up yet.

Although Dr. Burckhardt wouldn't allow Alice to leave with Dr. Longfellow, he did agree that having her parents near would do his patient good. He'd written to them, and they agreed to come straightaway and bring Alice's cat that she loved so much. They would be here tomorrow. They couldn't come fast enough.

"Doctor..."

Nurse Glass's rose perfume filled the hallway, and the clack of her heels reverberated along the tiled walls.

"It's dreadful," she said. "I just received a call from the gendarmerie. Alice's parents... their carriage... oh my..." Tears welled in her eyes. She held her hand to her face.

"Tell me," Dr. Burckhardt said.

"Their carriage went over a ravine in Reims. Something spooked the horses. A witness said it might have been a cat. Weren't they traveling with one?"

"Yes." Dr. Burckhardt took off his spectacles and rubbed his eyes. "I believe they were."

He looked at Alice and sighed. She had to be told, of course. He entered the room with Nurse Glass following behind. He kneeled before Alice, staring into blank eyes that seemed to peer into another world. He took Alice's limp hand into his own.

"Alice," he started. "Remember how we told you that your parents were coming? That we were going to have a lovely visit, and they were even going to bring your cat? What was its name? Dinah, I think. I know you must have been looking forwards to their visit and I...I don't quite know how to tell you this, but there was an accident..."

After he explained to Alice what had happened, she turned her head towards him, her eyes focusing, or trying to. He held his breath, hopeful she might say something, but Alice only sniffed and then retreated back to whatever place she had just come from.

"Don't despair," Dr. Burckhardt said, and glanced up at Nurse Glass. "We're going to take care of you. This is your home now. Do you understand? Alice?"

Her features remained expressionless. Alice was lost within her mind, and it was going to take time for her to find her way out again. When she did, he'd be there.

Dr. Burckhardt left Alice and went to his study. The medical conference was a month away. He needed to get all his notes in order if he was going to present his findings. He opened Alice's file and dipped his pen in ink.

Patient was admitted to Préfargier Asylum, suffering from a clear case of paranoia and exhibiting signs of hallucinations, delusions, and at times, aggression. The operation took place precisely at 7:37 AM. Following the surgery, the patient became substantially quieter.

Chapter 59
Alice
House of Hearts, Wonderland
Daisy 20, Year of the New Queen

Alice walked down the halls. With her newly red hair left in long waves down her back, she'd been changed into a sparkling red gown. The material rested heavily against her from all the inlaid jewels—more than Alice had ever seen. Her feet shuffled along the polished floor of the palace. Everything was still except for a humming in her ears.

Constance was waiting for her on the same balcony where the last Queen of Hearts had stood to watch Alice's execution. Now it was where Alice would be crowned. As she approached, she could see Constance, still in her black gown of the House of Spades, except her skin was brighter, and she had a crown of onyx on her head. Next to Constance were Thomas and Ralph, both wearing armor.

Flags and banners of the Houses of Hearts, Spades, Clubs, and Diamonds fluttered as far as she could see, and the grounds overflowed with animals and people, young and old, all standing on their tiptoes or propping each other up on their shoulders to get a glimpse of her.

No matter how much Alice kept telling herself this couldn't be happening, that it had to be a dream and she'd wake at any second, she couldn't help but swell with pride. This was all for her. It might end at any time, but not just now.

Two servants wearing the livery of the House of Hearts

came onto the balcony. One carried a scepter topped with a red heart on a velvet pillow, and the other carried a satin pillow with the rubied crown of the House of Hearts.

Constance took the scepter and presented it to Alice, bowing her head. Alice grasped the red-and-black marbled handle and held the scepter in front of her, its heart becoming her shield.

Next, Constance picked up the crown. "Now hold still," she said. "You'll feel a little pressure."

Alice faced the throng as her heart hammered in her chest. The weight of the crown settled upon her. It was heavier than she'd imagined. She winced as something pinched her skin. One of the rubies must have wiggled loose. She'd have to get it mended.

Constance shouted to the people, "Your new rose!"

The Remonstration Church bell started ringing, and all of Gardenia City—every home, garden, and shop—filled with cheering.

Ralph hopped next to her. "Right on time," he said.

Thomas nodded. "Indeed."

It all felt meant to be. As if she couldn't have been anything other than the Queen of Hearts and Wonderland wouldn't be Wonderland without her. It didn't make sense, and yet, somehow, it did.

Chester purred in her ear. "And it all begins again."

"You," Alice snapped. "Go away, you traitor."

"Traitor? Not me," he said. "I'm the most loyal one here. You might even want to make me the Chief Royal Cat of Wonderland someday."

"I highly doubt that."

Chester placed his head on his paws and stared at Alice in a way that made her feel like he was looking through her. "You know," he said. "Some would say you're the spitting image of the last Queen of Hearts—and probably all the ones before her too. I tried to warn her, the last one I mean, but she wouldn't listen. None of them ever do. You'll probably ignore my advice as well. Such a pity. But don't mind me, Alice, because I'm mad, you know."

He grinned. "We're all mad here."

Author's Note

This re-invention of Lewis Carrol's classic came to me in a flash: one of those old-school flashbulb types. In that yellowish light was a girl crouching near a tree, frightened of the creatures moving in the dark. The name "Alice" popped in my head and not just any Alice—Alice from Wonderland. With that, also came the knowledge that she had somehow made it back to Wonderland and she was hiding from Jabberwockies. Shortly thereafter, I fell down that proverbial rabbit hole and became busy with creating *Ever Alice* in an attempt to answer the question: *What is Wonderland?* Of all the novels I've worked on, this one has been the most fun. Since I started writing way back in 2002, the piece of advice I'd heard time and time again was to write the book you'd want to read. Well, this was it. It had all my favorite things: the twisted psychological to the fantastic, slapstick humor to satire, and glittery palace courts to suffocating asylums. Light and dark baked into one narrative.

The flashbulb moment came to me around 2009. By 2010, I'd completed a draft of *Ever Alice* that had been workshopped and edited. I had an agent at the time who shopped the manuscript and it made it to an acquisitions meeting with a reputable publishing house. The house eventually passed, and the manuscript went into a drawer. By then, I had already started my MFA program and had moved on to other writing projects. Even so, I never forgot about *Ever Alice*. I thought about the story over the years, but figured it would stay under the heading of "never-to-see-the-light-of-day" as some novels are fated to do.

Flash forward to New Years Eve 2016. On a whim, I opened the *Ever Alice* file that had sat for so long and decided that I would self-publish. I knew that if *Ever Alice* was going to have its best possible chance, I had to make it the best it could possibly be and I needed help. Luckily, I had a lot of people willing to do just that and they all deserve some space here.

First, I'd like to send a very grateful and loving thank-you to my original hometown critique group who read *Ever Alice* back in 2009-2010. Marilyn Ebbs, Samuel Hall, Darren Howard, Sandra Shaw-McDow, Mark Reed, Rachel Starbuck, and Frank Yates—your support and sound advice got me to that acquisitions meeting in the first place.

Second, I'd like to thank my new critique group. Nancy Bennet, Justin Colucci, Geri Copitch, Courtney Grela, Daniel Link, Michelle Modesto, and Ashley Rich—you guys have been so awesome and supportive and never once said (or showed) that you were sick of *Ever Alice*, not just with me bringing excerpts to group but taking the time to read the whole thing. Your feedback has been invaluable and has given me the assurance to press forward.

Daren Howard (darrenphoward@gmail.com). You were one of my initial readers way back when *Ever Alice* was just getting its start and then you were one of its final reviewers. Having you copyedit *Ever Alice* was one of the best decisions I made in this process. You caught so much—literally something on every page. I couldn't imagine having taken the next steps with this story without you looking at it first. You gave it a much-needed polish that would have been impossible for me to do on my own.

Gretchen Stelter with Cogitate Studios (CogitateStudios.com). You've always been amazing at what you do. You were amazing when you gave *Ever Alice* an initial read in 2010 and were again when I came to you with my plans on publishing it in 2018. I knew, without a doubt, that this novel could never be sent out into the world without it first having your careful eyes. Thanks to you, I had the confidence to hit the send button.

Caroline Holmes. Thank you for being the voice of *Ever Alice* for the audiobook and helping me with my British. You gave the story a sparkly shine and brought it to life in a new and exciting way.

My husband, Nick. Thank you for supporting this idea of mine, backing me up 200% because you have always been a 200%-er. And thank you for having so much creative talent that you were able to design a beautiful cover even while running a business, helping me with the kids, doing yardwork, and watching episodes of *The Prophet*.

Before I finish, I'd like to honor the readers of *Ever Alice*. I never thought this story would have anyone other than myself, other writers, and/or publishing professionals read these pages for any other reason other than to just enjoy the story. Thank you! You have made my dream finally come true and you'll never know how much that means to me.

Finally, I couldn't complete this acknowledgment section without thanking Lewis Carrol. The original creator of Alice and the Queen of Hearts and every other memorable character from that fantastic world. This re-imagining wouldn't have been possible without his amazing imagination. I hope, someday, I can create characters as timeless as these.

Yours in Wonderland,
H.J. Ramsay

Stay up to date with latest news from H.J. Ramsay at
HJRamsay.com

For information on other exciting projects offered through
Red Rogue Press, please visit our website at
RedRoguePress.org

Printed in Great Britain
by Amazon

74689770R00210